DARK MIST RISING

Also by Anna Kendall from Gollancz:

Crossing Over

DARK MIST RISING

Book Two of the Soulvine Moor Chronicles

Anna Kendall

GOLLANCZ

LONDON

The right of Anna Kendall to be identified as the author
of this work has been asserted by her in accordance
with the Copyright, Designs and Patents Act 1988.

First published in Great Britain in 2011 by Gollancz
An imprint of the Orion Publishing Group
Orion House, 5 Upper St Martin's Lane, London WC2H 9EA
An Hachette UK Company

A CIP catalogue record for this book is available
from the British Library

ISBN 978 0 575 09430 7 (Cased)
ISBN 978 0 575 09431 4 (Trade Paperback)

1 3 5 7 9 10 8 6 4 2

Typeset by Input Data Services Ltd, Bridgwater, Somerset

Printed in Great Britain by Clays Ltd, St Ives plc

The Orion Publishing Group's policy is to use papers that are
natural, renewable and recyclable products and made from wood
grown in sustainable forests. The logging and manufacturing
processes are expected to conform to the environmental
regulations of the country of origin.

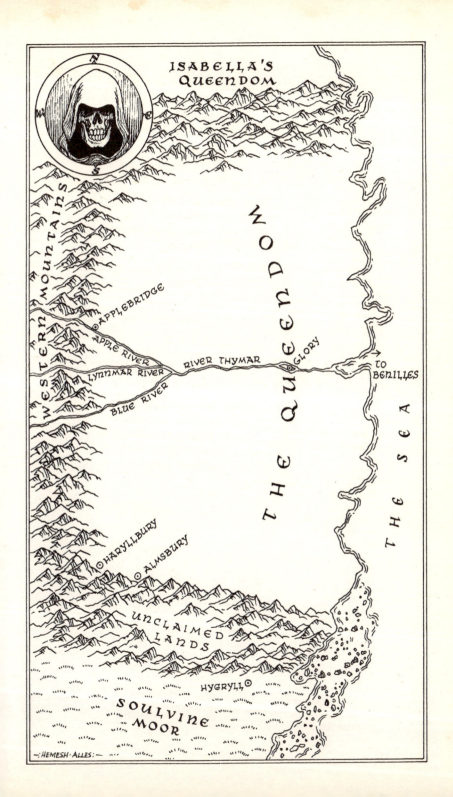

1

It is old women who are most willing to talk to me.

Not all of them, and not only them. Sometimes an old man could be coaxed into talk, especially if I tripped over him. Occasionally a halfwit who did not know where he was. And twice I have talked to queens. But usually, in the Country of the Dead, it was old women who would come out of their eerie trances to prattle of the lives they had lost, some very long ago. But I was not now in the Country of the Dead. I only dreamed that I was, and the dream was even more terrible than the reality had been.

A flat upland moor, with a round stone house. There is the taste of roasted meat in my mouth, succulent and greasy. In the shadows beyond my torch I sense things unseen. Inhuman things, things I have never met in this land or in that other beyond the grave. Moving—

'Peter!'

—among them is a woman's figure, and the voice coming to me from the dark is a woman's voice, and I can see the glint of a jewelled crown. The woman calls my name.

'But—'

'Peter! Wake up!'

'— you're dead,' I say.

'Eleven years dead,' she says, and gives a laugh that shivers my bones. And—

'Peter! Now!'

I struck out, blindly, crazed with fear of that monstrous laugh. My fist struck flesh. A cry, and I came fully awake, and Jee lay sprawled against the wall of the sheep shed,

1

his little hand going to the red mark on his cheek.

'Jee! I'm so sorry! Oh, Jee, I didn't mean to . . .'

He stared at me reproachfully, saying nothing. Early-morning light spilled through the door he had opened. The sheep – two ewes and three lambs – stared at me from their bed of straw.

'Jee . . .' But what could I say? I had already apologized, and it changed nothing. The blow could not be undone – like so much else in my life.

'*Eleven years dead.*'

I took Jee in my arms, and he did not resist. Under the fingers of my left hand his bones felt so small. Should a ten-year-old be so small? I didn't know, having so little experience with children. The village children avoid me, frightened perhaps of the stump where my other hand used to be. 'Peter One-Hand', they called me, not knowing how I lost the other, or that my name is not Peter.

Sometimes I think that even Maggie forgets the past. But I never forget.

Jee freed himself from my clumsy embrace. 'Maggie says ye maun kill a lamb for dinner. The fattest one.'

I blinked. 'Are there travellers?'

'Yes. And their servants. Come!'

Travellers with servants. Our rough inn, perched above the village of Applebridge in the foothills of the Western Mountains, seldom gets travellers, and never travellers with servants. They must have arrived very early in the morning. I had slept in the sheep shed because two days ago a wolf had carried off Samuel Brown's only lamb, killed it right in the enclosure by his cottage. Maggie had insisted that I build a stout shed, and I had chosen to sleep in it. 'There's no need, it's completely enclosed and has no window,' Maggie had said, her lips tightening. I hadn't answered. We both knew why I preferred to

2

sleep out here, and that neither of us could bear to discuss it.

I raised myself from the straw, brushed bits of it off my tunic and leggings, and pulled on my boots.

Maggie and I have run this inn for two years. It is due solely to her that we, two seventeen-year-old fugitives and Jee, have been able to make a living. It was Maggie who bartered the last of our coins for the rent on a falling-down cottage in Applebridge. Maggie who hammered and nailed and scrubbed and drove me relentlessly to do the same, until the cottage had a taproom, usable kitchen, and three tiny bedrooms above. Maggie who cooked stews from wild rabbit and kitchen-garden vegetables, stews so good that local farmers began leaving their own cottages to have dinner and sour ale at the inn, talking through the long winter nights and glad for a gathering place to do it. Maggie who bought the ale, driving such a hard bargain that she won the grudging respect of men three times her age. Maggie who acquired our chickens, sewed our tunics, baked and boiled and roasted. Maggie who, just this spring, bought the two ewes from the Widow Moore with our carefully hoarded money. Maggie who had saved my very life, with Mother Chilton's help. I owed Maggie everything.

But I could not give her the one thing she wanted from me. I could not love her. Cecilia stood between us, just as if she had not died. Twice. Cecilia and Queen Caroline and my talent, which I had not used in over two years but which still festered within me, like a sore that would not heal.

The sheep gazed at me meditatively with their silly faces. Stupid animals, they irritated me constantly. They belched, they farted, they got soremouth and ringworm. They fell on their backs and, when in full wool, couldn't get up without help. They chewed their cud until it was

3

a sloppy wad and then dropped it on my foot. They were afraid of new colours, strange smells and walking in a straight line. They smelled.

Still, I was not looking forward to killing the lamb. One of the ewes lay beside twin lambs, the other nursed a single offspring – which one did Maggie mean by 'fattest'? How many travellers were there, and where did they come from?

I should have been fearful of travellers, but I found I was not. Any change in the small, wearying, unchanging routine of Applebridge was welcome. And there should be nothing to fear: The Queendom had been at peace for two and a half years, ruled by Lord Protector Robert Hopewell for six-year-old Princess Stephanie. No one knew where or who I was. Travellers would be a pleasant break.

'I'm sorry,' I said to the larger and plumper of the twin lambs. It blinked at me and curled closer to its mother.

I left the sheep shed, carefully barring the wooden door, and walked the dirt path to the back of the cottage. The summer morning sparkled fresh and fair. Wild roses bloomed along the lanes, along with daisies and buttercups and bluebells. Birds twittered. The cottage stood on the side of a hill, backed by wooded slopes, and I could see the farms and orchards of Applebridge spread below me, fields and trees all coloured that tender yellow-green that comes but once a year. The river ran swift and blue, spanned by the ancient stone bridge that gave the village its name. Maggie's kitchen garden smelled of mint and lavender.

As I rounded the corner of our cottage to the stable yard, I stopped cold.

'Travellers,' Jee had said, 'and their servants.' But he had not told me of anything like this. Five mules, stronger than donkeys and sturdier than horses, were being

4

groomed and watered by a youth about my own age – although I knew that I, with all that had been done to and by me, looked older than seventeen. The mules were fine animals but looked as if they had been pushed hard to pull the four wagons now drawn off the road. Three of the wagons were farm carts such as everyone used to take crops to market, but they were piled high with polished wooden chests, with expensively carved furniture, with barrels and canvas bags. The fourth was a closed caravan with a double harness, such as faire folk use to take their booths around a more populated countryside than ours. This caravan, however, had gilded wheels and brass fittings and silver trim. Neither wagon nor coach, it was a room on wheels, and probably as rich within as without.

Where had such visitors come from, and what had driven them to travel on a night lit only by the thinnest of crescent moons?

'Good morrow,' I said to the youth. 'I am—'

He snapped something I could not understand through his thick, high-pitched accent.

'What?' I said.

This time I caught enough words. 'Be ... halfwit? Tell ... hurry ... My lady's breakfast!'

Hot words rose to my lips: I was the proprietor of this inn and he but a stable boy! But before I could lambaste him, the cottage door opened and Maggie rushed out.

'Peter! I need that lamb butchered now if I'm to have stew for noon dinner! They leave by mid-afternoon!'

She stood with her hands on her hips, her fair curls drooping from under her cap, kitchen heat filming her forehead with sweat. A white apron covered a trim grey gown of her own making. Maggie will wear grey or red or brown, but never green nor blue, the colours of the two queens for whom she had been a kitchen maid. Her

5

foot in its neat leather boot tapped on the ground. She looked pretty, and determined and very competent: Maggie as master and commander.

As always, this brought out in me a desire to resist, to not be ordered about. All my life I had been ordered about: by my stepfather, by a head laundress, by a queen. In my own cottage I would not be ordered and scolded.

'In good time,' I said testily to Maggie. 'I'm talking to this man here.'

The boy ignored me and went on feeding the mules.

'Peter, we must have—'

'In good time!'

Jee appeared at the door of the cottage. 'Maggie, ye maun come! They want—'

I didn't wait to hear what they wanted. Already my stupid fit of pique had passed. Maggie was working hard for both of us; the travellers were obviously rich and would pay us well; I was a fool to not do as I was told. I started back towards the sheep shed.

But then an old woman emerged from the door in the back of the caravan. She stumbled on the one step and I leaped forward to catch her. Her considerable bulk lurched against me and we both fell to the ground, me underneath. It was like being crushed by a very large, very dense mattress. 'Thank you!' she cried, in that same strange accent.

'Are you hurt, mistress?'

'No, but . . . Catch my breath, lad . . .'

I led her to the wooden bench in front of the cottage. She plopped heavily down. And then she began speaking.

It is old women who are most willing to talk to me. And once again everything in my world changed.

2

The old woman, a servant of some type, wore a simple brown dress and white cap not unlike Maggie's. The fabric, however, was richer than ever graced Maggie's back, and the white cap was embroidered with an intertwined C and S. Her broad, wrinkled face turned from red to white and back again as she answered my questions.

'Are you certain you are not hurt, mistress?'

'I ... am fine ... well-padded ... Just let me ...'

'I can bring some water. Or ale.'

'W ... wine?'

'No.' Wine was too grand for the inn.

'Then ... no.' Her breathing slowed.

'I am Peter Forest, proprietor of this inn. Where do you come from, mistress?'

To my surprise, she groaned. 'Gone! All gone!' She covered her eyes with her hands.

'Gone? What's gone?'

A torrent of words gushed from her, of which I caught every third word. 'Manor ... fire ... baby ... my lady ... all that be left ... baby ...'

I put a reassuring hand – my only hand – on her arm. 'A fire? There was a fire in your lady's manor house?'

'No!' And again the spill of anguished words. This time I caught only three. 'Destroyed ... army ... savages.'

Savages. A savage army.

I seized her arm so hard that the woman not only

jerked her whole massive body, she also actually stopped talking. 'An army? Of savage warriors in fur tunics? And you come from the west?'

'Yes, lad. *Don't!*'

I let her go. She stood up shakily from the bench, glaring at me, and I stood too.

'I'm sorry, mistress. Your news startled me. You are . . . you are sure? A savage army is marching from the west, from over the mountains, and destroying settlements on their way? Do you know who they are?'

She shook her head, still glaring, until a sudden high wail came from the caravan. A baby. The old woman waddled away. Once more I grabbed her with my good hand.

'Please, mistress, just one more question and—' But she shook me off and climbed into the caravan, closing its door behind her. I had a glimpse of a dim interior rich with rugs and embroidered pillows and a carved wooden cradle.

The nursemaid had not told me whose army marched from the west. But I knew.

For a long moment I stared at the closed door of the caravan, not seeing it nor anything else in the stableyard. Seeing only the past. Then my vision cleared and I pushed open the door to the inn and went inside.

Our taproom is small, with two long trestle tables neatly filling the space between hearth and door. Two men sat there. This fine summer morning no fire burned in the hearth, although of course there was one in the kitchen behind, and the two windows stood open to the light breeze. A narrow staircase led to the rooms above. A girl descended the staircase, one hand steadying herself against the wall, as if she might fall. The younger of the two men, both richly dressed in velvets creased and soiled from hard travel, jumped up from the table to help her.

'Joanna! Be careful!'

'I'm fine.' She smiled at him, a tremulous smile, full of love. Their accent was easier for me to understand than were the servants' outside. The girl was plain of face and very thin, dressed in a brocade gown worn too loose at waist and belly. She might have been pregnant, but I guessed instead that she had very recently given birth and had not yet fully recovered. Her young husband guided her to the table, where the older man sat tucking in to Maggie's bread, cheese and ale.

The young man said, 'Is that all there is? Joanna can't eat that!'

Joanna quavered, 'I could try some bread.' Sweat glistened on the woman's pale forehead, although the room was not warm. Her eyes shone too brightly.

The young man said desperately, 'The innkeeper's wife promised us spring lamb. You could eat that, couldn't you, sweetheart? It's so tender. It would slide right down, and give you strength.'

'Yes, Harry.' Maintaining her sweet smile was costing her tremendous effort. All at once she clutched the edge of the table. 'If I could just step outside for a moment . . .'

Harry helped her outside. The older man looked at me. 'Go ask if—'

'I am Peter Forest, the proprietor of this inn,' I said, as I have said so many times before, never without faint disbelief. He took me for a servant, and so I often feel.

'I beg your pardon, sir. Lord Carush Spenlow. When will the lamb stew be ready? We must get back on the road as soon as possible.'

The lamb stew was still on the hoof. I said with as much authority as I could muster, 'Stew takes time, my lord. And I was told that you need to rest both yourselves and your mules at least half a day.'

'True, true.' Lord Carush stood, his sword clanking against the side of the table. He looked around, sat down again, stared at his bread and cheese. Abruptly he blurted, 'My daughter-in-law is not well. Is there an apothecary in the village?'

'No, I am afraid not.'

'Where is the closest physician?'

'Probably Morsebury, two days' hard ride east.'

'Have you a midwife?'

'Yes. Mistress Johns. She is very skilled.'

'Send for her at once, please.'

'Yes, my lord.'

We looked at each other. Shadows moved behind his eyes. He knew, as did I, that if Lady Joanna had childbed fever, there was precious little even the most skilled midwife could do for her, nor a physician either. Young Harry Spenlow would be a widower soon enough, and the baby in the gilded caravan would be motherless. I said, 'Sir, you are travelling hard by night. What news from the west?'

'You haven't heard? I've tried to tell everyone we met along the way. There is an army marching over the mountains. They are pillaging estates as they go, slaughtering our animals for food, carrying off our goods, burning our manors. An army of savages – they scarcely look human in their furs and feathers – and they have terrible weapons they call *guns*. The weapons shoot bits of metal with great speed and force. Sir, you have never seen anything like it, or like them!'

Yes. I had.

Lord Carush continued, 'They burned my manor to the ground, and we barely escaped with our lives. My unfortunate cook ... The savages burned out my neighbours as well, or so I heard, although we mountain nobles live far apart and only runners informed me. But don't look like that, sir. Everything I've heard says that the savages are not burning villages, nor harming common people. Only the nobility.'

'Why?'

He shrugged with the frustrated helplessness of a man used to having his orders obeyed. 'Perhaps they are all mad, or halfwits. But more likely they intend to send a warning to the palace: "We will destroy your nobility until we get what we want."'

'And what is that?' My heart had begun a slow thud, painful as stones being dropped on my chest one by one by one.

The provincial lord was becoming impatient with talking to a country innkeeper as if to an equal. But he answered me. 'Don't you know? The savages were promised the Princess Stephanie in marriage to their chieftain's son. Three years ago, before Queen Caroline was burned for a witch. Now they are coming for the princess. The army is led by Lord Solek's son, the Young Chieftain.'

'But—'

'Please see to the lamb stew!'

'Yes, my lord.' I turned to stumble back to the sheep shed, and Carush Spenlow's last words caught me as I walked out into the sunlight. Their tone was apologetic; he regretted his rudeness to me. He was a good man.

'The runner from my neighbour's manor said, too, that the savages seek someone else besides the princess. They questioned servants, including my cook. Who knew nothing, of course. Brutes!'

My heart stopped all motion.

'Who ... who do they ...'

Lord Carush shook his head. 'I don't know. Now, please, that lamb stew.'

3

I slaughtered the lamb. Jee could not be spared to run for the midwife, so I went myself, since I am useless in the kitchen. Maggie made the stew, the travellers ate it at midday, and before the shadows lengthened on the grass, they were gone. Mistress Johns ate the rest of the lamb stew in the deserted taproom, sitting at the trestle table with Jee, Maggie and me. The room, with its thick walls and stone floor, was cool and dim. Gravy ran down Jee's chin. He sopped it off with a piece of bread.

'That girl, Lady Joanna, will die,' Mistress Johns said. 'There was nothing I could do.'

Maggie nodded. She had tidied her hair and changed her apron. She wore her master-and-commander look. I tried to avoid looking at her.

''Tis a pity, really,' Mistress Johns said. 'She seemed a nice enough little thing. No strength, though. Not made to bear children. Now you, Maggie, you could bear a dozen and still run the inn besides.'

I ate faster, my eyes on my plate.

Mistress Johns chewed regretfully on her last chunk of lamb and smacked her lips. 'You're a fine cook, Maggie, my girl. I daresay you could cook for such as that there lord. Did you know his own cook died on the journey here?'

'No,' Maggie said. She stacked the empty plates.

'Just beyond Applebridge, at Two Forks. They paid the Smallings to bury the poor woman – no time to do so themselves, with poor Lady Joanna so ill.'

'What did the cook die of?'

'Burns. In the fire she tried to save her special spices. All the way from Benilles, they was.'

Maggie made a face. I knew she had seen too much of death and danger to risk a life for spices, no matter how exotic or expensive they be.

'But the cook was old,' Mistress Johns added, with the comfortable tone of one who had barely reached middle age. 'I daresay her time would have come soon anyway. We all must go eventually, and that is no more than stone truth.'

Jee looked up. Recently Maggie had cut his hair, and short soft strands blew in the fresh breeze from the open door. His dark eyes turned to Maggie, whom he worshipped. And with good reason: she had rescued him from hunger and poverty and a father who beat him. He said, 'Maggie, be we fleeing the savage army, like those travellers?'

'No,' Maggie said.

'Yes,' I said.

Mistress Johns looked from one of us to the other. She drained her mug of ale. 'Well, I am not leaving Applebridge. My cousin at Starbury, she heard from *her* sister-in-law at Buckhurst, who had it direct from a villager where the savage army passed through, that the western warriors be not harming country people. Didn't touch so much as a hair on any virgin's head, not so much as a single hair. No burning, no thievery. It's just the nobility they're revenging themselves on. Nothing to do with us.'

I had heard the same thing from Lord Carush. I opened my mouth to say, 'But who's to say the savages will stay with that plan?' but Maggie got there first. As always.

'That's right,' she said eagerly. 'Their groom told me the same thing, when he was having his breakfast in the

13

kitchen. We at Applebridge are perfectly safe.'

I said, 'But who's to say the savages—'

'Perfectly safe!'

We glared at each other. Jee looked bewildered and shrank against Maggie's side. Mistress Johns stood. 'I'll just be away now. I'll say this for that Lord Carush, he warn't mean. Burned out and ruined like they are, he still paid me thrice what I usually get.' She opened her broad red palm to show us the silver coins reposing on it.

Maggie demanded fiercely, 'So you are not fleeing Applebridge, Mistress Johns?'

'No, no, child, I told you. No need.'

'Is your daughter's family fleeing?'

'No.'

'Are the Smallings or the Staffords or the Trentons?'

'No. Good morrow, my dears.'

Mistress Johns left, and Maggie stared at me triumphantly.

I said, 'I must see to the sheep.'

'Peter—'

I strode from the inn. But I knew it was only a temporary reprieve; she and I would have it out tonight.

Meanwhile, I checked the combs in the beehive – too early in the season for honey, as well I knew – brought water from the well to the sheep and mucked out their pen. They should have been taken to pasture today, but with all the business of the travellers, had not. I would take them now. In pasture they would meander aimlessly, chewing and chewing, starting at every strange sound or smell, taking flight and making me run after them. Maggie would disapprove, saying it was too late in the afternoon for pasturing sheep. However, I needed to be away from the cottage.

Lord Solek's son, leading an army to claim his child

14

bride, Princess Stephanie. By now Lord Robert Hopewell, who was not only lord protector but also commander of the army of The Queendom, must know of the invasion. The savages had *guns*; The Queendom did not.

No concern of mine. Maggie had said so.

I led the sheep further afield than they wanted to go, to the pasture above Two Forks. Dusk found us beside the Apple River. Lilies and green rushes grew thickly on the banks, and the meadows blazed orange with marigolds. The silver-green leaves of poplars quivered in the warm breeze. A frog, startled when I sat on a grassy hummock, splashed into a marshy pool. The long summer afternoon stretched golden around me, fragrant with clover and wild mint and the clean sharp smell of the river.

One of the ewes bleated piteously, either because it was exhausted or because I had slaughtered its other lamb. The ewe had not yet forgotten.

And I could not forget, either. Not anything, neither present nor past. The present was Maggie, waiting for me at the inn, ready to argue, undoubtedly getting more and more angry at my absence. Maggie, whom I had bedded once and once only, and who now believed she owned me. And the past was all else.

I could lie to Maggie. I could also lie to myself, but not for very long. It was not by chance that I had dragged the stupid sheep as far as Two Forks. It was here that Lord Carush Spenlow's cook had died of her burns, here that the Smallings would have buried her. 'The savages also seek someone else,' Lord Carush had said. 'They questioned servants.'

No, I was not here by chance.

I was going to cross over.

It had been over two years since my last time. But everything in me – nerves, bones, the prickling over my skin – remembered the ability I had been born with, and had used since I was six years old. No, that was not true – I had not used my ability. Others had used it, and me, for their own ends. Or else they had forced me into circumstances where I must perform or die. But not now. Here, now, in the Two Forks pasture above the Apple River, I would choose for myself to cross over to the Country of the Dead.

What if I could no longer do it? What if maturity, or lack of practice, or some other unfathomable agent had decayed my talent? That was what Queen Caroline and Mother Chilton had both called it: 'your talent'. I had hated that talent, and used it to stay alive, and finally abused it to rescue Maggie. After that, I had hated it all the more. But it was mine – was me – and life at Apple-bridge had sharpened my need for it again.

Pain is required, pain and a letting go that is, para-doxically, a matter of will. I tied the sheep to a hickory tree, lay down on the grassy hummock, and with my good hand drew my knife. Quickly, quickly, before I could change my mind, I drove the point of the knife into my thigh, and it happened.

Darkness—

Cold—

Dirt choking my mouth—

Worms in my eyes—

Earth imprisoning my fleshless arms and legs—

But only for a moment. I was not, after all, actually dead. The taste of death lasted only for the brief moment of crossing, the plunge through the barrier that no one except a *hisaf* can penetrate, not even the Dead them-selves. A heavy barrier, solid and large as earth itself, the barrier of the grave. I tried to cry out and could not for the dirt clogging my mouth. I tried to flail my arms and could not for the lack of muscle and flesh over my naked bones. Then it was over. The dirt gone, my bones restored, and I had crossed. I stood and gazed around me.

The Country of the Dead is like our country, but weirdly stretched out and sometimes distorted. A few steps in an upland pasture might be half a mile here, or two miles, or five. Or it might be the same. Sometimes our rivers and forests and hills existed here, but sometimes not. The Country of the Dead is vaster than ours and I think it changes over time, just as ours does, but not in the same way. It is our shadow made solid. Like a shadow, it shrinks and grows, but from some unseen influence that is not the sun. There is no sun here.

There is light, an even subdued glow, as on a cloudy day. The sky is always a low, featureless grey. In that cool light I saw the river, the pasture, the marshy pool where the frog had splashed. But here was no frog, of course, nor my sheep. Nothing lives here; there are only the Dead.

A few of them sat or lay scattered around the meadow. They never move far from where they died. They were doing what the Dead do: nothing. They sit – for days, years, perhaps centuries – gazing at emptiness, and on each of their faces is complete calm, a mindless tranquillity that never changes. Only the old can be roused at all, and then only briefly before lapsing back into their trances.

And tranced, too, was how my own body must look now, back in the land of the living, until I returned to animate it once again.

I made my way along the river towards where the Smallings' graveyard would be in the land of the living. I knew I had reached the right place not only by the marker of a great old oak, but by the greater numbers of the Dead. People had been buried here for a long time. The burial grove had stretched to accommodate them all, becoming almost the size of a respectable small forest. Some of the Dead sat in circles, as they often do; I don't know why. I walked among the trees, studying faces and clothing.

Lord Carush Spenlow's cook was not hard to find. Someone had dressed the body in the same brown dress and embroidered cap as Lady Joanna's nursemaid, and thus had the Smallings buried her. Now she sat gazing at a wildflower. Her wrinkled old face looked tranquil, with no sign of burns; the Dead do not bring their injuries or illnesses with them. Somewhere, just this mindless, my mother sat in the Country of the Dead. Once I had wanted desperately to find her, but that had been before I owed Maggie my every action, my every breath.

'Mistress,' I said to the cook. She didn't stir. But it is old women who are most willing to talk to me, if I persist hard enough. I knelt on the grass beside her, seized her shoulder, and shook it. 'Mistress Cook!'

Slowly the old eyes focused on me, then all at once snapped into awareness. 'What is wanted? Is it the rosemary bread again? I told them— Oh!'

I saw it come to her all at once, the awareness. But it didn't scare her; it seldom does.

'So I'm dead, then?'

'Yes, Mistress.'

'The bread—' She blinked once, then began to slip away from me. The Dead are not much interested in their recent lives, not after the first time they slide into tranquillity. That is what their loved ones left behind do not, cannot, understand. To talk at all to the Dead, you must either discuss their childhoods, which seem to stay with them better, or else be very quick with your questions. I was quick.

'Mistress, wait! The savage army—'

'Stop shaking me, young man! Leave me go!'

18

'I'm sorry. But the savage army that burned Lord Carush's manor'

'Lord Carush,' she said experimentally, as if trying out a strange language on her tongue.

'Yes, the manor. The fire. The savage soldiers were looking for someone and they asked the servants about him. Who was it?'

She was sliding back into mindless tranquillity. I shook her shoulders so hard that her head bobbled and the embroidered cap slipped sideways on her grey hair. The Dead cannot be hurt, but they can be annoyed. 'Leave me go!'

'I will stop as soon as you tell me who the savage soldiers sought. Who?'

She frowned in concentration. 'They wanted . . . they wanted . . .'

'*Who?*'

The creases on her face became ravines, hillocks, an entire landscape devoted to the effort at memory. Finally she brought out, 'The witch boy. The one who . . . who led the army of magic illusions against Lord Solek. Who killed his savage lordship, when Queen Caroline reigned. They seek . . . they seek . . .'

I stopped shaking her.

A final spasm passed across her face and triumphantly she brought out the name: 'Roger Kilbourne!'

I let her shoulders go. Immediately she lapsed back into the calm of the Dead. I stood gazing down at her, and then gazing at nothing at all.

I remembered the past, but so did the savage army. They too remembered the battle at the palace, where their leader's blood had spurted red on the green tiles of Queen Caroline's courtyard. They remembered the army I had sent into that battle that the folk of The Queendom had called 'magic illusions from Witchland' but that

I knew were actually soldiers I had briefly brought back from the country of the Dead. Those soldiers could not be killed again, and so had killed with impunity. The savage army remembered their losses, and their chieftain's death, and now they sought not only the princess promised them in marriage but also revenge.

They sought me, Roger Kilbourne.

4

I did not linger in the Country of the Dead. Crossing back to the land of the living takes far less pain than travelling the other way; I don't know why. It hurt enough to make me clamp my teeth lightly on the inside of my cheek.

Darkness—
Cold—
Dirt choking my mouth—
Worms in my eyes—
Earth imprisoning my fleshless arms and legs—

Then I lay again on the grassy hummock in the Two Forks pasture. The sky had turned dark blue. Time, like landscape, can stretch or shrink on the other side, and I had been gone for hours. The first stars appeared. The new moon was a thin crescent, cradling the old moon in its shining arms.

Something crashed through the rushes at the water's edge.

I leaped up. The ewes bleated and the lambs, who had fallen asleep at their dams' sides, mewled and tried to stand. The wolf that had taken Samuel Brown's lamb? I drew my knife, knowing that I was a fool to bring Maggie's tiny flock out this far, this late. No time to make a fire, and Peter One-Hand was no match for a wolf.

It was not a wolf.

A dog bounded from the rushes. It raced right up to me and licked my hand. A big dog, with short grey fur, a small tail and a huge snout. I glimpsed the double row of sharp teeth, but with its big pink tongue slobbering joyously over my fingers, it was impossible to be afraid of the beast.

'Hey, boy, hey . . . .'

A ewe gave a shrill, terrified cry. Her lamb rose to its wobbly feet and began to sob.

'No, it's all right, you stupid beasts. See, it's a *good* dog, aren't you, boy?'

The sheep continued to make noises I had never heard any sheep make. The dog ignored them. The younger ewe, her silly face contorted, ran, leaving her lamb behind. The ewe was much faster than I expected. I raced after her – Maggie would kill me if I lost one fourth of her prized flock – and tackled the idiot animal. It was like jumping on a blanket laid over moving stone. We rolled over each other on the spongy grass, sheep and man and then dog, who happily jumped aboard.

'Off! Get off!' I yelled. To my surprise, the dog did, lying down obediently a few feet away.

I tied a rope on the still terrified lead sheep, slung her lamb over my back (not easy to do one-handed) and started for home. The second ewe and lamb followed. The dog trailed several lengths behind, although not far enough to keep the sheep from occasionally taking fright all over again and racing ahead, dragging me along. I was no longer a *hisaf* who could travel beyond the grave; I was an inept one-handed shepherd making his stumbling way home in the dark, back to the inn to face Maggie.

She said nothing until very late. All evening local folk thronged the taproom, chewing over news of the invasion.

'The savages don't touch common folk, everybody says so.'

'Just the same, I be hiding my grandmother's pewter plate.'

'Best hide that pretty daughter of yours, Jack.'

'They don't touch common folk.'

'They want the princess. Like the young queen promised.'

'That witch! They were right to burn her!'

'Burned that nobleman right out of his manor. Killed his sister, too – a woman!'

'They want our princess to live away from The Queendom!'

'That be not right. Queens stay and rule; men defend. Savage bastards!'

'They're *savages*, Hal – what can you expect?'

'I hear they can turn into wolves by the full moon. They be beasts already 'neath their furs.'

'Don't talk like a halfwit! They wear furs but they be men.'

'Jeffries be taking his family away tomorrow morning.'

'Jeffries always was lily-livered.'

'They don't touch common folk.'

'Peter, Maggie, more ale!'

I filled tankards from the cask and carried them, one by one in my good hand, to the two trestle tables. Maggie worked in the kitchen, washing tankards and setting tomorrow's bread to rise and sending Jee out to the taproom with whatever cold food was asked for. It was late when the last man left, drunken old Riverton, staggering out the door and crashing into the jamb on his way out. Perhaps I should have seen him home, but the night was warm and if he spent it snoring somewhere on the dirt lane, it would not be the first time.

I shuttered the windows. Jee went upstairs. When there were no guests, we each took one of the three tiny bedchambers, as if we were nobility living in a great house. If the two guest bedrooms were occupied, Jee slept on a pallet on the floor of Maggie's room, and I in the taproom, 'to keep the fire going'. In summer there was no fire and I slept in the sheep shed. The taproom was lit by only two rush lights stuck in holders along the wall and two fat candles on the tables. One candle had burned down to a guttering wick. In the shuttered gloom its odour seemed to thicken as much as the congealing tallow.

As I moved to close and bar the door, the big grey dog bounded in. He licked my hand briefly and then lay on the stone floor beside the hearth as if he had slept there every day of his life.

'Hey, boy, you just dance in and take over, don't you?'

The dog wagged his negligible tail.

'I don't think Maggie will approve.'

She came through from the kitchen and sat on a bench. She didn't notice the dog behind the other table. 'Peter, sit down. We must talk.'

'The sheep—'

'Bother the sheep! They're fine in their shed and you know it. Why did you tell Jee that we will flee Applebridge?'

'Because we will.' I braced myself. In the dim light Maggie's face looked calm and weary, even vulnerable. In such a mood she was harder to oppose than when she was angry. She had taken off her cap and her fair curls straggled over eyes blue-shadowed with exhaustion.

'But, Peter,' she said reasonably, 'there is no danger in staying here. You heard what everyone said – the savage army is not harming common folk. Everybody said so.'

'Fourth-hand gossip from someone's wife's cousin's sister-in-law!'

'Lord Carush said it, too. I heard him.'

'Maggie, I am not common folk.' It came out wrong, as if I thought I was nobility, a laughable idea. Nonetheless, my words were true. I was a *hisaf*.

'Nobody here could ever connect Peter One-Hand, the

innkeeper, with Roger Kilbourne, the queen's fool.'

'The queen's fool who brought an army back from the Country of the Dead.'

'Hush!' Maggie glanced around, as if she expected to discover a listener hiding in the taproom, where there was no place to hide. Instead she saw the dog.

'What is that dog doing in here?'

'It's my dog.' The words came out spontaneously, defensively. I hated arguing with Maggie. I usually lost, and her stubborn knowledge that she was always right acted on me like itchy wool. At the same time, I liked the dog. It asked nothing of me.

'Since when do you have a dog?'

'Since this afternoon. The dog lives here now, Maggie. It can eat scraps, or maybe it will just hunt its own food and—' a sudden inspiration '—it can help herd the sheep.'

'It's not a herding dog. Look at it.'

'Well, perhaps not, but maybe if I—'

'Bother the dog!' Her face reddened, but she calmed herself – I could see it happen, like a feather bed being smoothed out by a rough hand – and resumed her reasonable tone. 'Peter, we've worked so hard. To get this inn, to get the local people to spend their money here, to get the chickens and sheep and bees, to—'

If I let her go on, she would name every single thing we had gotten, which was also every single thing I owed to her. I couldn't stand it.

'You've done a lot, Maggie. I know it. I am grateful to you for ever, but—'

'I didn't mean to say—'

'I know you didn't. But—'

'We'll lose everything if we leave now! And Lord Solek's son can have no idea who you are! Everyone thinks Roger Kilbourne is dead!'

'If the Young Chieftain thought that, he would not be searching for me.'

This was unarguable. I pushed down my triumph. The candle flickered one last time and went out, leaving Maggie's face lit only by the rush lights on the wall.

She said, 'It's *your* safety I'm thinking about. And – yes, I admit it – mine and Jee's. Applebridge is remote and unimportant. What makes you think that you'd be any safer anywhere else in The Queendom? The road from the west goes along the Apple River, and once they're through the mountains that's how the savage army will travel too. It's the road to the capital. You would be far more likely to be captured on the road than here.'

'If I left now, I would be ahead of the army.'

'And you don't think they'll send out scouts and advance patrols? Lord Solek was a fine soldier – you told me so yourself – and I'm sure his son is too.'

She was right again. I felt the ground grow slippery beneath my arguments. 'I can ... I can travel off the roads.'

'Where would you even go? If, as you claim, the Young Chieftain knows you're alive, then where in The Queendom would be safe for you? Nowhere!'

'I would have to go to the Unclaimed Lands.'

'And the only way to get there is by travelling through half The Queendom.'

She was right. But then she caught the meaning behind my words.

'The Unclaimed Lands. You mean you're going *there*. To search for *her*.'

She meant Soulvine Moor. She meant Cecilia. She meant search in the country of the Dead. But Cecilia, though no longer living, was not in the country of the Dead. Cecilia was nowhere and never would be anywhere again, and I would never tell Maggie any of that terrible story.

'No,' I said, 'I'm not going to search for Cecilia.'

'Then why go?' It came out a wail, which shocked me so much that I stood, clumsily knocking over the trestle. Maggie does not wail. Maggie does not sob. Maggie does not lose control. But she did so now in a manner that I had not seen for over two years. She put her head in her hands and cried, her fair springy curls shaking with each gasping sob. She cried as if she would never stop.

'Oh, Roger—' she never called me Roger '—it's so unfair! You want us to give up everything, and I did it all for you! I worked only for you and tried so hard with the inn only for you, and you won't bed me or love me or ... The savages will find you out there on the road, and even if they *are* looking for you it wouldn't occur to them that Roger Kilbourne would be in a place like this, not after a palace and a queen, and ... they'll kill you!'

I did it all for you.

You won't bed me or love me.

We'll lose everything if we go now.

Each sentence was a stone in my mouth, gagging my throat, lying heavy in my belly. Each word was true, and next to their granite solidity my desire to leave seemed insubstantial as fog. I didn't really believe that we were in danger here, or that the Young Chieftain knew enough to seek me in Applebridge, or to recognize Roger Kilbourne in Peter One-Hand. I wanted to leave Applebridge because I was so bored and restless here. Because I was more discontented with what I had than grateful for what I had been spared. Because I was still, and for ever, a fool.

'Don't cry, Maggie. Don't cry.' I couldn't make myself walk around the table and put my arms around her. But

I could make myself force out my next words, and I did so. 'You're right. We'll stay here.'

On the hearth, the dog suddenly raised his huge head and howled.

5

That night, the dreams were particularly bad. As vivid as real life – no, more vivid.

A flat upland moor, with a round stone house. There is the taste of roasted meat in my mouth, succulent and greasy. In the shadows beyond my torch I sense things unseen. Inhuman things, things I have never met in this land or in that other beyond the grave. Moving among them is a woman's figure, and the voice coming to me from the dark is a woman's voice, and I can see the glint of a jewelled crown: 'Roger. Hisaf.*'*

'But you're dead,' I say.

'Eleven years dead,' she says, and gives a laugh that shivers my bones.

I woke in the sheep pen, to the pungent smell of the ewes and the bleating of one of the lambs. Outside lay another fine summer morning. Down the hillside, Jack Lambert's pretty daughter walked their goats to pasture. She waved to me. I waved back, the dream still on me, and picked straw off my clothing. The chickens squawked in their coop. Jee came out of the inn to draw water from the well.

Everything as usual, everything normal. Nothing indicated that somewhere to the west a savage and invading army was on the move.

The dog had spent the night lying outside the sheep shed, although it was unclear whether this was to protect the livestock or to eat it. For the first time I noticed that the dog wore a collar, a thin strip of leather the exact colour of his short grey fur. Burned into the leather was a meaningless design of squiggles. I traced the squiggles with my fingers while the dog tried to twist his head to lick me. 'Do you belong to someone else, boy? Do you?'

He wagged his tail.

With the dog here, the sheep would not leave their shed. I pushed and pulled and smacked the lead ewe on her flank and then on her stubborn head, but she would not budge. All I got for my pains was a boot-sole of sheep dung. This thwarted my idea of taking them directly to pasture, thus skipping breakfast and avoiding Maggie. Cursing, I closed the sheep inside the shed – maybe Jee would do better with them later – washed my boot at the well and went into the kitchen, hoping desperately for no more tears.

There were none. Maggie smiled at me and said, 'I have your breakfast ready in the taproom, Peter. I'm sure you're hungry.'

The trestle table, freshly scrubbed, was set with a wooden trencher and tin tankard. Cheese, new eggs, wild berries with clotted cream and small cakes dusted thickly with sugar. Maggie must have been up since before dawn, cooking this compensation prize for the loser in our quarrel. *Noblesse oblige*.

All at once I was not hungry. But to not eat would only make things worse. 'How fine!' I said heartily, sat down and ate a strawberry. Maggie sat across from me. She wore a fresh smock, tightly laced black stomacher and skirt of red wool hiked up over a striped petticoat – her best clothes. Her light curls, freshly washed, were tied with a red ribbon. All this looked dangerous.

'Peter, I've been thinking.'

Maggie was always thinking. I nibbled at a cake. It tasted wonderful. 'Oh?'

'Yes. We need ... Good morning, dog.'

He had followed me inside and now sat on his enormous haunches, eyeing the food. I gave him a sugar cake and waited defiantly for Maggie to protest that sugar was too expensive to waste on a beast. She did not. Instead she said brightly, 'What will you name him?'

I hadn't thought of that, but of course he must have a name. And Maggie was trying to please me. I said, 'I don't know. Do you have any ideas?'

She studied the huge grey dog. 'His eyes are so strange. I don't think I've seen that colour eyes on a dog before.'

I hadn't noticed the dog's eyes. Now I did, and was startled. They were the same colour that Cecilia's had been: a clear bright green. But surely I would have noticed that yesterday? Hadn't the dog's eyes been a different colour, or less bright, or ... something? But that was impossible. It must have been the difference in light that had made me not notice how green they were. Light can play tricks on the eyes.

Evidently Maggie was not reminded of Cecilia, for which I was grateful. She said, 'I've seen a cat with eyes that colour, but never a dog. You could call him Greenie.'

It was the stupidest name I'd ever heard. 'No, I don't think so. It doesn't ... fit him.'

'Captain?'

'No.'

'Rex?'

'No.'

'Hunter?'

'No.'

'Bandit?'

'No.'

'Are you saying no because you don't like those names or because I'm the one suggesting them?'

I didn't answer her right away. A strange sensation rose in my mind, as if a dream had flitted lightly through my skull and then dissolved like smoke in a strong breeze.

31

I said slowly, 'Shadow. His name is Shadow.'

The dog looked up at me. His eyes were clear green water.

'That's a fine name,' Maggie said warmly. 'And by coincidence it's naming that I wish to talk to you about. I think we should choose a name for the inn.'

'A name?'

'Yes. And have a sign painted and hung.'

'A sign?'

'So people will know where they've come to.'

Nearly all our custom was local folk, who knew very well where they'd come to because this was the only inn for five miles around. All at once I noticed things in the taproom that I had scarcely paid attention to before: a tankard of daisies on the other trestle table, a small bit of weaving hung on one wall, a carved wooden rabbit on the broad windowsill – where had Maggie got that? And did all women feel this need to nest, to transform what had been perfectly adequate before?

She gazed at me with hopeful, shining eyes in which I nonetheless saw something determined, even ruthless. But then if she had not had those qualities, she could not have rescued me from death in the last days of Queen Caroline's reign. I could not deny her a sign for the inn, no matter how much I disliked the notion. And why did I even dislike it? I didn't know.

'That's a good idea,' I said with as much enthusiasm as I could force. 'What shall we call the inn?'

'I thought perhaps the Red Boar.' She pointed at the weaving, which, I now saw, depicted a boar stitched in red wool.

'Fine.'

'Unless you prefer something else.'

'No, that's fine.'

'If you prefer something else, Peter, just say so.'

'It's fine!' *Now leave off about it!*

'Good. Then let me show you something.' She went into the kitchen, returning a moment later with a wooden board painted with a red boar and the words 'Red Boar' written below.

I can read. Maggie taught me. I recognized her bold letters from the patient instruction she'd given me on winter afternoons. She had had this sign ready before we even discussed it.

She said, 'Jee painted the picture. I didn't know he could do so well; nor did he. Do you think you can make a bracket and hang it over the door?'

'Yes.'

'Today?'

'Yes.'

'This morning?'

'Yes, yes, yes!'

Maggie is not without perception. She said quietly, 'You think I'm pushing you.'

She *was* pushing me. But it wasn't Maggie that was wrong. I was wrong, in some deep way I didn't understand. This life was wrong.

'I'm sorry, Maggie,' I said, and I meant it. 'It's a perfect sign, and I'll hang it this morning.' I walked around the table and did something I rarely do: I kissed the top of her head. She went still. Before she could desire – ask for, compel, quarrel over – anything more, I was out the door, Shadow at my heels.

Piss pots! I hadn't eaten more than a few bites of her elaborate breakfast.

I took the sheep to their usual pasture, first tying up Shadow in the stable yard. Ten minutes after we left, Shadow came bounding after me, his rope broken in two. I had not realized the dog was so strong. Immediately the sheep began to make shrill, terrified noises.

33

'You're a bad dog,' I told Shadow, who wagged his tail.

I tied him to a tree by what was left of his rope and took the sheep far enough away that they stopped bleating. A few minutes later Shadow broke his rope and raced after us. The younger ewe broke away, and both of us ran after her, leaving the others bawling behind. I tripped over a bayroot. Shadow caught the ewe by leaping on its back.

'No! Shadow, no!' He would maul the sheep, kill it, eat it – I stumbled to my feet.

But the dog had not hurt the ewe. He stood casually beside her, and every time the stupid animal moved, Shadow moved to block her escape. I blinked. I had seen dogs herd sheep before, but not Shadow's breed (whatever that was). And he had not exhibited this behaviour yesterday.

The sheep still bleated and wailed. In this state of mind – if the silly things even have minds – they were not going to feed. I sighed, led the errant ewe back to the others, slung her lamb over my shoulders and started back to the inn. The rest of my small hungry flock followed. Another futile excursion. And what awaited me seemed equally futile. Muck out the chicken yard. Weed the kitchen garden. Hang the new sign. Help with the laundry.

Only it did not happen that way. I entered the inn through the kitchen. Maggie wasn't there. She and Jee stood in the taproom, both staring at the hearth. Maggie pointed. A rock sat on the cold stones of the empty hearth.

'It . . . it came down the chimney,' Maggie whispered. Her face had gone white as her smock. 'A moment ago. And . . . there was no one on the roof.'

Jee clutched at Maggie's skirts, as if he were five years old instead of ten.

Gingerly I approached the rock. It was a perfect disc, a

full hand-span across and flat on top and bottom, heavy on my one palm. What I could see was featureless, an even grey, but as I picked it up I saw flecks of green in the stone, malachite or chrysoprase. I turned the stone over. On the other side, as flat as the first, the green flecks formed letters, not bonded on but an integral part of the rock itself. Maggie, reading the impossible lettering over my shoulder, gasped.

DANGER – LEAVE NOW – MC

6

Mother Chilton. She must have known where I was – for how long? That fragile web of women who 'studied the soul arts' with varying degrees of skill, how far did it extend? Was there someone here in Applebridge, someone I saw every fortnight . . .

Maggie said, 'It's from . . . from . . .'

'Yes. Jee, were you outside when this stone fell down the chimney?'

'Yes.'

'What did you see?'

'Naught.' The boy touched each of his eyes and squeezed them shut, the country folks' charm against witches. And yet he knew what I was.

'Nothing?' I said. 'Think hard, Jee!'

'Naught. Except . . .'

'What?'

'There be a hawk, circling high up.'

I hefted the stone – too heavy for a hawk to carry, especially 'high up'.

Maggie had recovered from her shakiness. She had always respected Mother Chilton, the 'great apothecary', and now her fear of Mother Chilton's message catapulted Maggie into what was most natural to her, getting things done.

'We can leave within the hour, Peter. I'll pack food. Jee, fill that old water bag from the cupboard under the stairs, and mind that you rinse it out three times first. Then roll up our winter cloaks as tight as you can and

36

bind them with the string from the peg in the kitchen. Peter, you should— Oh, what about the animals? I don't think we can take them with us, although maybe if you kill a chicken – no, two – I'm sure there's time . . .'

I put my one hand on her shoulder and turned her to face me. No avoiding this battle. As Jee ran off to do Maggie's bidding, I took a deep breath.

But she was there first. 'No, Roger,' she said quietly, using my true name. 'You can't leave me behind. Nor Jee, either. There are savages in that army who will recognize me. They captured me once before in order to get to you, remember? If the Young Chieftain is as smart as you say he is, then he will use those men again. I am in as much danger as you. And so is Jee. You can't leave us behind, even though—' and being Maggie, she could not leave off the last phrase '—even though you want to.'

Yet last night she had argued that none of us would be recognized. Still, she was right on both of today's points. The Young Chieftain would use her, as his father had, to get to me. And I wanted to leave her and Jee behind.

Her face had the crumpled, defiant look it got whenever we alluded to our living arrangements. Not for the first time, I wished that Maggie did not feel so compelled to name hard truths. I capitulated – for now.

'Maggie, you said yourself that we have little time. We are all three going, and within the hour. Pack the food and I'll kill the chickens. We must be away before anyone comes to the inn.'

She nodded vigorously and sped into the kitchen, where I could hear the rattle of pots and slamming of keeping-box covers. I strode outside, caught two chickens, killed and blooded them. All I could do for the sheep was open the door to their shed and hope that they would wander to pasture and into some farmer's flock, or that an inn patron would find us all gone and take them, along with the rest of the chickens.

Within the half-hour we had left the inn, slipping into the wooded slope behind the cottage. Shadow followed. When we were deep enough into the woods to not be seen, Jee stopped and said, 'Where be we going?'

A reasonable question. The child looked at me expectantly, and with some pride. Jee, snarer of rabbits and gatherer of nuts and berries, knew the countryside for miles around. Wherever I said we were going, Jee knew he could guide us there.

I hoped that Maggie had exhausted her week's supply of hurt outrage. But I doubted it. I said, 'We head towards the capital, Jee. But not along the river.' Along the river ran roads, villages, armies.

Maggie said, 'Towards *Glory*? But that's where the savage army will go, to claim the princess!'

'We're not going into Glory, Maggie. Just near it.'

'Now she was suspicious. 'Near it where?'

There was no help for it. I wouldn't lie to her. 'Tanwell.'

'You ... you want to leave me and Jee with my sister.'

I said nothing.

'My miserable piss pot of a sister, who will use me like a slavey and Jee like a dog.'

At the word dog, Shadow wagged his tail.

'No,' Maggie said.

Despite myself, I was impressed. No arguing, no crumpled face, no hurt tears. Just a simple no, smooth and hard as the stone that had inexplicably fallen down my chimney. I said nothing.

'We can travel south, staying in hills and woods,' Maggie said, 'and still reach the Unclaimed Lands by a longer route. Settle in some rough farming village on the border between The Queendom and the Unclaimed Lands

– that would be safest. We can get work as labourers until we can start over. Jee, lead on.'

Jee looked from Maggie to me and back again. Silently he picked up his pack and led off. Maggie followed him, I followed her, and Shadow followed me. For now.

Travel in early summer. Long days of walking under the hot sun, short nights of sleeping off exhaustion. We avoided villages unless we needed supplies, and then we sent Jee to buy them, accompanied by Shadow. But we needed to purchase very little. Jee set rabbit snares each evening. Shadow too hunted small game and, surprisingly, laid it untouched at my feet. This endeared him to Maggie, who could pluck a wild partridge faster than anyone in Applebridge. Once Shadow even brought a suckling pig, stolen from some farmer's wallow. Maggie scolded him, but I think even a dog could tell that her heart wasn't in it. She roasted the pig and we ate it, the rich juices filling our bellies and the skin crackling and crisp in our mouths. Swift clear streams kept the water bag full. We slept wrapped in our cloaks, or upon them, under bright summer stars.

We spoke only of the journey, never of the reason for it. When Jee went into a village to buy bread and cheese, he brought back little news. These remote villages heard even less than Applebridge, which at least had travellers along the river. No one mentioned an army of savages invading The Queendom, and neither did we talk of it among ourselves. It was almost as if that fortnight was detached from the rest of the world, holding the three of us in a moving bubble, transparent and softly coloured as the soap bubbles a child will make on wash day. There was no rain, no high winds, no storms. The nights were clear and warm, scented with wild thyme and woodland flowers. I did not dream. We had, however falsely, a kind of gentle peace.

The Queendom is a vast plain, circled to north, west and south by mountains and to the east by the sea. The northern mountains are little more than hills; beyond them lies the queendom of Isabella, kin by marriage to little Princess Stephanie. The Western Mountains are high and jagged. To the south lay neither hills nor mountains but a wild country all its own: high plateaux and deep ravines and tiny valleys, rough and infertile, inhabited only by hard-scrabble farmers and hunters who barely wrested a living from the grudging earth. The Unclaimed Lands. Jee had been born there.

And beyond the Unclaimed Lands lay Soulvine Moor.

Maggie did not know what I planned. I was sure of it. And if I travelled this fortnight with a kind of steady easiness that rose almost to light-heartedness, I was glad to deceive her. For although I was not light-hearted, I did feel a kind of pleasure, which brought its own kind of guilt. The pleasure was at escaping the inn at Applebridge and the life which went with it. The guilt was because I had wanted that kind of peaceful life, and had built it along with Maggie, and it seemed terrible to me that I wanted it no longer while she still did.

She had said we would find work as labourers 'until we can start again'. And I had no doubt that she *would* start again. Within two years of choosing some village, Maggie would again run an inn, or a cookshop or a barter house. She would learn a cobbler's trade or a cooper's or an apothecary's. She could learn and do anything, anything at all, and she would not let me do what I wanted, which was what I had always wanted: go to Soulvine Moor, cross over, and find my mother in the Country of the Dead. Only from my mother could I learn who was my father, who was the crowned woman in my terrible dreams, who I was myself.

'You will seek your mother. Despite anything I would tell you,' Mother Chilton had said two years ago. But I had not. Now the chance had come, and I would not rest until I found my mother and she told me what I must know.

So I walked with Maggie as we moved south-east and the countryside grew steeper, more wooded, less peopled. I joked with her, slept at night across a banked campfire from her, and said nothing about my plans. And so we came to Haryllbury.

'This is the place,' Maggie said.

In mid-afternoon we stood on a high rise, looking down at a village beside a small lake. It was larger than most hill settlements, perhaps because of the lake. A small river fed it, tumbling down from the mountains and winding like a slim swift snake among the steep hills and through the sudden ravines. Farm plots, tiny and irregularly laid out, but nonetheless under cultivation. I didn't know if we still stood in The Queendom or over the border in the Unclaimed Lands, and later, when I came to learn the village's name, I still didn't know. 'Haryll' sounded like the latter, 'bury' like the former. The place was a cross-breed, and so likely to belong to neither.

'It's big enough to afford us work,' Maggie said. 'But small enough to be unnoticed.'

'Yes, I agree. Jee, take Shadow and buy some bread.' I gave him a penny.

Jee started down the hillside, Shadow bounding alongside. Maggie and I sat on the thick grass, grateful for the chance to rest our legs. She began to pull up daisies and braid them together into a chain. Bees hummed around us, drinking of the red clover, and a rabbit leaped by. Lucky for it that both Jee and Shadow had gone.

Maggie said quietly, 'Don't go, Peter.'

She knew. Perhaps she had always known. I couldn't look at her.

'Don't leave us. You were going to slip away at night, weren't you? Make sure we had work and a place to sleep, and then set out alone. Leaving me. Again.'

Once before I had tried to leave her behind, when I had forsaken the palace and gone to search for Cecilia. That time she had insisted on following. I sensed that it would be different now. She would not follow a second time. Maggie had her pride, and it had suffered enough where I was concerned. She wouldn't insist on coming with me, but she would do everything she could to prevent me from going.

She said, not without dignity, 'Please don't lie to me. You are planning on going to Soulvine Moor, aren't you? To search for your mother over ... over there. Please don't lie. to me!'

'*Ye will seek your mother. Despite anything I would tell ye.*'

'Yes,' I said, so softly that she bent her head towards me to hear, 'I'm going. I must go, Maggie.'

'No,' she said simply, 'you choose to go.'

And to that there was no answer. She didn't rage, she didn't argue, she didn't even cry, and I found myself thinking that I would rather any of those things than this quiet hurt, deep as the sea. The chain of daisies lay in her lap. Her head bowed over them, and her fair springy curls fell forward to hide her face. She stayed still, so still that except for the tension in her neck, she might have been dead. Might have been one of those motionless Dead on the other side, eternally sitting in their tranquil circles.

The thought chilled me. I couldn't stand seeing her like

this – Maggie, who was all bustle and energy and plans. I couldn't stand it.

'Maggie . . .' I reached out my one good hand and laid it on her shoulder.

So swiftly that she startled me, Maggie turned to face me. No tears, but she put her arms around me and hung on like a drowning woman to a raft. Her mouth breathed hot near mine.

'Then if you're really going, you cannot deny me this. One last time, Peter. I may never see you again. You can't deny me this. You can't, oh you *can't* . . .'

And I could not. Her anguish touched me to my soul. Her body was warm and soft next to mine. The sun shone hotly on us both, the heavy drone of the bees brought its own trance, the fragrant grasses rustled in a sweet breeze. We were seventeen, and my member throbbed with life. I laid Maggie gently on the wildflowers and raised the skirt of her gown.

Afterwards, she slept. Jee and Shadow had not yet returned. Quietly I took the least I needed from our packs and left her there, asleep on the sunny hillside. I turned my steps south, climbing alone into the Unclaimed Lands.

7

By evening I had reached an upland meadow, a tiny flat grassland amid steep wooded slopes and jutting boulders. The last time I had travelled through this wild country-side, I had had two hands. I was finding it much more difficult with one, even leaning on a stout oak branch as a walking staff. As darkness fell, exhaustion took me. I made a fire, ate some bread and cold mutton, and rolled loosely in my cloak to sleep. Shadow was a warm dark bulk beside me, and with the fire on my other side, I thought I would sleep easy. I was wrong.

An hour slid by while the stars came out and the moon rose, full and round and yellow as a good cheese. Until this journey, it had been over two years since I had slept without a roof over my head. The night sky brought up all sorts of feelings, all sorts of memories. Myself as a child and youth, travelling with Aunt Jo and the brute she married, Hartah. What Hartah had forced me to do at summer faires to earn a few coins from grieving and susceptible countrywomen. Hidden in our tent, I had listened to their tales of lost mothers, children, husbands. Then I had crossed over, roused some old woman to tell me details about the family, and returned with false messages of love and happiness beyond the grave. Even now, remembering these lies, I burned with shame and humiliation.

But what Hartah had made me do was nothing com-pared to what I had, as Queen Caroline's court fool, done for her. And to her.

So many Dead I had roused! All of them old, for only the old can be roused from their deep trance; perhaps only they live long enough to retain memories of life. The Dead are waiting, I think, but neither I nor anyone else knows for what. And I could be wrong. Perhaps they are not waiting at all. Perhaps this unmoving tranquillity is what they have lived in order to attain.

I would like to think that. It would mean that I had not deprived Cecilia of so very much after all. Cecilia and all the others I had brought back to life from the far country, only to ensure that now they existed in neither place, and never would again. That was the unceasing anguish in my mind. Not that Cecilia had died, but that because of me she was not among the Dead. But if death was no more than this rigid stillness, I had not taken from her anything worth having.

It was Maggie that I had robbed of everything she wanted.

But to bring Maggie with me would have been to endanger yet another woman. I was right to leave Maggie behind. But she did not think so, and even to me the thought was cold comfort. I wanted more than that, and only my mother could give it to me. I remembered her in her lavender gown, holding me on her knees and singing to me. Lavender ribbons in her hair. I remembered her scent and her bright eyes and her gentle touch

'Eleven years dead.'

No. The woman in my monstrous dream was not my mother. My mother had not worn a crown, had not been queen of anything. And the voice in my dream was lighter than my mother's, higher in pitch. Nor was it the voice of Queen Caroline, who had anyway been dead for only two and a half years, and whom I had last seen quiet and motionless in the Country of the Dead. No, this woman was only a bad dream, an insubstantial thing fashioned of air and anguished memory, not real in this land nor that other. Merely a dream.

Finally, I slept. It seemed only a few minutes later that I was wakened by a kick in the ribs. Thrashing to turn over, tangled in my blanket and blinking against the morning sunlight, I woke to two warriors standing above me, short knives drawn and pointed downward at my throat.

'*Aleyk ta nodree!*'

'*Hent!*'

I struggled, but it did me little good. One savage hauled me to my feet and pinned my arms from behind. The other peered into my face, as if trying to decide who I was. I had no idea who he was, except that he was a soldier in the Young Chieftain's army. He wore their shaggy fur tunic with leather belt and metal-capped boots. His long hair, braided away from his sunburned face, sported no feathers and he wore no short feathered cape, so he was not an officer. Some sort of scout, perhaps. Like most of them, his eyes were blue, not the brilliant piece-of-sky blue that Solek's had been, but rather a dull blue-grey. In the palace I had learned some of their guttural language, but not the words they'd uttered so far. But I understood the next exchange.

'*Mit?*' Him?

'*Tento.*' I don't know.

'*Jun fee kal.*'

That last I did not understand. However, it took no language to understand the hands that went roughly over my body and through my pack. They took my big hunting blade but left the tiny shaving knife in my boot. They pushed me forward and we began walking, off the meadow and down the mountain.

I was a prisoner. But so far I had not been hurt in any way. And the savages were not sure who I was. In two and a half years I had changed: filled out in the body, gone gaunt and sunburned in the face, grown a beard, lost a hand. *They were not sure who I was.* Desperately I clung to that, because there was little else to cling to. The savages were big men, in the prime of their strength and manhood, and the larger outweighed me by at least three stone. Running from them would only get me hurt.

How had they found me? Had they already captured Maggie and forced her to talk? Maggie, whom I had left peacefully asleep on the hillside fragrant with clover. She wouldn't betray me unless they forced her. But under torture, anyone will betray anything. And Jee, with his thin small bones ...

I stumbled, going down heavily, unable to catch myself with only one hand. The savages halted and waited for me to get up. They did not touch me. I staggered upright and we carried on down the steep slope. As we descended, the mountain rose behind us, blocking out the morning sun, so that it seemed as if it were setting instead of rising.

We were heading north, back to The Queendom. Towards Haryllbury? Fear for Maggie and Jee rumbled through me like summer thunder.

After several hours, the savages paused for food. They let me drink from my water bag and pull cheese from my pack. My throat was so parched it was difficult to swallow. The savages, who said little even to each other, seemed to feel no fatigue from the half-day's hard march over rough terrain. I had thought myself hardy from long hours of labour at the inn, but tending sheep and nailing boards could not compare with whatever training these men had. Nor could what now seemed the leisurely pace with which Maggie, Jee, and I had come from Apple-bridge. Ten minutes to eat and to fill the water bags at a swift stream, and we were off again.

'*Alt!*' one savage said, whipped his *gun* off his shoulder

47

and fired. Twenty feet away, a deer that had burst from cover was cast into the air and then fell back to earth.

It was the first time I had seen a *gun* fire up close. The terrific noise echoed off the mountains. The deer was dead, its head bloody. This was the weapon that had given Lord Solek's army control of The Queendom once before, and apparently was doing so again, for these soldiers were taking no trouble to conceal their presence from any nearby farms. My ears were still deafened from the *gun*. Swords were no match for this.

The savage skinned and butchered the deer with his short knife. This was useful information: Unlike Lord Solek's knife that had taken my hand, this one was not tipped with poison. The savage wielded it even more swiftly than Maggie skinning rabbits. The venison was cut, salted and stored in his pack in less time that I would have thought possible.

Even such a short rest was welcome. But then we were off again, and by now I had another piece of information. The sun was setting in the west, and it dyed the sky behind us, not ahead. We were marching north-east, towards the sea. I had climbed into the Unclaimed Lands heading south-east. So we were not headed towards the village where I had left Maggie and Jee, but to some point further east. Of course, the savages could still have captured them and brought them east, but why would they do that instead of bringing me to them? So I hoped that Maggie was safe, that the savages did not recognize me, that I might be let go.

My very bones ached with weariness. More than once I thought I could not go on, that my legs could carry me no further. The savages made me continue, however, and at an even quicker pace as the land grew flatter. We were now well within the borders of The Queendom. Through twilight gloom I glimpsed prosperity all around me in this fertile valley. Even more, I smelled it and heard it. Here, cattle dung fertilized a field, the pungent odour carried on the evening breeze. There, frogs croaked beside a mill pond. The scents of mint and thyme drifted from an herb plot. Geese, penned for the night, squawked and settled.

Finally we came to a village. Although the summer night was warm and the moon full, the cottages were all shuttered and barred. No women gossiped at the well, no lovers strolled hand in hand, no young people danced on the green. We walked past gardens set behind painted gates, the hollyhocks and delphiniums and roses silvered by moonlight, and entered one of the cottages.

Two more men waited there. And I lost my last chance of not being recognized.

The cottage belonged to some prosperous farmer. Two-storeyed, it was built of soft red brick and thatched with straw gone green with moss and lichens. We stood in the kitchen, its door open to the warm summer night. Clean flagstoned floor, big fireplace hung around with polished pots of copper and pewter, bunches of herbs dangling from overhead beams. A woman lived here, caring diligently for a large family, but neither woman nor family was evident now. I smelled soap and tallow and lavender.

My mother in a lavender gown ...

Maggie safe, or bound and helpless in an upstairs chamber?

Moths circling rush lights set into holders on the walls.

A man coming toward me, wiping ale from his mouth with the back of one hand.

My skittering thoughts settled on the man, who walked towards me with a pewter tankard in his hand. He peered closely into my face, but there was no need. '*Ven,*' he said to the others. Yes. And to me, in my own language harshly accented, 'Roger the queen's fool.'

I said nothing. There was nothing to say.

Two and a half years since I had last seen him, and he had been a boy then, a singer with a voice as powerful as a war drum. I had watched him sing Lord Solek's army into the throne room of the palace, the savages marching into Queen Caroline's presence in seemingly endless numbers, pounding their cudgels on the floor and chanting a battle song. Later I had seen him sing that army into battle against a rival queen's soldiers, a battle the savages won easily with their *guns* and their superb training. The young singer had worn twigs braided into his hair and red dye on his face, as I had worn the yellow dye of the queen's fool.

He was a singer no longer. No dye, no twigs, no music. He had become a warrior. But I was still a fool.

'*Tel mit.*'

The singer-warrior's lieutenant seized me and dragged me to a narrow steep stairwell. The two men who had brought me here remained below. On the floor above we passed two chambers, both with open doors, both empty. Maggie and Jee were not in the cottage. In a third, only slightly larger bedchamber at the end of the corridor, the lieutenant pushed me into a straight-backed chair and expertly bound me to it with rope. I could move neither arms nor legs. The singer-that-was followed at his leisure, still carrying his tankard. He drained it and set the mug on a polished oak chest. He searched for words in the language not his own.

'You . . . kill . . . Solek.'

'No.' I had not been the one to thrust the swords into Solek's body, not the one to cut off his head and set it on a pike over the east gate of the city. The Blue army had done the first, Lord Robert Hopewell the second. But I had brought the Blue army, which the savages thought of as magic illusions, to the palace. I had brought them from further than anyone, including me, had believed possible: from the Country of the Dead.

'Yes,' he said. 'Now Tarek son of Solek son of Taryn ...' He lost the words. But I knew who he meant: the Young Chieftain, who wanted revenge for his father.

Hope is a strange bloom, struggling to survive in even the rockiest soil. Bound to a chair, facing the murderous blue eyes of the singer-turned-warrior, I still hoped. I hoped that revenge would not be exacted this moment. Hoped that Tarek son of Solek son of Taryn would wish to watch me die. Hoped that the Young Chieftain was not in this village and that tomorrow we would travel to wherever he was, and so give me a few more days of life.

Below me, in the kitchen, I heard the two savages who had brought me there talking and laughing and drinking. The scent of smoked ham drifted up the staircase. Disbelief seized my mind. Surely I was not going to die with the good smell of ham in my nostrils; surely I was not going to die in this small chamber with its polished oak chest and bright quilted bedcover; *surely I was not going to die—*

Then the older warrior took something from a fold of his shaggy tunic. I had never seen such a thing before, but it had been described to me once, three years ago, by an apprentice stable boy. And I knew that indeed I was not going to die, at least not right away, but that, instead of this, death would be welcome.

'No!' The scream came out of me unbidden, even as I was ashamed of it. But it would not be the last. The device was simple, a knotted cord tied in a circle, with a stick bound into it. The older savage fitted the cord tight around my forehead. He twisted the stick a half-turn, and the hard knots cut into my skull.

I cried out again. The pain was excruciating.

'You kill Solek son of Taryn,' the singer-who-was said.

Another twist of the stick. I writhed and screamed. My bladder let go.

'You kill Solek son of Taryn.'

If the stick were twisted long enough, it would force my eyeballs to pop from my head.

'You kill—'

I escaped the pain the only way possible. I crossed over.

8

Darkness—
Cold—
Dirt choking my mouth—
Worms in my eyes—
Earth imprisoning my fleshless arms and legs—

But this time, for the first time, I did not mind those terrible sensations. They were preferable to the agony I had left behind. For several minutes I sat in the Country of the Dead, gasping with remembered terror but not with pain. I could feel pain here, but only from injuries inflicted here. However, although it did not hurt, the knotted rope still bound my skull, and my arms and legs were still tied to the chair, since whatever I wear on my person travels with me. Never before had I crossed over wearing a chair.

A short distance from me sat one of the Dead, a gentleman dressed in an old-fashioned slashed doublet, full short breeches and green hose, but of course he took no notice of me whatsoever.

Carefully I rocked my chair until it tipped over. Then I wriggled my body like some sort of clothed and booted earthworm, until my one good hand closed on a stone. Not really sharp, but it would do. Patiently I worried it across the rope around my arms. This was made easier because the savage had not been able to bind me at my wrists – the stump of my missing hand would have slipped out too easily from the bonds. So he had tied me to the high-backed chair at my shoulders, and I could bend my good arm at the elbow. Still, it took a long time to cut my upper body free of the chair.

When my hand was free, I tore the knotted rope from my skull and threw it to the ground. Gingerly I fingered my temples, where the knots had been. My fingers came away bloody. Rolling onto my side, I cut my ankles free of the chair.

For several more moments I lay still, breathing heavily, wondering what would happen if the savages killed my body in the land of the living. My guess was that I would not be able to return. But would I lapse into the unknowing serenity of the rest of the Dead? Or – terrible thought – would I stay as I was now, the only person awake and moving in the Country of the Dead? *For ever?* A shudder ran through my entire body, convulsing limbs already stiff from their imprisonment on the chair.

Slowly I stood and looked around me. Since I had come here a fortnight ago, something had happened to the Country of the Dead.

Not storms, winds and quakes such I had caused here two years ago. No, this was different. Sky and landscape lay as quiet as ever. The mill stream, without the mill or its race, flowed placidly. The trees under the featureless sky did not rustle their leaves. But a little distance off, low to the ground, floated a patch of motionless grey fog. My legs almost gave way again. I had seen such a thing once before. But perhaps I was wrong. Cautiously I approached the cloud.

In the land of the living, this valley was fertile and fair. People had lived there for a long time, which meant they had died there for a long time. Many Dead dotted the landscape. Some, like the gentleman in doublet and hose, were alone, gazing serenely at the ground or the sky or a flower or a stone. But since I first crossed over at the age of six, many of the Dead I had seen had sat in circles. It was around one of these circles that the fog had coalesced. Three women and two men sat facing each other, not touching, staring fixedly at the centre of the circle, which held nothing except more pearl-grey fog. The same fog enveloped each of the motionless figures, but so lightly that I had no trouble seeing their faces and clothing. All were young men and women, and their dress said they had died in different eras. Their circle looked like those I had seen for over a decade, but the fog was new.

I moved closer.

Two years ago I had crossed over while upon Soulvine Moor and had found that a grey fog had accompanied me: a crowd of the men and women of Soulvine, invisible but somehow *there*. I had felt them, pressing close to me like heat, until I screamed and ran. A few steps and I had been out of the fog, but the fog itself had remained. The Soulviners could not manifest their solid bodies here, as I could, could not move about the countryside, could not talk to the elderly Dead. They were not *hisafs*. But in some strange sense they had crossed over with me, and their shadowy presence had taken the form of a dense dank dark-grey fog.

This fog was neither dense nor dark but merely wispy grey. And we were a long way from Soulvine Moor. Perhaps I was mistaken and this was just fog. But the Country of the Dead had no weather, not before my meddling and not after. I had not meddled now. For over two years I had not crossed over at all, until the brief crossing at Two Forks pasture. Whatever this fog was, it was not my doing.

What was it?

I reached out my hand and placed it within the fog, resting my palm on the head of one of the Dead, a man dressed in the rough tunic and leggings of a farm labourer.

He, of course, did not stir. My hand felt nothing, not even the moistness of natural fog. I moved closer, knelt down, moved closer still, until the dead labourer and I were pressed against each other and my head, as well as his, was enveloped in fog.

Did I feel a faint sensation in my mind? I wasn't sure. The slight quickening within my head might be due merely to the hard beating of my heart and rapid breathing of my lungs. The labourer, of course, moved neither heart nor lungs. His body was neither warm nor cold. He just *was*, and whether anything at all was happening in his brain, I could not know. If anything was happening in the Country of the Dead, I could not know that, either.

One thing I did know, however. If this fog was not natural, if it was indeed some sort of shadowy presence here of those who lived in Soulvine, then the only way it could have crossed over was in the company of a *hisaf* like me. And I had not brought this fog with me. I had brought a chair, some rope, a cruel instrument of torture and a bloody head, but no fog. So who had? Was there another *hisaf* here?

The only other *hisaf* I had ever heard mentioned was my father, who had left my mother and me before I could remember him. But a green-eyed old man on Soulvine Moor, the leader at Hygryll, had once told me what my sire was: '*Your father be* hisaf. *Or you could not be.*'

Carefully, as if I might break, I pulled myself away from the dead labourer, out of the fog, and up onto my feet. I turned around slowly, studying everything I could see. Grass, a small wood, a pond, some boulders and bushes and weeds and the Dead. At the very edge of my vision there was a faint shimmering in the still air. I walked towards it.

It was another circle of the Dead, this time ten people, one of the largest circles I had ever seen. Wispy pearl-grey fog hung around each figure, with a patch of fog in the middle of the circle. Again I knelt beside one of the Dead, an old woman, and put my head close to hers. Again I seemed to feel that faint tingle in my mind, too unlike the strong fog presence I had felt on Soulvine Moor for me to be sure I felt anything at all.

It is old women who are most willing to talk to me. I pulled away from this one and shook her roughly until she roused.

'Lord-a-mercy, lad, what the dung d'ye think ye be doing? Leave off!' She pushed me hard, and I tumbled back onto the grass. She might be dead, but she was strong.

'Good madam—'

'Aye, and ye'll call me by my name, if ye call me at all!'

'I'm . . . I'm sorry. What is your name?'

'Ye don't recognize me?' She heaved a great sigh, theatrical in its exaggeration, and batted her eyelashes at me. Finally I had the wit to notice her clothing: a gown cut so low that it would have put the queen's ladies-in-waiting to shame. Her flabby, brown-spotted breasts were in danger of escaping from the sweat-stained satin, and her skirt was short to show silk stockings fastened just below the knees with garters trimmed with fake diamonds. Pink-white paint lay thickly on her lined face. I had roused an old bawd who had died as lusty as in her youth.

'There was a time, lad, when ye'd have known my name, all right. I'm Sally Cleggers, sometime lady-love to – but I musn't say, should I? Your great men keep their secret lives secret, if they can!' She winked at me and looked around. 'So I'm dead, am I?'

'Yes, Mistress Cleggers. Can you tell me—'

'Well, we all must die sometime. I had a long life and

a merry one. Why, I remember once when I was a child—'

'Yes,' I said hastily. The elderly Dead will prattle happily about their childhoods; in fact, usually it's all they will talk about. Their adult selves, their lost lives, the families they left behind – these mean nothing to them. But themselves as small children, that will sometimes animate them. Sometimes, anyway. Perhaps it is because little children, in their simplicity, are closer to what the Dead are now. I don't know. None of the actual children here, nor any adults less than sixty years, have ever talked to me, or even seemed to see me. 'You were a captivating child, Mistress Cleggers.'

'That I was!' she said, sticking out her chin at me and narrowing her eyes. 'And don't ye doubt it, lad!'

'But now you're dead.'

'So it seems.' A puzzled look crossed her face, and I could see her lapsing again into the calm rigidity of the Dead. Again I shook her arm, saying desperately, 'You were the prettiest little girl in your . . .' Village? Neighbourhood? 'Your area!'

She revived. 'Well, no, I cannot say that, lad. Nell Goodman was prettier. Why, one time Nell and me—'

'Mistress, is there a *hisaf* here?'

'A what?'

'A *hisaf*'

'Speak plain, lad. That be not a word. No "*hisaf*" on Barrington Heath, where Nell Goodman and me—'

'But here, now! When you sit and wait, what are you waiting for? What do you feel?'

Her puzzlement was giving way to anger. 'I be dead, lad! I wait for nothing!'

'And do you feel anyone else here with you?'

'*Ye* be here, and a more troublesome idiot I never did see!'

'But is there anyone in your mind that—'

She was gone. Tranquillity had reclaimed her. If I shook her arm again, all I would hear was a tedious story of Nell Goodman sixty years ago. I had learned nothing.

Or perhaps I had. If Mistress Sally Cleggers had been experiencing the presence of Soulviners while in her serene trance, wouldn't she know that? Wouldn't she have awakened frightened, as I had been frightened two years ago when I crossed over to find that dense dank fog touching my mind? Perhaps not. I didn't know what the Dead felt. I was among the living.

Or perhaps I was not. I didn't know what the Young Chieftain's soldiers, back in the upstairs bedchamber of that snug cottage, were doing to my helpless body. It was possible I was already among the Dead, and would not know it until I returned – if I could return.

And now another terror came to me. I had brought Cecilia back from the dead. I had brought back the sailor Bat. I had brought back the entire Blue army, which had defeated Solek's men because the Blues could not be hurt or killed a second time. But a fortnight after each return all of them had melted away, leaving not even dust. They had vanished for ever, to be found neither among the living nor the Dead. Would that now happen to me?

If I was even now being tortured to death in the land of the living, and then I crossed back over, would it be as if I brought *myself* back from the dead? Would I live a fortnight on the other side, whole and invulnerable, and then melt grotesquely away, my chance at eternity forfeit?

I didn't know. I didn't know anything. I was afraid to stay here and afraid to go back. Fear tightened around my chest until my breath came fast and shallow, and my heart pounded hard enough to hurt. I put my head in my hands and there, in the quiet Country of the Dead, I wept and sobbed like the six-year-old I had once been, who lost his mother to a death he could not understand.

9

I stayed longer in the Country of the Dead, but I could not stay for ever. There was no way to know if more or less time had passed here than in the land of the living; time is not the same in the two realms. However, if the pain on the other side was too great, I could always cross back again. My torturers could not take that escape away from me. It was mine.

Despite my fear, I had to know if I was I already dead in that tiny bedchamber in The Queendom. I took a last look at the puzzling grey fog, wispy and motionless around the circle of the Dead. Then I bit my tongue and crossed back over.

Darkness—

Cold—

Dirt choking my mouth—

Worms in my eyes—

Earth imprisoning my fleshless arms and legs—

I was back in my body in the cottage bedchamber, again tied to the chair and with the knotted cord bound painfully around my head. A burst of agony around my eyes as I returned, and a moment to clear my blood-soaked vision. *So much blood.* And then I saw that it was not all mine. Only a small portion of it was mine.

The two savage soldiers, the singer-warrior and his lieutenant, lay on the floor. I could see the lieutenant clearly, but the singer-that-was lay mostly behind the bed, where he must have fallen. On the quilted bedcover the pattern of wildflowers was spattered with sprays of blood. The lieutenant's throat had been torn out in fleshy gobbets of meat and blood. His hands were flung helplessly above his head and one arm lay at a grotesque angle to his still body. Beside him sat Shadow, wagging his tail.

It was a moment before I could speak. When I did, my voice came out thick and high. 'Shadow . . . did you . . . ?'

Of course he had. The huge dog gazed at me expectantly, eager for praise. His green eyes shone. Blood matted his grey coat. In the dim light from the single tallow candle on the dresser, the blood looked almost black, oily and viscous as tar.

I felt sickened, and relieved, and grateful. Mostly, however, I felt scared. Where were the other two savages, the ones who had brought me here? At any moment they could come pounding up the stairs, *guns* drawn, and I didn't think even Shadow would be a match for guns. Why hadn't they come up already? They must have heard some noise – a dog cannot kill two men without noise.

Someone was climbing the stairs.

'Shadow, go! *Kill!*'

The dog wagged his tail harder.

A figure filled the doorway. All I could see was his outline, and then he came carefully into the room.

Not a savage. It was a youth of about my own age, at least six and a half feet tall, his considerable bulk made even larger by a pack strapped to his shoulders. Yellow-haired and stubble-bearded, he was dressed like the son of a prosperous farmer in wool tunic and leggings, with thick leather boots. In one enormous hand he carried a pig-butchering knife. We stared at each other for a moment, he looming huge above me, before he loosened the knotted cord from my head. I gasped with relief. The boy's knife slashed through the ropes that bound me to the chair.

Finally he spoke. 'Who are you?'

How to answer that? I gave the simplest answer. 'Peter Forest.'

'I heard a . . . I was bringing the sheep back from high pasture and . . . Your dog ain't never done *that*?' He waved at the dead soldiers.

Shadow bounded over and licked his hand. The dog's short tail wagged. I said, 'Help me up – please.'

He hesitated, but evidently decided I was harmless. To someone of his bulk and strength, armed with a butchering knife, I most certainly was. With one hand he pulled me to my feet, but I could not stand. I collapsed upon the bed. The reek of fresh blood filled the room.

I said urgently, 'There are two more savages—'

'Dead in the kitchen. More of their soldiers hold the roads. Are *you* the reason they have taken Almsbury?'

'No.' Was I? It seemed possible, but I didn't want to tell that to this stranger who looked at me with such frank, fearless curiosity. Yes, fearless. He stood absently patting Shadow's blood-spattered head with no trace of alarm about the four murdered men, the dog that had killed them or the Young Chieftain's soldiers occupying his village.

'If you ain't the reason they came here, then why were they torturing you?' He stared at my head, where the bloody wounds left by the knotted cord still burned like fire.

'I don't know,' I lied. 'How many more savages are in . . . in Almsbury?'

'Dunno. I been several days at high pasture with my father's sheep. I came down at twilight to visit Betsy Turner. She's Almsbury's whore, you know. She told me, all a-fright, that some of the Young Chieftain's army was here, searching cottages and barns for something. Or,

I suppose, someone.' He eyed me speculatively. 'Do those wounds hurt?'

'Of course they hurt!'

'Did the soldiers cut off your hand, too?'

'No. I lost it long ago.'

He nodded, studying the stump of my wrist.

Again I tried to stand. This time my legs held me, if I kept one hand on the bedstead. My head throbbed and burned but that pain could be borne. I had to get away now. More savages could appear at any moment. Trying to make my voice as authoritative as possible, I said, 'Listen to me, boy. I will give you a silver if you will say nothing to anyone about seeing me here. If you leave now, go back to your sheep or to the . . . the whore, or to your father's house, the savages will never know you've been here. You won't be harmed. And you will be a silver richer.' I hoped he was young enough, sheltered enough, that a silver would seem like a fortune, rather than what it had seemed to me: a week's rent on the inn at Applebridge.

He said instantly, 'Take me with you instead.'

I stared at him. 'Take you *with* me? But you . . . I . . .'

'Yes!' Enthusiasm flooded him, along with that naive fearlessness, and I realized he must be younger than I had first supposed from his height and bulk. 'You don't know the countryside and I do. You're weak from torture. You have only one hand.'

If he had left out any of my disadvantages, I didn't know what it was.

'Besides,' he added, 'if the savages are looking for one man, two may mislead them. We could pretend to be cousins. Or brothers. We could make up names that fit together.'

'This is not a game!'

'I know. But I would nonetheless go with you. You and

the dog.' His fingers nuzzled Shadow's ears. The dog licked his hand.

'Your father would send men after you.'

'No. I am not due back from the sheep pasture for another day. I came down for Betsy.'

'But if your father—'

'Leave off about my father,' he said in a different tone, harsh and bitter. 'The stinking old pinchpenny ain't going to look for me. He hates me and I hate him, He'd be glad if he thought I disappeared or – better yet – died.'

I said nothing, remembering my own step-uncle, Hartah.

'I can be of use to you. I know the countryside as well as I know Betsy Turner's bottom. Also, I'm the best tracker in three counties. But we must start right away, you know. The townspeople are all shut in their cottages, scared as mice, but they ain't going to stay inside for ever.'

He was right. I made a sudden decision. After all, I could always leave him once we were in the Unclaimed Lands, creeping away while he slept, as I had crept away from Maggie. 'All right. I am glad for your help.'

'Then let us go!' he said, too happily.

We went downstairs, me holding on to the wall every step in the narrow stairwell. The kitchen door still stood open to the soft summer night. Shadow had had no trouble entering. The other two savages sprawled on the floor, one with his feet still draped over the wooden bench beside the table. Blood and ale mingled on the flagstones. In one corner stood the four long *guns* that Shadow had given the savages no time to use. The boy snatched up one.

'You can't take that,' I said. 'It makes too much noise. And do you even know how to use it?'

'I can learn.' He bent over the dead soldiers.

'Come, we have no time!'

'Just one moment.' Swiftly he went through both men's pockets, put several items I did not see into his own and grabbed a half-drunk tankard of ale off the table. He drained it and grinned at me, for all the world like a boy who has just won some cheap prize at a summer faire. In the greater light of the torches stuck in wall sconces, I saw that he was indeed younger than his body suggested and that he was extraordinarily handsome. He seemed to feel no fear whatsoever at striding out the door into an occupied village with a man he did not know, a weapon he could not use and a dog that killed.

He was an idiot.

But I needed him.

10

His name was Tom Jenkins and he was sixteen years old. Confidently he led me out the kitchen door into the moonlight, around the well house, and into a thick hedgerow bordering a small lane. A long, thin patch of bare ground had been scraped clean in the very centre of the hedge, completely invisible from either side. Tom whispered, 'Made it for Joan Westfield and me. Biggest teats in Almsbury! Stay here while I look around.'

He was enjoying this.

I huddled in the tiny space, scratched by twigs, the reek of blood still in my nostrils and the real thing clotting on my aching temples. Tom returned in a few minutes. 'This way, Peter.'

He led me along the lane, within the deep shadow of the hedgerow. When we left the shadows, Tom went first, running across fields silvered by moonlight. We ran crouched low, and once I stumbled and sprawled flat. Something small and fast skittered away from me in the half-grown hay.

We passed a barn but Tom whispered, 'No, that's the first place they'll search for you.' We kept moving until I could go no further. My legs simply refused to carry me. I collapsed onto the ground beside a ditch.

'Peter, you have to go on!'

'I ... I can't.'

I felt him crouch beside me and then he heaved me onto his great shoulders on top of the pack he already carried and set off.

'Put me down! You ... you can't ...'

He carried me another hundred yards. He was immensely strong, but he could not have kept it up much longer. This was a theatrical bit of business, a display of his great strength. When I wriggled off his shoulders he was panting heavily, and I was shamed into staggering forward on my own. Which may have been what he intended in the first place.

The full moon shed clear, cruel light. Once I heard shouting in the distance. Soldiers? Had the carnage in the cottage been discovered?

For the first time, I wondered why Shadow was not with us. Or was he, trailing along somewhere behind? Had the dog taken injuries I had not, in my own pain, even noticed?

'Shadow ...'

'Don't try to talk,' Tom said 'We're almost there.'

'There' turned out to be a cave on the side of a hill, its entrance hidden by bushes. Inside, it was so dark that I could see neither the cave's dimensions nor its interior. I had no cloak with me, nothing to lie upon, but Tom produced one from his pack. 'Sleep,' he said softly, suddenly tender as a woman.

I slept.

I woke with my left side much warmer than my right. Shadow lay pressed up against me. Tom Jenkins was gone.

Sunlight filtered weakly through the brush in front of the cave. Sitting up, I saw it was about the size of a cottage kitchen, but roofed low with irregular rock. A man could not stand upright. In the back, water dripped slowly down the rock, and the space smelled dank. Rocks and logs had been dragged inside to form a table and stools, such as children might make for their play.

Tom Jenkins's pack lay open and its contents scattered on the ground. He'd been several days at high pasture with his father's sheep, he'd told me, and the pack held flint and steel to strike a fire, a thin blanket, small cookpot, tin tankard, pewter spoon, salt in a twist of paper. The butchering knife was gone. The *gun* he'd taken from the cottage leaned against the cave wall, but I did not know how to shoot it and in any case I had no *bullets*.

Shadow stirred. 'Hey, boy, hey . . .' I could barely get the words out. My throat was swollen, my mouth dry, my head throbbing. Every muscle ached. Worse, I didn't know what to do next. Where was I? Would Tom Jenkins return, and if he did, would he bring with him savage soldiers? If the Young Chieftain had offered a reward for the man who had killed four of his soldiers . . .

The thought was like a hot sword in the ribs. Immediately I crawled out of the cave, blinking in the sunlight, to get away as fast as I could. Tom Jenkins, alone, strode towards me, swinging a full water bag.

'Good morrow, Peter! How are you today?'

How was I? No simple answer suggested itself, but Tom didn't wait for one anyway.

'I have water and food. Here, back into the cave – you can't come out till night. Almsbury's swarming with savages. Pepper my arse, but they look fierce! Here, you best eat.'

He was as cheerful as if returning from a morning stroll through a garden. Not sure what else to do, I retreated back into the cave. If Tom had set soldiers coming this way, he was more than capable of holding me here until they arrived. I possessed only my little shaving knife, which was about as dangerous as a woman's sewing needle. The savages had not even bothered to take it from me. So I sat with Tom in the dank gloom of the cave and drank the fresh water he'd brought in his water bag, ate the good bread and cheese, listened to him chatter as he tore into his own breakfast.

'Got the bread from Agnes Coldwater. She's been after me to lie with her for a month or more. Too ugly, though it's a pity because she bakes the best bread and pies and sweet cakes in Almsbury. Good, ain't it? I'm going to have to stay here with you in the cave today, you know. Pretty soon my father'll miss me, the doddering old bastard! We used to play here when I was a boy, me and John Crenshaw. John died of plague three years ago. We pretended to be highwaymen and ... Here, dog, you want some cheese, boy? Shake paws, then!'

Shadow did not shake paws. His eyes fastened on the cheese and he went utterly still, as if to ensorcel the cheese, or Tom, or both.

'He don't shake paws? Well, we can cure that, can't we. Here, boy, sit!'

Shadow was already sitting. Tom began to teach him to shake paws, using bits of cheese, talking all the while. Tom's energy was boundless. It wearied me, already weakened by pain and fear. The good food stretched my belly taut as a drum. I had just woken up, but drowsiness took me, and despite myself, I fell back asleep.

A dream came.

Not the dream of the crowned figure moving through the Country of the Dead. This was worse, a dream I had had two years ago and hoped to never have again, a dream of my mother:

She sat in her lavender gown with a child on her lap. I was both the watcher and the child, safe and warm in my mother's arms. She sang to me softly, a tune that I heard at first without words. Then the words became clear, and Roger the watcher's blood froze. 'Die, my baby, die die, my little one, die die . . .' But Roger the child listened to the monstrous song and nestled closer, a smile on his small face and the pretty tune in his ears. 'Die, my baby, die die, my little one, die die . . .'

I woke with a great cry. Shadow crashed through the underbrush and into the cave, looking for whatever had attacked me. A moment later Tom stuck his head in.

'Peter, what is it? A bear?'

'No, I . . . I . . .'

'No bear?' He crawled into the cave. He carried the savage's *gun*. The sight of it banished the last of the terrible dream.

'Tom, you can't shoot that thing out there. It makes a great noise – soldiers will come running from miles away.'

'I know,' he said cheerfully, 'but I wanted to practise holding it. There might come bears. I can shoot it once we're in the Unclaimed Lands. I took metal pellets from that savage in the cottage – that's what the weapon shoots, you know, big metal pellets – and I—'

'No! You cannot shoot that *gun*. Not even in the Unclaimed Lands.'

'Sure I can. It ain't hard. See, you open this small chamber here and—'

'Tom, you *cannot*.'

He grinned at me. 'Do you always worry so, Peter Forest? Damn, but you're tetchy as a girl. Although not so pretty. Here, have some more of Agnes's cheese.'

I didn't want some more of Agnes's cheese. Tom pointed the *gun* at me, sighted along it as if along a tautly strung bow, and said, 'Kwong!' He laughed.

I put my head into my hands.

No bears appeared. Shadow was taught to 'shake paw'. Tom fidgeted in the cave until twilight, ducked outside

71

periodically, slept briefly and fidgeted some more. Whenever he was awake, he talked. Whenever he was asleep, I worried. About Tom – was he reliable? About the savages – would they catch me? And about Maggie, whom I had abandoned. Not that Maggie couldn't take care of herself, and of Jee as well. But she had given me everything she had, and I had left her with nothing. Guilt gnawed at me like rats.

So it was almost a relief when night came and Tom led me out of the cave. Unfortunately, the weather had changed. A cold drizzle fell and the countryside was so black that I could see neither Tom nor my own feet. But he seemed to know where he was going. He took my hand and led me, stumbling, away from the cave.

'Tom, we can't travel in this. It's too dark.'

'Just wait,' he said, and pulled me around the side of the hill. 'Stay here.'

I shivered in the rain while he vanished into the blackness. Several moments later I saw a light bobbing along. It was a small lantern, a single thick candle encased in a glass housing, with holes on each side for air. Tom said triumphantly, 'Surprise! I got the lantern from Agnes this morning when I got the bread and cheese. I hid it to surprise you. Ain't you pleased?'

I was apprehensive. 'If soldiers see a light—'

'Oh, piss pots! In this rain they can't see nothing. I daresay they're all inside anyway, fucking our girls. Give you six to one odds on it. Peter, you surely can ruin a surprise.'

'I'm sorry, Tom. I am grateful, only I think—'

'You think too much,' he said shortly.

'I merely—'

'I daresay you would not have thought to ask Agnes for a lantern.'

72

It seemed best to mollify him. 'No, I would not have.'

'What do the savages want you for, anyway?'

It was the first time he had asked. I had prepared an answer designed to both fit whatever he might have heard in Almsbury and to mislead him. 'They think I am kin to the man who led that raid upon Wellford and killed three of their number. They wish to find him through me.'

He stared at me, his eyes widening. Rain ran, unheeded, from his hair and over his face. 'Someone led a raid on the savages?'

'Yes. In Wellford.'

'Where is that?'

'I don't know.' I had made up the name.

'And the raiders killed the savages and got away clean?'

'So I heard.'

'By damn, I wish I'd been there!'

He seemed to have lost track of the main idea. I said, 'Someone described the leader of the raid to the savages and said that the man had a young cousin with one hand, so they thought it was me.'

'But you told them naught about your cousin, right?'

'He's not my cousin,' I said patiently. 'He is no relation to me.'

'Oh.' His voice held disappointment. And then, 'How did you lose your hand?'

For this too I had prepared, devising the least interesting explanation I could think of. 'I misjudged while splitting wood with an axe.'

'Oh,' he said, clearly disappointed a second time. 'I thought perhaps you were having an adventure with your cousin. Come on, then!'

I followed his great bulk through the rain, trying my

best to keep within the jiggling little light of the lantern. Shadow followed me. We began the long slow climb towards the Unclaimed Lands, from which a few days ago I had descended as a prisoner.

11

We walked by night, slept by day. Tom cut both of us stout walking staffs, which helped with the steeper ascents. The weather continued foul although mercifully warm, and I began to think I would never be dry again. Tom had an uncanny ability to find safe sleeping places and trails in wild countryside beyond where he had travelled before. Each morning he built a small fire sheltered from the rain, cooked a rabbit caught by Shadow or toasted some cheese – while we still had any – and then banked the embers to relight his precious lantern at evening. He nursed those embers like a mother with a new infant, glancing at me frequently to be sure I noticed.

'You're amazing, the way you can do that,' I said, and there was sincerity mixed in with my flattery. I did not point out that he could just as well have lit the lantern anew with his flint and steel.

'Well, I do think I'm pretty fair at it,' Tom said.

'You are.'

'Three to one odds that not even your cousin could do better!'

'I'm sure not.' There was no dissuading him about my adventurous cousin. The idea had caught Tom's fancy, and therefore to him it was fact.

'What is your cousin's name again?'

'George.'

'Yes, that's right. George could do no better.' Tom smiled at his embers, protected by a large flat rock suspended above them on stout twigs, while I fell asleep in the rain. A long wet sleep, to awake again at twilight, eat a cold meal and stumble after Tom. Still, while Shadow was with me, catching small game and lying beside me, I was less fearful than I might have been. And the bad weather covered our trail and made pursuit less likely. Or so I thought.

We were now high into the Unclaimed Lands. Steadily the countryside grew wilder, less fertile, rockier. Fields of crops gave way to pastures for cattle, then to sheep, and finally to goats. No villages, merely isolated farms, poor and small, where Tom bought supplies with the last of my coins.

'I hope you don't ever tell any of these farm folk your name,' I said as we camped beside a rocky landslide that barely blocked the wind.

'Oh no,' Tom said. He grinned. 'I tell them I'm George. Like your cousin. Peter, how many girls have you bedded?'

'Girls?' I wrapped myself tighter in Tom's cloak while he took the less warm blanket. Tom was never cold. It had finally stopped raining but I was still wet, seemingly clear through to my bones. Shadow pressed closer to my side, as if he knew how much I needed warmth. The large campfire that we now permitted ourselves danced in the breeze, sending sparks snapping. I don't know how Tom found dry wood each morning. But he always did; there was little he didn't know about the woods.

'Yes, *girls*. How many?'

There had been only Maggie. I had never bedded Cecilia. I had only held her, adored her, destroyed her. I said, 'That is personal, Tom.'

'Oh, piss pots! Why should it be? Me, I've had thirteen.'

Was he telling the truth? I peered at him in the early-morning light. After walking all night, I was exhausted and wanted to sleep. Were there even thirteen willing young girls in the villages around Almsbury? But it didn't matter if he was telling the truth. All that mattered was that I keep the peace with him, so that I could survive.

In that, it was no different from being at court.

'Thirteen?' I said sleepily. 'Really?'

'Yes. I already told you of Betsy Turner and Joan West-field. My first was Annie Palmer. I was only twelve but well grown, almost like I am now, see, and she was fifteen. One day Annie caught me stealing apples in her father's orchard, and she said ... And then we ... the barn ... only I ...'

His voice faded in and out. The sun rose, its warmth welcome on my wet cloak but making me even drowsier. 'Really,' I murmured.

'Nell Potter ... in the dairy house ... Annie found out that she ... Susannah Tenler ... Peter, you ain't listening!'

The tone, reproachful and impatient, brought me awake instantly. One learns that at court: to recognize anything threatening. I needed Tom Jenkins.

'Yes, I was listening! Susannah, and ... and the dairy house.'

'No, *Nell* was in the dairy house, and Susannah and I met in the woods. She could milk me like I was a nursing ewe, by damn!'

I knew what I should say, what was expected of me. 'So many girls! I am envious.'

Satisfaction spread across his handsome face. 'I daresay not even George had that many girls at my age, did he?'

'Not half as many.'

'Nor you, neither?'

'Only three,' I said. Three seemed a good number, enough to be respectable but not so many as to seem rivalrous.

Tom was one of those whom victory turned generous.

'Well, I daresay you'll have more girls eventually. Two to one odds on it. Even with one hand.'

'Perhaps.'

'Sleep now, Peter. You look tired. You ain't very strong, are you?'

'Not as strong as you.' The mountain beneath us was not as strong as Tom Jenkins.

He leaned over, tucked his cloak more tightly around me, and said, 'Are you hungry before you sleep? There's the last of that rabbit.'

'You eat it.'

'No, I'll save it for you, when you wake. Sleep now.' He turned away, as if the sight of his vitality might somehow interfere with my rest.

It was impossible not to be fond of him. Brash, vain, only thinly connected to reality, there was nonetheless not a mean fibre in his unthinking brain. Just before I drifted off, I realized that Tom Jenkins made me feel as Cecilia once had: superior. Something I had almost never felt with Maggie.

Maggie. What were she and Jee doing now? I had thought to leave Shadow with them for protection, but he stuck to me as his fleas stuck to him. He scratched now, reaching his leg up to his neck, and it was to the comforting sound of the dog's scratching that I finally slept.

When I woke, Shadow was gone.

At first, I thought nothing of the dog's disappearance. He was off hunting, or marking territory, or chasing a squirrel. Shadow carried on unceasing warfare with all squirrels. I rose, stretched and got to my feet. My cloak had dried in the day-long sunshine. When I removed it, even my tunic had begun to dry, and gratefully I lifted my face to the sun.

Tom, as was his custom, woke all at once and immediately examined his banked embers. 'Still some fire. By damn, but I am good. Where's Shadow?'

'Away somewhere.' I stretched again, luxuriating in the hot sun, the sweet air of a golden late afternoon.

'Away? Why did you take his collar off?'

Tom's eyes were sharper than mine. He scooted over to my side of the campfire, where Shadow's grey leather collar lay on the ground. Picking it up, Tom ran his fingers over the squiggles etched into the leather.

'I didn't take the collar off,' I said. 'He must have worked it loose.'

'Oh. Well, he don't need it anyway. I wish I knew what these letters mean.'

'They're not real letters.'

He stared at me. 'Can you *read*?'

'Yes.'

This seemed to unsettle him. He scowled. I now had something he did not have. I should not have admitted that I could read. I said, lying, 'But not very well. Just a few words.'

'Can George read?'

'No, not at all.'

'Oh. Well, I have some bad news, Peter.'

My belly tightened. Tom's face looked uncharacteristically grave. So it was not my reading, after all, that had unsettled him. He said, 'Last night, after you slept, I walked to the edge of that cliff we passed yesterday, the one that slants down into that ravine with the creek on the bottom, you remember?'

Of course I did. We had spent hours feeling our way along the further cliff edge in the dark, with me apprehensive of slipping and tumbling over the edge. We needed to cross the ravine in order to follow the Southern Star. Finally we had found a crude rope bridge strung by the folk of the Unclaimed Lands, and we made our way across just as dawn broke. There was no forgetting that ravine, nor the wobbling of the old rope beneath my feet. Had it broken, we could not have survived the fall. But Tom always spoke as if I were so hopeless in this wild terrain that not only could I not navigate it alone, I could barely remember it.

I said stiffly, 'I remember the cliff.'

'On the other side, on that great upland meadow we passed through – you remember – I saw lights. Three or four fires.'

Cold slid along my spine. 'A hunting expedition, maybe.' Two years ago Jee had once mentioned that his father, whose cabin stood near the border of Soulvine Moor, had gone on 'the long hunt' with several other men.

'That may be,' Tom said. 'Or they could be savage soldiers.'

He smiled, and I saw my mistake. What I had taken for gravity, and then for disturbance, was actually Tom's version of quiet excitement. In one sense, he welcomed pursuit by the savages. Things had been too quiet for Tom Jenkins.

Before I could speak, he said, 'I cut the rope bridge with my knife. So they can't cross the ravine where we did. Ain't that smart?'

'Yes, it is,' I said with all the enthusiasm I could drag from my numbed brain. The Young Chieftain's men in pursuit . . . Again I felt the cord around my skull, the cruel knots cutting into my temples, my eyes straining from their sockets in agony.

'I daresay George wouldn't have thought to cut the bridge,' Tom said with satisfaction. 'Would he, Peter? Would he? And now we have a nice supply of rope, to boot.'

'Very smart,' I said. My lips had trouble forming the words. 'We need to go now.'

'Fine.' And then, for the very first time, 'Where are we going, Peter? Will George be there?'

12

I did not tell Tom where we were going, and he forgot about his question in the excitement of a deer breaking cover and streaking by not ten feet from us, pursued by a wolf. Tom let out a wild whoop and ran after them, coming back panting and flushed.

'Peter! Did you see that? Did you?'

'I did. What were you going to do if you caught up with them?'

'Oh, I'd never be able to catch up with them,' Tom said cheerfully. 'But it's fun trying.'

Not an idiot. A child.

'I could have tracked them much further, you know. I daresay I'm the best tracker in The Queendom. My father, the old piss pot, don't ever believe that. Wouldn't let me track nor even hardly hunt. Just watch those stinking sheep.' His voice turned bitter. '"Tom Feeble-Wit" he called me. "Tom Half-Brain". Just because that one time John Crenshaw and me . . . I *hate* sheep. I hope all of his get the black rot and that he hisself dies a-choking. Peter, you don't have a father, do you?'

'No.'

'You're lucky. Your mother's dead?'

'Yes.'

'Mine's not, but she don't never stand up for me. You can't trust women, you know. They're great fun to bed, but either they betray you or they want to own you. And they *cry*. Half the time they don't even mean it, nothing like so untrustworthy as a girl's tears. Women's weapons,

I call 'em.' Tom brooded silently by the fire for all of two minutes before grinning and asking, 'Which of the three girls you bedded was the best?'

All that night we walked at double time, or as close to double time as I could manage, south-east through the Unclaimed Lands. My journey here two years ago had taken only a fortnight, but I had been travelling from Glory, capital of The Queendom. Now I came from the far north-west, and Tom and I had already been on the road three weeks. The moon was waxing, half full. This made night journeying easier, although presumably it would also make easier pursuit by the savage soldiers.

Were they in fact pursuing me? We did not see them again. Sometimes, striding along after Tom, climbing steep trails or balancing on mossy stones as we crossed small streams, I persuaded myself that the Young Chieftain had better things to do than chase me. He had a child bride to capture, Lord Robert Hopewell's army to defeat, The Queendom to subdue and occupy. He would not spare the soldiers to pursue me.

Other times I saw the singer-turned-soldier sprawled along with three of his men on the cottage floor in Almsbury, their throats torn out by Shadow. Saw Lord Solek fall in the palace, in the green-tiled courtyard outside the queen's barred door, cursing me as he died. Saw the countless savage soldiers killed by the invulnerable Blues brought back from the Country of the Dead by the 'witch boy' that had been me. At those times I thought that the Young Chieftain would pursue me to the farthest edges of creation.

What I did not know, but hoped for desperately, was that he would not pursue me onto Soulvine Moor. Soldiers are the most superstitious people in the world. Surely by now the savages would have heard from the people of The Queendom what supposedly happens on

Soulvine Moor. Not even the wild folk of the Unclaimed Lands ventured past that border. Neither would I, who knew what actually occurred there. I hoped that should I be closely pursued, the savages would go away if I could make them believe that I had sought refuge on Soulvine Moor.

But I did not know for sure.

However, we saw no soldiers that day, nor the next, and no campfires in the night. Shadow did not return. I missed him, that warm bulk beside me. And without the dog often we had no meat. Tom was a fine tracker, as he had boasted, but he had not Jee's skill with snares and had no bow and arrows to attempt larger game. I would not let him shoot the stolen *gun*. That evening there was nothing to eat but a handful of wild strawberries gathered in the slanting rays of the setting sun. My belly growled with hunger.

Tom said, 'This looks like a real track, Peter, not just a hunting trail. It must lead somewhere. Give me some money and I'll find a farm and buy bread.'

'There's no money left.'

'No more *money*?' he said, incredulous, as if money were a thing I could manufacture but had somehow neglected to do so.

'No more money!'

'Oh.' He contemplated this. 'What will we do?'

I was weary. I was hungry. I was afraid. I was tired of travelling with pretty children to care for: Tom, Cecilia. And the dreams were back, haunting me each night. *'Die, my baby, die die, my little one, die die . . .'* I snapped, 'What will we do? We'll go hungry!'

'Oh.'

We did not speak again. Tom made the campfire, lay down and fell instantly asleep like the healthy young animal he was. I lay awake, dreading that monstrous dream, but when I finally did fall into a fitful sleep, I dreamed instead of food. Fragrant rosemary bread, fresh from the oven. Maggie's thick pea soup with crusty little meatballs floating in it. Roast mutton, sweet cakes shiny with melted sugar, big bowls of—

Crack!

The *gun* fired in the woods somewhere to my left. I jumped to my feet and grabbed, stupidly, for my walking staff – as if it would be any use against the savages' weapons! Dawn coloured the sky with red and orange, and it seemed to my terrified, sleep-dazed brain that the unseen *gun* had spattered the colours across the sky, as it would soon spatter my brains across the wild grass.

Crack!

Tom was gone.

I leaped up, fury replacing my fear. 'Tom!'

Crack!

'Tom, you son of a whoremaster!'

No answer. It was another ten minutes before he came crashing through the brush holding up a brace of dead partridges, his face all a-glow, the gun hanging limply from his other hand. 'Look, Peter! Breakfast! I did it!'

'You idiot!' I was on him before he knew what to expect, hitting him about his face and great shoulders with my one good hand, shouting that he was a halfwit, a birdbrain, a clod of senseless dirt—

He pushed me away with a single shove, his face hurt and uncomprehending. 'What? Look – breakfast! I killed them for us!'

'You fired that *gun*!'

'It ain't hard. I figured it out easy. You simply—'

'*Tom.*' I willed myself to calm. I – who had kept my temper under Hartah's beatings, Queen Caroline's scheming, Cecilia's moods – had just lost it, and with it, control over myself. We could not afford that.

'Tom, the *gun* made a huge noise. If the savages are anywhere within miles, they heard it. Now they know where we are.'

'Oh, piss pots. I cut the rope bridge.'

'That was two days ago! They could have found another way across the ravine.'

He turned sulky. 'I saw no sign of them in the woods. And I thought you'd be pleased by my partridges.'

How had he survived till age sixteen? I began to have sympathy with the father who had used him so harshly. Tom would try the patience of a statue. And yet he gazed at me so reproachfully – so crushed that I was not thrilled with the partridges he had shot for breakfast.

I sighed. 'Just don't fire the gun again. All right?'

'All right. But I still think the savages are far away. And I daresay you ain't never tasted a partridge as good as this one will be! Four to one odds on it!'

He was right. There is no sauce like hunger. The plump partridges, roasted over a hickory fire, seasoned with wild onions and washed down with cold water from a mountain stream, were the best breakfast I had ever eaten. 'I told you so!' Tom crowed, belched, and froze, his eyes going wide.

I turned to look over my shoulder. Two savages stood at the edge of the clearing, *guns* pointed at us.

Tom scrambled wildly for his stolen *gun*, and I slammed my boot down upon it. He had no chance of shooting before they did. They would kill him. They were going to kill me, but the Young Chieftain had no grudge against Tom Jenkins. Maybe I could—

'*Aleyk ta nodree!*'

'*Hent!*'

'You sons of thieving bastards!' Tom screamed. 'Don't you dare—'

'Tom! Don't!' I yelled – futilely. Tom had jumped to his

feet and drawn his knife. He charged forward. There was at least twenty feet between us and the strangers. Casually one savage sighted along the smooth metal tube of his *gun*. In another moment he would fire. I cried out again, something wordless and despairing.

A grey shape crashed into the savage and he went down, the *gun* firing harmlessly into the air.

The second savage let out a shout and spun in a quarter-circle, pointing his weapon away from me and onto the grey shape. By that time the dog had the first man on the ground. Tom sprinted across the remaining ten feet of ground and grabbed the second savage.

When Shadow had killed the four soldiers in the cottage in Almsbury, I had been gone to the Country of the Dead. I had not seen it. Now it seemed that every second was not only slowed but also exquisitely detailed, like the miniatures painted by court artists. I saw every-thing, and everything etched itself into my brain: the dog covering the fallen soldier and bending over him, graceful as a lover, to find his throat. The blood spurting in a strong jet, even as the soldier's eyes rolled in his skull and his body shook in agony. The other savage grappling with Tom. The clash of strong male bodies, the soldier older, but Tom larger and with his knife already drawn, as the savage had not. They fell to the ground so close to the other pair that the dog, now shaking his dead savage like a terrier with a rat, sent sprays of blood flying onto Tom. I saw the glint of sunlight on Tom's raised knife and the more brilliant flash as the knife descended, and all at once that blended in my mind with the flash I had once seen in the Country of the Dead, as something bright and terrible rent the sky in the second I crossed back over with my stolen army of the Dead. Bright and terrible – here, and there.

Then it was over, and Tom staggered to his feet, bloody

and triumphant. 'Hey! Oh, by damn, did you *see* that? Peter, are you all right? We got 'em, didn't we, Shadow? Hey, Shadow, good dog!'

I said numbly, 'That's not Shadow.'

Tom didn't hear me. He was patting the dog, play-cuffing him. Was examining the dead savages. Was admiring his own prowess. 'Hey, look, they better not cross *us*, let me swear to you! We're too much for them, ain't we, Shadow? By damn, Peter! I daresay your cousin George couldn't have done much better! Could he, Shadow? Good dog, what a brave killer—'

'That's not Shadow.'

This time Tom heard. He stopped burbling, looked puzzled and gazed down at the dog.

'Sure it is. What ails you, Peter?'

I walked forward and stood beside Tom. The dog looked up at me and wagged his tail. Blood still stained his muzzle. I don't know how I knew this was not Shadow. This dog had the same short grey fur, small tail and great snout, green eyes. But just as a man knows which of two twin sisters he has married, despite how alike they may seem to others, I knew this was not Shadow.

Tom knelt. 'Shake paw, boy.'

The dog kept his gaze on me and did nothing.

Tom straightened. 'You're right, Peter, it ain't Shadow. This one don't know how to shake paw. Well, here's a strange coil! Two dogs that look so much alike, and both saved your life! A strange coil! Hey, now we have two more *guns*, and maybe the bastards had money, or food!'

Strange coils did not much bother Tom Jenkins. Whereas they froze my blood and haunted my dreams.

Tom, not at all squeamish, went through the corpses' pockets and packs. I crouched before the dog and said softly, inanely, 'What are you?'

The dog did not answer, of course. Whatever else it was,

or wherever else it had come from, it was a indubitably a dog. It licked my hand and wagged its tail, and bounded over to Tom when he found on one of the bodies a hunk of roasted rabbit wrapped in a clean cloth.

I straightened. 'Tom, there could be more savages around. We need to go. Now.'

'Yes ... just one more minute to get ... By damn! Silvers!'

He held out his huge hand. On it rested six or seven silvers of The Queendom, stamped still with Queen Caroline's picture. Her lovely profile rested upon his grimy palm, delicate silvery lines upon smears of drying blood.

13

Each day we climbed higher into the Unclaimed Lands, followed by the new dog. Tom named him Shep. I said, 'I thought you told me you hated the sheep your father raised.'

'I did. Stupid beasts.'

'Then why name him Shep?'

Tom shrugged. 'Why not? He's a good ol' dog, ain't you, boy? Good boy! Let's fight!' He rolled on the ground, the dog jumped enthusiastically on top of him, and they mock-fought for several minutes, both rising up muddy and satisfied. I watched, feeling like someone's indulgent grandfather.

I had been fond of Shadow, but this dog made me uneasy. Not his manner, which was just as affectionate and devoted as Shadow's had been – the same wagging tail, the same licking tongue, the same willingness to hunt and bring back game for Tom to cook. Shep had no collar – but what were the chances of two otherwise identical dogs adopting me within a month's time? But there was no use explaining this to Tom.

'Tom, think. What are the chances of two identical dogs adopting us within one month's time?'

'I don't know. What?'

'I don't know exactly either, but—'

'Then why ask me? By damn, I wish we had a pair of dice! Can you play sichbo?'

'No.' More lies. Sichbo had been played at court. I had

played it once with Cecilia, for a forfeit I had not understood at the time.

'I could teach you. But we have no dice. I know – I'll whittle some!'

In the last few days, with The Queendom far behind us, we'd reverted to travelling by day and sleeping at night. That evening Tom sat at the campfire and laboriously carved a section of a branch into two lumpy cubes. On each face he gouged notches.

'Now, see, Peter, you cast one die first, and if six comes facing up—'

'Tom, I don't want to play sichbo.'

'Oh, but it's the greatest fun! Let me show you!'

'No.' I seldom gave him a direct refusal, but I could not bear to cast dice with him. All I could see was Cecilia in her green gown, her beautiful hair loose on her shoulders, her green eyes glowing with feverish excitement that was almost hysteria. *Roger! I shall wager with you! For a silver coin with Her Grace's image stamped upon it! Come!*

'I didn't take you for such a spoil-joy,' Tom said sulkily.

'I'll play with you tomorrow night,' I said.

'Oh, all right.' He rolled over on his belly and instantly fell asleep.

By tomorrow night I would be gone.

For now I knew where we were. Our rough track had joined another, equally rough but with landmarks I recognized. I had come this way before, more than once. Soulvine Moor lay a day's strenuous journey to the south. Tom obviously did not know that. Although a splendid tracker, he had never been far from his village of Almsbury, and the geography of the world was as unknown to him as it had once been to me. I dared not enter Soulvine itself, but at the border I could stay in the Unclaimed Lands in body, and enter the Moor only in the Country of the Dead. That way I could search safely for my mother. More safely, anyway.

But I could not do so and also keep company with Tom. What would he do if I stayed too long in my tranced state? Drag me to some rough cabin, shouting for a healer? Decide I was dead and bury me? Try to revive me by dumping so much water on my head that I drowned?

Worst of all, he might actually recognize my trance for what it was. Country folk were usually more willing to believe in the old ways, the old powers. No one at court, save Queen Caroline, had believed that I could cross over. But the country people Hartah had cheated through me at summer faires too often knew that the gift was real. However, many of them also believed it was witchcraft, and what would Tom Jenkins do if he decided I was a witch? I didn't believe that he would betray me deliberately, but there was no wall between his brain and his mouth. Always he babbled the first thing that came into his head. The less he knew about me, the less he could tell ... anyone.

So I had made a plan. The next evening, I put it in motion.

Never trust plans.

We stood in a place I recognized all too well, the homestead of Jee's family.

The cabin, always ramshackle, was now deserted. In the strong afternoon sunlight the door hung crazily, half off its rope hinges. A hole gaped in the roof. The straw pallets swarmed with lice and spiders, and not even rats could find any food to tempt them to nest-build.

'Nobody lives here,' Tom said, wrinkling his nose in disgust.

'No, not now,' I said. But they had lived here, two and a half years ago. Jee had run away from here, leaving a father much more brutal than Tom's. Here I had left Maggie, furious and tearful, in order to venture alone onto Soulvine Moor. And here, or rather in its counterpart in the Country of the Dead, I had lain with Cecilia in my arms, she dead and tranquil, unknowing that I held her. Behind the cabin, the little waterfall beside the pine grove where we had lain still tumbled over rocks into its shallow cold pool.

'Peter?' Tom said. 'What is it?' And then, with perception unusual for him, 'Have you been here before?'

'Yes,' I said, forcing myself back to the present. 'And the water is good to drink. We should fill the bag.'

'All right. Shep didn't hunt today – bad dog! Bad dog! But I can try to, although maybe I should ... I think I smell wild onion.'

'We don't need it,' I said absently, my mind still on the past. 'The dried meat you took from the dead savage is already seasoned well.'

He stopped and turned to look at me. 'How do you know that?'

I stared at him.

'That the savages' meat is well seasoned already,' he repeated, his forehead wrinkling. 'Have you eaten it before?'

'No, of course not. George told me.'

Tom nodded, willing as always to accept my mythical adventurer cousin as the best authority on anything. Lies – I could not open my mouth without adding to my store of lies, which now loomed over me large as any mountain. And now I must add more.

'Tom, it's George I want to talk to you about.'

'George?' He looked around, the limp water bag dangling from one huge hand, as if he expected to see George stride out from the trees.

'Yes. George. Remember I told you that George killed

93

savage soldiers, and that's why they are looking for me – to tell them where he is?'

'But you didn't tell,' Tom breathed. 'And you never would, not even under torture!'

'No, I didn't tell them where George is,' I said, and truer words have never been uttered. 'But I am going to tell you. Because George needs our help.'

Tom's eyes glowed. 'Anything!'

'George is planning a rebellion against the savage army. To fight them. Not in a big battle, such as happened before at Glory, but in small raids. By night, and using our superior knowledge of the countryside. We can do it, George says. And he needs soldiers.'

'He wants us!'

'He wants you, Tom. I have only one hand, remember? I am no use as a fighter.'

Tom frowned. I could almost see the slow turning of his brain, like a millstone ponderously grinding sparse grains of wheat. Finally he said, 'But you could help George in other ways, maybe.'

He was casting his dice to my numbers, did he but know it. 'Yes, I can. And George has a task for me to do. I cannot tell you what it is, but I can tell you what George wants *you* to do. He wants you to travel this track here north-east. In two days' time you will come to an inn. Wait near there for George and his men. Stay hidden in the woods.'

'How will I recognize George?'

'He looks a lot like me, but older and stronger. And he will be wearing an emblem embroidered on ... on the shoulder of his tunic – the left shoulder. A ... a red boar.'

'A red boar,' Tom repeated. 'On the left shoulder. Yes, I understand. But, Peter, how does George know about me? You and I ain't spoken to anybody since we met.'

'Shadow took him a message. That's why he left us, you know. I sent him to George.'

'You use dogs to send messages! What a good idea! And is Shep—'

'Yes, he brought me a message.'

'And when you said it was strange to find two identical dogs, why, you were testing me, weren't you, you rascal! To see what knowledge I already had about all this!'

'Yes.' He was doing half my lying for me. Shame and relief mingled in me. But surely the shame was misplaced. Weren't all these lies for Tom's protection as much as mine? He would travel for two days and discover there was no inn, no George, no red-boar band of fighters against the savage occupation of The Queendom. Tom would be disappointed, but he would otherwise not be harmed, and he would be away from my dangerous company. The savages had caught me before; they might do so again. I was, in one sense, saving Tom's life, as he had saved mine.

Tom said, 'When should I start for the inn?'

I squinted through the pine trees at the sun. 'There are still several hours of travel possible this day.'

'You're right! I'll go immediately. Peter, I'll leave you one *gun* and take the other two. Oh, wait – can you hold and fire it with one hand? No, you cannot, and perhaps George's men can use the *guns*. Yes, of course they can! A good thought! I'll leave you my big knife – here, take it – and also the water bag and the savages' meat because – no, you'll have Shep to hunt for you. He prefers you to me, but that's all right because I have two hands so it's fair you have Shep. You can keep my cloak and—'

I could not stand it: his enthusiasm, his good-hearted concern for me, his simple mind. I said, 'You should go now, Tom. The sooner you reach George, the sooner you will be of aid to the rebellion.'

'Yes, of course. Goodbye then.'

He held out his hand and I shook it. He had forgotten about the water bag in his other hand, and it flapped against his thigh as he strode off, the three *guns* strapped on his back. I watched him disappear down the faint track, a healthy young man eager to fight in a rebellion that existed only in my deceitful brain.

When I was sure he had gone, I turned my steps towards Soulvine Moor.

14

I walked south until nightfall and made camp beside a woodland pool. Frogs croaked in the darkness, splashing into the pool when I bent my lips to the water to drink. The moon spilled silvery light across the water, and in the branches of a tall pine an owl hooted, mournful and low.

Shep brought back a rabbit. Slowly, without Tom's deft, two-handed energy, I made a fire, skinned the rabbit with Tom's knife and roasted it. After dinner I destroyed all signs of my fire and hid myself in a thick deadfall of branches and rotting logs. Shep crawled in beside me. My bed of moss was comfortable, but I could not sleep. Soulvine Moor was less than half a day's journey. Soulvine Moor, and my mother.

She would talk to me. She must. I would rouse her from her death trance. (*But*, whispered my logical self, *you have never yet roused anyone who died so young.*) She would tell me how she died and why my father abandoned me to my Aunt Jo. (*But Mother Chilton told you to not seek that very knowledge.*) She would tell me who my father was. (*But always the dead speak only of their own childhoods.*) Most of all, she would tell me what I am, why I am cursed with this 'gift', and what I must do to live in the peace I had never yet found: not with Hartah, not at court, not at Applebridge with Maggie. I remembered her so clearly, my mother in her lavender gown with lavender ribbons in her hair, and myself safe and happy in her arms. She would tell me where I must go, how I must live, to be safe and happy again.

Looking up at the one brilliant star I could see from my hiding place, I could wait no longer. I was still half a day's journey from the border between the Unclaimed Lands and Soulvine Moor. But both time and distance were different in the Country of the Dead, and it may be that I did not need to be directly on the border.

I pulled my little shaving knife from my boot, pricked my thigh and rode the pain to cross over. The last thing I was aware of in the land of the living was Shep stirring frantically beside me.

Darkness—

Cold—

Dirt choking my mouth—

Worms in my eyes—

Earth imprisoning my fleshless arms and legs—

But only for a moment, and then I lay in the Country of the Dead. The deadfall was gone and I lay in the open. Scrambling to my feet, I looked around. For a long, dazed moment, I recognized nothing.

All was hidden in fog.

It hung heavily over the landscape, obscuring anything further away than an arm's length. I could not even tell if the countryside here matched that in the land of the living or if it had stretched or shrunk, as it often had before. All I could see was light grey fog: motionless, silent, parting effortlessly as I moved through it.

I tripped over one of the Dead, a man dressed in winter hunting clothes, too young to be roused. Next I fell into the shallow woodland pool. The bank, which I could not see clearly, gave way beneath my feet and I splashed into a foot of water, climbing out wet and muddy to my knees. But at least now I knew that the landscapes matched. However, without much visibility, how would I know in which direction I must walk to reach Soulvine Moor? Here there were never stars to guide me, never sun, never moon.

But I could not face the idea of returning to the land of the living. Not yet, not after having come so far. Not without at least trying to find my mother.

Carefully I walked around the woodland pool, judging as well as I could when I had reached halfway. Then I set myself to walking away from the pool, which should be south, in as straight a line as I could manage. The fog became a little less dense. I had gone less than a hundred yards, water from the pool sloshing in my left boot, when I came upon one of the circles of the Dead, and my blood stopped in its veins.

The Dead often sat in circles of four to eight people, sometimes touching, sometimes not. This was a larger circle, fourteen Dead, and they all held hands. I could see their clasped hands resting on the grass by their sides, and their legs, crossed under them or stretched out on the ground before them. But their heads were all enveloped in patches of the fog denser and darker than any on the landscape, so thick it completely shrouded each of the Dead from the neck up. And another, equally dense patch of fog rested in the centre of the circle.

When I had meddled before in the Country of the Dead, keeping the Blue army artificially roused and then bringing the Dead soldiers temporarily back to the land of the living, the landscape had reflected my meddling. Winds, storms, quakes and finally the tearing of the sky itself, so that there roared out of it that bright and terrible thing I had glimpsed for only a brief second. Trying to change death itself had monstrously roiled the landscape of death. But that was not happening now. This ground was as stable, the air as motionless, the woods as silent as the grave that in fact they were. Only the fog was different. And it had increased hugely since I last crossed over.

Cautiously I approached the circle. Closest to me was, judging from the shabby homespun skirt and wrinkled bare feet that were all I could see, an old woman from some poor upland farm. It is old women who are most willing to talk to me. I put my hand within the dark fog and laid it upon her head.

Immediately I jerked my hand away and cried out. Her head *vibrated*. It felt like touching the outside of a hive humming with bees. My hand was not injured, and the lower half of the old woman's body rested as tranquilly on the grass as before.

'Mistress! Wake up!' With the toe of my wet boot I nudged her leg. Nothing. I pushed harder. Nothing. Finally I kicked her, knowing that the Dead cannot be hurt, but although my kick knocked her over, she did not rouse. However, her hands slipped from those on either side of her in the circle.

All at once the patches of dense fog dissolved from around each head; what remained were thirteen Dead holding hands and one lying peacefully on the grass. I could see each clearly. No heads vibrated. But the dark patch of fog in the centre of the circle began to hum angrily.

Those were the watchers from Soulvine Moor.

I dared not approach that angry central fog. The cloud could not, as far as I knew, move from that one spot, but what did I really know about what was happening here? Nothing. This was new, and troubling, and there was no one to help me understand it – unless my mother was that one.

In the land of the living, Soulvine Moor had lain a half-day's walk from where I had crossed over. The Moor might be closer here – or further. I had crossed over soon after dark. I had the whole night and, should I need it, the whole of the next day to spend in the Country of the Dead. My body could go that long tranced. It was a risk, but I was well hidden in the deadfall from any savage soldiers, and Shep would protect me from four-legged predators. Skirting widely around the remains of the circle, I again moved south through the fog.

It was not easy to keep my bearings. But as the land rose and the woods thinned out, I was sure that I approached the Moor. I passed two more large circles of the Dead, all holding hands, each head shrouded in impenetrable dark fog. In the centre of each circle was a patch of even darker fog. I did not approach the circles.

Finally, after hours of climbing steadily upwards, the ground levelled and began to feel springy under my feet, squishing slightly as I walked. *Peat.* I was on Soulvine Moor.

Another hour of walking and I came to the largest circle yet. Twenty-one Dead. Except for its size, it looked like the three circles I had seen in the Unclaimed Lands. But I knew how people died on Soulvine Moor – at least those people who either were strangers or natives who left and then returned. It was how Cecilia had died.

Don't think of it.

And then I saw something that wiped away all thoughts of the past. *Figures moved in the fog.* Figures, where heretofore nothing had moved except me.

They came towards me very slowly, three of them, as shrouded as the immobile circled Dead. Their dense mist moved with them, dark patches in the lighter fog that hung everywhere. Slowly, so slowly, they approached me, then stopped on the far side of the circle of twenty-one Dead.

'What . . . what are you?' I quavered, and realized that I had said the same thing, on the other side, to Shep. But

101

Shep was a dog – familiar, solid, known – at least in form. I could not see these forms beneath the fog. I did not know if they were solid. I could not imagine what they might be.

None of the three answered.

We stood there, on opposite sides of an immobile circle of the Dead, in the grey silence. I don't know how long we stayed thus, I waiting fearfully for what might happen next, and they waiting for ... what? It seemed a long time. Perhaps it was, perhaps not.

A woman's voice spoke from behind me. 'Roger.'

I screamed and whirled around. Now the pervasive light grey fog had thickened, although without growing darker. A wall of it stood behind me, and it swirled as if in a light breeze. Through that swirling pale fog it seemed I glimpsed shapes, shifting and inhuman, and among the shapes the glint of a crown.

The voice was the voice of my dream.

'Roger,' she said again, and then, 'Eleven years dead.' And she laughed.

It was a laugh to shiver bones, to shatter minds. When the wall of swirling fog moved towards me, I bit my tongue and crossed back over.

Darkness—

Cold—

Dirt choking my mouth—

Worms in my eyes—

Earth imprisoning my fleshless arms and legs—

Horrible, but not so horrible as what I had left. For the second time in my life, my travel through the cold and maggoty grave was actually welcome. Then I lay back in the land of the living, wrapped in Tom's cloak, hidden in the deadfall in the Unclaimed Lands. Shep was gone.

I had crossed over early in the night. Now the sky was pale grey. Dawn? I crawled out of the deadfall to see red streaking the western sky. Sunset. Time is different in the Country of the Dead, and I had been gone nearly twenty-four hours. Hunger twisted my belly. Where was Shep?

The dog waited outside the deadfall, and beside him waited Tom Jenkins, his face stiff with anger.

15

'Tom,' I said, inadequately. He was supposed to be on his journey to join George's mythical rebellion. I was supposed to have time to think on what I had seen in the Country of the Dead. Nothing was as I had planned. 'Tom—'

'Roger,' he said, and my growling belly clenched like a fist.

'That's your name, ain't it?' he said. 'Not "Peter Forest". Roger Something, and you lied to me all along.'

What could I say? He was right. I had lied to him, and chances were I would now have to lie again. My lies might be for his own protection, but it was clear that Tom was not interested in being protected. He had no idea of the forces against which he might need that protection. Neither, for that matter, did I. *'Eleven years dead . . .'*

'I went as fast as I could down the track,' Tom continued, 'and I came last night to a farm. There were only two women and a passel of young children there; the men were away on what the head woman called a "long hunt". It was a poor hard-scrabble kind of place, but they gave me something to eat and a place to sleep in the goat shed.'

Now I could smell the goats on him. I had underestimated the speed with which his strong body could travel. Shep sat on his haunches, looking back and forth between us.

'But before I went out to the goat shed, I sat with the women and children around their hearth. I cut them wood and fetched water, and they were kind to me. Also, I think they were glad of any company.'

Of course they were. The huts in the wild, infertile Unclaimed Lands were far apart and the living very hard. I could see it clearly: the hearth blazing with logs cut by this handsome young stranger who talked so easily. The two ragged women, old before their time, their men gone on a hunt, listening to Tom talk. Watching his yellow hair fall over his forehead. Abashed and yet intrigued by the flirting that was as inseparable a part of him as breathing. The children hugging the shadows, staring in wonder at this visitor from another world, just as Jee had once stared at Maggie and me.

'It was hard at first to get those women to talk personal to me. They don't like strangers. But soon enough I got at least the younger one to speak. Her name was Karha, and the two were sisters. Karha told me an interesting story. She said that two years ago a man and a woman stole her sister's oldest boy, a youngster named Jee. Just stole him. She described the man to me. Except for having two hands, the man looked exactly like you. Ain't that a strange coincidence? More strange, even, than two identical dogs.'

Tom's anger was growing with his recitation. I must find a way to damp down that anger. 'Tom, many men would fit my description, I think. What did she say? "So tall, such-and-such colouring—"'

'No more lies!' Tom shouted. 'I won't have it! You've called out in your sleep both "Jee" and "Maggie", and Maggie was the name of the woman with Roger! It was you!'

Called out in my sleep – my old problem. What else had I said?

'And that's not all that those women told me, *Roger*. There ain't no inn two days' travel from here. It's much longer travel before there is *any* inn. The women ain't never left their ugly little farms but their men have, and so they knew. And they told me. From beginning to end, you gave me nothing but lies!'

He stood and advanced on me. I was no match for him; not even with two hands would I have been a match for him. Tom's huge hands balled into fists, and I braced myself for the blow I could not hope to evade.

But he didn't hit me. When he was close enough that the smell of the goat shed enveloped us both like fog, his face suddenly crumpled. Tears sprang into his eyes.

'Why did you lie to me, Peter? Why? I liked you, I thought we were going to have adventures together. You sent me to George—'

His slow brain had finally got there. The tears vanished and the anger returned. 'Is there even any George? Is George a lie too? He is, ain't he, you stinking bastard!' Tom raised his fist. The rest he might have borne, but not the loss of George.

'No!' a voice cried. 'Don't hit him!'

Tom whirled around. A girl stood there, her outstretched hand beseeching. Then her eyes rolled back in her head. Tom, cat-fast, leaped forward and caught her as she fell, just as Shep began to howl and howl as if he would never stop.

She was beautiful. That was the first thing my dazed mind noticed. Black hair falling loose around her shoulders, skin white as lilies, lips nearly as pale as her skin. The girl wore a simple gown of homespun grey, apron of the same material and boots of tanned hide. Both dress and boots looked worn, with a rent in the skirt of the gown. Tom laid her on the ground.

'Where did she come from?' Tom said. 'By damn,

I didn't hear her! Why didn't Shep bark before she got so close? Hush, you stupid dog, it's just a girl!'

'Quiet,' I said to Shep. He stopped howling and lay on the ground, his head on his front paws. But I had no time for dog jealousy. 'Tom, is she dead?'

'No. Just fainted. Get the water bag.'

It was with his pack, and full. I handed it to Tom, who gently flicked droplets into the girl's face. After a moment she stirred in Tom's arms and opened her eyes. I felt the breath go out of me. They were Cecilia's eyes. The same bright clear green, not emerald nor moss nor any other easily named shade but only their own colour. This was not Cecilia; this girl was taller, less delicate in feature, though no less beautiful. She was not Cecilia. But she had Cecilia's eyes.

Those green eyes stared straight at me.

Tom said tenderly, 'Are you all right, mistress? How came you here?'

'I . . . I hardly know.' Her voice was soft and guttural, not Cecilia's voice at all. And also – although I hadn't realized I'd feared this until the fear was gone – not the voice of the crowned woman in the Country of the Dead.

Tom said, 'Can you sit up?'

'I can stand.' She pulled herself upright, leaning on his arm, and smiled at him. The three of us stared at each other. All at once I realized that my member was hard as stone, and from the state of his breeches, so was Tom's. His voice came out low and intimate.

'You said you don't know where you come from?'

The girl frowned. 'No. I . . . I can't remember.'

'It don't signify,' he said reassuringly. 'Do you know your name?'

'Fia.'

'Come now, that's a start. Fia what?'

107

She hesitated. 'I don't know.'

'No need then. Fia is enough.' He flashed her his most devastating grin. 'I'm Tom Jenkins. And this is . . .' He scowled, remembering my betrayal. It was difficult for Tom to keep more than one thing in his mind at a time, but the betrayal still lay there, sharp and dangerous as a sword, and I knew I must sheathe it before he turned on me again. He finished, pointedly, '*Roger.*'

The girl curtseyed to each of us.

Tom's mouth fell open, as did mine, but undoubtedly from different causes. He was astonished that anyone should curtsey to him, Tom Jenkins, sometime shepherd and his father's fool. I was astonished that a girl who dressed and spoke in the manner of the Unclaimed Lands should have this court gesture at her automatic command. Certainly no other woman in the Unclaimed Lands had ever curtseyed to me. Who was Fia?

'Who are you?' Tom blurted.

'I . . . I hardly know.'

'Oh!' Tom said. And then, 'Stay right there, sweetheart, for just a moment.' He grabbed me by the arm and pulled me beyond her earshot. 'I seen this before, in Almsbury. Will Larkin got hit on the head in a fight with some stranger at a summer faire, both of them drunk as piss pots. Will got his memory knocked clean out his head. Didn't know who he was nor what had happened nor anything else for two weeks, and then it all come back, but slowly. That must have happened to this girl too.'

I nodded. She did not look to me like anyone who had been knocked in the head. Where were the bruises? But I had no better explanation. And I did not want to anger Tom any further.

'We have to take care of her till she recovers,' Tom said with perhaps too much enthusiasm. 'But don't think I've forgotten your lies, *Roger*. And don't try to run me off again, or to run off yourself!' He stalked back to Fia.

She waited, swaying a little on her feet, gazing at me steadily from Cecilia's green eyes.

16

Tom, usually so feckless, actually made a plan. We would go back to the deserted hut by the waterfall – Jee's family's hut, although of course Tom did not know that – and make it habitable. He and Shep would hunt. I would gather nuts and berries. Fia would rest and recover her memory. He did not say, although I suspected, that part of his plan was that he would bed Fia while I was out nut-and-berry-gathering. What Tom did say was, 'At least this way she will have a roof over her head until she gets well.'

'It wasn't much of a roof,' I said, remembering the gaping hole open to the sky, the sagging walls.

'I'll fix it,' Tom said. 'I'm good at such things.'

Of course he was. Tom was good at anything physical. He had washed his face in the pool, combed his yellow hair, strapped one of the *guns* to his back. He looked manly and confident. Fia sat a little way away beside a roaring campfire, even though it was only slightly past sunset and not even the first stars had appeared.

In truth, she looked like she needed the warmth. Tom had spread his cloak – which up till now had been my cloak – close to the fire. She sat on it with her head bowed, her shoulders in their drab gown hunched forward. Her slender body looked barely able to support the sorrow in that bent neck and drooping shoulders. As I watched her from the corner of my eye, all the while listening to Tom's plans, her shoulders shook with might have been a single silent sob.

'. . . and then we can— Peter, you ain't listening!'

'Yes, I am.' And I was, alert to every inflection, uncertain how and when Tom might punish me for my lies to him. I was 'Roger' when he was thinking about my betrayal, 'Peter' when he was not. 'It's a fine plan.'

'Well, I think so,' he said with satisfaction.

'What if she does not recover her memory?'

'Oh, she will,' he said confidently. 'Will Larkin did. And then he was just as much a piss pot as before. Everybody in Almsbury preferred him when he didn't know who he was. But *she* will only be better.' He glanced tenderly at Fia. 'Come, let's tell her.'

The plan was explained. 'No,' Fia said.

'No?' Tom seemed genuinely shocked; that she might refuse had not occurred to him. 'No what?'

'No, I cannot stay here in this . . . this wild country. I must go to The Queendom.'

I stared at her. The very words 'The Queendom' sounded strange in her upcountry accent. I would bet my life that she had never been there. She came from the Unclaimed Lands, or even from Soulvine Moor. She had the same green eyes as Cecilia, as the old man at Hygryll who had—

Don't think about that.

—but on the other hand, she curtseyed like a lady-in-waiting. Who was she?

Tom, stupefied, said, 'Go to The Queendom?'

'Yes.'

'You?'

She smiled faintly. 'Me.'

'But why?'

'I don't know.' She looked steadily at Tom, not so much as glancing at me. 'I only know I must go.'

'Do you have family in The Queendom?' A deep

frown creased his forehead. He was trying his best to understand.

'Perhaps. I don't know. I think ... I think I may have been a shepherdess there.'

'Oh.' He seemed at a loss for anything else to say.

I said, 'Is your memory becoming clearer, Fia? Is that why you think you may have been a shepherdess?'

'I don't know.' Still she did not look at me.

'Then why?'

'I ... I seem to see sheep – rams and ewes ...'

'A flock,' I said.

'Yes.'

'A small flock?'

Now she did turn her eyes towards me, and under that clear green gaze my mind clouded as my member hardened. I felt the colour rise in my face. She must notice my erection, surely she must notice.

'Yes,' she said gently, 'a small flock.'

'Sheep,' Tom said in disgust. 'I hate sheep.' But then he brightened. 'But you're not strong enough to travel all the way to The Queendom!'

'I am stronger than I look.' She turned her face back towards Tom, and I could breathe again. 'You will see. We should start north now.'

'Now?' His plans were crumbling all around him. He had perhaps envisioned a cosy evening by the fire, me falling asleep early, intimate flirting between him and Fia by moonlight and flickering flames. And who knew what might happen after that?

She said, 'Well, perhaps we can start tomorrow.'

I said, 'I cannot travel to The Queendom.'

There was a little silence.

Tom broke it, enthusiasm back in his voice. 'No, by damn, he cannot! Peter has savage soldiers chasing him!'

Fia did not ask why these soldiers chased me. She

merely bowed her head and hunched her shoulders. On another woman such sagging might have marred her beauty, but on Fia it merely aroused my protectiveness. She seemed both tense and profoundly sad, a cord stretched taut which somehow knew it must soon break. But then, who would not be so, if all memory had gone? If you did not know who you were, were you anyone at all?

I said, 'It's true, my lady. I have savage soldiers chasing me.' Actually, I did not know if it were true or not. Nor did I know why that 'my lady' had slipped from my mouth. Whoever this girl was, she was not Lady Cecilia.

Fia did not react to my slip, and I doubt that Tom even heard it. All his attention was on her. He said, 'Well then, that settles it. Roger must stay here, and I will take you back to The Queendom.' Conveniently for him, all the savage soldiers who had seen Tom's face were now dead.

Fia said again, 'No.'

Tom said again, 'No? No what?'

'No, we cannot leave Roger alone.'

Tom glared at me but spoke to Fia. 'Why not? He's a grown man!'

'I need you both,' she said simply. 'I'm . . . I'm afraid.'

I said gently, 'What are you afraid of, Fia?'

She shook her head from side to side.

Tom said, 'Well, of course you're afraid, sweetheart! No memory, no weapons, a woman up here in the Unclaimed Lands – but you may rely on Tom Jenkins! Roger must stay here but I'll take you back home right enough. We'll find this flock of sheep of yours and mayhap that will jolt your memory. See, I knew this farmer, Will Larkin, and at a summer faire he . . .'

Tom prattled on, his big hand on Fia's arm, offering reassurance and protection and travel plans and everything but his life-long fealty, although I had no doubt

113

that would be offered too, if he thought it necessary to bed her. Fia listened gravely, saying nothing. But her green eyes slid sideways to meet mine, and I read their message, somewhere between a command and a plea: *Don't leave me alone with him.*

And I knew I would not. I did not think Tom would ever force a woman, but I could easily believe that he would wear one down. After all, there had been Betsy and Joan and Agnes and Nell and all the others he had bragged of as we lay on opposite sides of many campfires, stranding me between envy and disdain. The only woman I had ever bedded was Maggie. And if Tom *did* try to force Fia, I must be here—

No. It was not that. I wanted to be here, with her. It was true that I was safer high in the Unclaimed Lands than I could ever be in The Queendom. But it was also true that I had planned to cross over again into Soulvine Moor and search for my mother in the Country of the Dead. That was why I had come here in the first place.

And the largest truth of all: I was afraid to cross over again.

Those dark patches of fog moving towards me in the mist, with figures moving inside them. *Nothing* moved in the Country of the Dead, save I. Those immobile, humming fogs in the middle of the circles of the Dead, which I knew to be watchers from Soulvine. The eerie silence of the pervasive mist. And most of all, the woman's voice from the fog, saying my name. Saying the words from my dream: *'Eleven years dead.'* And then the laughter that shivered along my bones.

I was afraid to cross over again. All my plans to find my mother – I would still carry out those plans, *must* carry them out. But not yet. For now I would stay with Fia, would 'protect' her against Tom and so put off again facing those terrifying figures in the fog, that voice that shivered along my bones. Put them off for at least a little while.

I was not conscious of having changed expression. But Fia interrupted Tom to say, 'Good. Then that is decided. Roger will stay with us, and tomorrow we will discuss travelling to The Queendom. Tom, do you think ... do you think you could get me some more water? I find I am so thirsty.'

She smiled at him in the gathering dusk.

17

Perhaps no one is what they seem to be.

Fia, looking so fragile, without any memory of who she was, drooping so sadly last night by the campfire, was already awake by the time I stirred the next morning. She sat picking over berries gathered in her apron. The fire had been built up from last night's embers and Tom's cookpot sat over it on a lattice of green twigs.

'Good morrow, Roger,' Fia said. 'Would you like some tea?'

I sat up. 'Tea?'

'Yes. It's good.' Carefully she poured brown liquid from the cookpot into one of our two tankards, Tom's of tin and the pewter one stolen from the Almsbury cottage. I sniffed the tea. Some sort of wild herb, not sweet but strong and flavourful. Its warmth spread through my night-chilled body. Tom snored loudly on the other side of the fire.

'Thank you,' I said. 'How did you know how to brew this?'

'I don't know. Perhaps I worked in the kitchen of some manor house?'

'I don't think the Unclaimed Lands have manor houses.' And yet the night before, she had curtseyed.

'I don't know.'

'You said yesterday that you thought you were a shepherdess.'

'I just don't know. Oh, Shep – good dog!'

He bounded up with a rabbit in his jaws and laid it at

Fia's feet. Hers, not mine, although until now all Shep's kills had been presented to me. Fia put the berries onto a wide leaf, picked up Tom's knife from the ground beside her, and began to skin and clean the rabbit with expert speed and no squeamishness whatsoever.

'Would you like some berries? They're very sweet.'

'Fia, how long have you been awake?'

'I don't know exactly.'

'Did you sleep badly?'

'No, I slept fine. No, Shep, this is for Roger. Go get your own breakfast.'

I was feeling dizzy. The tea? No, it was Fia. She sat at her bloody task looking so beautiful in the morning sunshine that every sinew in my body ached to reach for her. I wanted her with the intensity that I had once wanted Cecilia, more than I had ever wanted Maggie. But at the same time Fia's brisk competence reminded me of Maggie. This confused me completely, and filled me with shame. I did not expect to ever see Maggie again. I was too dangerous to her and Jee. We had broken with each other, there on the sunny hillside where I had left her asleep. So why did my yearning to touch Fia fill me with such a sense of disloyalty to Maggie?

So I sat bewildered into silence, vainly trying to hold my cup of tea in such a way that Fia did not see my erection. Fia leaned forward to put the skinned rabbit onto the fire, and her breasts strained against the bodice of her gown. I closed my eyes.

'Well now, roast rabbit!'

For the first time ever, I was glad of Tom's hearty obliviousness.

'This is great, sweetheart, by damn! What a nice thing for a man to wake up to!'

'Let me pour you some tea,' Fia said. 'Roger, are you done with the tankard?'

117

By mid-morning she had us well fed and on the move. In the lead was Tom, who was importantly armed with his knife and all three guns, and who turned to help Fia over logs that she could very well step over unaided. I was next, my walking staff in my good hand. Shep brought up the rear. Every few minutes he bounded away to investigate animal holes or deer spore. The morning was fair and very warm, and birds sang in every branch.

We moved north, back towards The Queendom, but I did not intend to go further than the deserted hut of Jee's family. That kept me within a day's walk of Soulvine Moor. It also kept me far enough south that – I hoped – the Young Chieftain's soldiers would not find me. I would do all I could to keep Fia at the hut as long as possible. I had no idea how long that would be. She seemed determined to travel to The Queendom. How could someone with no memory have a destination?

I watched the play of sunlight on the smooth black waves of her unbound hair.

'Don't trip on the big stone there,' Tom said. 'Are you tired?'

'Not at all.' And over her shoulder, 'Roger? Are you tired?'

I was tired, yes. I was sore. My feet hurt, and the stump of my wrist, and my heart. Fia's dress caught on a berry bramble and Tom freed it for her. He had a strong whole body and a handsome face and yellow hair.

In the late afternoon we reached the hut beside the mountain waterfall. Fia looked at it carefully and said, 'Hmmmm.'

Tom and I looked at each other. What did 'Hmmmm' mean?

'Hmmmm,' Fia repeated. 'Not fit for so much as goats.'

Tom, trying to be witty, said, 'Luckily we have no goats.'

'No people could live here.'

I did not tell her that people had.

'There are still hours of daylight,' Fia said. 'We could travel further. If we— What was that?'

Tom said, 'I didn't hear anything.'

But I had. The sound came again, distant and faint. Fia looked puzzled, and I had another piece of information about her. She had not, after all, come from The Queendom, at least not recently.

She said, 'What is that strange noise?'

'*Guns*,' I said.

We did not hear the *guns* again that day. Perhaps a hunting party of the savages had been shooting game; soldiers must eat the same as anyone else. Or perhaps some folk of the Unclaimed Lands had acquired *guns*, as Tom had, and were putting them to good use. Or perhaps the Young Chieftain's scouts were indeed still looking for me.

'I will go no further,' I told Fia. 'I can't.' Soldiers to the north, Soulvine Moor to the south, and I in the middle, fearing both. I didn't know what I was going to do eventually, but I knew I was going to do nothing right now. Nothing seemed my safest choice. In the mountains sound carries a very long way, echoing off cliff faces and amplified by canyons. The soldiers – if there were soldiers – could be very far away. Or not.

Fia did not look at me when I spoke; at first I thought she hadn't even heard me. She went on gazing at the ramshackle roof of the hut. Then she went inside and looked up at the sky through the hole in the roof. Tom and I trailed after her.

'Hmmmm,' she said.

'Sweetheart,' Tom said, 'why don't I build a fire in that pine grove over there and—'

'This hut can be made very snug for us,' Fia said.

I blinked. Tom looked confused, as well he might. Hadn't she just said it wasn't fit for so much as goats? She turned to both of us and gave us her enchanting smile. 'You are right, Tom,' she said. 'I'm more tired than I thought. As soon as we stopped walking, weariness caught me. I think . . . I think I may not be well. Do you mind if we stop here for a few days?'

'Of course not, sweetheart!' Tom looked as if he would stop there with her for a few days, a few months, for ever. Fia sank gracefully to the ground.

'If I could have a little water . . .'

He ran outside for the water bag. Fia looked up at me and her smile was gone, replaced by a look of such sadness that I was struck dumb. Dumber. In such moments she reminded me so strongly of Cecilia that it was like a blow. And yet Cecilia had never shown such sadness. Nor, I suspected, such duplicity. Cecilia had been an artless kitten, adorable and helpless. Fia was something different, but I did not know what.

'Fia,' I said softly, 'who are you?'

'I don't know,' she said and shook her head, and my heart split down its seam with sorrow for her. Or desire.

'Why do you want to go to The Queendom?'

She only shook her head again. Then Tom returned with the water bag and her sadness vanished, replaced by a flurry of nesting that would have done a robin proud. 'Thank you, Tom. We have several hours of daylight yet. Have you an axe? No? A pity. Well, if you can break off branches as thick as your wrist, I will gather grasses from that clearing over there for thatch, and we can have the roof patched by dark. Roger, if you will clean out the hearth and make a fire, that would be a great help. Send Shep out to hunt. I saw some wild onions growing by the waterfall . . .'

120

I said, more harshly than I intended, 'I thought you were weary.'

'I am,' she said calmly, 'but this work must be done despite all our weariness.'

The words, and the tone, might have been Maggie's.

'Of course the work must be done!' Tom said. 'We should start now.' He dashed out to find branches as thick as his wrist. Fia followed, not looking at me.

I gazed at the hearth, full of old ashes and mouse droppings, and then began to clean it out with my one hand.

By nightfall the hut was, if not snug, at least habitable. We slept inside, by a real hearth fire. Fia had kept us working past dark, and we had walked much of the day before that, so all three of us fell asleep quickly and hard. But towards morning the dreams came. Never before had I dreamed my two terrible dreams brought together into one.

My mother sits in her lavender gown with a child on her lap. I am both the watcher and the child, safe and warm in my mother's arms. She sings to me softly, a tune that I hear at first without words. Then the words become clear, and Roger the watcher's blood goes cold: 'Die, my baby, die die, my little one, die die . . .' Then the scene enlarges and I see that mother and child sit outside, on a flat upland moor, at night. There comes to my mouth the taste of roasted meat, succulent and greasy. Moving among the shadows are inhuman things and one woman, her voice coming to me from the darkness under the glint of a jewelled crown: 'Roger. Hisaf.'

'But you're dead,' I say.

'Eleven years dead,' she says, and gives a laugh that shivers my bones. My mother cries No no no no . . . .'

'Roger! By damn, wake up!'

Tom, shaking my shoulder. Fia lay asleep, wrapped in Tom's cloak. The fire had died to glowing embers that cast dim ruddy light on Tom's angry face.

'By damn, how can a man sleep with you yowling like that? And you might have woken *Fia*, and with her unwell!'

'I'm sorry.' I said, inadequately. The dream swirled in my mind like bile.

'Well, stop *doing* that,' Tom grumbled. 'It startles a man!' All at once his face became more alert. He was always more wakeful at night than I, who preferred mornings. 'Look here, Roger, I think it's time you explained about George. And that rebellion that don't exist.'

'I'm sorry,' I said again. However, I had had hours of walking to prepare my lies. 'But only think, Tom, I was just trying to do right by you. We knew the savages were after me. Every one of them that saw your face, on the other hand, is already dead. But if they find us together, they will kill you as well as me. They might even torture you, as they once did me. So—'

'So you made up that piss pot story about George and a rebellion in order to send me away to safety?'

'Yes.'

Tom considered. I saw, even in the gloom of the hut, the moment he accepted my story as truth. His was a generous and unsuspicious nature, and moreover his brain moved so slowly that nearly all lies could outrun it. All at once he, rather than Fia, reminded me of Cecilia. He was, despite that muscular bulk, a kitten.

'I see,' Tom said. His face broke into a grin. 'I'm so glad, Peter. Although I always knew you wouldn't really betray me. You *couldn't*. We're adventurers together. Still, you musn't try to protect me – that ain't your part. It's my part to protect you!'

'All right,' I agreed. Tom had no idea what I actually

122

needed protection from, nor how little he would have been able to supply it.

'You're shivering,' Tom said. 'Are you cold? Fia has my cloak but if you want my tunic to put atop your blanket—'

'No, no, I'm fine.'

'Are you certain?'

'Yes. Let us go back to sleep, Tom.'

'All right.'

But neither of us did. I feigned snoring, but my mind would not leave my monstrous dream. Tom tossed and turned, and twice he said softly, 'Peter?' He wanted company. I did not. Eventually he grew quiet and his breathing deepened.

I did not sleep until nearly dawn, afraid of what dreams might come. But none did. When Tom and I woke, within moments of each other, the morning was far advanced, and Fia was gone. So was Shep.

18

Fia returned at noon, with Tom. 'I told you I'd find her!' he exulted to me. 'I can track any game!'

'I am not game,' Fia said crossly. 'Nor was I lost. I was merely gathering things we need.' Her apron was tied in front of her in a sort of bag; I had often seen countrywomen carry things in such a way. She sank gracefully to the ground and untied the apron. The pungent scent of wild onions tickled my nostrils. With them were several handfuls of nuts, various other plants I did not recognize, a packet of leaves tied with vine, a large bunch of greens and twelve black stones worn smooth by some stream. Fia untied the leaf packet. It held four quail eggs.

'By damn!' Tom said enthusiastically. 'I love quail eggs!'

'Then both of you clear out and let me make a meal,' Fia said.

I said, 'What are the stones for?'

She smiled at me and my heart turned over. She had washed her hair and clothing, perhaps in the same stream where she found the stones, and damp tendrils clung to her lovely neck. I pictured her bathing, naked in cold rushing water, and all at once my body responded like a soldier on parade. Had she noticed? I hoped not.

'Call me when the food is ready. I need to ... to go and find Shep.' Hurriedly I moved away from the cabin, calling, 'Shep! Shep!'

Behind me, Fia chuckled softly.

*

She made a delicious salad, with boiled eggs, for the midday meal. She made rabbit stew for dinner. Over the next few days she made pallets of pine boughs whose sweet smell almost banished the mustiness of the cabin. She made a woven basket to gather berries. She made rush lights dipped in pine resin. She made fish hooks of carved bone, and caught fish with them. She made Tom scour the woods for logs and the stream for large flat rocks, and of them made benches and a table. She found hickory nuts and summer apples in the woods, mussels in the stream, cattails in a marsh. Maggie herself could not have accomplished more.

'But, sweetheart,' Tom said, setting a large flat rock on an upended log and eyeing the resulting wobble with the sure knowledge that Fia would make him fix it, 'we don't need Peter's snares. Shep can catch game.'

Fia raised her face from the nuts she was pounding into some sort of flour. Her look of sadness was back, so profound that even Tom noticed.

'What's wrong, sweetheart? Shep still ain't back?' She didn't answer, and he turned to me. 'Peter, is Shep back?'

I said to Fia, 'He's not coming back, is he?'

She had once more bent her head over her work. 'How should I know? I am here with you.'

But she knew.

Tom said, 'Of course Shep'll come back! Good ol' dog! Peter, I wish to talk to you outside.'

We left Fia to her pounding – *whap whap whap* of stone on nut meat – and went outside. Tom dragged me away from the cabin.

'Listen to me, Peter. This girl likes me, and I like her. That's obvious. So will you please leave us right after dinner for – oh – several hours? Until full dark?'

I didn't know what to say. All at once Tom's face darkened. He said bluntly, 'You don't want her for yourself, do you? Because she don't want you.'

Did she? Lately she had smiled more at me than at Tom, and once or twice in the sway of her full-breasted body I thought I had seen an invitation . . . but I must be wrong. Here was Tom, so confident, so handsome, so much more experienced with women than I was. For me there had been only Cecilia, whom I had loved but not bedded, and Maggie, whom I had bedded but did not love. I knew nothing of women, and knew that I knew nothing. And Tom had saved my life.

'No,' I said miserably. 'I don't want her for myself. But, Tom, you wouldn't . . . you wouldn't ever insist, would you? Try to . . . to force her?'

I thought he might become angry, might even strike me, and I braced myself for the blow. Instead he burst into hearty laughter.

'Force her? Lad, Tom Jenkins need force no woman! If a man can't make a girl lie down and open her legs willingly, he don't deserve her! And I can! Now, go find an errand in the woods, right after dinner.'

Not waiting for my acquiescence, he turned and strode back towards the cabin, and not even Lord Robert Hopewell, lord protector for the Princess Stephanie, could have exuded more confident, masculine power. As I watched him go, I fingered Shadow's leather collar, still in my pocket. I wondered where Shep had gone. I wondered why Fia wished to go to The Queendom and why she tarried here. I wondered how long after dinner it would take Tom to get Fia's dress off. I wondered why I was destined to lose everything, always, that I desperately wanted.

But Fia had other ideas.

We had no sooner finished our meal than Tom began giving me significant looks. That evening we ate outside, sitting on the bare ground before the hut, and long slanting sunlight touched the tops of the forest trees and turned them green-gold. Fia produced the twelve smooth stones from her apron and cast them before us. 'We will play at baz! It's great fun! I will teach you both.'

That sweet, beseeching smile, so at odds with her commanding tone. She was Cecilia, she was Maggie, she was herself.

Tom scowled. 'What is *baz*?'

'A game of chance.'

His face cleared. 'Oh, a good thought, that! I have dice! Tell you what, sweetheart, you and I will wager while Peter gathers the wood for the night fire – it's his turn.'

Fia said, 'I have already gathered tonight's wood.'

'Oh! Then Peter will ... will—'

'I must check the snares,' I said miserably. 'It's good you made rush lights, Fia. I can take one to light my way, since I expect to be gone quite a while. In fact, I am looking forward to a good long walk.'

'Then you shall have it tomorrow,' she said pertly. 'For tonight, we play baz. Tom shall go first. You take six of the twelve stones in hand, Tom, and cast them into this triangle I draw in the dirt.'

There were many triangles drawn in the dirt, and many casts of stones, and despite myself I became interested. Baz turned out to be only in part a game of chance. It also involved strategy, as in battle, where one must outthink one's opponent. Fia did this well, but I did it better.

Tom was wretched at the game, and soon bored. His mood grew disgruntled and sulky and he shot meaningful glances at me: *Leave us!* But I found no pretext to do so, and Fia insisted that we play on.

'That was a very good move, Roger,' she said to me, and my heart glowed for just as long as it took to glimpse Tom's face. 'I can scarcely believe you have never played before.'

But she knew we had never played before; she hadn't even asked if we knew the rules before explaining them. This was a foreign game, brought from wherever Fia came from, and already she knew that it would be foreign to the folk of The Queendom. How?

Tom lost the last of his stones. 'Goodnight,' he said abruptly, not troubling to hide either his humiliation or his displeasure. His glance at me was ugly. 'Will you two play very late?'

I understood him. 'No, I am too sleepy. Goodnight.' Ostentatiously I went to my pallet of pine boughs, my face turned to the hut wall. A spider spun a web inches from my eyes.

'Goodnight, then,' Fia said, and went to bed, wrapped in Tom's cloak as in an impenetrable castle.

Tom swore softly in the darkness. I watched the spider. It had trapped a fly and was slowly, surely enveloping it in silken snares too strong to break.

Tom was outwardly cheerful in the morning, his natural confidence again claiming his mind, although something of last night's anger remained beneath the good cheer. At the first opportunity he jerked his head towards Fia and winked at me. I set off to check the snares before Fia could ask me to do something else instead. As I walked, this time leaving my staff behind, I fingered Shadow's collar in the pocket of my tunic. Once I even pulled it out and gazed at the strange markings etched into the leather. I missed Shadow. I missed Shep.

The morning gained me two rabbits and a sore heart.

But Tom gained nothing. When I returned to the hut at midday, he was sweaty and hot from building a dam across the stream just below the waterfall, deepening the shallow pool. 'No luck,' he growled. 'She's slippery as a greased pole, that girl! And she's been gone the whole morning again, "gathering food", leaving me to this stupid work – a "bathing pool"! Why does she want a bathing pool? People needn't bathe more than a few times a year. It ain't healthy.'

Fia bathed every day, but neither of us saw her do it. The bathing pool, it turned out, was for us. Fia expected daily washing. Moreover, she expected it when she was gone on her morning food gathering, from which she returned this time with more eggs, more greens for salad, bulbs of dog-tooth violet to roast in coals, more nuts and berries and strange herbs, and even some of the first wild honey.

'How did you get it away from the bees?' I asked, my mouth watering. 'Didn't they sting you?'

'No,' she said with her sad lovely smile but no explanation. Tom was not interested in explanations, nor in honey; his mood was turning dangerous. He was not used to girls evading him. Scowling, he watched Fia through eyes narrowed to blue slits.

But she was encouraging to him at the midday meal, which we ate outdoors beside the new bathing pool. She smiled at Tom, even flirted a little. 'Tom, the pool looks wonderful. How did you ever get that log in place? It must be so heavy!'

'It was.'

'Yet you managed it.'

'Oh piss pots, I've lifted things heavier than that.' He straightened and expanded his chest like a pigeon during courtship.

'You must show me.'

'I will, sweetheart.' As Fia went inside to fetch him another tankard of honey-sweetened tea from the hearth, Tom whispered to me, 'I've got her! Go away again this afternoon, Peter!'

I did. I sat on a fallen log well away from the cabin

129

and, having nothing to do, did nothing. But I could not tolerate that for very long. And an idea, monstrous and horrible, had been growing in my mind. I must know the answer.

But there was only one course of action to discover it, or to have even a faint hope of discovering it. And I was afraid of that course. Three times I pulled out my little shaving knife to poke myself and cross over, and three times I stopped myself. I was afraid to go again to the Country of the Dead.

Those figures in the fog, that woman saying my name in tones that froze my blood ... It was not really Fia that kept me from crossing over. It was myself.

So I sat on my log, wretched and cowardly, and late that afternoon dragged myself back to the hut. Fia, on the watch for me, came running to the edge of the clearing. 'Roger! Where have you been? Why did you go away so long? Tom is very sick and I cannot lift him myself!'

19

Tom lay on the ground beside the bathing pool. His tongue had swollen to three times its normal size, filling his mouth. His eyes were swollen shut. He moaned in pain, and every so often his limbs spasmed helplessly. I knelt beside him. 'Tom, what happened?'

Groans.

Fia said, 'We were just inspecting the pool when this illness seized him. I think . . . Did Tom eat any mushrooms in the forest?'

'I don't know.' It was possible. With Tom, any impulsive act was possible. 'Have you seen such an illness before, from eating mushrooms?'

'I . . . I think so. At any rate, somehow I know what to do for it.'

'How do you know?' I said bluntly.

'I don't know. Perhaps I was once a healer?'

'And a shepherdess and a lady's maid and a kitchen girl.'

She looked from Tom, groaning and oblivious, to me. Her lovely face creased with hurt. 'Roger, are you angry with me?'

Yes. No. I had no idea, except that it was less anger than fear. But all I said was, 'The sun is full in his poor eyes. We must move him inside.'

It took both of us to shift Tom's bulk. I took his arms, and Fia, stronger than she looked, took his legs. Somehow we got him inside, and I built up the fire. Tom had begun to shiver uncontrollably and to cry out with pain.

Fia said, 'I can make him a tea that will at least shrink his tongue.'

'Do so!' I didn't know what else to do for him. I didn't know anything.

She brewed the tea from her store of gathered plants, and together we dribbled it down his throat. Within a few minutes, Tom's tongue began to shrink, giving him some relief. He grew quiet, then slept. I loosened his belt and raised his tunic, my heart hammering. But there was no rash, no pustules, no discoloration on his broad chest. It was not plague.

I said, 'I think it might have been mushrooms, after all.'

'I think so too,' Fia said, and began to cry.

I put my arm around her, and so it happened – or rather, it did not happen.

She turned in my arms and her tears flowed hard and silent, wetting my shoulder. I tried to say, 'He will not die,' for Tom was already sleeping deeply and his colour was better, and anyway if the mushrooms were the type to kill him, he would have stomach cramps and vomiting. But it was my words that were killed, for Fia raised her head and kissed me.

At the first touch of her soft lips on mine, my member rose and hardened to stone. Her breasts pressed against my body. Her hand reached for me, and I found my voice, although it came out hoarse. 'Not here ...' Not beside Tom, who had also desired her, even though he lay oblivious.

Fia nodded, took me by the hand and led me outside and a little way from the cabin. She put her arms around me and kissed me again. We sank to the ground, kissing wildly, and I whispered, 'Me ... not Tom? Why?'

'It was always you.' She lay back on the pine needles and raised her skirt, smiling at me.

Maybe it was the smile, which wavered between tears and encouragement. Maybe it was the gesture of raising her skirt. But I think it was the scent of pine needles. For it was here, in this grove, that I had once rested in the Country of the Dead with Cecilia in my arms. And it was here I had found Maggie when I returned from Soulvine Moor. She had been digging edible roots, and her face had flushed with both pleasure and fury at my return, and I had taken her away from here and back to The Queendom. Maggie, whose face always surged with pleasure when she saw me, who loved me better than I had loved her or than I deserved. Maggie, whom I had left on a sunny hillside after taking her as I was now prepared to take Fia: without a future or the promise of a future. Maggie, whom I had deserted. My mind filled with Maggie, and with guilt, and my member wilted under Fia's hand.

Nothing more humiliating can happen to a man. And although Fia tried, she could not revive me. I covered my eyes with my one hand.

'Roger, it is all right. Truly. You are tired. You must have walked all morning, and the shock over Tom's illness—'

'I will see to Tom now,' I said, to escape her and my shame. I would have got to my feet, but she clung to me.

'Don't go,' she said, 'please don't go. We can try again in a little space of time.'

No words were ever said more seductively, more softly. They had no effect on the softness in my breeches. Scarlet-faced, close to tears, I went to see to Tom.

Then began a time of frustration such as I had never known. Tom's pain stopped and the colour returned to his face, but he slept deeply for many hours each day. In the mornings he was awake but weak, and Fia tended him gently, while I brought in game from the snares.

When she was gone to gather plants, I watched over Tom. He was fretful, impatient with illness in a body that had scarcely known it before. 'By damn, I'm weak as a kitten, Peter. I hate this!'

By noon he would be asleep again. In the afternoon heat Fia bathed in the pool beneath the waterfall. Each day I would say I would not join her, and each day I did. My arms held her slender naked body with its full breasts, and the blood sang in my veins. My member gorged and rose. Then we lay on the sweet grass beside the pool, and the thoughts of Maggie would douse me as the cold mountain water had not. I could not take Fia.

'It's all right, Roger,' she would say and hold me tighter, until I broke from her in shame and confusion and growing suspicion. It was not just thoughts of Maggie that wilted my member. I was suspicious of Fia – why she had wanted to journey to The Queendom, why she now stopped here, where she had come from. When I asked her these questions, she always replied that she didn't know. If my suspicions proved wrong, and Fia discovered them, she would push me away in horror. I did not want that. But if my suspicions were right ...

No. My doubts were baseless, without foundation. And even if they *had* had foundation, they would have dissolved in the strength of my desire for her and its continual frustration.

Sometimes I heard *guns* in the distance, always in the distance, but with the echoes in the hills, I could not be sure how far away. However, even if I had known them to be very close and hunting me, how could I leave Tom ill and Fia for the savage soldiers? She was strong and resourceful, but no woman can stand against soldiers bent on taking her. And if they found out she knew me ...

Fear, like guilt and suspicion, does not help a man lie with a woman.

Fia was endlessly patient with me. But as the days passed, her patience took on an edge of desperation. Tom grew steadily better. He slept less. He began to watch Fia and me.

'Roger, are you bedding her?' The dangerous glint was back in his eyes, and once more I was 'Roger'.

I said, truthfully, 'No.'

His face cleared immediately. 'I knew you ain't. I knew you wouldn't go back on your word to me. By damn, forgive me for even doubting you for a moment. It's this stupid piss pot sickness, it makes a man not himself. I hate it!'

'You'll be better soon,' I said, because I must say something, and I no longer had any idea what was or was not true.

That evening Tom was awake at dinner. Fia had prepared something new: small cakes made from the nut flour she had been laboriously pounding and hoarding for a fortnight. The cakes were baked in leaves on the hearth and sweetened with honey robbed from bees. Each of the three morsels was decorated with berries arranged in a different pattern. They had a delicious distinctive scent, a smell like every dream of food a hungry man ever had.

'How fine!' Tom said. He sat on a log at our rock 'table', looking almost like his old robust self. We were eating dinner later than usual, due to the long time Fia had needed to bake her cakes. Two rush lights lit either side of the cabin. They cast eerie shadows in the dim hut. By their subdued glow Tom looked even bigger than he was, and Fia even more desirable. She sat with eyes downcast, holding her honey cake, and her lashes threw spidery shadows on her pale cheeks. Tom swallowed his cake in two bites and shifted his gaze to mine. Hastily I ate it, letting the sweetness dissolve slowly on my tongue.

'By damn, sweetheart,' Tom said, 'but you're a treasure! And it's a wonder how those bees never sting you. They'd perforate me a dozen times over if I got within a field's length of their hive. Are you going to eat that or not, Fia? By damn, you didn't eat no more than a crumb!'

She laughed and held it out to him. 'I'm not hungry. You eat it.'

He did. We went on laughing and talking, the three of us, and all the while Tom grew larger and larger. I didn't understand how that could be. Suddenly he filled the whole cabin, then abruptly shrank again to a normal-sized man. The rush lights grew to the ceiling and then shrank to nothing but glowing flames, which danced across the floor and then up onto Fia's white arms, turning them pink and gold and orange. I was admiring this when Tom said, 'So tired ... just rest a moment ... tired ...'

He staggered to his pallet and fell upon it, and the pine boughs enclosed him tenderly and began to hum. I knew their song; I had heard it once before; I almost had it in mind. But then Fia was leading me outside and we were in the pine grove.

The pine grove, hadn't I been here before? I had been here with ... with ...

'Roger,' Fia breathed, and her dress was half off, her white breasts gleaming in the moonlight filtering between the dark branches of pine.

I took her then, with a ferocity I had not known I was capable of and a joy I had never known either. We loved once, twice, and when I lay spent on the fragrant pine needles, Fia cradled in my arms, she whispered in my ear.

'Roger, love, will you promise me something?'

136

'Anything,' I said and meant it, even though I was having trouble with the pine branches above us – they shrank and grew and shrank again. Now they were great sheltering arms, humming, and then they were mere twigs, silent. How odd! And yet it was not odd, it was just as it should be. Everything was just as it should be, and my member stirred faintly, a third time, at the press of Fia's body against mine. Pine needles damp with dew had become trapped between our bodies, and their slight sting only inflamed my love for her.

She said softly, 'Don't cross over again into the Country of the Dead.'

'All right,' I said, watching the branches shrink and grow, shrink and grow, even as her words sank into my brain, no stranger than anything else in this strange night.

'Do you promise?'

'Promise what?' Shrink and grow, shrink and grow.

'Do you promise me to never cross again into the Country of the Dead?'

'Yes.'

'Do you promise on your mother's grave?'

'Yes.' And then, 'Does my mother have a grave?'

'No,' Fia said with profound sorrow. I did not under-stand the sorrow. My mind floated, high in the branches that were still shrinking and growing, shrinking and growing. 'Do you promise on your mother's soul?'

'Yes,' I said.

'Remember that you have promised me.'

'I will remember,' I said.

She clutched at me. 'They are almost ready!'

'Oh,' I said, without interest, for her clutching had aroused me again, and I reached for her. But before we could proceed, I fell abruptly asleep.

When I woke in the early morning, she was gone. And

knowing all at once what had happened, what she had done, I started after her in rage, far more rage than I had ever felt towards any savage soldier who had only tried to kill me.

20

Tom still slept, as affected by his drug as I had been by mine. Those little cakes, each so sweetly scented and each individually marked with berries ... But now my head was clear. I dashed into the cabin only long enough to be sure Fia was not there, grabbed the water bag and Tom's knife, and set out after her.

I was not the tracker Tom was, but she could not have gone far. When I had last held her close to me under the pines—

The branches shrinking and growing.

—the sky had already begun to pale in the east. Now the sun—

'Do you promise on your mother's grave?'

—had barely cleared the trees. And it must have rained a little overnight, my clothes were damp, so—

'Does my mother have a grave?'

'No.'

—there should be traces of her in the mud of the track leading away from the hut. I could find her. I would find her. And when I did ...

She had not stayed on the track, but neither had she gone very far. I circled the hut in ever-spiralling circles, as Tom had taught me. This was not as easy as I had hoped, but I could follow her course. A footprint here, smeared sideways where she had slipped slightly. A small piece of cloth on a bramble where she had caught her gown. A flattened place in the weeds where she had sat to rest. She must be tired; we had been awake much of

139

the night. I was not tired. Rage is a great strengthener.

I first glimpsed her through the trees, resting below me in a dell of wildflowers. She must have seen or heard me at the same time because she leaped to her feet and began to run. I caught her easily, threw her to the ground and straddled her slim body. Only with great effort did I keep from striking her.

'You drugged me,' I said, barely getting the words out through clenched teeth, 'and you made Tom ill so you could do it.'

She said sadly, but with no surprise, 'Yes, I did. I was a healer.'

'I thought you said you were a shepherdess! Or a lady's maid! Or a kitchen girl!'

'No.' And then with despair, 'You know what I am, Roger.'

'Bees don't sting you. Or they do, but you are not injured by them. You appear suddenly in the deep woods of the Unclaimed Lands, clean and fresh as if from court. You tell me . . . you tell me that my mother has no grave.'

I could not go on. And all at once I could not touch her either. I stood. Fia got unsteadily to her feet. We stood there facing each other in that little dell full of wild-flowers, sunlight falling all around us and birds singing in the freshness after rain.

I said, 'You come from the Country of the Dead.'

'Yes,' Fia said, suddenly fierce, 'and you have given me your promise. Remember that. Your promise on your mother's soul! You will not cross over again.'

'You exacted that promise from me unfairly. With drugs and sex!'

'Nonetheless, you have given the promise.' Her face suddenly crumpled. She repeated quietly, 'You have given that promise.'

'How . . . ? Who . . . ?'

'You know how – there is only one way. A *hisaf* brought me.'

'But why?' I cried. 'You have lost your chance at eternity! You will—'

'Yes,' she said. 'I know. I have lost my chance at eternity. As did Cecilia, as did all the Blue soldiers you brought over once before. All gone for ever. So remember your promise!'

I seized her by the shoulders and shook her. 'Why? Why?'

'They are almost ready!'

'On Soulvine Moor? Ready for *what*?'

But she only looked at me, a gaze of such profound despair that I clasped her to me. And so it happened in my arms. A fortnight had passed, the same fortnight that Bat had had, that Cecilia had had, that the Blues had had. Fia *melted*. All at once her face and body twisted and decayed, flowing into grotesque shapes, her mouth open in a silent scream. In moments she was gone. Her gown and apron and boots lay in a puddle amid the flowers.

I sat there beside them the entire morning. I could not move. Fia was neither in the land of the living nor the Country of the Dead; she was nowhere. Her soul had been extinguished, giving up its chance at eternity in order to exact my promise to never again cross over. To give up my quest to find my mother. That was why she had destroyed herself – to gain my promise.

No. That did not ring true. Fia had insisted on travelling north, towards The Queendom, to put more distance between herself and Soulvine Moor. That I could believe. But I did not believe that she had forfeited all existence, both here and in the Country of the Dead, solely to keep me from crossing over. There was more to Fia that I did not understand, much more, just as there was more to the fog on Soulvine Moor and to the figures I had glimpsed in that fog. *'They are almost ready.'*

For what?

A great lassitude came over me. I had been up most of the night. Fia was gone. My body had been put through drugging and lovemaking and tracking. She was gone. I would never now talk to my dead mother, not unless I broke a vow sworn on her grave. Fia was gone. I lay on the ground and buried my face in her gown. It bore her scent still. I wept.

Then I fell asleep.

I woke to the sound of *guns* not far off.

Carefully I rolled Fia's clothing into a tight ball, and so found the miniature. It had been sewn into a secret pocket of her gown. I held it in my hand, where it lay small on my palm, and turned it to the light to make out the tiny image. Shining waves of black hair, green eyes, sad half-smile. The miniature was undoubtedly Fia, and yet it reminded me so much of Cecilia. Even though, except for the green eyes, the girls' features did not look much alike. The resemblance was more shadowy, impossible to define, but real.

I stared at the miniature until I nearly went blind. I suspected that both Fia and Cecilia had had some connection with that shadowy web of women who practised, or at least knew of, the soul arts. Cecilia, artless, had not practised them at all, but Mother Chilton had nonetheless once gone to great trouble to smuggle her out of the palace and to the Unclaimed Lands. Fia had been a healer, and perhaps more. Mother Chilton had known I was in Applebridge and perhaps had used a strengthening potion on a hawk – as she had once, two years ago used it on me – to enable the bird to drop a rock down my chimney.

Putting the miniature in my pocket, I carried Fia's clothing a half-mile into the woods and buried it in a copse thick with dead leaves. I had no doubt that Tom, a far better tracker than I, would follow her trail to this dell, but he would not be interested in following mine. I replaced the leaves.

Then I went home to see if Tom had woken from the drugged sleep that Fia had given him instead of her body.

He was awake and fully recovered. Standing in front of the hut, hands on his hips, he glowered at me. 'Where did you go?'

I feigned surprise. 'To check the snares, of course. As I do every morning. But no game today.'

'Then where's Fia?'

'Fia? Isn't she here with you?'

He scowled uncertainly. 'No, I thought ... Ain't she with you?'

'No. Well then, she must be off gathering plants.'

'Oh! I thought—'

'What?' I could feel false innocence on my face like a suffocating mask.

'Nothing,' Tom said, too heartily. But he was never good at withholding information. He blurted, 'By damn, I thought she was with you! The truth is, I been feeling very strange this last week, Peter. And last night I thought I would finally bed Fia, but then I fell asleep as if I'd been drinking ale all night with the lads at the Ram and Crown! But I feel fine now. Fia must just be off on one of her food gatherings. Come, then – I have something to show you. Behind the hut!'

I followed him reluctantly, glad that he accepted my story but wanting only to be alone to grieve for Fia. Why had she done it? Why give up eternity – even an eternity of sitting tranquilly in the Country of the Dead – for a fortnight of subsistence living in the Unclaimed Lands? What did I not yet know?

Everything, it seemed. I was as ignorant as Tom, and

far more beset. He beamed as he led me behind the hut to a full-grown deer, a buck in summer antlers, lying dead on its side. But there was no arrow in its flesh, and anyway Tom had no bow. I had to squat down and look closely to see the single small hole in the skull, between the animal's staring eyes.

I said, 'You killed it with a *gun*!'

'And got it on the second shot! Pepper my arse, but I'm good!'

'You stupid fool!'

Tom's swift change from pride to bewilderment to anger would have been almost comical if I had been in the mood for comedy. I was not. He said hotly, 'Don't call me names! I got us a deer, and Fia will want the meat for her stews.'

'Your *gun* folly will bring savage soldiers down on us!'

'Oh piss pots. We ain't seen any soldiers in a fortnight. They don't come this far into the Unclaimed Lands. You know that.'

I did not know that. But Tom had the capacity to believe whatever he wanted. All at once I saw my chance to both protect him and shed him. I said, 'I think they will come here. Attracted by your *gun* noise.'

'Well, even if they do, I can defend myself!'

'I cannot.'

His anger vanished as quickly as it had come. 'I'll defend you, Peter. You know that.' He smiled at me, confident and big and an utter idiot.

'I can't take the chance. I'm going now.'

'Going? Going where?'

'Away. It's not safe here.'

'But . . . but . . . where will you go?'

'I don't know. But I'm going.' I went inside the hut and packed the water bag and some left-over food. 'May I take your knife?'

'Yes, of course, I have the *guns* and— Wait. What do you mean, *you* are going? Ain't we all going?'

'Fia may not be back for hours. You know how she is about her gathering. And she'll want to stay here. We just made the bathing pool.'

'But I can track her! I can track anything, you know that. I'll go find her and we can all—' He stopped. His face changed. Finally he said, 'You would go without her.'

'You'll be here to take care of her.'

That struck him powerfully. I watched him struggle between the desire to have me gone and the desire to have us all together. Tom Jenkins, who feared nothing but being alone, finally said slowly, 'You're a coward, Roger. You would leave her to save yourself from the soldiers.'

I shrugged, letting him think so. He would be safer without me. He would wait in vain for Fia to return, and when she did not, he would search for her. By the time he came to believe that he couldn't find her, my trail would be too cold for even him to track. The Young Chieftain's soldiers had no business with Tom Jenkins. I would have saved his life as he had once saved mine, and we would be quit of debt to each other.

His broad face furrowed with contempt. 'A coward,' he repeated, and I shrugged again. He turned his back to me. I packed some of the useful things Fia had made. Then I picked up Tom's knife from the floor beside his pallet, and in its place I put the miniature of Fia, half-hidden by pine boughs.

I did not want it. It hurt too much. Let Tom think she had left it for him. When she did not return, it might give him comfort. Despite everything, I would miss Tom Jenkins.

He did not turn around or say goodbye. I walked out of the hut that Fia had briefly made into a home and turned my steps towards Soulvine Moor.

21

I was not going to enter Soulvine Moor; my plan was to walk only a half-day's journey south, away from the savage *guns*. I knew from my days at court that the savages were as fully superstitious as the people of The Queendom. During their occupation of the palace they must have learned from servants that the Soulviners 'stole your soul'. That was not true, but the truth was equally horrendous. And since no one ever returned from Soulvine to tell that truth, the stories and folk tales grew. It was said that inhuman things lived on Soulvine Moor. That too was false; the human things were terrible enough. I was fairly sure that savage soldiers would not enter Soulvine Moor.

And I knew beyond doubt that Soulviners would not enter the Unclaimed Lands. Anyone leaving the Moor and then attempting to return met the same fate as a stranger. It had been Cecilia's fate, and she—

Don't think of that.

I walked the entire afternoon, sometimes sure I was too exhausted to take the next step, and yet I did. Long before sunset I ate the food I had brought, hid myself under a deadfall and fell into sleep as down a dark well. When I woke it was morning again, and raining. Soggy, cold, hungry, I contemplated my future.

Where was I to go?

How was I to live?

The savage army's main purpose in making the hard mountain trek to The Queendom seemed to be to lay siege to the capital, abduct six-year-old Princess Stephanie and carry her back over the mountains to marry the Young Chieftain. If they succeeded in capturing the princess, perhaps they would leave. Then I could return to Maggie and Jee. Unless the savages both carried off the princess and also left enough soldiers here to hold The Queendom. Was their army large enough to do both? I had no idea.

I could stay here, on the southern edge of the Unclaimed Lands, build a shelter and eke out some sort of living by hunting and gathering plants. In two years I had learned much about living off the land – from Jee, from Maggie, from Tom, even from Fia. That might suffice for summer, but eventually winter would come. I did not know how to survive a winter in the wild.

No, I must find people who would take me in as the lowliest kind of labourer. I must find these people in the Unclaimed Lands, mountain folk who kept to themselves and would be unlikely to give me up to savage soldiers. But mountain folk lived so poor, on such hard-scrabble farms, that they were unlikely to need extra labourers. And I had but one hand.

Lying under my deadfall, I felt tears spill from my eyes, mingling with the rain. I had but one talent, and I was afraid of that too. As a child I had lived, under Hartah's brutal direction, by crossing over and selling to grieving women whatever information I learned from old women in the Country of the Dead. The thought of doing that again filled me with horror. And now I was afraid to cross over, afraid of that crowned figure in the fog, whispering my name. And I had promised Fia.

'*They are almost ready*,' she had said. Ready for what?

I had no answers, not to anything. But I must at least have breakfast. My stomach ached with hunger.

I found a stream, and with Fia's carved fish hook and a line of stout vine caught two fish. Gutted with Tom's knife and cooked over a fire, they would at least give me strength to further contemplate my misery. I was searching for dry wood when I heard voices.

Guttural. Loud. Calling to each other, the words unknown. Savage soldiers.

Wildly I looked around. The stream flowed shallowly through the large clearing, and there was nowhere to hide. Any moment the soldiers might break through the trees and raise their deadly *guns*. I ran.

I gained the woods and was several yards into the trees when I heard their shouts. They had discovered my fish on the bank of the stream. But they did not know which direction I had gone. Standing still, afraid to call attention to myself by even the slightest motion, I listened intently, trying to discover by the different voices how many they were.

At least three. The Young Chieftain was serious about capturing me.

Carefully and slowly, raising one foot and then setting it down, I moved deeper into the woods, looking for another deadfall, a cave, anywhere I might feel safe. I didn't find it.

Neither did they find me. But they hunted me, fanning out and spiralling in, driving me as a wolf pack drives its prey. Had the savages been Tom Jenkins, they could have followed my trail, but these were no trackers. They relied on numbers and their *guns*, and all day they drove me relentlessly south. I had slept but not eaten, and I could feel myself weakening. I hid when I could, but no hiding place felt safe enough.

Each hour the pack drew closer.

Finally, at dusk on that agonizing day, desperate and starving and exhausted, I came to the border of Soulvine Moor.

This was not the place where I had entered Soulvine

two years ago, but in its great sweep of empty land and huge sky, the moor everywhere looked almost the same. Ground springy with peat under my boots. Outcroppings of rock, ranging in size from mossy stones the size of my head to great naked tors jutting up against the sky. Patches of purple heather, patches of wet and treacherous bog, patches of acidic soil either bare or barely nourishing poor grasses. I stood in the last stand of trees before the border, heard the soldiers shout behind me and knew that I had run out of choices. In a few more minutes they would be on me. I sprinted across the open space to the nearest large boulder, a quarter-mile away, and dived behind it.

More shouts, fading away. Did they know where I was? I couldn't tell. But they did not enter Soulvine Moor – from fear, from military orders, from who-knew-what. I sat with my back pressed against the side of the granite, trying to hurry darkness. Night would hide me.

The first bright stars came out. Then the second group, less bright. The stone at my back lost what little warmth it had held from the fitful sun. I peered cautiously around the boulder and saw a campfire at the edge of the woods. The savages were not going away.

But if I made no fire, at least the Soulviners would not find me. My belly groaned with hunger. My clothes were still damp with the morning's rain. The summer night was warm, but not warm enough. I must keep moving. At full dark I would move – crawling if necessary – across the moor and re-enter the Unclaimed Lands at some point east of the savage encampment. Perhaps that way I could escape.

But it did not happen like that. Instead, lights bobbed towards me from deeper into Soulvine. At first I thought they were merely marsh gas. Then I knew they were not. They headed unerringly towards my boulder.

Impossible. The inhabitants of the moor could not know

I was here. This was coincidence: a hunting party or else some peculiar ritual, nothing to do with me . . .

The lights came straight towards my boulder.

I dashed away in the dusk, running east, trying to keep from the bogs that could mire me to the waist. But then figures also loomed ahead of me, and I changed direction. More figures, then shouts from the savage camp, and then a body hurled itself on mine. We went down. I struggled, but I was no match for him, a strong young man with two good hands. I struck out blindly, he struck back, and everything went black just as the first *guns* sent shots over our heads and someone screamed.

I came to in a place I knew well. A low windowless round room built of stone. A fire smouldered in the centre, the smoke going up through a hole in the roof. Torches burned in holders on the walls. Stone benches heaped with fur blankets ringed the central space, with baskets resting under each bench. The only other furnishing was a large drum. When I had been here two years ago, the stone room had held many men and women, and they had—

Don't think of that.

—had crowded the space. I had sat with them on furs thrown on the floor. Now I lay bound on the stone, and a single man was with me. He sat on a bench, gazing down at me. It was the ancient white-bearded man with the same green eyes as Cecilia, as Fia.

'So, *hisaf*,' he said gently. 'You return.'

I strained against the ropes that bound me. The ropes held.

'No one returns to Soulvine Moor,' he said.

But I was a *hisaf*! They killed foreigners, but two years ago they had not killed me because I was a *hisaf*. So at least one rule was different for *hisafs* and surely other

151

rules would go on being different, the old man didn't mean to imply—

'I am a *hisaf*!' I cried.

'Yes,' he agreed. 'And because that is so, your flesh will give us great power.'

And then there was no telling myself not to think of it, no holding the memory back. The roasted meat, succulent and greasy, my eating it while the fire blazed with the sweet-smelling powder thrown onto it ...

Cecilia ... *Cecilia* ...

'Do not wail so,' the old man said, his wrinkled face wrinkling even more with disgust. 'You are a *hisaf*. You should find it in yourself to die like one.'

22

It was my dream come monstrously true. I lay on the flat upland moor outside the round stone house. A torch stuck into the ground beside me burned brightly, and beyond the circle of its light moved inhuman things – men but bent on inhumanity.

I was tied on a broad flat stone, face up to the starlit sky. The ropes that held me circled the stone. Someone had moved the drum outside, and now the drummer began a slow steady rhythm: *boom boom-boom-boom booooom*. One by one, the older men and women, middle-aged or more, came up to me and stared deeply into my eyes. The torchlight cast weird shadows on their faces. All their eyes were green.

'I thank you for your flesh,' each said solemnly, 'which will gain me the power of your soul.'

'You will gain nothing!' I screamed. 'You know that! You have been in the Country of the Dead in the dark mist – you know you cannot have my soul!'

Boom boom-boom-boom booooom . . .

'I thank you for your flesh,' said the next one, a wrinkled and bent woman, 'which will gain me the power of your soul.'

'It does not happen that way! You know that!'

Boom boom-boom-boom booooom . . .

I squeezed my eyes shut, so that they could not gaze into mine. The next person pried them open.

'I thank you for your flesh, which will gain me the power of your soul.'

'But I am a *hisaf*!'

'I thank you for your flesh, which will gain me the power of your soul.'

Boom boom-boom-boom booooom . . .

I strained against my bonds. As my head thrashed from side to side, I saw a fire burning beside the stone house, and over it a large iron pot.

For me.

'I thank you for your flesh, which will gain me the power of your soul.'

As the Soulviners left me, each entered the round house. A scent floated towards me from within, sweet and pungent. I had smelled that powder thrown onto fire before, two years ago, when I had sat inside the stone house, feasting on meat . . . greasy and succulent—

All at once I grew calm. This, then, was how I ended in the land of the living. It was no different for me than for anyone else; death must claim us all. And if in the Country of the Dead I lapsed into mindless tranquillity, at least I would be free of the memories and dreams that tormented me. But if I could not escape death, I could at least escape the pain of dying.

The old man with white beard and Cecilia's green eyes was the last to come to me. He held a long curved knife with a carved wooden handle. We gazed at each other, and in the shifting torchlight I seemed to see strange shapes deep in his eyes. I bit my tongue hard and, to the beat of the unseen drum and without so much as hesitating about my promise to Fia, I crossed over.

Darkness—

Cold—

Dirt choking my mouth—

Worms in my eyes—

Earth imprisoning my fleshless arms and legs—

Then I was in the Country of the Dead, and the drum

beat had stopped. It was the upland moor swaddled in fog, even denser and thicker than before. Blindly I stumbled forward, senselessly fleeing the round stone house. But of course there was no stone house here. Nothing but fog and the circles of the Dead.

I came across the first one almost immediately. It was huge, perhaps thirty Dead. Soon I might be one of them. The Dead held hands. Each head was shrouded in opaque dark mist.

'You are monsters!' I shouted, but not to the Dead. To whom, then?

I charged towards the middle of the enormous circle. There would be a humming mist there, a collection of watchers from Soulvine, made up of the men and women now sitting in the round stone house. Breathing the drug thrown onto the fire. Preparing themselves to feast on my flesh. I could not reach them in the land of the living, but here I would – what? I didn't know. I only knew an insane rage to destroy that mist, to somehow beat on it, to—

There was no mist in the centre of the circle. Instead a single figure sat there, and all around it the fog had dispersed, leaving a clear area of almost bright air. The single figure was one of the Dead, and she sat with her hands folded in her lap, her legs tucked under her, her head slightly bent.

It was my mother.

Vertigo took me. For a moment I could neither see nor hear. Then my head cleared and I lurched forward, falling to my knees before her motionless figure.

'Mother!'

She wore her lavender gown, and lavender ribbons bound her hair. A slight smile curved her pale lips. She was just as tranquil and mindless as the rest of the Dead. I clasped her to me. When my embrace did not rouse her,

155

I grabbed her by the shoulders and shook her. 'Mother! Mother!' When that did not rouse her, I hauled her to her feet, and her folded hands, with their long lace-trimmed sleeves, fell away from her lap. Blood soaked the front of her gown.

I eased her back to the ground and stared. This was not old blood, brownish and dried. This was fresh, bright red, and now I could smell its coppery scent. When I touched my fingers to her gown, they came away smeared with blood.

'*Mother!*'

'Roger,' said a woman's voice, 'you are here.'

She moved towards me in dark mist, and other figures moved with her. I could see none of them clearly. Through the fog a crown glinted.

'Who are you?' I cried.

'Eleven years dead.'

'*Who?*' I clutched my mother tighter, as if I could somehow protect her, she who was already Dead!

The crowned figure gave the laugh that shivered along my bones. And then, 'You don't belong here, not like this. But soon.'

And all at once I was not there. I was back on Soulvine Moor, tied on the flat rock under the stars.

But I had not sent myself back. It did not happen like that; always I had chosen to return from the Country of the Dead; always I had had to inflict some slight pain, concentrate my will, and only then pass through the grave with flesh gone from my bones. Always I had a *choice*.

'You do not escape that way,' the old green-eyed man said. More shapes moved behind his eyes. He raised his knife and carefully cut open my tunic. Cool night breeze played across my bare chest. The drum had fallen silent.

I cried, 'What happened to my mother!'

It was as if I hadn't spoken, as I were already dead. He whispered ritual words in a language I did not know and raised his knife over my body. I closed my eyes.

The crack of a *gun*. My eyes flew open in time to see the old man's look of surprise, just before his body tumbled back out of my sight.

'Peter!' a voice cried. Tom Jenkins. And then he was running towards me out of the darkness. But so were men and women – not the middle-aged and old, who sat drugged in the round stone house, but the able-bodied young of Hygryll. The warriors. They rushed out of the darkness with knives drawn, shrieking, their faces contorted with shock and ferocious rage. A young woman threw herself on the fallen old man. The rest made for Tom, just visible at the edge of the circle of torchlight.

He stopped, his face confused and uncertain. Then he began firing. But he had told me that a *gun* could shoot only three times before more *bullets* needed to be fitted into it. Tom fired twice more and reached for a second *gun* from the sling on his back. I could see that he would never make it. A warrior leaped towards him. Tom Jenkins would join me in the Country of the Dead.

A grey shape hurtled towards the warrior. It caught him in mid-air and they crashed to the ground.

Then, as I blinked in disbelief, there were two of the grey shapes, three, a half-dozen. They did not run in from the moor; they were just *there*, as air is there.

Or fog.

'Peter!' Tom cried from somewhere on the ground below me. The warriors screamed. Tied to the rock, I could see little but hear everything: the human shrieks of agony, the inhuman snap of jaws on flesh, the sudden howl of an animal, sharp and shrill with pain. Above all, a gurgle I cannot forget, as blood and air mixed from throats torn out. I could not see it happen, but I saw it in imagination, and that was the more terrible of the two. The carnage seemed to go on for ever, but of course it did not. It lasted only a few minutes. The landscape of horror, like that of the Country of the Dead, distorts time.

Then silence.

'Peter.' Tom rose beside me, blood streaming down his clothes and his face ashen. 'Are you all right?'

I couldn't speak. My helplessness seemed to steady Tom. Colour flooded back into his face. His hand did not shake as he cut my bonds.

I sat up on the rock. Young men and women lay dead or dying all over the ground. A few moaned. Amid the carnage sat a single large dog.

Shadow.

Shep.

My voice came out shaky. 'There were many dogs . . .'

Tom looked puzzled, but only briefly. 'Must have run off. Come, Peter, we have to get away from this cursed place!'

The dogs had not run off. Lying helpless, my pre-ternaturally sharp hearing attuned to the brutish killing around me, I had heard and seen many dogs, and I had not heard them leave. I choked out, 'Did you see—'

'Come on, Peter!'

Tom grabbed me by the hand and pulled me forward. I looked back over my shoulder at the round stone house. No one had emerged from it. The elders of Soulvine Moor sat in their drugged state, watching someplace, somewhere in the Country of the Dead.

I ran with Tom until I could run no further. When I faltered and fell, he caught me. We rested briefly in the darkness, and then he made me start again. I lost track of time, place, everything but the terrible pictures in my head.

My mother, fresh blood on the lap of her lavender gown—

A crowned figure in the fog—

'Come on, Peter!' said Tom.

'You don't belong here, not like this. But soon.'

Boom boom-boom-boom booooom ...

The snap of jaws on flesh and bone—

My mother, fresh blood on the lap of her lavender gown—

'Come on – just a little further.'

We went a little further. Further still. We stopped. I tumbled to the ground in the greatest exhaustion I have ever known and then I was asleep, and mercifully without dreams.

23

I woke in a forest, under a huge oak tree. Beside me slept a large grey dog. Tom crouched over a pile of kindling, blowing gently on sparks struck from his steel and flint. He couldn't stop blowing long enough to speak, so he waved one hand at me. The dog stirred, stood and stretched. A bird sang, stopped, sang again.

The scene was so quiet, so mundane, that unreality took me. Had I really seen last night's horror at Hygryll? Had I really lain bound, ready to be killed while the elders of Soulvine Moor waited for my flesh? Had a pack of dogs really materialized from nowhere and—

Nothing could materialize from nowhere, and I knew only one place from which a solid body could be brought from empty air. But that required being brought by a *hisaf*, and anyway there were no dogs in the Country of the Dead.

The dog wagged his tail and brought me a stick to throw.

Tom had got his fire going. He said, 'You slept a long time. Shep here already brought back a fat rabbit – didn't you, boy, good old dog! Well, I guess you needed the sleep, after what almost ... Peter, I owe you an apology.'

It was the last thing I expected. I blinked at him. His face was solemn.

'You see, I thought you tricked me. After you left, letting me think you were afraid of the savage soldiers, I decided that you told me a flock of lies and ran off yourself with Fia. So I tracked you. But you didn't go away with her, did you?'

'No.'

'So where is she?'

His face wrinkled with pain. For the first time I considered that Fia might have been to him what Cecilia had been to me. Not just a possible bedmate, but a lost love. I said, and they were among the truest words I had ever spoken, 'I don't know where Fia went.'

Tom's gaze dropped. I knew he was not seeing the fire, nor the skinned rabbit beside him, but only his loss. Despite all else, it moved me.

He said, 'She wanted to go to The Queendom. I suppose she went. But I would have taken her there, or anywhere else she desired!'

'I know,' I said gently.

'The worst is, I couldn't track her. I followed her easily enough to a little dell full of wildflowers, but then the trail just disappeared. I found a lot of other tracks, though. Savage soldiers.'

So they had come as far south as the dell where Fia's time had ended. I must have missed them by only a few hours. And their blundering about had covered my trail. 'Tom—'

'She left me this.' He held out the miniature, smaller in his huge palm than it had ever looked in mine, and Fia's face gazed back at me. But I knew that, if I squinted, I would see not only Fia but also Cecilia.

Abruptly Tom said, 'If I didn't know better, almost I would think that she met those savage soldiers there by design. That she *wanted* to go away with them.'

'I don't think that, Tom.'

He shrugged, and now his eyes were hard, and the pain gone from them. 'It could be so. You can't trust women, after all. They are fun to bed, but they ain't men.'

161

He shrugged again, thrust the miniature into his pocket and laid the rabbit on the fire.

Did he mean his words – were women to him a pleasurable distraction when present but dismissible when not? Or was he only telling himself that in order to lessen real hurt over Fia? Watching him cook the rabbit, whistling tunelessly as he poked at the fire, I genuinely could not tell. Tom Jenkins was so different from me that he might have been another form of creature altogether. I did not know what he was.

The dog solemnly watched us both. I did not know what he was either. But I did not think he was Shep, although he looked as much like him as Shep had looked like Shadow.

Grey dogs, materializing out of the fog.

I said slowly, 'Tom, why weren't you afraid to go onto Soulvine Moor?'

He looked up and grinned. 'Why, Peter, you don't believe those tales made up to scare children, do you? Old women talking.' His grin faded. 'Although what was in that place was fearsome enough. Why were they going to kill you? Are they in league with the savage army?'

'I . . . I don't think so.' He utterly confounded me. Even the palace servants had been afraid to so much as speak the words 'Soulvine Moor'. But the palace servants perhaps had more actual knowledge of the place. Could knowledge increase rather than lessen superstition? But no, the country folk of innumerable summer faires had believed all the old ways. This was just Tom: fearless, feckless, cutting his beliefs to suit his whim, unwilling to share beliefs held by old women.

He said scornfully, 'I suppose you believe in witches too.'

Did I? What else to call Mother Chilton? But that was not what Tom meant. 'No,' I said.

162

'Well, come now, that's good at any rate. Still, you hesitated before you spoke, Peter. Next you'll tell me that you believe men can cross over to the Country of the Dead!' He gave his hearty laugh and turned the smoking rabbit on the fire.

I ate ravenously, slept again and ate again when I woke, this time fish caught in some mountain stream. Tom kept low the fire of some hard wood that smoked very little. Once I thought I heard *guns* in the far distance, but I could not be sure. By mid-afternoon, when the sun sent the oak tree's shadow long over an open patch of buttercups and daisies, I felt ready to travel again.

Tom looked at me expectantly. 'Peter, what do we do now?'

'Journey,' I said.

'Why?'

'There is a place I must visit, and someone I must see, but I cannot tell you more about either. If you are willing to travel with me in such a way, I am glad of your company. If you do not wish to come, I understand.'

His face clouded. 'You do not trust me.'

'I do trust you,' I said, and it both was and was not a lie. There was no one more loyal, useful and tireless than Tom. There was also no one more likely to commit some impulsive act that could get us both killed. 'But none-theless I cannot answer your questions. Will you come anyway?'

He chewed his thumbnail and stared at me resentfully. 'You won't tell me?'

'I can't.'

'Is this more lies?'

'No. I am telling you nothing so that I don't have to lie to you.'

He considered this, trying to work it out. Was I com-plimenting him or deceiving him? The workings of his slow brain were clear to me – clearer, in fact, than the workings of my own.

My mother, fresh blood on the lap of her lavender gown—
A crowned figure in the fog—
Fia—

And I had been *sent* back from the Country of the Dead. I had not chosen to cross back over; I had been yanked away, a thing that had never happened before. I did not know who could possibly possess such power, nor what was going on in the Country of the Dead, and I knew of only one person who could tell me for sure. But I had no idea where Mother Chilton was. That left only one other who might have any useful information. My plan – if it even deserved that name – was a desperate one. But it was all I could think of.

'I will come,' Tom said and kicked dirt over the fire. He rolled up his cloak, in which I had been sleeping, and efficiently packed up knife, cook pot, tankard, *guns*. All packed, he looked at me expectantly.

'Where are we going?'

'East,' I said.

It took more than a fortnight. We kept to the northern edge of Soulvine Moor, sometimes within sight of the Moor itself down the long wooded slope of some hill. I caught glimpses of empty land, of bogs marked by green moss, of towering rocky tors, but never of any settlements. The walking was easier here than it would have been further north in the heart of the Unclaimed Lands. One night I drew in the dirt a rough map for Tom, as Kit Beale had long ago drawn it for me.

'See, here are the Unclaimed Lands, and north of that is The Queendom. This is the sea, here to the east. We are heading towards the sea.'

'Oh,' Tom said. He knew better, now, than to ask me

why. Nor did he show much interest in my map. He could not read and had no interest in my teaching him letters. For Tom Jenkins, the world existed not in symbols, not in superstitions, not in memory, but only in what he could see and feel directly in front of him. He had never again mentioned Fia, nor had I ever seen him look at her miniature.

Sometimes I envied him.

'When we reach the sea,' I said, pointing with my stick at the dirt map, 'we turn north along the coast.'

'Oh. Is there any rabbit left? Hey, Shep, you lazy dog, you didn't catch a big enough rabbit, you wastrel! Must do better tomorrow, Shep, old boy, old good dog!'

Shep, who was not Shep, wagged his tail.

The going became harder once we reached the sea. The coast was wild here, with deep hidden coves, high cliffs and no dwellings. However, as the land descended, rough tracks appeared, and then the occasional isolated cabin. The weather held clear and warm, and Shep found ample food. When Tom talked to cabin folk, they were suspicious and uncommunicative, but we did learn that the savage soldiers had not appeared in this remote area. At some point, unmarked, we passed from the Unclaimed Lands into The Queendom.

And then, after long days of hard travel, when a rich summer haze lay over the land, we came to a place I knew well. A deserted cabin in a clearing, with a track leading to a steep cliff above a pebbly beach. Huge, half-submerged rocks stretched out to sea. I stood at the top of that cliff, gazing at the calm blue sea, and the scene in my mind was different and terrible.

'Peter,' Tom said, with one of his isolated, unexpected flashes of insight, 'What is it? You look so ... so ...'

'It is nothing.'

He said quietly, 'You have been here before. And in

that clearing with the cabin a rotted noose hangs from the oak tree.'

The body of the yellow-haired youth – his hair the same colour as Tom's – was long gone. It had been three years since Hartah and his murderous crew had wrecked the *Frances Ormund* on the rocks below and had been caught by the queen's soldiers. Now no ships sailed that quiet horizon, and the beach was lit by the sun, not the burning of a treacherous bonfire to make a ship think it a safe harbour in a wild storm. Somewhere on that beach, unseen, sat the Dead. Killed in the wreck, killed by Hartah's men, killed by soldiers. Plus one killed by Hartah, and one by me.

'Yes,' I said to Tom, 'I have been here before.'

24

That night, as Tom slept beside our fire in the clearing, I broke my promise to Fia for the second time. I crossed over.

First I had to make my way down to the beach. I remembered from three years ago that in the Country of the Dead, whose landscape resembles but does not duplicate the land of the living, there had been no track from the cliff down to the beach. This was where I had first seen the sailor Bat fly up through the air, and so had realized that the Dead – if not lapsed into quiet trance – had power I had not realized. But I was not dead and could not fly though the air, neither here nor there. So before I crossed over, I picked my way carefully down the steep, overgrown but fortunately moonlit path to the beach.

The dog followed me. He sniffed with interest at bushes, at holes in the ground, at spoor. When finally I reached the beach, he lost interest, lay down on the pebbles and went to sleep.

A little breeze had risen with the sunset, ruffling the water into wavelets against the shore. I stood for a long time, watching the water break gently against the rocks, gathering my courage. Then I lay down close to the cliff edge, bashed my thigh with a stone and crossed over.

Darkness—
Cold—
Dirt choking my mouth—
Worms in my eyes—

Earth imprisoning my fleshless arms and legs—

Night was replaced by the steady low light of the Country of the Dead. The fog was wispy here, hanging in sparse pale patches that I could easily see through. For a long moment I stood motionless, waiting to see if I would be sent back, as I had been on Soulvine Moor. But nothing yanked me away, and so I made my way through the fog towards the Dead.

They sat on the beach or on the rocks, some far out to sea. No waves threatened their perch. There was one circle of Dead, but it contained only four sailors; they did not hold hands, and no thick mist shrouded their heads. Whatever Soulvine Moor was doing to the Country of the Dead, it had not yet reached this eastern shore.

Not all of the Dead on the little beach were sailors or wreckers. Over time, other people had died here. I saw two small children dressed in old-fashioned smocks, a fisherman and a barefoot man dressed in crude furs. There was only one woman on the beach. I went over and crouched beside her.

'Aunt Jo?'

She didn't answer, of course. It was odd to see such a tranquil expression on her face, which I had known only pinched with worry or distorted with fear. A little way off sat Hartah, the source of all those years of worry and fear. I did not look at him directly, my aunt's brutish husband, who had terrorized both her and me. There was nothing I wished from him now. All accounts between us had been settled the night of the wreck, when I drove his own knife between his ribs.

'Aunt Jo, it's Roger. Roger Kilbourne.'

She gazed serenely at nothing, from eyes the light brown of my own. My mother's eyes were darker, the colour of rich spring earth. Aunt Jo was – had been – her older sister, but I didn't know by how many years. Nor

168

did I know how old my mother had been when she died and I was sent to live with Aunt Jo. I was seventeen now. If my mother had been, say, twenty when I was born and her sister ten years older, that would make my aunt forty-four when she died. Not yet an old woman, and it is old women who are most willing to talk to me.

'Wake up, Aunt Jo!' I shook her shoulder. She did not stir.

'You must wake up! I don't know where Mother Chilton is, and you are the only other person one who can tell me about . . . I need to . . . Wake up!'

She did not rouse. I grabbed her thin, frail body and shook her hard. My voice rose to a shout: 'Aunt Jo!' She did not wake.

Was she really too young to be roused, or did her dreaming mind prefer the tranquillity of the death trance to the horror that had been her life? The gash that had torn open her head when Hartah hit her with the brass-bound wooden box – that gash was gone. The Dead do not carry their fatal injuries beyond the grave. But I could nonetheless see her terrible life with Hartah in the starved thinness of her body and the gauntness of her sunken cheeks. She looked older than forty-four, old enough to be wakened as I had wakened other old women in the Country of the Dead, and perhaps she was older and merely choosing to stay tranced.

The idea enraged me. I shook her again. 'Wake up! Wake up! There are things I need to know and only you can tell me. Who calls my name in the Country of the Dead? Why is there fresh blood on my mother's gown? Who was my father? Damn you, Aunt Jo, wake up or I'll . . . I'll . . .'

I could not say it. But I was prepared to do it: *Wake up or I'll carry you back with me to the land of the living and make you talk.*

I could do it. I had done it before. And if I did, Aunt Jo would have a fortnight of renewed life and then she would vanish for ever, would rot away in less than a minute, and would exist no longer in either realm. Whatever the Dead waited for – if they waited – she would not receive it; death could not be cheated for long. I would have my answers, but at the price of my aunt's eternity.

'Curse you! Answer me, or I *will* do it! Wake up! Wake up! Who calls my name in the Country of the Dead? Who was my father? Who? Who?'

She flopped like a doll in my one good hand. No emotion, no recognition, no life crossed her face. I pulled her close and prepared to cross back over.

At the last moment, I could not do it.

This woman had not protected me from Hartah, but she had taken me in when my mother died and own father did not come for me. Aunt Jo had shared with me what little food Hartah gave us. She had urged me, on that terrible day of the shipwreck, to flee Hartah while I still could ('Go, Roger! Go!'). For eight years, whatever kindness I had experienced had come from her, and if it had not been much, she had nonetheless strained to give it to me. I could not repay her by robbing her of this existence, the nature of which I did not even understand in the first place. For all I knew, the Dead were ecstatically happy inside their oblivious bodies. For all I knew.

I laid Aunt Jo back onto the pebbles of the little beach. To Hartah I gave a vicious, utterly pointless kick, sending him sprawling onto his calm face. Then I bit my tongue and crossed back over.

It was a good thing I did. Although I had spent only a few moments in the Country of the Dead, hours had passed in the land of the living. The tide was coming in and water half-covered my senseless body; in another few minutes I would have drowned. It was dawn and mist swirled across the little beach.

I stood, soggy and chilled. A figure came towards me in the fog.

For a dazed, horrified moment I thought I was still in the Country of the Dead, and the figure, crowned, would give that terrible laugh that shivered along my bones. But I was in the land of the living, the fog was only morning mist rapidly burning off as the sun rose, and the woman was not crowned. She wore a grey dress and grey cap. She looked neither young nor old, fat nor thin, pretty nor ugly. She *did* look angry.

It was Mother Chilton.

25

'So you can still think of someone else, Roger Kilbourne,' Mother Chilton said. 'That may be the only good you have done – or rather not done – this summer.'

All I could do was stare at her and stammer. 'How ... how ...'

'How did I know that you thought to bring back your poor aunt but did not do so? Don't be so stupid, Roger. I know that you did not because your aunt is not here, is she? And I know you thought to do so because why else would you come to this place? It's not as if you have fond memories of this beach or the clearing above.'

'But how did ... did you know I was here?'

She gazed at me, and under that calm disapproving stare I felt fifteen again, a lovesick blunderer coming to her shop for a milady-posset without knowing what it was or why Cecilia needed it. I lay again in an empty apple cellar while Mother Chilton cured me of black pus by cutting off my hand. I stood, drugged by her potions, in a secret chamber of the palace and watched Queen Caroline burn at the stake. With me again was every terrible mistake I had ever made since I last stood on this damp beach. And here *we* were again, Roger the fool and Mother Chilton the rescuer. Nothing had changed.

'All has changed,' she said severely, without answering my question. 'Roger Kilbourne, you must stop crossing over. But first you must come up from the tide.'

The water had nearly reached the tops of my boots in the few moments we had stood talking. The small beach acted as a funnel, drawing in the tide. Mother Chilton and I climbed back up the rough track, she first. Behind us the sun rose, burning off the mist below, and the sea lay calm and blue and hard.

At the top of the track, in the shade of a stand of pine twisted by salt wind, she turned to me. Disapproval turned into urgency. 'Roger, you must give me your promise that you will not cross over again, not ever. It is more important than you can know. Promise me!'

For the first time ever, I felt the balance between us shift. I had something she wanted. Meanly – and I knew it was mean even as I said it, for I owed her my life – I said, 'I will promise only if you first give me answers.'

Her expression did not change, but her old-young eyes glittered with anger. She did not answer me, and I took the absence of denial as cause enough to press ahead.

'What was Fia?'

'I think you already know what Fia was.' Mother Chilton folded her arms across her chest. She would give me nothing I did not work for.

'Fia was ... was ...' Difficult words to say, to even think. I postponed them for a moment by saying, 'There are many of you ... you women who know the soul arts. Aren't there?'

'Yes.'

'Is the ability passed from mother to daughter?'

'Sometimes. Not always. Neither Caroline nor her mother had talent, but her grandmother did.' Arms still folded, she waited for me to reach my question.

'And Fia was one of you?'

'No. She was not.'

'Then who was she?'

Mother Chilton said nothing.

'But she was ... was brought back from the Country of the Dead, wasn't she?'

'Yes.'

'And now she exists nowhere, and never will?'

'That is true.' Sudden pain crossed Mother Chilton's face, and I saw that she too mourned Fia.

'But *why*?' I cried. 'Why do that to her? Why?'

'It was not done *to* her, Roger. She chose it.'

'The Dead cannot choose anything! They are quiescent! You cannot tell me—'

'I can tell you truth, ' she said, her composure vanishing, 'but you will not listen to it. Fia chose to do this while she still dwelt in the land of the living. She chose to die and be brought back over, and die again, as a fighter against those forces you cannot understand. She had a task to do, and she did it.'

My knees gave way, and I grasped a pine tree for support. 'Fia ... Fia did that to persuade me to stop crossing over?'

'No. Don't be so arrogant. Before she died, Fia did not even know that you existed.'

'Then what ... She came originally from Soulvine Moor?' Those green eyes, so much like Cecilia's.

'Yes.' Mother Chilton's expression shifted. She unfolded her arms, as if coming to some decision. My breath stopped in my chest. She had decided to tell me the truth.

'Fia was a Soulviner, from Galtryf, the heart of the enemy. I use that word advisedly, Roger Kilbourne. Soulvine Moor is the enemy of all that lives. Fia saw what was happening there, and it sickened her. She escaped. She thought to find any of the women who practise the soul arts and tell us of Soulvine's plans. She actually reached the border of the Unclaimed Lands. To have got that far, already dying—'

'Dying?'

'Galtryf had poisoned her. It keeps all of its young on

a steady low dose of poison until it is sure it has snared their minds. Without the antidote in the food that Fia ate every day, the sickness took her. But she kept going, dragging herself over the border, where no Soulviner would go. You know why.'

I knew. Anyone who left Soulvine Moor and attempted to return would meet with the same death I had only barely escaped.

'A boy found her in the Unclaimed Lands. An ignorant boy, not very intelligent. But before she died, Fia made him promise to find a *hisaf* to cross her back over. The boy did so. The people of the Unclaimed Lands, most of them anyway, still respect the old truths.'

Like Jee. I could picture Fia, dying in pain, gasping out her last request to a rough young lout – who would honour it. Also like Jee.

'You can guess the rest,' Mother Chilton said. 'A *hisaf* brought Fia back over, and she found women of the soul arts to tell what she had learned. Then, during the rest of the fortnight left to her, wanting to be as useful as possible, she was taken to you to obtain your promise to never cross over again. A promise you broke the very next day.'

'She tricked me! She—'

'I know what she did,' Mother Chilton said severely. 'Do you still not understand, Roger? This is a *war*. It is much, much larger than your petty concerns. And you must stay out of it.'

'Why?' It came out a howl, and two birds in a nearby bush took frightened wing. 'And a war against what? What is Soulvine trying to do?'

'They are doing it,' Mother Chilton said grimly. 'Listen to me. The Dead grow in power over years, over centuries – how could it be otherwise? Even stupid youths like you know how much power death has. You have good reason

175

to know it. All thoughtful men and women spend their lives aware that they will someday die and that nothing at all, neither riches nor beauty nor love, can thwart that ultimate power. And when death finally enters into them, so does some of death's power. The power of the Dead is their own – unique, even when shared in their circles. That power grows slowly, like a huge oak from a tiny seed, until each of the Dead is ready to let it take them on to eternity. If it were otherwise, the Country of the Dead would contain many, many more than it does. Have you never noticed that no clothing there dates from further back than the last few hundred years? No, of course you have not noticed, and your ignorance would not know the dates of clothing anyway.'

I would not let her scorn deter me from my questions. 'But Soulvine Moor . . .'

'Soulvine has found a way to visit the Country of the Dead. You have seen the men and women of the Moor over there, have you not?'

'As a dark, humming fog. But I thought only *hisafs* could cross over!'

'Originally, yes. But there are faithless *hisafs*, corrupt and self-seeking, and some of those . . . I have told you enough!'

I had never before seen Mother Chilton distressed. I did not know she *could* be distressed. She covered her face with her hands, and her whole body trembled. The sight terrified me; it was like seeing a mountain tremble or an oak tree weep. But I could not let up. This was my only chance to learn what I so desperately needed to know.

'It's not enough, Mother Chilton. What do Soulvine and these "faithless *hisafs*" seek to do? Tell me, or else I will promise nothing.'

Her spasm ended as soon as it had begun. She took her hands from her face, and in the shade under the pines

I could not tell if there were tears on her face. Had it been but an act, then? To move me and so end my questions?

She said simply, 'They are trying to draw the power of the Dead to themselves, and so live for ever.'

I stared, appalled beyond any words.

'They would rob the Dead of eternity and take it into themselves. They would thus destroy the Dead over there, just as you destroyed them here – Bat and Cecilia and the Blue army. Now do you understand what is at stake?'

Rob the Dead of eternity. I thought of those large circles, hands joined and heads shrouded in dark fog that agitated each of the Dead. In the centre of the circles, humming clouds of watchers from Soulvine. But to rob the Dead of eternity . . .

'Can they *do* that?' I whispered.

'Yes. No. It's unknown as a certainty, but we believe they can. After all, *you* robbed people of eternity in this realm – why should it be impossible in that other?'

I could say nothing.

'Roger,' she said, more quietly now but with urgency somehow aided by that quiet, 'you must not cross over again. I told you once before to not seek your mother. Now you really must not try to find her.'

'I found her,' I said. Mother Chilton's eyes widened. So she did not know everything that I did, or everything that happened in the Country of the Dead. This knowledge gave me courage to ask more. 'Why is there fresh blood on my mother's gown when no blood is fresh beyond the grave? And who is that woman in the mist who knows my name? The woman who says, "Eleven years dead"?'

Mother Chilton groaned. 'She has seen you, then.'

'Yes.'

'And spoken to you?'

'Yes.'

'This is very bad.'

'Who is she? Tell me, or I will promise nothing.'

'You threaten me, you ignorant meddling boy?'

'I am no longer a boy,' I said hotly, 'and if I have meddled, it is because no one has ever given me the knowledge to act wisely. So tell me, Mother Chilton, or I will make you no promises, who is that woman?'

'She is not a woman. She is a girl, born eleven years ago. She is a girl, and she is your sister.'

The words did not make sense to me, did not map onto anything real. 'My—'

'Your mother married a *hisaf*. *Hisafs* do not marry girls from The Queendom, but they fell in love. She was beautiful and he was headstrong. None of us approved the marriage but—'

'Who are "us"?'

She continued as if I had not spoken. 'They married, and you were born. Six years later your mother gave birth again, and it killed her. Many women die in childbirth, you know.'

I remembered the visitors to the inn at Applebridge months ago, a lifetime ago. Lord Carush Spenlow's daughter-in-law fresh from childbed, pale and feverish. The midwife saying, *'That girl, Lady Joanna, will die. There was nothing I could do.'* The baby wailing in the caravan. *''Tis a pity, really.'*

Mother Chilton said, 'But your mother was different, Roger. She carried the child of a *hisaf*, and she died at the very moment before giving birth. Such a thing had never happened before. Your sister was born wholly in the Country of the Dead, in that brief moment before the Dead lapse into tranquillity. Do you understand? The infant had no body in the land of the living. She never existed here. She has grown up beyond the grave.'

'I don't understand, no.'

Mother Chilton said, 'Yet it is so.'

'But how could an infant even survive? If my mother lapsed into the tranquil trance of the Dead, how could she care for the baby?'

'She could not. Did not. Your sister was raised in the early years by a succession of Dead, old women briefly roused by the corrupt *hisafs* who saw their chance in this bizarre birth. When the child grew a little older, they themselves brought her food. But she has spent most of her life alone, there among the Dead. She is a source of enormous power to the rogue *hisafs*, those who work with Soulvine. Even a *hisaf* must die, and these faithless ones do not wish to do so. But your sister is not a *hisaf*. She cannot cross back over, and if someone brought her over, she would wink out of all existence like a gutted candle. She knows this. What she is, Roger, is a link between the living and the Dead. She lives, and yet she never lived. And—'

She stopped, but I knew what she was going to say, and I said it for her. That laugh that shivered along my bones, turned my blood to ice.

I said, 'My sister is mad.'

'Wouldn't you be, with such an existence for so long?'

'Yes.'

'*Eleven years dead* ...' And yet not dead.

Mother Chilton said wearily, 'Go back to Maggie, Roger Kilbourne. Give me your promise that you will never cross over again, and then go back to that poor girl who so unaccountably loves you. I have told you enough.'

'No, you have not! Why must I not cross over? What can my sister do to me?'

'We do not know for certain. We do know that she is in the power of the rogue *hisafs*, who seek to use her for their own ends. She is unique, neither living nor dead –

179

who can say what her powers may be? And we suspect that they seek to use you as well, through her, although we do not yet know how. Try to remember, Roger Kilbourne, that you are not alone in this world – in either of these worlds. You are not a speck of dust floating in empty air. What you do has consequences for the entire web of being.'

'But I am a *hisaf*!' It came out sounding like the wail of a child.

'There are many *hisafs*. But you are different from the others.'

Fury filled me. She was so elusive, this woman standing in the shadow of a wind-warped pine, her eyes somehow reflecting all light back to me. She would tell me nothing straight. I wanted to strike her with my one good hand – I, who have never hit a woman in my life – but I knew that if I did, she would best me yet again.

'I am different *how*? And why think so at all?'

She said, 'Because you and your mad sister are linked by blood. And because your father is different from other *hisafs*.'

I gaped at her. She had said it simply, just as if the sentence had not the power to knock me off my feet. And she continued on in the same tone.

'He is horribly mistaken about the nature of this war. But he is nonetheless doing the best he can. As are we all.'

'My father is *alive*? And never has he seen me or even—'

'Hush! Listen!'

I heard it then, shouts through the trees. They came from the direction of the cabin in the clearing.

Mother Chilton seized my arm. 'Give me your promise! You will never cross over again!'

'Soldiers—'

'Say it! I have kept my part of this unholy bargain!'

I said, 'I promise I will never cross over again. My father—'

Four soldiers burst from the trees. We stood, Mother Chilton and I, our backs to the cliff. No escape. But these were not savage soldiers of the Young Chieftain's army; they wore the purple tunics and shoulder emblems of Princess Stephanie, of The Queendom. I could have wept with relief – but only for a moment.

'That's him!' one man cried. In a moment they had seized both Mother Chilton and me. They dragged us along the track to the clearing. Tom Jenkins lay outside the cabin, beside our fire. Blood caked his blond head. He was not moving.

A tall man with the tunic emblem of a captain studied my face. He nodded and made a gesture, and one of the others hurried inside. The captain, who had the thin sharp-chinned face of a weasel, said, 'You are Roger Kilbourne.'

I said nothing. A rusty voice quavered, 'Master . . .'

The captain said impatiently to the others, 'Let the crone go. We have no orders about feeble old servants!'

I turned to look at Mother Chilton. Her face had wrinkled fantastically; her head bent forward on its knotted neck; her eyes were filmed with the rheum of age. The soldier released her. Again she whined to me, despairing and obsequious, 'Master . . .' The soldier shoved her, and she nearly fell. Righting herself, she shuffled off. Not once did she look back at me.

'Roger Kilbourne,' said a voice behind me, and I turned. The voice was both thick and heavily accented. I think I knew, even before I turned, who it was.

The savage singer-turned-warrior had not, after all, died from Shadow's attack in the Almsbury cottage. Unlike the other three soldiers, he had somehow survived

181

that brutal maiming. But his handsome young face was horribly disfigured. One eye was covered with a patch. His mouth twisted in a grotesque line, the lips half torn off and still not healed. His voice came thick and garbled from a throat swaddled in bandages. His one eye sparkled with hatred.

This time, I knew, there would be no dog to rescue me. Shep-who-was-not-Shep had not followed me up from the beach. His time in the land of the living was done, and so was he. As I would soon be as well.

In moments of despair the mind can fasten on to strange notions. Knowing that soon I would die under torture, one irrelevant thought stabbed me with regret.

I wished that I had asked my mother's name.

26

I was not tortured. Tom was not dead. Once again, nothing was as I had thought.

'*Tel mit*,' the savage once-a-singer growled at the soldiers of The Queendom, and I saw from the puzzled look on their faces that they too had difficulty understanding the words coming from that swaddled, maimed throat. The savage was evidently in charge of this detail of Princess Stephanie's soldiers, and he spoke to them in his own language, not ours. I understood 'Take him' but not the string of garbled syllables that followed. I didn't think the captain could follow it either, but he must have already had his orders.

His men handled me roughly but with no intent to cause pain. They bound my arms behind my back and pushed me into a supply wagon at the edge of the clearing. They also dumped Tom into the wagon. He groaned briefly before lapsing again into unconsciousness. The savage singer came towards the wagon and said sharply, '*Ka! Ka mit!*'

A soldier grabbed Tom and dumped him out again, back on the ground. The driver lashed his donkey and we started forward. Whatever was going to happen to me was not going to happen here.

All morning we travelled. I lay bound on the bed of the supply wagon, along with sacks of flour and dried meat and a barrel of ale that sloshed, half-empty, with every jolt. The driver sat on the wagon, and the other three soldiers walked behind. The maimed savage walked ahead, alone. Under the trees the shade was cool, but each time the track took us into the open, the sun beat down on my uncovered head. I had nothing to do but think.

When would the torture start?

Was Tom dying, left in the clearing, or would Mother Chilton go back for him?

She had turned herself into a shuffling helpless crone – how? And was the change for the moment only or for ever?

My mother, the blood fresh on her lavender gown ...

My sister, alive and mad in the Country of the Dead – *'You don't belong here, not like this. But soon.'*

My father, the bastard who had deserted both his children ...

No. Stop. No. Think.

I was seventeen. My father had left my mother and me before I could remember him, and had never returned. My sister had been born eleven years ago. So my father was not also hers. She was my half-sister, and different *hisafs* must have fathered us. I tore through my memory, searching for ... what? Some recollection of a man with my mother and my six-year-old self watching, observing, noticing anything at all ... There was no memory.

Who was he?

Was Tom dead?

How could the 'rogue *hisafs*' harness the power of the Dead unto themselves? Could my sister really be used to aid in that unholy quest?

And when would the torture start?

Around and around my thoughts went, and the sun beat down, and the ale sloshed in its barrel, and dust rose up from the track and enveloped me in a dry, choking fog.

When the sun stood high in the sky, we stopped. I was given meat and bread, plus a long draught of water that was the sweetest thing I had ever drunk. After that, everyone ignored me. The savage sat apart and was served by the driver. Every line of the driver's body spoke his dislike of this duty, but it was clear who was in command here. When we resumed travel after the noon meal, one of the other soldiers of the Purple joined the driver on the wagon seat. I pretended to be asleep and listened to their low conversation.

'Fucking prince, he thinks he is.'

'Shut up. He will hear.'

'He don't hear us here, ye idiot.'

'They hear everything. Anyways, *he* will hear.'

'He be asleep.'

I snored loudly.

'What'd he do, anyways?'

'Dunno. The Young Chieftain wants him, is all I know or care.'

'Ye care only for the triple pay.'

'By damn, I do. And ye, too. Samuel, when we reach Tidewell, will ye . . . will ye stay with the army?'

A long pause. 'Will ye?'

'I asked ye first.'

Another pause, even longer. Then Samuel said, 'I will desert if ye will. After we get our pay.'

'A bargain? Seal it.'

I heard spitting and hand-slapping. Were these soldiers typical? Was most of the army of The Queendom held under savage command only by the promise of triple pay? I could easily believe that. So the Young Chieftain could hope to hold The Queendom by force only briefly. Why would he even . . . ?

I knew the answer. He was here to claim his six-year-old bride, his future hold on The Queendom. And to take his revenge on me for his father's death.

At nightfall we reached Tidewell, a poor fishing village somewhere on the coast. I slept on the floor of a cottage, its terrified owner having been roughly evicted. My ankle was chained to the bed occupied by a savage soldier. There were more savages here, entire cadres, and the princess's Purples were paid. The next morning they had gone.

The savage singer-turned-warrior never came near me. Not yet. Perhaps he did not trust himself.

For a few weeks we travelled south-west, our travel slowed by the cumbersome wagons and by many long halts. By the third day I knew, from the arc of the late-summer sun, where we were headed. Each night we stayed at a village or inn, and the folk of The Queendom were ousted from their beds and kitchens. But no one, as far as I could observe, was harmed or robbed, and the savage soldiers left the women alone. Even absent, the Young Chieftain kept the same strong discipline among his troops that his father had kept. If there were soldiers at the villages, they left with us at dawn the next day. And so the number of savages around my supply wagon grew, until they were a small army.

Now a boy, a younger singer with red dye on his face and twigs braided into his hair, stood in the bed of my wagon. The soldiers marched all day, tireless. The singer chanted, with equal tirelessness, the same song that I had heard three years ago, at The Queendom's first sight of the savage army under Lord Solek.

'Ay-la ay-la mechel ah!
Ay-la ay-la mechel ah!
Bee-la kor-so tarel ah!
Ay-la ay-la mechel ah!'

Thus, with savages chanting and marching, as I lay bound and sunburned on the bed of a donkey wagon, I caught my first glimpse of a purple banner flying from the top of a slender stone tower. And so at dusk of a fair autumn night I returned to Glory, the capital city that I hoped to never see again, where I was thought a traitor and a murderer and a witch.

Now there were two groups of people with reason to kill me.

27

The city had not changed in three years; it had not changed much in two hundred. It filled its island in the placid River Thymar, behind the high stone wall that ringed the entire island right to the water's edge. Stone bridges, their arches high enough to permit barges to pass underneath, connected the riverbanks to the island. Set into the wall at each bridge were massive iron gates, now all raised. Other gates had no bridges but instead docks. The city's single slender tower soared above the walls.

The soldiers patrolling the ramparts wore purple, but those guarding the bridges were all savages, dressed in their furs and feathers, their *guns* on their backs and their curved knives at their belts. We passed over the bridges, through the crowded cacophony of the city, and through a high wooden door into the quiet of the palace.

I tried to sit up on the wagon bed, but a savage soldier pushed me roughly down again. So all I saw of the palace was the sky above and the upper storeys of buildings. Gardens festooned some of the flat roofs, but no people appeared. I had no idea where I was among the vast, sprawling, exquisite courtyards of my memory. As Queen Caroline's fool, I had seen all of the palace – except the dungeons. Fear gripped me. Was that where we were headed now?

It was not. The wagon stopped and a savage hauled me, just as if I were a sack of grain, through a door. He dropped me on the floor. I hit my head and for a moment saw nothing but swirling colours. Then a woman cried, 'Roger?'

My vision cleared. Bending over me was the broad, ruddy, utterly incredulous face of head laundress Joan Campford. She had recognized me despite my beard, my sunburn, my filth.

'Clean it,' the savage said, the words barely understandable through his thick accent. A flash of knife and my bonds were cut. A kick of his boot and I tumbled, numb from being so long bound, into the pool of the laundry where I had once worked. I flailed madly until I could stand, waist deep in soapy water, surrounded by soaking bed sheets.

Without a moment's hesitation, Joan waded her stout personage into the pool beside me and handed me a lump of the rough yellow soap I knew so well. 'Roger, lad, be ye all right? We all thought ye dead!'

'Clean! Clean!' the savage soldier said.

'Hold your piss-soaked tongue,' Joan said, but her back was to the soldier and her words were muttered. The next ones addressed me. 'They all said ye be dead, lad, and such terrible things – that ye be a witch, that ye be a traitor, that ye . . . Faughhh! He's naught but Roger the queen's fool, I said, and before that he was Roger the laundress, and the best worker I ever had!'

'Clean! Clean!' The savage brandished his knife.

I stripped off my filthy tunic and, below the sudsy water and floating cloths, my boots and breeches and small clothes. The yellow soap stung, just as I remembered. I said to Joan, 'Thank you.'

'I told them, I did – I told them that I saw ye kill Lord Solek! With my own eyes I saw it! Ye led the . . . the magic illusions that did the deed! Be ye now a prisoner then? The Young Chieftain holds the palace.'

'I know,' I said, and ducked under the water to scrub

my hair. Also to avoid any more talk. Joan had always been kind to me, in her rough way. She knew as well as I what must happen to me now. Had this been one of the washing areas built out over the river, I might have swum out under the palace walls, as I had once swum in under them. But this was an enclosed soaking pool, full of bed sheets, and there was no escape. When I surfaced, Joan knelt beside the pool, scrubbing my clothing. Her eyes watched me with sadness.

But hope survives in even the most desperate places. Why would the savages make me bathe if I were going to be killed? Did torturers have such delicate noses that my stink would offend them as they tore at my bones and blood and nerves?

When my guard judged me clean enough, he said, 'Out! Out!' I came out. Joan followed and handed me a towel. I dressed again in my wet clothes. My little shaving knife was still in the inner pocket of one waterlogged boot, but it did me no good. The savage retied my arms behind my back. Then, because it was all I could say to her, I whispered to Joan, 'Goodbye.'

Her eyes filled with tears as the savage led me away.

Through the laundry courtyard. Then the courtyard of the baths. Then courtyard after courtyard – I knew exactly where we were at any given moment. But where were the people? The courtyards, each becoming more elaborate as we left the servants' part of the palace and walked through that of the courtiers, were all empty. Not so much as a gardener or pageboy or carpenter was to be seen. Only a few savage soldiers patrolling the rooftops. The palace was the reverse of the Country of the Dead – all structures, no inhabitants – but just as silent. The only sound was my guard's boots, first on cobblestone and then on painted tiles, and the soft squish of my wet feet in my wet boots.

But then we came to the royal apartments, and I had my answer.

The massive carved doors to the throne room, three storeys tall, stood open. Inside the enormous room, torches and candles along the walls made twilight almost as bright as day. The nobility stood massed on both sides of the throne dais, just as I remembered from Queen Caroline's reign, but now they wore purple instead of green. Purple velvets, satins, brocades, silks. The gowns of the ladies were cut low over their breasts; the tunics of the courtiers were slashed over cloth of gold; the long robes of the elderly advisers were richly embroidered at hems and full sleeves. And all of them were utterly silent.

Along the left wall stood the servants of the palace, scrubbed and clad in whatever passed for their best. Cooks, gardeners, kitchen maids, carpenters, serving men, couriers, grooms, scrub women, ladies' maids. I recognized some of them. The faces of the few who recognized me went slack with shock.

Scattered among the silent crowd were soldiers dressed in purple but carrying *guns*. Before now I had seen soldiers of The Queendom serving the savage army, but never before had I seen them carrying *guns*. What did the people think of those who turned against their own folk?

But I already knew.

At the door to the vast room, the savage relinquished me to another, a captain in helmet and metal armbands, a short feathered cape over his sleeveless fur tunic. He seized my arm and pulled me forward. And so we walked that whole huge length of the hall, all eyes upon us: a captain of the conqueror and a traitor of the conquered, and not one person made a single sound.

I kept my eyes straight ahead. On the dais stood a sacrilege: not one but two thrones.

When we reached the dais, the captain pulled me to

one side. A murmur rose behind me, so faint that it might have been a breeze ruffling the arras, rather than the mutterings I knew it to be. The savage kept tight hold of my arm. We all waited. Everyone apparently knew what we waited for. And now, with a sickening lurch of my belly, so did I.

28

Ten minutes went by. Fifteen, twenty. It was a long time to neither speak nor move, but no one did.

The servants standing closest to the massive doors must have heard it first. Their gazes turned towards the court-yard outside, and those furthest away turned their heads and took on the expressions of people listening hard. Then all of us could hear it. For me, the throne room took on the aspect of a dream, something between memory and fresh experience. For I had seen this all before, three years ago, and to see it again was to believe for a moment that I was again Roger the fool, the boy who understood nothing instead of the man who understood too much.

A boy singer entered first. He wore red dye on his face and twigs in his hair. He could have been the singer from three years ago – except that particular singer had become a man and a soldier, and a dog from the Country of the Dead had torn into his throat and ripped out his eye. But even this voice, powerful enough to reach to the high vaulted ceiling and echo off the stone walls, was the same.

> *'Ay-la ay-la mechel ah!*
> *Ay-la ay-la mechel ah!*
> *Bee-la kor-so tarel ah!*
> *Ay-la ay-la mechel ah!'*

The boy sang as he walked the entire length of the throne room. When he reached the empty dais, he moved to one side, so close that, had my arms not been bound behind my back, I could have reached out and touched him. He sang the savage army into the throne room. They marched in two abreast, pounding their cudgels on the floor and chanting along with the boy.

'Ay-la ay-la mechel ah!
Ay-la ay-la mechel ah!
Bee-la kor-so tarel ah!
Ay-la ay-la mechel ah!'

This time there were not as many savage soldiers as when Queen Caroline had awaited them on her throne. Part of their army was holding the palace, part holding The Queendom, part perhaps still searching the Unclaimed Lands for me. Still, enough soldiers, followed by their captains, marched in to fill the right side of the room, with a wide aisle between them and the palace servants. Both groups strained with tension in every line of their bodies.

The savages fell silent, and the boy singer paused. Then he began again, a song I had not heard. If before his voice had swelled with the chant, now it soared with an exuberant joy I had not thought that guttural language could express. This song had no words. It was pure sound, and yet in it there seemed to be both the trill of birds and the drumbeats of victory.

A single figure appeared in the doorway. Swiftly, as if he were borne on the music, the Young Chieftain crossed the hall towards the throne. He wore the same helmet, sleeveless fur tunic and boots as his captains, but the feathers of his short cape were every colour of every bird that ever existed, and the gold bands on his upper arms glittered with red jewels. I saw Lord Solek's features on a younger face, and Lord Solek's eyes, so blue that they looked like pieces of sky. The Young Chieftain had not his father's great height and muscled bulk, but he had the strength and health of a young man of twenty.

Without a moment's hesitation, he mounted the steps of the dais and sat on one of the thrones.

Behind me rose a groan, from everyone and no one. The savage soldiers tightened their grips on their knives. But not one courtier, adviser, or servant made another sound. I could only imagine how much pain must have gone into acquiring that restraint.

Now three girls appeared in the doorway. This was the first time I had ever seen any females of the savages, and for a moment astonishment overrode fear. The crowd behind me gasped.

They were very young, no more than thirteen or fourteen, and at first appeared to be naked. They were not, but the cloth that drifted around their barely budded bodies was so light and fine that it looked like mist. Their little pink nipples were visible through that thin drapery, and the pale hair of their sex. All three had hair so fair it seemed white, and the long unbound hair drifted around them as lightly as the transparent draperies. They seemed completely unafraid.

They moved forward, singing the same wordless song as the boy. It was as if the girls *floated* across the floor. When they were a quarter of the way to the dais, a tiny figure appeared in the doorway, following them. It was Princess Stephanie.

When I had seen her last, she was three years old. Now she was six, and scarcely larger than before. Always sickly, she looked as if her trembling frame could barely support all the jewels sewn on to her purple velvet gown. Her lank brown hair fell down her back. How much did she understand of what was happening?

The princess followed the singing, nearly naked girls who, compared to her, suddenly looked like mature women. Stephanie had none of her mother's boldness, nor her grandmother's dignity. She was a quaking little girl trying not to cry, and as she drew closer, pity flooded me for the fear in her huge grey eyes.

At the dais the girls stopped singing and sat gracefully on the steps. The princess climbed between them and sat on the second throne. Her feet in their jewelled slippers did not reach the floor.

Two old men stepped out from the group of advisers, Lord Rathbone and Lord Carstill. I knew them both from Queen Caroline's reign, when they had been not advisers but ordeals for her. The queen's fool witnesses much. Great landholders in the northern part of The Queendom, both had tried, and failed, to marry their sons to the widowed queen. Their sons were as stupid and untrustworthy as themselves. Over the generations, the blood had run thin. But those without intelligence may nonetheless have a kind of low cunning, and it was clear that my lords Rathbone and Carstill had sold their loyalty, bargained it to the Young Chieftain in exchange for position and power. They mounted the steps of the dais with confidence, smiling, and behind me in the crowd of courtiers ran a low hiss.

The Young Chieftain ignored it. He stood and took Stephanie's hand. She flinched. He pulled her to her feet. Lord Carstill, I remembered, was a cleric.

The marriage ceremony was brief, cut to its essential words, all poetry and joy gone. 'Your Grace,' said Lord Carstill, smirking, 'will you accept High Lord Tarek son of Solek son of Taryn as your husband?'

Stephanie nodded. The Young Chieftain pulled on her hand. She whispered, barely audible, 'Y-yes.'

'High Lord Tarek son of Solek son of Taryn, will you

accept Princess Stephanie of The Queendom as your wife?'

'Yes.' His voice was guttural but clear in the single word of a language not his own. His eyes – how could eyes be that blue? – glinted with determination. He did not look at his trembling bride but instead turned his gaze on the people of The Queendom, nobles and advisers and common folk alike, and the message of that blue stare was clear: *Do not challenge me.*

And no one did. Where was Lord Robert Hopewell, Lord Protector for the princess until she came of age? Once Lord Robert had raised an army in an attempt to save Queen Caroline – surely he would do the same for her daughter? He must be dead, along with any loyal others who had not been cowed or beaten or bribed into accepting this marriage, which was in violation not only of decency but of the customs of The Queendom since time began. The princess royal always married at seventeen. She was, unless her mother died earlier, crowned at thirty-five, when her mother abdicated. One woman must not rule too long, lest tyranny establish itself. Women, the life givers, ruled. Men, the defenders, protected that rule. That was the way of The Queendom, and the law of life itself. The only way Lord Robert would have failed in that law was if the Young Chieftain had killed him.

Tarek son of Solek son of Taryn, and now consort to the Princess Stephanie, stood grimly,. Never had two people looked less like a bridal couple. A frightened little girl and a savage warrior clad in feathers and fur, claiming what had been promised to his father.

All at once a cry ran through the crowd, and this time no one, neither nobles nor common folk, tried to stifle it. Another of the boy singers walked alone across the throne room. On a huge pillow he carried two crowns. One was a simple silver circlet. The other was the Crown of Glory.

Fashioned of heavy beaten gold, the Crown of Glory was set with jewels of every hue, a rainbow of the colours of every queen who had ruled The Queendom. Emeralds, sapphires, rubies, amethysts, diamonds. Onyx, beryl, opal, topaz. Jewels I could not name, neither the stone nor the colour. The Crown of Glory had been set on the head of every new queen on her thirty-fifth birthday, and thereafter worn only upon state occasions. I had last seen it on Queen Caroline's beautiful dark hair.

Standing beside her bridegroom, Stephanie began to cry. The Young Chieftain said something sharp, and her sobs stopped. But silent tears continued to roll down her thin cheeks.

A woman broke from the crowd and ran towards the dais. Not a lady-in-waiting, not a courtier, not an adviser, not anyone of the nobility, who should have had their princess's welfare as their first duty. This was a stout middle-aged woman in white apron and stiff little cap with white lappets: a nursemaid. Before she could reach the steps, two savage soldiers caught her and dragged her behind the dais.

'Nana!' the princess cried.

One of the ladies-in-waiting spoke loudly, clearly, in defiance of whatever threats had been made earlier: 'It is all right, Your Grace. They will not hurt your nana. I will see to her now. Just stay a little while longer, my dear.' The lady walked with defiant dignity after the two savages. She did not run. She did not look at the Young Chieftain. But her purple satin skirts rustled and her head was held high, without trembling at whatever retaliation might come.

Well done, Lady Margaret.

There was no retaliation. The Young Chieftain made a slight gesture with his hand, and no soldier seized Lady

Margaret. All this while the boy singer with the two crowns had continued to advance across the throne room. Now he reached the steps of the dais and knelt. When he rose again, I saw under the red dye his strong resemblance to the Young Chieftain. This was a young brother or cousin, a prince in his own right, chosen to crown Stephanie in lieu of the lords of The Queendom who should have done it. And still the crowd in the throne room did not protest. What punishment had they been threatened with if this premature crowning of their little princess did not proceed a-right? Whatever it was, only Lady Margaret had defied it, and she in only a small way.

Tears still rolled down Stephanie's face. Her skinny little neck did not look strong enough to support the Crown of Glory. The red-dyed prince carried the crown up the steps. The first singer burst again into that wordless, weirdly beautiful song of victory. Princess Stephanie bent her neck.

And the savage prince placed the Crown of Glory upon the head of the Young Chieftain.

A moment of long terrible silence while people struggled to believe what they had just seen. And then the crowd broke.

Courtiers reached for the swords that were not by their sides. Ladies screamed insults. The common folk broke ranks and rushed at the dais, murder in their eyes. The savages were ready for them, and the soldiers were armed. From the left side of the room they sprang towards the attackers. The Young Chieftain drew the knife at his belt.

I saw that knife plunge into the heart of the gardener who reached the dais first. I saw a savage's cudgel come down on the head of a courtier fighting to get to the princess. I saw blood on the throne room floor. Then I saw no more because a savage soldier dragged me behind the dais and through the same door through which Stephanie's nursemaid had been taken. I struggled and shouted, but I was bound and one-handed, and he handled me as easily as if it were I who were six years old. The door was yanked closed behind us and I heard no more of the revolt in the throne room. A revolt that I, and everyone else, knew would be futile.

The soldier opened another door, thrust me inside and slammed the door shut, locking it behind him. I was in a small guardroom, now stripped of all weapons, with one barred window set high in the wall, and with me were the nursemaid and Lady Margaret.

29

Despite the dim light and the two years gone by, Lady Margaret recognized me. 'Roger the queen's fool.'

'No. Not any more.' As if that mattered now!

'Roger the avenger then.' She smiled thinly, as if knowing that her words could be taken two ways. By bringing back the Blue army from the Country of the Dead, I had broken Solek's power over the palace and avenged The Queendom. But that Blue army had also killed the Greens allied with Solek, and then the Blues had proved only 'magic illusions' that had vanished. Everyone in the palace had been related to soldiers in one army or the other. So I had killed them all, avenging myself on Queen Caroline even as I rescued Maggie. You could view events either way, but most people cannot hold in their minds two views at once. Lady Margaret was one of the few who could. I saw in her eyes that I was, all at the same time, a rescuer, a murderer, a deceiver, a witch and still and always the queen's fool.

The nurse, whom I did not know and who did not know me, cried, 'What of the princess? What is happening? Did they dare crown her?'

'No. They crowned the Young Chieftain.'

Both women gaped at me. The nursemaid gasped, 'With the *Crown of Glory*?'

'Yes.'

The nurse began to curse, a string of foul oaths more to be expected from a bargeman than from a maid of nursery. Lady Margaret stood motionless for a long moment. Then, always practical, she drew tiny embroidery scissors from the pocket of her gown and sawed laboriously through my bonds, pausing only a second when she first saw the stump of my right wrist.

'Roger, what else can you tell us?'

'When the savages crowned the Young Chieftain, the palace folk rioted. There was ... there was bloodshed. I don't know how bad it became. But it cannot last long. None of our people are armed.'

'They are not your people,' Lady Margaret said tartly. 'You forfeited that right, I think.'

'No,' I said, 'I did not. And you, you must remember, helped me do what I did.'

'I did not know your intent. And I will not dispute with you now, when both of us are probably going to die. But, Nana,' she said, turning to the nurse, 'I think you will be safe. The Young Chieftain has no women with him except those naked whores, and he will not want to be bothered with the care of a child on the long journey over the mountains. He will need you.'

This was much more information than I had had until now. The savages were going to take a princess royal away from The Queendom? No princess or queen ever left her own queendom except once, during her betrothal journey, to inspect the lands brought to her by her consort. But no one could expect a six-year-old to inspect anything intelligently. Nor did I expect the Young Chieftain to return Princess Stephanie – now Queen Stephanie, if the riot in the throne room had ceased long enough to crown her – to The Queendom. She would be a prisoner in that far western land that none of us had ever seen.

The nurse said hotly, 'If he dares to harm her—'

'Surely he will not,' Lady Margaret said.

The nurse, in her fear, turned on the lady-in-waiting. 'You cannot know that!'

'I know he has gone to great trouble to wed her, and that keeping her well is the only thing that will hold The Queendom for him.'

'True, true,' the nurse said distractedly. 'My poor motherless lamb! And her so often unwell, and plagued by nightmares!' She began to pound both fists on the door.

'Stop that,' Lady Margaret said in a tone I remembered well. The nurse stopped pounding. Lady Margaret, older and far less foolish than had been the rest of Queen Caroline's ladies, was usually obeyed. She was plain and severe-looking, and no courtier had chosen her to wife. One of them should have, for she had dignity and strength. Looking at her settle her skirts on a three-legged stool and fold her hands in her lap while still looking alertly around in case there should be anything useful to do, I was reminded all at once of Maggie. What was Maggie doing now? How would she learn of my death?

All of my fear for my own life, a river diverted by concern for the little princess, rushed back in a torrent. My belly clenched and my throat closed, making each breath an ordeal.

No one spoke again, although the nurse muttered to herself. We were not left alone for long. The door flew open and two savages entered. The first seized the women, one in each hand, and dragged them out.

Lady Margaret looked back at me. 'Goodbye, Roger,' she said. Both of us knew she meant more than a common farewell.

'Goodbye, my lady.'

'Whatever you say under pain does not matter. It cannot diminish you.'

There was no time to answer; the soldier hurried her down the corridor. Lady Margaret had done what Mother Chilton had urged me to do: think of another. As my

captor yanked me along a different corridor, not bothering to retie my wrists, I tried to think of others, in order
to not think of what awaited me.

Maggie stirring stew on the hearth at Applebridge, her
fair curls falling over her forehead . . .

Jee blowing on a willow whistle . . .

Tom triumphantly bringing back a rabbit for dinner . . .

None of it helped. Fear infested me like lice, and my
whole body and mind itched with it.

The savage led me to the stable courtyard. Here, even
though it was full dark, all was activity. The army's stables
were outside the city, but the royal hunters and coach
horses and courier mounts were kept here, along with
coaches and wagons. Torches flickered in their holders
on the courtyard walls. Savage soldiers shouted orders.
Palace grooms and stable boys leaped to obey. Horses,
catching the tension, pawed the cobblestones and whin-
nied. Three men pulled a wagon from its housing.

Whatever revolt had happened in the throne room
must have been quickly put down. How many had been
injured or killed? I would never know.

My captor pulled me into a coach house, at the back
of which stood a small oak door, not quite the height of
a man. He took a torch from the wall, unlocked the door,
pulled me through and locked the door again. We stood
on a narrow wooden landing at the top of a flight of stone
steps. In my months at the palace I had never learned
the location of the dungeons. Here they were.

'Dungeons' – such a grand name for such squalor. At
the bottom of the steps a short corridor had been dug
into the earth. Its rough walls, fortified with wooden
beams, stretched no more than twenty feet. The floor of
hard-packed dirt felt uneven under my still-wet boots.
On each side of the corridor two wooden doors with
barred windows were set into the earthen walls, and one

more door at the corridor's end. Between the windows torch holders, now empty, were fastened to the walls. No one called out in response to our torchlight; no one screamed in agony. The place resembled nothing so much as an empty grave.

But it was not empty. The savage unlocked one of the wooden doors. A stench hit me: unwashed bodies and slop buckets. The soldier thrust me into the darkness within. He hesitated. Then he closed the door but the light did not go away. He had left the torch to burn, for as long as it lasted, in the holder outside the door.

'Who are ye, that ye merit such consideration from a savage?' a voice asked, not gently.

It took a moment for my eyes to accustom themselves to light so dim that beyond the circle of torchlight only shapes were visible. The shapes resolved themselves into four men, three sitting with their backs against the far wall and one prone on the floor.

'Speak! Who are you?' said a much different voice. It robbed me of my own. I knew that voice.

'Come into yer own light then,' growled the first man. 'Why be ye unchained?'

I stayed with my back to the door, keeping my face shadowed from the small wavering circle of light from the torch outside the cell. 'I am ... am Peter Forest.'

'I know no Peter Forest.'

But the second man, he with the accent of nobility, jerked in surprise. 'Roger? *Roger the fool?*'

My eyes had adjusted enough to see that they were all chained to the wall. It was that which gave me courage enough to answer. 'Yes, Lord Robert. Roger the fool.'

The first man lunged in his chains. 'It was ye who led the Blue army against us! The magic illusions that killed all those Greens! Yer a traitor, a murderer, a witch!' If he could have reached me, he would have torn me apart.

But my death would have to wait for the savages. Their chains kept all three men in place, with only a limited range of movement.

Lord Robert Hopewell, lover of the queen whom my Blues had burned, said nothing. But I could feel his hatred flaming into me, palpable as the torch outside the barred door. Carefully I edged to the corner furthest from the three men, where the prone figure lay face down. He was also in chains and did not move.

The first man continued to curse me. I said nothing, my eyes adjusting further to the gloom. The man beside Lord Robert, closest of the three to my corner, seemed young. Slightly built, he was dressed in the riding clothes of a courier, although the garments were not purple. But it was impossible in the darkness and the courier's dirt, to see what colour. His stare at me did not carry the rage of the other two men.

Eventually the curses of the first man wore themselves out. Shortly after, to my surprise, both the first man and Lord Robert began to snore.

'They sleep often. They have been here a long time, and they are weak,' said the courier in a hoarse whisper. He had a slight accent, not of the south. 'Are you really Roger Kilbourne?'

I said, 'Who are you?'

'David Arlen, courier to Her Highness Queen Isabelle.'

Isabelle, ruler of the queendom to the north, bride to Queen Caroline's brother Rupert. Isabelle, who had failed to come to her sister-in-law's aid against the savage army. Once again I stood on the roof of the tower beside Queen Caroline as she scanned the horizon, day after day, for help that did not come.

The courier spoke again, and now I recognized the tone in his voice: panic. He was one of those who babbled to keep hysteria at bay. Cecilia had been the same.

'I was captured while bringing a message from Her Grace – a promise to Princess Stephanie – I mean to Lord Robert of course on Her Grace's behalf – a promise of help – the savages – they caught me two days ago – Lord Robert's groom says they use torture here – the savages – although no, of course those instruments were Queen Caroline's—'

Those instruments. I said, 'You have seen them?'

'Yes – I was briefly in the room across the corridor – before they brought me here – and I saw—'

'Don't tell me!'

'Hush! Keep your voice down; you will wake Lord Robert!'

He was right. I didn't want to wake Lord Robert. This jittery lad, obviously chosen for courier because his slight body could ride fast and hard, was my only source of information. I needed to keep him talking. 'How long have you been here?'

'I'm not sure. It's hard to tell in the dark.'

'But Lord Robert was here first?'

'Oh yes, as soon as the palace was seized.' Being asked questions seemed to steady him. In the corridor the torch sputtered.

'And you are fed?'

'Yes, and the slop bucket is emptied twice a day, and the water fresh. We have not been that ill-treated. But in that other room—'

'Don't think of it. Who is the man with Lord Robert?'

'A groom. He struck a savage soldier.'

'And this man lying here? Can he usually sleep like this through anything?'

'He's not asleep,' David Arlen said. 'He is unconscious, and has been for a day now, although he bears no injury. He was put here with all his wits, and then suddenly it came over him like that. The groom is an ignorant countryman. He called him some name but I can't remember it. The instruments in that other room—'

'What name?' I did not care what the unconscious man was called, but the young courier had begun to shudder, long racking spasms that shook his whole body. I must keep him talking, if only to distract him. 'What is his name?'

'I don't remember!'

'Try,' I said gently. *Think of others.*

'It wasn't a name but a word. Not even really a word.'

'What was it?'

He said, *'Hisaf.'*

30

At first I thought I hadn't heard right, that I couldn't have heard right. Stupidly I said, 'Oh . . . oh . . . what?'

'*Hisaf,*' the courier repeated. 'Oh, what does it matter? We are all going to die in horrible pain! I heard that they—'

But I had stopped listening, had stopped caring about the courier's fear. Laying a rough hand on the prone man's shoulder, I shook him. He did not wake. I shook harder. Nothing.

I rolled him over on his back. Every muscle was slack, his body an unresisting weight, his eyes closed. He could have been in a *hisaf*'s trance, but he could just as easily have been unconscious, or dead. By the dim light of the flickering torch in the corridor I could not see his features clearly. With my one good hand I seized his left leg and awkwardly dragged him as far into the light as his chains and my strength would permit.

'Hey!' the courier said. 'What are you doing?'

The light was still not good, but it was enough. When I pulled back the man's eyelids, his unseeing eyes were green. And his face was mine.

No. It was not possible.

The man was clean-shaven except for a day's light stubble, while I had a wild beard from weeks in the wilderness. I was thinner in the cheeks, and my hair and eyes were brown, like my mother's. But the man's face was an older version of the one I saw in the mirror, when I had a mirror, and the heavy unconsciousness that had 'suddenly came over him like that' could certainly be a *hisaf*'s trance. Was I looking at my father?

No. Not possible.

But many things had happened that did not seem possible, and none of them were coincidences. If this was indeed my father, he had come or been brought here for some purpose. Why?

The courier said, 'Do you know him?'

I gazed at the unconscious face beside me. This was the man who had abandoned my mother and me. Who had left her to be taken by whatever man had begotten my sister upon her. Who was thus indirectly responsible for my mother's death, and directly responsible for the miserable childhood years I had spent with Hartah and Aunt Jo. This man, who even now was probably crossed over, engaged in some terrible business in the Country of the Dead.

The courier repeated, 'Do you know this man?'

In the corridor the torch flickered one last time and went out, its pine pitch consumed. I spoke into total darkness. 'No,' I said without even trying to keep the bitterness out of my voice. 'I do not know him at all.'

It had been evening when I was brought to the dungeon. For that whole night nothing happened. In the dankness my wet clothing could not dry but it did turn slightly less damp, smelling of wool and sweat. I could not sleep, but the others snored steadily, even – eventually – the terrified young courier. Every so often I groped around in the total darkness for the shoulder of the prone man and shook it hard. Once I slapped his face. He never stirred.

In the morning I was going to die, the Young Chieftain's vengeance for the death of Lord Solek. When the torturers had finished with me, I would cross over for the last time and sit in a circle somewhere in the Country of the Dead, to be used by Soulvine Moor as just one more wellspring of power in their bid to live for ever. Dark fog would shroud my head. I would vibrate like a hive of bees, and then I would be cheated of eternity. Whereas if I crossed over now—

I had sworn to Mother Chilton that I would not cross over ever again. *'It is more important than you can know. Promise me!'*

But I had no idea what would happen if my body died in the land of the living while I was in the Country of the Dead. Would death take me just the same, so that I simply sat down in that thickening fog and lapsed into the same mindless serenity as all the other Dead? Or, being a *hisaf*, would I stay awake for eternity in that shadowy realm, as my sister had? My sister was mad.

I had promised Mother Chilton.

I did not think I could face torture.

When she extracted my promise, Mother Chilton had not known that I would be captured and would face torture. She probably thought I would do as I was bid and go back to Maggie and Jee. And I noticed that *she* had escaped torture for herself handily enough, by turning herself into a frail and ancient crone not worth bothering with. Why should I have to face what she had not?

But I had given my promise.

Somewhere tantalizingly close my father walked in the Country of the Dead. I could finally have the answers that not even Mother Chilton had given me. How dare she deprive me of them? She had told me much but not all. Not about my father, nor why he was 'different' from other *hisafs*.

And so my thoughts went back and forth, around and around, like a donkey lashed to a millstone and just as helpless to break free. All the while rage built in me: at

Mother Chilton, at my father, at the savages, at the world. Both worlds. I was in this state, choked with both anger and the fetid smells of the cell, when Lord Robert Hopewell spoke to me out of the darkness.

'Roger the fool.'

'Do not call me that!'

'I will call you whatever I choose. I have something to say to you.' His voice could have frozen the River Thymar in high summer.

'I am not interested in anything you have to say.'

'You will hear it anyway,' he said, and I recognized a rage as great as mine, and under better self-control. 'You are the cause of all this.'

'I am not,' I said loudly, not caring if I woke the others, not caring if I woke the entire treacherous and stinking palace. 'Your lover was the cause of this. It was Queen Caroline who tried to cast the savage army against her mother's Blues, as if men were so many dice. She used the savage army, she used me, and she used *you*, my lord. Lay blame on the grave where it belongs!'

'Close your lying mouth or I will kill you.'

He said it calmly but I knew he meant every word. Despite myself, I inched away from him towards the cell door.

'Do not mention her name again,' Lord Robert said in that same even voice. 'You understand nothing. But it is not of her that I would speak now, but of the Princess Stephanie.'

'She is Queen Stephanie now,' I said meanly, to hurt him. 'She was crowned at the same time the Young Chieftain was given the Crown of Glory, and married to him as well.'

'So I expected. And now she must be rescued. And by you, who have brought things to this pass.'

Rescued? By me? He must be as mad as my sister. I gasped, 'How?'

'The only way you can. You have that obscene talent at your disposal; the queen made use of it often enough. I witnessed that. And you brought back the army of Blues from ... from that place. You can do so again. Bring another army, and I will lead them.'

'I cannot do so again,' I said hotly. 'This time there is no army awake in the Country of the Dead.'

'I do not understand that.'

'You understand nothing,' I said, giving him his own words back. 'I can bring no one back again.'

'Then you can at least bring back weapons to get us free of this dungeon.'

I had not thought of this. In my rage at my father, my fear of torture, my indecision about my promise to Mother Chilton, I had not thought of the simple expedient of robbing the Dead of weapons. Now my mind leaped forward. Throughout history there must have been large battles on this island where the palace had stood for so long. The Dead would have swords, knives, even *guns*. Perhaps I could even find among them something to cut through chains.

I said, 'I cannot cross over.'

'Yes. You can. You owe this debt to the princess.'

I did not owe the princess anything. But his certainty provided the final ounce on my invisible scales. On *this* side of the scale, my rage and my fear and my desire – my right! – to confront my father. On *that* side, my promise to Mother Chilton. Lord Robert's certainty added to the first side, not because he was persuasive but because I was looking for that extra ounce. We can always find reasons for what we wish to do anyway.

'Yes,' I said, bit my tongue hard and crossed over.

Darkness—

Cold—
Dirt choking my mouth—
Worms in my eyes—
Earth imprisoning my fleshless arms and legs–

The fog, thicker and blacker than ever, did not obscure the figure waiting for me. He sat on a boulder right beside the place where I'd crossed over, and his green eyes gazed steadily into mine.

'What delayed you so long?' my father said.

31

I stared at him for a long moment, two moments, three, unable to speak. Choked with astonishment and rage. Those befuddle a man, so that the first thing I blurted out – of all the things I might have said to this man – was, 'Was it the dog collar in my pocket?'

He smiled faintly. 'How did you know?'

'Mother Chilton said, long ago . . .' I could not go on. Two and a half years ago and I a much different Roger Kilbourne, starting out to look for Cecilia, and Mother Chilton scowling at me: *'Give me that gold piece in your pocket and Caroline's ring too. How stupid are you, to carry markers like those two around with you?'* Shadow's collar was also a marker. It was how Mother Chilton had found me on the tiny pebbled beach. This had all come to me during the long wagon ride to the palace. Not even Joan Campford's fierce hasty scrubbing had dislodged the collar from my pocket. The collar was how my father had known where I was, guessing further that I would be taken to the palace dungeon.

He said, 'You are quick, Roger. You will need that, where you are going.'

'Where I am going is *here*, permanently! After torture and—'

'No. The savages do not torture. They consider it beneath them.'

'I happen to know otherwise!'

His face changed then. All at once he looked older and sadder, and yet impatience was there too. 'You mean the knotted cord in the cottage at Almsbury. We could not get the dogs to you fast enough. And we trusted that the singer-warrior would carry out his orders, instead of what he chose to do. He was sent to bring you to the Young Chieftain, no more. But Solek was his war-father and he is young and hot-blooded. He has himself in control now, and already anticipates what trouble that knotted cord has brought upon himself from the Young Chieftain.'

'And you know all this about the savage army?' I said bitterly. 'Do you work for them then? Have you betrayed your queendom as well as betraying my mother?'

His mouth tightened. 'I am not a subject of The Queendom, and we will not talk of your mother.'

'Yes, by damn, we will!' I shouted. 'You left her and you left me and then some other man ... did you *give* her to him? Is that another of your filthy customs on Soulvine, where—'

He was on me so fast that I did not see his fist until it had connected with my jaw. I went down, tripping over one of the Dead. Uselessly I flailed with my one hand, pushing at the serene dead soldier until I flipped over onto my back, my father looming over me in the drifting fog. My one hand snaked out towards the Dead, searching for a weapon.

'You know nothing,' my father said, and I became motionless when I saw that it was taking every last ounce of will he possessed to control himself. 'You are an ignorant boy. Get up.'

I did, but only because it was worse to lie there at his feet. My father's green eyes glittered. His body, taut as a line about to snap, leaned forward slightly on the balls of his feet.

'Listen to me, Roger. We have not much time, so I will tell this briefly and only once before I do what

216

I came here for. I loved your mother and she loved me. I did not "betray" her; I left both of you because my presence at her side put both your lives at risk. Even then Soulvine Moor had begun its monstrous quest to steal eternity from the Dead and give it to the living. Do you understand me? This war began when you were an infant in Katharine's arms, and there is more at stake than you can imagine. I left Katharine for her own safety, and yours, and what happened four years later ...'

He turned away until he had mastered himself and could continue. Now his voice was dry and hard, a soldier's voice. 'You came here to take weapons from the Dead. Do not do so. If you attack the savages, they may very well kill you from necessity. If you do not attack them, they will not harm you. At least, not now. The Young Chieftain has something else in mind, and we can turn it to our advantage. There is a task for you to do. That is what I came here to tell you, what I risked my own life to tell you. You will—'

'Don't tell me what I will and will not do!' And then, because I sounded like a sulky child, I added, 'Why should I believe you? Mother Chilton told me to go home. If I had some large "task", she would have told me so.'

'The women of the soul arts are not soldiers. They do not really understand the situation.'

'Neither do I!' Caught somewhere between tears and fury, I folded my arms and made a pathetic attempt to look demanding. 'Explain it to me.'

Carefully my father scanned the landscape. There was nothing to be seen but the Dead. 'Then listen well. There is a natural wall between the living and the dead and that wall is the grave. A *hisaf* can pass through that wall. You know this.'

Dirt choking my mouth – worms in my eyes – earth imprisoning my fleshless arms and legs—

'Yes,' I said. 'I know this.'

'Soulvine Moor is chipping away at that wall. The first chink was created when your sister was born bodily in the country of the Dead. Such a thing had never happened before. Then when you brought back first that sailor, then a woman, then an entire army—'

I grimaced, but he was relentless.

'—you widened that chink in the barrier more than you ever knew. It is like a fortification around a castle – once the wall is breached, each object or person forced through that gap widens it more. The soul-arts women do not seem to understand, or perhaps just accept, that *hisafs'* crossings are different. That we are different.'

'*You are different from the others, because your father is different from other hisafs,*' Mother Chilton had said. But she had not meant what my father meant now. I said, 'But just the same, I was told to—'

'Forget what you were told! The soul-arts women and my *hisafs* both fight against Soulvine Moor and the rogue *hisafs*, but we do not fight together. The women are not soldiers. They have their uses but are badly organized and ineffective.'

Mother Chilton had never seemed ineffective. 'But—'

He seized me by the shoulders. 'Roger, I do not have time to argue with you! Do you not hear that noise?'

And now that he had mentioned it, I did hear it: a faint baying, as of royal hounds on a stag hunt. But there were no royal hunts in the Country of the Dead, no stags, no *noise*. I did not know what I was hearing.

My father put his mouth close to my ear. 'You will be

218

taken with the princess over the Western Mountains, to the Young Chieftain's kingdom. He wants the "magic illusions" that he believes you created in order to defeat his father. He believes not only that you are a witch but also that you can teach him to become one too. Go along with this idea. Do whatever you can *except* bring anyone or anything back from the Country of the Dead to the land of the living. Pretend to teach the Young Chieftain, for that is the only way you can remain alive until we can rescue you. And I *will* rescue you; you have my solemn promise. We—'

'Rescue me now!' I said, and it was the sudden cry of a child to a parent. Instantly I regretted it. My face grew warm with shame.

'Do you not think I would if I could? All those years I thought you had died when Katharine did, all those years of searching for you on this side of the grave—' The baying grew louder. My father's words tumbled out. 'We cannot stay here any longer. Cross back over, Roger. *Now.*'

A loud noise like a cliff falling, where there were no cliffs. I chomped hard on my tongue. Blood spurted into my mouth and I crossed back over.

In the dark dungeon men stirred. I heard Lord Robert curse softly, and the country groom groaned with some unseen pain. Someone pissed into the tin slop bucket. But my father did not stir, not even when I poked him sharply. He had not come back with me from the Country of the Dead.

My father.

Even now I could not believe it. My head ached with all he had told me, as if the knowledge were raw splinters shoved into my brain. My mother and the 'war' with Soulvine Moor. *Hisaf* disagreements with 'the women of the soul arts', though both claimed to fight on the same side. My father had spoken of a 'breach in the fortifications between the land of the living and the Country of the Dead, but Mother Chilton spoke of the 'web of being'. I pictured a huge spider's web spanning the grave, woven alike of the living and the Dead, and in the middle sat the spider. She twitched on a silken strand and the entire web vibrated. *'You don't belong here, not like this. But soon.'* *'Eleven years dead.'*

'Light,' said Lord Robert's groom. A faint glow through the cell bars, growing stronger. A key scraped in the lock. More light, as a soldier of the Purple held up a flaming torch. Two savages strode into the cell, studied us all and hauled me to my feet.

But not before I had, when there was just enough light to see, flung to Lord Robert the knife I had taken from the dead soldier on the other side. My father had not seen me take it then, and he did not see me give it now. It was a small stupid act of defiance towards the man who had abandoned me, come back to me, promised me a rescue that I wanted desperately to believe in. Yet why should I trust him, or his counsel, especially since it conflicted with Mother Chilton's? *'You must never cross over again, and you must go home.'* *'You may cross over as you choose, and you must go with the Young Chieftain and teach him.'* Who was right?

I didn't know. But at least Lord Robert could use the stolen knife to defend himself, perhaps even to escape. Or, failing that, to choose for himself the time of his death. *'You must think of others as well as yourself.'*

The savage soldiers shoved me from the cell and locked the door behind us. The other prisoners were left behind. I was marched along the dank stone-and-earth corridor, up the steps, through the massive door and into the coach house. I gulped huge draughts of fresh air. The smells of horses and wheel oil seemed to me the sweetest I had ever known. I was still alive.

And now I knew my mother's name.

Katharine.

32

In what seemed to me a very short time, the stableyard was cleared of all horses, carriages and carts save one. This was a heavy high-sided wagon crammed with chests bound with iron. Someone had thrown a pile of straw and a few blankets into the small remaining space. Even I could see that none of horses in the stableyard was strong enough to draw the wagon. A pair of draught horses would be needed. The last of the grooms, shouting at each other, went off to commandeer such beasts. I was left alone with one savage soldier. He motioned for me to climb into the wagon, chained me to an iron bolt driven into one side and closed the wagon back. I heard his boots tramp away on the cobblestones.

What was happening to my father in the Country of the Dead? What had that baying been, moving closer to us, and had he escaped it? Or joined it?

I believed now that he had left my mother and me for my own safety – and yet that was not the whole truth. I had seen the quickening on his features as he faced whatever was coming at him in that other realm. I had seen the sudden sharp light in his green eyes. He was a *hisaf*, with a larger destiny to fulfil than merely living with a wife and child, and some part of him welcomed that destiny. Despite the real danger, despite the real anguish, despite the separation from loved ones. My father had left us with reluctance, but also with a heightening of his senses that was almost desire.

I recognized all that because it was what I had felt about leaving Maggie and Jee.

Lying upon the straw in the wagon bed, I thought about Maggie. I remembered so many small things: the way her fair curls fell over her forehead as she stirred a savoury stew in the big pot over the hearth fire. Her strong arms kneading bread. Her laugh as we sat at day's end over tankards of ale at the trestle table in the inn. And her body moving under mine on the sunlit hillside, the last day I had seen her. Somehow, my father's story had brought Maggie sharp again into my mind. It made no sense, but there it was.

'*Ven tek fraghir! Klen!*'

A horse neighed. The wagon jolted as the traces were put on. More shouting in the savages' tongue. Then we were moving, the iron wheels rolling noisily across the cobbled stableyard and not stopping. The wagon sides were high enough that I could not see over the sides unless I stood. The length of my chain permitted that, but I was not about to do so. Already more people than I'd expected had recognized me, and many in the city had reason to hate me. So I lay flat in the wagon, and again all I saw of the palace as we rolled through it were sky and the single grey thrust of the stone tower flying its meaningless banner of purple. Stephanie may have been crowned, but she did not rule here.

A halt to open the palace gates, and then the wagon moved through Glory, a city gone curiously silent. Eventually the sound of the horses' hooves changed to a steady ringing clop. We were crossing one of the great stone bridges spanning the River Thymar. On the other bank, all silence was gone. Cautiously I stood and peered over the side of the wagon.

Three great groups spread across the plain by the river. Furthest from me was the bulk of the savage army, in

223

perfect formation twelve abreast, armoured and ready to march. The land was dense with them, as with a plague of furry locusts. Next came a convoy such as The Queendom had never witnessed. Six brightly painted caravans were being hitched to draught horses. Each caravan had been constructed on a long wagon bed, with walls and roofs and curtained windows. They were garish colours – apple red, glaring yellow, the poisonous green of a haft-snake. The workmen of the palace, who had painted and tiled its subtle courtyards in soft blues and delicate purples, must have hated using the flat lurid colours. In each caravan closed curtains matched the paint. Iron wheels shone brightly, and the horses stamped in their leather-and-wood harnesses.

The savages did not ride. I had never seen a savage soldier on a horse. Beside each caravan stood soldiers, six on each side. But mounted soldiers of the Purple, some so young and slight that they must have been couriers or scouts, rode before and after the caravans. Other palace folk milled through the noisy chaos, amid the flocks of sheep that would be slaughtered to feed the army on its march home, the supply wagons holding crates of squawking chickens, casks of ale, bags of flour, and me. The plain rang with cackles, bleats and shouts in the guttural savage tongue. A drum sounded, and then, from the third group, the rearguard of soldiers, the voice of a savage singer, powerful and strong.

Everything began to move. The Young Chieftain's army was leaving The Queendom.

Why would he go after invading and conquering us? A moment's thought brought the answer. The savages did not have a large enough army in The Queendom to hold it indefinitely. This was but a very large raiding party, sent to capture the princess and me. But after I had taught the Young Chieftain to become a 'witch', as my father had said was the savage leader's intention, all would be altered. The Young Chieftain could then return over the mountains in a year or two at the head of an army of the Dead, invincible and infinitely renewable. There were always more Dead. Tarek could retake The Queendom with no losses to his own men, and rule through his child wife. Or so he thought.

And the entire insane plan depended on me.

For a moment, caravans, soldiers, sheep, wagons all blurred as vertigo took me. When my vision cleared, I saw that people had begun to appear on the ramparts of the city. They were too far away for me to see their faces, but I knew they would be weeping. For their dead lost to the savages, for their six-year-old princess being taken away from her heritage, for the traitors among them who had chosen to throw in their lot with the conquerors and so made conquest possible. And then, my eyes practically leaping from my head, I saw something I had never expected to see again.

Tom Jenkins.

Impossible, yet there he was, dodging lumbering wagons and marching cooks and stray sheep, one of which he nearly tripped over. A soldier of the Purple grabbed for him, but he knocked the man down and kept weaving and shouting, frantically searching for something. For me?

'Tom!' I called, but there was no way he could hear me over the din. All at once the back of my wagon, which had started forward, was jerked open and a soldier leaped in. I braced myself for a blow, which did not come. The savage muttered something I did not catch, unlocked the chain that held me to the wagon and leaped back to the ground. Urgently he motioned me to get out. No savage had motioned to me before; they had grabbed and shoved and pulled. I stared at him, uncertain, and then, even as the wagon pulled away from him, he bent his head and knelt.

I swivelled my head, looking for the Young Chieftain. He was not there. The soldier was kneeling to *me*.

When I gazed at him in stupefaction, all the while being borne away on the moving wagon, he jumped to his feet, ran after me and again gestured for me to get out. He did not touch me. His face creased in anxiety. He was young, blue-eyed as were all of them, heavily armed, and I would have sworn he was embarrassed. None of this made sense.

Tom saw me standing in the open wagon bed and ran towards me, shouting something I could not distinguish over the noise.

I climbed down from the wagon, which kept on moving. Relief flooded the young savage's face. He pointed in the direction I was to go. Tom was seized by a savage soldier, with whom he immediately began to fight.

'Tom! No!' I ran towards them, expecting to be grabbed in turn. But my guard – captor, guide, whatever he was – did not touch me. Tom was bigger than the savage, but the savage was not only superbly trained but also armed. If Tom pulled a knife—

He did. The savage leaped backward, graceful as a court dancer, and pulled his own wickedly curved blade. I screamed, '*Ka! Ka! Aleyk ka flul! Ka!*'

Nobody paid me the least attention. Tom and the savage circled each other, the soldier faintly smiling. Then another voice cut through the din, repeating what I had said in a commanding tone that would have made wild boars obey. '*Ka. Alyek ka flul.*' 'No. Do not attack.'

The soldier circling Tom did not look up but immediately shifted his stance to one that even I could recognize as defence only. Tom whooped and dived forward. His knife was expertly parried and a moment later he was disarmed and lying flat on his back, blinking up at the sky.

I tried to say to the captain in his own language, 'Please do not hurt him,' and hoped I hadn't said something entirely different.

'He is yours, *antek*?'

I didn't know what *antek* meant, and Tom was most certainly not mine, but I nodded. Tom tried to get up. The soldier put a boot on his chest and pointed his *gun* at him.

The captain scowled and had a rapid exchange with the soldier. I understood none of it except one word: *nel*. Again Tom began to get up.

I said, 'Don't move. They'll kill you, you stupid oaf! They think you're my servant. Just lie still!' And for a wonder, he actually did.

The captain stared at me, hatred in his blue eyes. They all hated me, of course they did, these soldiers whose high lord I had defeated two and a half years ago. But the captain, like the rest, was too disciplined to disobey Tarek's orders. He spoke curtly to his men. Both savages, the one who had released me from the wagon and the one with his boot on Tom's chest, gave their clenched-fist salute. The captain strode off. The boot was removed. Tom scrambled up.

I said, 'Don't move quickly, don't do anything stupid, don't say *anything*, just follow me!'

He nodded. My guide gestured me forward. I went and Tom followed, although I had no idea to what.

We were led towards a yellow caravan. One of the savages opened the door in the back and pointed. I peered in, desperately trying to make out whatever or whoever was inside. As far as my sun-blinded eyes could see, the caravan was empty of people, and of almost everything else. Knowing I had no real choice, I climbed the one step to the open door.

'Wait!' Tom cried. 'We can't go in there!'

'*Tom*—'

'No, wait, we can't! She can't find us in there!'

'Who?' Both savages frowned, and the gestures of my guide grew stronger. *Get in, get in*. The other five caravans began to move forward. 'Tom, if you don't get in now—'

'I can't! You can't! She won't be able to find us!'

'*Who?*'

Tom glared at me. 'Maggie. She's here.'

33

I stood on the step at the back of the caravan; the caravan moved slowly forward; all else stopped. Time, thought, meaning – all stopped. Maggie. Here.

Both Tom and my savage guide trotted forward, the savage trying to get me into the yellow caravan so he could close the door, Tom trying to – what? Make me understand. I could not understand, not anything.

'Maggie? Here? But how—'

'I told her not to come!' Tom said furiously. 'But have you ever tried to argue with that woman? By damn, make this stupid caravan *stop*!'

But it did not stop; it picked up speed. The horses trotted over the level plain, following the marching army. The savage still did not dare touch me, yet another thing I did not understand. Tom had no such scruples. He grabbed my good arm and yanked me off the caravan steps. We both tumbled into the dust. The savage howled and drew his knife.

'*Nel!*' I screamed. '*Nel, nel!* He's my piss-pot damn *nel*! *Ka!*'

The soldier, his short supply of patience evidently used up, picked me up, trotted after the caravan and shoved me inside. Then he looked around fearfully to see who had observed him. Tom sped after us and jumped in. A second later the door slammed and I heard a key turn in the lock. Instantly Tom threw himself against the door and bawled, 'Let us out! Damn you!'

'Stop,' I said and seized him. 'What about Maggie?

Why is she here? Why are *you* here? How—'

'Let me go, Peter, or you'll wish you had!' Tom glared down at me from his great height, fists clenched and face almost purple with rage. I let him go.

He stood there, panting and glaring and clenching, for several moments longer. Finally he said, 'This is flimsy wood. I can tear this caravan apart! Four to one odds that I can!'

'Yes, but don't. If you can do it now, you can do it later, and I want some answers first. Please, Tom. I need your help!'

That calmed him, as it always had. Tom was born to help, however ineptly. The rage drained from his face. 'Well, I need answers too, but meanwhile we're getting further and further away from Maggie!'

'Where is she?'

'Hidden, don't worry about that. I got a cottager to take her in overnight. Said she was my widowed sister. The savages aren't molesting cottagers, they just want to leave The Queendom. You're right, Peter, I can tear this place apart and go get Maggie just as well in half an hour. Do you have anything to eat? Why aren't you in a dungeon someplace? Or dead?'

I wasn't in a dungeon, I wasn't dead, and – equally surprising – I did have something to eat. This caravan was much smaller than the other five, furnished with only a low table and, against the far wall, a few rugs obviously stolen from the palace and still rolled up. On the table were a basket of fruit, two loaves of bread, a wheel of yellow cheese and a few bottles of wine. Tom collapsed onto the floor, grabbed an apple and began to munch, eyeing the wine.

'Tom,' I said, and heard the desperation in my voice, 'please tell me what happened. Start at the beginning and don't leave anything out.'

230

'Much the best way,' he agreed. The apple disappeared in three bites. He uncorked a bottle of wine, drained it in two gulps, and tore off a hunk of bread. 'Well, after the savages knocked me out and carried you off, your grandmother nursed—'

'My what?'

'Your grandmother,' Tom said patiently. 'Are you all right, Peter? She'd just found you at the top of the cliff above that little beach and you two were talking when the savage soldiers arrived – remember?'

Mother Chilton. She who'd somehow turned herself so old and dithering that the soldiers had dismissed her as not worth bothering with. Later she'd gone back for Tom and told him she was my grandmother.

'I ... I remember now,' I got out.

'Good. For a minute there I thought something was wrong with your brain, that the bastards had tortured you or something. They didn't torture you, did they? Why not? I thought that savage whose face got messed up by Shadow wanted to—'

'Tom,' I said desperately, 'please just tell me your story. I'll tell you mine afterwards.'

'Except,' he said with one of his sudden disconcerting flashes of shrewdness, 'you won't tell me all of it, will you? You never do. All right, your grandmother bandaged my head and gave me some herbs to chew and they healed me very well. That's a useful grandmother to have, Peter. I wonder you ain't never mentioned her sooner. Your cousin George told me—'

'My ... my ...'

'Didn't you tell me to say my story straight through?' Tom said reasonably. 'Then don't interrupt so much. Your grandmother and I stayed in that cabin above the cliffs that night while I got healed. I ain't never slept so well or so long. Not even when Fia ... well. When I woke up,

231

George was there, and between 'em they explained to me—'

'What did George look like?'

Tom stared at me. 'Don't you know what your own cousin looks like?'

'I ... I haven't seen him in a long time.'

'Oh. Well then, I'm sorry to tell you he's aged a great deal. He looks old enough to be your father. Grey hair, green eyes. But still strong as a mountain. In fact, I was wondering if he could take me in a fair fight, and I really wanted to find out, but it ain't good to fight people who are helping you. Anyway, George and your grandmother explained to me that the savages wanted you because they believe you can cross over to the Country of the Dead. Well, they're savages; they'll believe anything, not that a lot of women in Almsbury don't believe the same nonsense! George also explained to me that the rebellion against the savages is real, and you told me it ain't, just to protect me. You shouldn't of done that, Peter. I can take care of myself.'

He scowled at me and then devoured an entire loaf of bread. I was speechless.

'George told me the best thing I could do right now was go find your wife and ... Why didn't you never tell me that you are married, Peter? I wouldn't have devilled you about Fia – not that the lying bitch turned out to be worth it after all, and when I think how sodden I was about her for a while ... This is damn good bread. Want some of the other loaf?'

'No.'

'All right. George wanted me to go to where you left your wife at Haryllbury and stay to take care of her, but what kind of task is that for a man when there's a rebellion going on? Still, I thought I might just go there first, and then I could take you word of her. But when I told her

232

about you, she threw a pot at my head, and then she cried, and then she swore she was coming with me. And even though I tried to sneak out in the middle of the night, she heard me and she came. Her and your little brother. Women!'

My 'little brother'. Jee. I could picture it all: Maggie's fury, Tom's high-minded consternation, Jee's stubborn determination to go wherever Maggie went. My head whirled.

'Although I will say this for that boy – he's useful. He laid snares and caught nearly as much game as ol' Shep ever did – what happened to Shep?'

'He ran off.'

'Oh. Too bad. Good ol' Shep. So do you think we should bust out of here now?'

I pulled my wits around me. It was not an easy task; Tom had effectively tattered them. I said, 'No. No, Tom, listen to me. George didn't tell you everything because he didn't know everything. I'm not going to bust out of here. George was right about why the Young Chieftain wants me – he believes I can cross over to the Country of the Dead. He wants me to teach him how. Eventually he'll send for me. I think I'm the only one who can get that close to him, do you see?'

'Yes!' Tom glanced around the caravan, bounded to my side and whispered in my ear, 'You'll get close to him and then you'll be able to kill him! Good plan! Only they'll disarm you, won't they? And ...' He trailed off, pulled away and gazed meaningfully at the stump of my wrist.

I leaned close to his ear and breathed, 'My grandmother's herbs.'

'Ahhh.' He nodded and smiled.

Poison made sense to him, at least if it came from a woman. Women used herbs and women believed in superstitions and women were to bed, not marry. Men

233

used knives and men joined rebellions and this was a great adventure, thrilling and important. We were going to kill the Young Chieftain, Tom and I. His impulsive brain did not think what would happen next if we actually succeeded in such an impossible plan. Tom did not look as far ahead as the punishment, or the consequences for The Queendom, or the subsequent fate of little Princess Stephanie. He lived moment to moment, inventing reality as he went along.

Yet, was I so very different? I did not know either what would happen on this journey to the Young Chieftain's homeland. All I had were the orders of my father – who may or may not have been the man posing as my 'cousin George' – to go along with the idea that I could teach witchcraft to the Young Chieftain. My orders were—

'The only thing is,' Tom said, his face clouding, 'what about Maggie?'

—to stay alive until I could be rescued, and—

'On second thoughts, she really can't come with us,' Tom said.

—to do 'whatever you can *except* bring anyone or anything back from the Country of the Dead'.

Tom said, 'It will be much too dangerous for a woman, don't you think?'

How was I to teach the Young Chieftain what was unteachable?

'Much too dangerous,' Tom repeated. 'Maggie will have to stay behind. I didn't even want her to come with me this far. After all, a pregnant woman really should be more careful.'

34

'Peter? *Peter!*'

Tom, looming over me.

'Peter, by damn, when was the last time these piss pots fed you? You fainted!'

I had not fainted; I had been conscious every single second of my legs giving way, of the caravan walls swooping around me, of what Tom had just said. Of that afternoon on the sunlit hill, with Jee and Shadow gone into the village spread below us, to buy bread and cheese. Of the heavy drone of bees and the fragrant grasses rustling in a sweet breeze. Of Maggie crying, 'Then if you're really going, you cannot deny me this. You can't, oh you *can't* ...' Of her body so warm and soft next to mine ... *Pregnant.*

'Here,' Tom said, 'eat this!' He thrust an apple at me. 'All this food sitting right here and you fainting with hunger. Sometimes, Peter, I think you don't have the sense of a rabbit.'

'No,' I said, 'I don't.'

Pregnant. I had never thought. But perhaps Mother Chilton had: 'Go back to where you left that poor girl who so unaccountably loves you.' Had she known that Maggie carried my child?

Fresh guilt washed through me. I had not only abandoned Maggie at Haryllbury, I had abandoned her pregnant. She seemed to have managed – Maggie could always manage – but that did not excuse me. What had Mother Chilton said to me? 'You are not a speck of dust

235

floating in empty air. What you do has consequences . . .'

Tom said, 'Well, don't just hold that apple, Peter, eat it! I'll open another bottle of wine.'

My child. The child of a *hisaf*, carried by a woman of The Queendom. As I myself had been seventeen years ago. As my sister had been, when my mother died in childbirth.

'Tom,' I said swiftly, 'you can't come with me. You have to go back and take care of Maggie.'

'Me?'

'Yes. There's no one else, don't you see? I'm a prisoner here. And I—'

'I ain't going back to take care of Maggie. What do you think I am, Peter, a midwife? You said this is —' he leaned close to my ear again '—a rebellion, and we're going to poison you-know-who, and you want me to desert to take care of a *woman*?' He pulled away and scowled ferociously. 'No.'

'But she has no one to—'

'She has the cottagers I left her with. She can work there, or in the palace, or someplace – she's a worker, that one! Two to one she finds a really good place. Besides, if I was with her, more than likely she'd throw more pots at my head. You married a furious girl, Peter. I don't envy you, I'll tell you that.'

Maggie had good reason to be furious. But it was clear that Tom was not going to be budged. He stretched, yawned hugely, looked around the caravan. 'Comfortable, ain't it? I don't think I've had any sleep for two days. Well, maybe one hour. I'll just pull out one of those rugs and . . . You should sleep too, Peter; you'll need your strength.' He looked doubtfully at my gaunt body. 'Well, maybe not strength, but all your wits for . . . *you know.*'

'Tom—'

But he was already asleep, with the instant transition

of the blameless. His bulk took up half the floor of the small caravan.

I stepped over him and pushed aside the yellow curtain. Behind it, the window was barred. It looked towards the city, but the stone walls of the island were all but hidden by the great clouds of dust raised by wagons, animals and soldiers. Now everything was on the move.

Including Maggie? Was she somewhere behind the rearguard of the army, following on foot? I would not put it past her. In the last two and a half years she had followed me from the palace to the Unclaimed Lands, from Soulvine Moor to Applebridge, from Applebridge to the hillside above Haryllbury, from Haryllbury to this caravan. On the other hand, now she had the child to think of. My child.

If it was a boy, he might well be a *hisaf*.

All at once I hoped passionately that Maggie would not risk coming after me. When my father succeeded in rescuing me ... Although how was he going to do that, locked in the palace dungeon? He might in fact already have been executed, along with Lord Robert Hopewell and his two hapless cell mates. My father might already be a permanent dweller in the Country of the Dead. But I did not believe that. He had got himself put in the dungeon specifically to confront me, and he would have a plan to get himself out again. And he *must* rescue me before the Young Chieftain realized I could not teach him witchcraft. Otherwise I too would be sent to the Country of the Dead, and my son would grow up as fatherless as I had. But at least my child would have Maggie, who would take better care of him than poor Aunt Jo had taken of me.

Maggie, don't follow me again. I am not worth it.

At my feet, Tom snored on his thick rug. I unrolled another, thick soft wool with a design of stylized flowers, and stretched out beside him. I felt weary in every muscle and did not expect to sleep. I was wrong. Within two minutes I slept, and within three minutes the dream came. But this time different.

Not at first. It began as it always did, with a *flat upland moor, with a round stone house. There is the taste of roasted meat in my mouth, succulent and greasy. In the shadows beyond my torch I sense things unseen. Inhuman things, things I have never met in this land or in that other beyond the grave. Moving among them is a woman's figure, and the voice coming to me from the dark is a woman's voice, and I can see the glint of a jewelled crown: 'Roger.* Hisaf.'

'But you're dead.'

'*Eleven years dead,' she says, and gives a laugh that shivers my bones.*

Always before, the dream ended there. *But now my sister emerges from the fog and I see her for the first time. She is not a woman but a girl, although tall and well grown. She wears a simple lavender gown like my mother's, but without blood on the skirt. Her eyes too are my mother's, dark brown, although my sister's eyes are open, as my mother's will never be again. Those eyes look wild; they look mad. And she speaks to me directly, as if I inhabit the dream beside her.*

'*You will not succeed, Roger. Nor will they. I am queen of this realm, and what queen willingly gives up her throne? Eleanor did not, Caroline did not, Stephanie does not. But now all three are mine. As you will be too.' Again that bone-shattering laugh.*

I woke, screaming. Tom, amazingly, snored on, and if everyone at the palace had slept so soundly three years ago so that no one overheard my sleep-talking, I would not be here now. Here, in a caravan moving forward to an unknown country, awaiting a rescue I did not believe in, threatened by a phantom in a realm that my father said I may cross into and Mother Chilton said I may not.

And I had not gone there. My sister had come to me.

She had used sleep, that little death, to cross over into my mind, as she could not do in body. She had spoken to me directly. *'All three are mine.'*

Queen Eleanor, Queen Caroline – both dead. I had seen both of them there, in the Country of the Dead, both quiescent and unknowing. But the little princess was alive, being carried off by her bridegroom in one of the caravans accompanying mine. Stephanie was not dead. So in what sense did she belong to my mad half-sister?

'As you will be too.'

It was a long time before I could sleep again. When I did, slumber must have lasted the whole night through.

Pale light filtered through a crack in the yellow curtains, and when I pushed them aside the sun was just rising. We had halted. Cook fires burned beside the caravans, with folk of The Queendom bent busily over them. Were they captives, slaves, deserters, traitors who had switched allegiance to the savages? I had no idea.

Tom stirred, woke. 'By damn, I'm hungry! But first where's the piss pot?'

I had found it last night, behind one of the rolled-up rugs. Before it could be used, the caravan door opened. A young savage stood there. He said something unintelligible and motioned for me to go outside.

'Let me go first,' Tom said, 'in case you need defending.'

I ignored him, climbing down the one step. Tom cursed and followed me. We were led to an efficiently dug piss pit and then to one of the cook fires, where a silent boy ladled thick gruel into two bowls and handed us tankards of ale from a great cask on one of the wagons. The savage guard watched our every move, his *gun* in his hands. He especially watched Tom, who was more interested in the young cook.

'Were you stolen from the palace, boy?'

The boy looked at him. He was perhaps fourteen, the same age as I when I killed Hartah. This boy looked capable of murder. He had small narrow eyes, shiny with contempt, and a sneer on his wide mouth. Clearly he considered Tom's question stupid. This boy was one who would always side with the victor, no matter who that might be. There would be others like him. He turned from Tom without answering and began to scour the gruel pot with sand.

We were the last to eat. The caravan was packing up for the day's travel. Far ahead, clouds of dust said that the main army was already on the move. Behind the rearguard, the sun rose red and gold. Our guard motioned me back to the caravan.

'Hey, you,' Tom said to him. 'We can't just stay in there all day. My ... my master needs exercise. You know, exercise? Look!' He pantomimed running in place, jumping high, flailing his arms. The savage, alarmed, pointed his *gun*.

I grabbed Tom's arm. 'Stop that. He thinks you're attacking.'

'Then he's a moron,' Tom said hotly. 'If I wanted to attack, I would. Listen, Peter, I really can't stay still all day in that travelling box. A man needs to move.'

I didn't need to move. It seemed that for months I had been moving, or being moved. Everything in me was weary: muscles, mind, heart. Where was Maggie? Was she safe?

I said, 'I'll ask about it later. For now, Tom, just do what they say. That's what George would advise, you know. Go along with the enemy until the best moment.'

Tom nodded soberly. 'I daresay you're right. Well, at least we got fed.' Resignedly he walked back to the caravan, forgetting that he was my servant and was supposed to follow me. The savage looked puzzled but guided us back inside.

Someone had done minor housekeeping. The empty wine bottles and cheese rind were gone, replaced with fresh food on the low table. The piss pot had been rinsed. One of the rugs had been rolled up again at the far end of the caravan.

The savage soldier locked us in, and a few moments later the caravan jolted forward. Tom pushed aside the curtain to look out the barred window. 'I wonder which caravan has the princess. By damn, to think that Tom Jenkins might see a princess! I daresay George has seen scores of them. Oh, that must be her caravan, the purple one. "Purple for the princess," my father used to say, damn his black soul. Did your grandmother tell you that the savage chieftain actually married that little girl? They're barbarians, for certain. Do you think there are any girls with the caravans? Not that I'd bed a traitor to The Queendom like that foul cook, but if there's a girl captive . . . Of course it ain't likely the— *What's that?'*

Tom leaped towards the back of the caravan, his expression ferocious. One huge fist clenched as the other hand clawed at a rolled-up rug. He threw the rug open and dragged out a small form wriggling and flailing his legs.

It was Jee.

35

I said immediately, 'Is Maggie with you?'

'No.' Jee gave the question the scorn he evidently thought it deserved. 'Maggie maun stay.' Further questioning elicited that he had slipped into camp during the night; Jee could move as unseen and quiet as a small animal. He had slept under the caravan, crept inside while Tom and I were at our brief breakfast and hidden himself in the rug. Now he eyed the food on the low table.

'Eat,' I said, and he fell on the bread and cheese.

Tom said, 'Are we taking him with us? Maybe he should go back the next time the door is unlocked.'

'No,' Jee said around a mouthful of bread. 'Maggie said I maun stay.'

'That woman orders everybody around,' Tom said, then glanced at me. 'Sorry, Peter. I'm sure your wife is ... is really a wonderful person.'

He was sure of no such thing, and Maggie was not my wife, and I had no idea what to do with the dirty boy gobbling enough food for three children. How was I going to explain him to the savages? Another 'servant'? But one thing was clear.

'Tom, you can't tell anyone that Jee is my brother. It could put him in real danger. Promise me!'

'All right,' Tom said. His face lit up. 'I know. I'll say he's my servant! Like I'm yours.'

Jee scowled ferociously. 'Not your servant.'

'Yes, you are, Jee,' I said. 'It's for your own protection.

What was in Maggie's thoughts that she sent you into such danger?'

'I maun give you this.' Jee undid the string that held his breeches around his waist. Under the full material, strapped to his skinny thighs, were two crude leather packages. When Jee unwrapped them, Tom's face lit up.

'Knives! All right, I take my words back, Peter. Your wife is a treasure. Give those to me, boy; I can wield them much better than your big brother.'

'Thank you, Jee,' I said. 'But now that you've delivered the knives, I think you should leave the next time you can and go back to Maggie.'

'She said I maun stay.'

Tom said, 'Listen to your brother!'

But of course Jee did not, no more than Tom ever listened to me. Jee obeyed Maggie, Tom obeyed my non-existent cousin George, and I was a straw on the wind, blown about by a savage army, a *hisaf* father and Mother Chilton.

We spent the morning cooped up in the moving caravan, slowly fraying each other's nerves. Jee played plaintive tunes on his willow whistle: *tweet tweet tweety-tweet*. Tom paced the small space, restless as a caged fox, or peered out the barred window, keeping up a constant commentary.

'That really must be the princess's caravan, no one else would have purple. Ho, there's a woman coming out of the caravan. Old and ugly, though. She must be a servant. Still, she hopped off the step pretty lively . . . Do you think any young women from The Queendom were brought along to attend Princess Stephanie? Must be, yes? Do you think the Young Chieftain rides in one of the other caravans? Probably not. He's a soldier, curse his damn bones . . . There's a fellow jumping off one of the supply wagons. I wish they'd bring us more wine or better yet some ale. Pepper my arse! There's a savage girl! At least I think she was. She went by so fast, but she wore a fur cloak like— No, it's only one of their boy singers. Red dye on his face and why do they braid those stupid twigs into their hair like that? It don't look— There goes the green caravan pulling ahead of the red one ... No, the red one is a length ahead now ...'

Tweet tweet tweety-tweet.

Hours of this. Then more hours, until the sun stood directly overhead (or so said Tom) and the door opened.

Our savage guard stood on the step of the moving caravan, his knife drawn. As his eyes adjusted to the dimness within, his gaze fell on Jee, who had had no time to roll himself again into a rug. The guard's eyes widened and his face creased into an expression I had never yet seen on any savage's face: fear.

Of a small scrawny boy?

The man's face had gone white as swansdown. Hastily he thrust a basket of foodstuffs into the caravan. Before he could slam and lock the door, I jammed the basket into the opening. 'Wait! Please!'

He stared past me at Jee.

I struggled to summon the words of the guttural savage language; the word for 'exercise' eluded me. 'Out – go out ... Yes, we go out to walk! We must walk!'

Slowly the savage swivelled his head to look at me, and both colour and scowl returned to his face. He pointed to me. *'Ven.'* To Tom: *'Nel, ven.'* Jee he ignored. Then he jumped down the step and gestured for me and Tom to follow.

Apparently all I had had to do was ask.

More bewildered than ever, I descended the step, followed by an eager Tom. We walked behind the caravan, its door widely ajar, and the guard walked behind us. Inside, Jee investigated the foodstuffs in the basket.

'Well, this is much better,' Tom said. 'Getting stuffy in there. Jee needs to sleep anyway – little toad must have been up all night. Where'd you learn to talk their speech, Peter?'

At court, as Queen Caroline's fool. But Tom knew nothing of that part of my life, so I didn't answer, instead pretending to choke on the dust raised by the caravan.

'I'll get you some ale!' Tom said, bounding back into the caravan. He bounced out with two uncorked bottles of wine. 'No ale, worse luck, but this'll do – here.'

We swigged the wine while trotting behind the caravan. Soon I had had enough exercise, and I climbed back inside. Jee was asleep in one corner. Tom and the guard, equally tireless, jogged along for hours. I sat inside alone with my thoughts, which were all and only questions, questions, questions.

The next three days passed exactly like the first. Tom and I slept; we walked behind the caravan under close guard; we were fed. Always I felt the hatred of the savage army rise around us, real as the shimmering clouds of dust. Jee stayed inside at first, until he discovered that no one would stop him from leaving the caravan, nor from re-entering it. None of the soldiers would even look directly at Jee. They seemed to pretend that he did not exist, which neither Tom nor I understood. 'Dirty little beggar can go anywhere,' Tom grumbled. 'You'd think he was a gnat. Or a bat. Or a rat.' He laughed, delighted with his own rhyming wit.

On the fourth day, villagers attacked the caravan.

We had halted the night before on the north bank of a river, undoubtedly a tributary of the River Thymar. All day the land had been rising as The Queendom's vast central plain gradually gave way to foothills that, in their turn, would become the steep Western Mountains. The

245

wide road grew narrower, less travelled, rockier. Nights became sharply colder; it was already the month of Styln. At night Tom, always restless when caged, pushed aside the curtain, and a huge autumn moon shone yellow through the barred window. Our guard, averting his eyes from Jee, brought us two thick furry cloaks, warmer than any we'd had.

But afternoons were still warm. Tom and I walked behind the caravan, which had slowed as the horses negotiated a steep rocky stretch of road. Jee slept inside. Across fields golden with hay lay a village, smoke rising from the cottage chimneys. Thick stands of trees, oak and birch and laurel cast long shadows across the road. Tom broke into little running circles that made the guard frown and raise his *gun*.

'I ain't going any place, you furry bastard,' Tom said. 'By damn, that piss pot is jittery today, Peter. I wish I could just run and run and run, but then he— What was *that*?'

A shout, a scream. Men erupted from the woods.

'It's the rebellion!' Tom cried.

It's the rescue, I thought. *My father*—

It was neither. The men rushed forward, farmers armed with pitchforks and clubs and ancient family swords. 'Our princess!' an old man screamed. 'Give us our princess!'

'No!' I called. 'Don't! They'll shoot!'

'*Haflug! Halflug!*' the guard said, pushing me towards the caravan. 'Get in!'

'Don't come any closer,' I cried to the farmers. The old man's gaze swivelled towards me. My eyes met his, fierce with anger, before a savage soldier fired and a *bullet* struck him in the chest.

The guard picked me up and threw me into the caravan. Tom swung a fist at him and missed. Before Tom could draw either of his knives I screamed, 'Tom, if you let him kill you I'll never ever forgive you and neither will

246

George!' There is apparently no limit to the stupidities that people in panic will say.

Or listen to. Tom paused, looked at the savage's *gun*, looked at me and jumped into the caravan. The guard slammed and locked the door. Tom bounded to the window. It was a measure of what he saw that he said nothing, just watched, his face contorting in hatred and grief.

It was all over in less than five minutes.

Into the silence I said softly, 'How many dead?'

'I can't tell.'

But I already knew. The death toll would be all of them – all the brave, stupid, loyal men pathetically trying to rescue their six-year-old sovereign.

Tom burst out, 'Why them? Why not a real attack? Where's Lord what's-his-name, who's supposed to be ruling until the princess grows up? Where's the army The Queendom used to have?'

Lord Robert Hopewell might still be in the dungeon, or possibly dead. The army too was dead, and by my doing. Rumours must have reached even remote Almsbury about what had happened two and a half years ago. Had Tom disbelieved the rumours, or just ignored them in his preoccupation with girls and ale and fighting his pinchpenny father? I couldn't ask. He did not know who I was.

Jee, who did, stared at me from his corner.

That was the end of walking behind the caravan for Tom and me. We were now let out only at breakfast and dinner. Tom muttered and paced and cursed, filling the small space with his huge discontent until I could barely stand to look at him. Jee slept fourteen hours a day, like a small animal preparing for winter hibernation. This went on for another fortnight, with each day the caravan horses labouring more as we ascended into the mountains, until finally the road became no more than a narrow track and the caravans could go no further.

'I think we've left The Queendom,' I said to Tom.

'So what will happen now?'

'I don't know. But I think we will have to walk over the mountains.'

'Walk!' His eyes lit up as though he had just been promised a treasure chest. He pounded on the caravan door. Immediately it opened, but not for him.

'*Klef, antek,*' said the guard, who hardly ever spoke to me, not even to address me by the mysterious title of *antek*. Until now. '*Ka mit. Bay Tarek.*'

'He wants me to go with him,' I said to Tom, 'but without you.'

'I go too. I'm your what-d'ye-call-it, your *nel*. Your servant.'

'*Ka mit! Ka mit!*' the guard said, raising his gun.

'Don't irritate him,' I snapped at Tom. 'You'll only get yourself killed.'

Jee said, 'Don't ye go, Peter.'

'Listen to the boy,' Tom said.

'Both of you be quiet and stay still.' I descended the single step.

Tom called, 'But where is he taking you?'

'I don't know.'

I was lying. *Bay Tarek*, the guard had said. To Tarek. The Young Chieftain.

36

The caravan had halted in a wide upland meadow thick with tough-stemmed mountain wildflowers. Jagged peaks covered with snow rose to the north and south, but I could see a break directly in front of us to the west, a high pass through the mountains. Beyond the pass, the setting sun shone red like a bloody beacon. The air was sharp and cold.

All over the meadow cook fires and torches burned. The six caravans huddled at one end with the exhausted horses. They had been pulling uphill for weeks now. Servants scuttled between the painted wagons. The rest of the meadow was filled with the savage army. Each cadre of twelve savages sat with its captain around its own fire, eating, singing and talking. Even to an outsider the voices sounded jubilant. These were soldiers going home. My guard and I wended our way among the fires, and for once no one paid us the slightest attention.

At the far end of the meadow, just before a steep descent into a small valley, were pitched four or five tents of animal hide. By the closed flap of the largest of these tents two guards stood at attention. Unlike the common soldiers we had just passed, these men eyed me with hostility, with fear, with awe. What did they think they knew about me? What did the Young Chieftain think he knew?

My chest tightened, squeezing my lungs. It was hard to breathe.

One of the soldiers broke attention to step forward and

search me roughly. He showed none of my own guard's reluctance to touch me, and I was glad I had not brought one of Jee's stolen knives. The savage found my small shaving knife, shrugged contemptuously and let me keep it. He barked something I didn't catch. *'Klef klen,'* my guard said to me. The language used the same word for 'come' and 'go'. 'Go now.' Hesitantly I approached the tent. When no one stopped me, I raised the flap and went in.

Coals glowed in a small fire pit in the centre of the tent. The back flap was open, giving a magnificent view of the sunset over the valley beyond. Thick furs made a pallet in one corner. Two men stood beside the fire pit. One was the Young Chieftain, his dark hair loose upon his shoulders, his powerful body in its sleeveless fur tunic giving off a strong smell of sweat and travel. At his marriage in the palace he had worn a many-coloured feather cape and gold-and-jewelled armbands, now both absent. The older man wore clothes like those of The Queendom, sturdy woven tunic and breeches, but his boots were metal-toed like the savages'. In the dimness I could see neither man's face.

Should I kneel? I would not – *could* not. Not to this man, who had seized my queendom and Queen Caroline's daughter, whose father's death I had caused.

Tarek son of Solek son of Taryn did not seem to expect kneeling. He turned his head slightly to inspect me, and his blue eyes caught the firelight. Only savages had eyes that blue, like the sea under bright sun. But his gaze held no savagery. No anger, no vengeance, not even the cold brutality of the men of Soulvine Moor. Tarek watched me with cool, intelligent curiosity. He looked at me as Queen Caroline had once done, as one might look at a hammer or an awl or a fire flint: a useful tool that might aid in accomplishing one's own ends.

The older man said in a strong, strange accent, 'I am Perb. A translator. The Young Chieftain welcomes you, *antek.*'

I said nothing, afraid that whatever I said would be wrong. In the silence a log in the fire pit popped. I jumped at the sudden sound. The Young Chieftain smiled coldly, never taking his eyes off me, and said something too quickly for me to catch more than a few words.

'He says to not be afraid, *antek,*' Perb said. 'Tarek means you no harm.'

Why not? I had killed his father, brought back from the Country of the Dead enough soldiers to defeat the savages' first army, maimed one of his singer-soldiers and had – as far as he knew – commanded dogs to tear out the throats of three more. How could Tarek *not* mean me harm? I realized that until now I had not fully believed my father's words: 'The savages do not torture. They consider it beneath them.' And that other, more devastating statement: 'He wants the "magic illusions" that he believes you created in order to defeat his father. He believes you are a witch, and that you can teach him to become one too.'

Underneath Tarek's control of himself must lie resentment of me, even rage. I must be careful not to wake it.

Perb said, 'You should be asking questions now, *antek.*'

I should be asking questions? I blurted, 'What's an *antek*?'

'A term of respect for the third of the three human states.'

'What are those?'

Tarek spoke sharply, and this time I caught his words: *What does the antek say?*

Perb translated. Perb's accent was actually harder for me to follow than Tarek's, provided the Young Chieftain did not speak too quickly. I had heard Tarek's accent from

251

his father, when I was Roger the queen's fool. Perb was neither savage nor Queendom. And so our three-way conversation lurched forward, with neither man knowing I could follow some of what Tarek said before Perb translated it. But the more I heard, the more confused I became.

'The three states of being human are, first, soldier; second, mother; third, *antek*. And all are the same state.'

Which explained nothing, including what made an *antek*, or why I was one. Nor why I was supposed to ask the questions here. I said, 'What is everyone else? All the people who are not soldiers or mothers or *anteks*?'

'They are slaves,' Perb said. Tarek spoke and Perb added, 'And they deserve to be slaves.'

'Why?'

'Because they have not attained the three human states.'

This was not helping. I tried a different approach. 'Who in The Queendom is an *antek*?'

'Only you. Else The Queendom would have *guns*.'

That made no sense. I did not have a *gun*. I said, 'Then is . . . is everyone in The Queendom a slave?'

'Of course. And you deserve to be slaves, because you let that happen.'

'But we have soldiers. And we have mothers—'

'You have no mothers of savage soldiers. Your Queendom is conquered. Defeated soldiers are slaves.'

My temper rose. 'Two years ago the Blue army defeated yours. Did that make Lord Solek a slave?'

For the first time Perb showed emotion. He looked appalled. 'I cannot translate that!'

Tarek said something to him and Perb replied. Listening intently, I followed most of what Perb said. It was not what I had said. Perb explained that I did not want my mother to be considered a slave.

My mother. All at once she was sharp in my mind's eye, and now there were two of her: the woman in the lavender dress cuddling me on her lap, and the tranced, quiescent body in the Country of the Dead with blood on her gown. Both images were hard-edged enough to cut glass, unnaturally clear, and both sliced into my brain.

Perb said, 'Are you ill, *antek*?'

'N-no.'

'Tarek agrees that your mother is not a slave. And you have asked your six questions. Now you will answer.'

Six questions. Six caravans travelling beside the army., cadres of twelve soldiers each. Evidently six was an important number to the savages. And I still did not know what an *antek* was.

Tarek said, 'Ask him where Witchland lies.' Perb translated.

What would they believe? My father had said to go along with the Young Chieftain's belief that I could teach him witchcraft until such time as my father's *hisafs* would rescue me. No rescue had come yet. My life, as well as Tom's and Jee's, depended on convincing Tarek that I could do the impossible.

I said, 'Witchland lies beyond the moon, below the sun.' And I held my breath.

Tarek nodded as if this actually made sense, but his blue eyes were speculative. I would not get away with too many such fanciful answers.

'He asks how long you studied to learn your art.'

'Since I was a small child.'

'How long did you study to bring soldiers back from Witchland?'

So my father had been correct about what Tarek wanted. Lord Robert Hopewell had wanted the same thing from me. Tarek had his father's direct, simple practicality. He would accept even his father's murderer if that would give him a second army to conquer the world, and he would believe that his father would approve.

'*Antek*, I asked how long you required to learn—'

'A long time. Years.'

Perb translated, and disappointment crossed the Young Chieftain's face. It was gone in an instant.

Perb said, 'How long to teach him this art? Since he is not a small child.'

I could not say years. That would not be an acceptable answer. I didn't know what answer might serve me best. I waffled. 'It depends.'

'Depends upon what?'

'On how much undiscovered talent his lordship was born with.' Mother Chilton's voice flickered at the edge of my mind: '*Caroline studied the soul arts but she has no talent.*'

Perb translated. Tarek said something I did not catch, but before Perb could translate I said, 'My turn now. That was six questions I have answered.'

Perb looked surprised. 'No, it was five.'

'You asked if I am ill. That was a question.'

Perb scowled. Tarek demanded to know what I had said. Perb translated, and the Young Chieftain gave a sudden bark of laughter. His eyes shone with appreciation. Mine blinked with relief, but mixed with the relief was resentment.

Another ruler who valued my wit but who would kill me if I did not deliver more than wit. Like Queen Caroline. Was it always thus with those in power?

Perb said sourly, 'Ask your six questions then.'

What answers would serve me best? I needed to understand Tarek's mind if I were to survive it. I said, 'If the Young Chieftain wishes me to teach him, why did he have his lieutenant – the soldier who was once one of his singers – torture me in the village of Almsbury?' Even as

Perb translated, it seems I could again feel the knotted cord around my temples, tightening until I screamed . . .

Perb said, 'That one has been dealt with.'

'How—'

'He exceeded orders. You will not see him again.'

I nodded. Perb's expression conveyed much more than those nine words. It was a warning of what would happen to me if I too disobeyed orders. I said, 'Can I keep my two servants with me once we reach Tarek's queendom?'

Perb scowled. 'It is a kingdom, not a queendom. By marrying your princess, Tarek has rescued your land from unnatural barbarity.'

'Unnatural barbarity! Is it natural to marry a six-year-old?'

Perb said, without first translating for Tarek, 'The princess will not be harmed. We are not savages, *antek*.'

'*You* are not anything – neither a man of The Queendom nor of the savages. You're like a mule, neither horse nor donkey.'

'I am paid well,' Perb said coolly, 'which is more than you will be. You have already taken a dangerous liberty in bringing that boy from Witchland. I advise you to not take any more liberties.'

Jee. The savages thought Jee, who had slipped unnoticed through their guard to sneak into my caravan, was a product of my witchcraft. No wonder my soldier-keeper was so frightened of him, while the other soldiers tried so hard to pretend he did not exist. I stored away this nugget of fear ('A witch child!') and arrogance. ('There is no other way the child could have penetrated our lines.') It might eventually prove useful.

Tarek, his blue eyes darkening, demanded to know what we had said. Perb said that I had asked after the welfare of his new queen – neither a lie nor the truth – and also about the fate of my servants.

255

'The fate of his servants depends upon his own teaching,' Tarek said.

Tom and Jee's lives depended on a task I could not perform. Both were hostages to my hopeless masque.

Perb said, 'Ask your last three questions.'

But I was suddenly weary of the whole pointless ritual. I could not do this. My father would not rescue me in time. Tom and Jee and I would die, and the best I could hope for was that at least my father had been right about the savages' considering torture beneath their strange code of honour. But both Tarek and Perb stared at me, waiting, and I must ask something.

'When will the instruction begin?'

'Tomorrow.'

'When will we reach the ... the kingdom?'

'Two more twelve-days of travel.'

'What is the most important value to his lordship?'

'We do not use those titles. You will address him as Tarek son of Solek son of Taryn, if you must address him at all. And the most important value is discipline.'

Perb translated all this. Tarek listened, then looked directly at me. In my own language he said, 'You go now.'

So he understood some of my words, just as I understood some of his. Had he grasped my insults to his people? If so, the understanding had not shown on his face.

Discipline.

Perb led me to the door, where my guard waited to conduct me to my last night of imprisonment in the bright yellow caravan.

37

Night had fallen during my interview with the Young Chieftain. The savages had finished dinner. Some had rolled into their cloaks and already fallen asleep, while others still sat around the fires of their cadres, talking. Somewhere flames snapped on dry wood and all at once the soldiers reminded me horribly of the circles of the Dead, grouped around the humming fog of Soulvine watchers.

We threaded our way through the cadres – so many soldiers! – until we reached the caravans. Here was more bustle. Men, both savage and from The Queendom, unloaded half-empty chests from wagons and sorted the contents into bundles which, I guessed, could be carried on foot. I had wondered how the little princess could walk so far on such rough terrain, and now I saw two objects being unloaded. Each consisted of two long poles with a platform mounted between. On each platform was a large chair surrounded by a curtained frame; at the moment the curtains were drawn aside. Four huge men, savages but not dressed as soldiers, picked up the ends of the pole, hefted them experimentally onto their shoulders and nodded. I had never seen such a conveyance before, but I was reassured that the princess would be carried over the mountains.

Then I saw her.

Beside the purple caravan Princess Stephanie – no, Queen Stephanie now, although I could not think of someone so small as a queen – sat hunched on a low stool beside a bright fire. She was crying. Two women crouched beside her. I could see the firelit face of the nurse who had rushed at the Young Chieftain's throne during the marriage ceremony. The nurse patted Stephanie reassuringly, then took her into her arms. The other woman, whose back was to me, shook her head. The two seemed to be arguing. The other must have won, because the nurse, frowning, replaced the princess on her stool and the little girl straightened her back and tilted her face up at the second woman, who turned enough for me to recognize her.

Heedless of my guard, I rushed forward pell-mell, hurtling into the circle of firelight. Six men pulled knives. My guard shouted something and the men retreated, but not very far. I cried, 'Lady Margaret!'

She blinked, then smiled. 'Roger. I thought you dead.'

'So did I.' I was absurdly glad to see her, this older woman who thought of me, all at the same time, as a saviour, a murderer, a deceiver, a witch and still and always Queen Caroline's fool. I was glad that such a practical, principled woman was the little princess's guardian.

The child looked up at me curiously; her nurse frowned.

Stephanie said, 'Who are you?' Her voice was thin, high and fearful. She wore not the purple she was entitled to, but a grey gown of sturdy weave, well made but without ornamentation. Lady Margaret and the nurse wore the same.

I knelt. 'I am Roger Kilbourne, Your Grace. I . . . I served your mother.'

'Oh.' She looked away, without expression. I could not tell if she remembered her mother, now two and a half years dead. Certainly she did not resemble that fiery and sensual queen, neither in temperament nor beauty.

The nurse said, 'Your Grace, it's time you were in bed.'

To me Stephanie said, 'This is my last night in the caravan. Tomorrow I shall have to walk, and it will be very tiring.'

'No, Your Grace,' I said, 'you will not have to walk. I have seen your ... your conveyance. It is a chair with little curtains all around it, and you will be carried in it very high and secret, and you can pretend you are an invisible bird.'

'Really?' For the first time she smiled. Her eyes, red-rimmed from crying, lit up, and I saw that she had her own charm. Not her mother's passion nor her grand-mother's dignity, but a gentle and childish sweetness.

'Nana, Lady Margaret, did you hear that? Roger says I shall not have to walk! And I can be an invisible bird!'

'A good notion,' Lady Margaret said. 'And now to bed, Your Grace.'

Stephanie obeyed, rising from her stool. Graciously she raised her little hand to me. 'You may rise, Roger. I like you.'

'I am Your Grace's servant.'

'But I don't like *them*,' Stephanie said, pointing to the poisonously green caravan. 'They're bad.'

Three girls climbed down from the green caravan. Although they wore more clothes, I recognized the three half-naked savage girls who had 'attended' the princess at her marriage. Now they laughed and chattered to each other, but I was too far away to catch the words. The savages' customs were strange, and I did not know what these girls were, although I knew what Tom Jenkins would have considered them to be. But surely not even

259

savages would have whores attend a queen-to-be at her wedding? They must be something else, but I had no idea what.

The nurse said, 'Come along now, lambie.'

'Goodnight, Lady Margaret. Goodnight, Roger,' the child said. She was led away by the nurse. My guard, who still never touched me, motioned for the sixth or seventh time for me to follow him. I ignored the gesture and said quietly to Lady Margaret, 'The princess is well?'

'She has nightmares. Sometimes they seem like more than just dreams.'

My blood froze.

'What is it, Roger? Do you know something about these nightmares? Are you *causing* them?'

'No.' But I guessed who was. Was that possible? *'Caroline studied the soul arts but had no talent,'* Mother Chilton had once told me, *'but her grandmother did.'* Did that mean that Stephanie had possibly inherited . . .

No. I was being fanciful. No one's dreams but mine, a *hisaf*, were invaded by anyone from that other realm. *'Eleven years dead–'*

I watched Stephanie mount the step to her caravan, followed by the nurse. In the doorway she turned and waved at me and at Lady Margaret, perhaps a last attempt to delay bedtime. Children used as weapons in war: the princess, my mad sister, the giggling half-budded girls by the other caravan. At least my own unborn child, who was never far from my thoughts, was not being so used. He or she was safe with Maggie in The Queendom.

'Klef! Klef!' my guard insisted; finally he was worked up enough to lay a hand on my arm and pull me forward. The hand felt like iron closing on my soul. I was taken away.

'Roger, help Her Grace,' Lady Margaret said urgently. But then she had no idea how little I could help myself.

As the guard closed the door of the caravan behind me, Tom let out a whoop. 'You're back then. Nobody hurt you?'

'No, no. I'm fine.' I was not fine.

'Where did they take you? Look, there's ale, not just that piss-pot wine. Are we going to start walking tomorrow, like you said? By damn, I wish George was here to help us with the you-know-what. George is the man we need. Where did they take you, Peter?'

'To see the Young Chieftain.'

Silence. Tom paused with a tankard of ale halfway to his lips. Jee, always quiet, somehow went quieter, like a mouse within scent of a cat. Finally Tom whispered, 'Did you—'

'I had nothing with me.' Tom would never learn discretion. How did we know who would hear if he mentioned the mythical poison?

'No, of course not. But ain't you ... you *are* going back?'

'Yes. Listen, Tom, Jee. I am to give instruction every day to the Young Chieftain, about how to bring soldiers back from the dead, which—'

Tom snorted. 'That nonsense again!'

Jee gazed at me without blinking.

'—which of course I cannot teach him to do.' That would mean one thing to Tom, another to Jee. 'But if I pretend to do so, it will—'

'Say no more!' Tom said. He winked, and said more. 'That will give you the chance to ... but say no more!'

'*You* say no more. I mean it, Tom.'

'Yes.' He beamed at me, made happy by our supposed plot to poison Tarek. 'What do you want me to do?'

261

I dropped my voice to a whisper. 'I want you to do nothing, Tom. Keep those knives sheathed, fight with neither savages nor traitors to The Queendom, say nothing to anyone. Nothing at all. Can you do that?'

His face fell. 'Nothing?'

'Nothing. Only walk.'

Tom brightened again. 'Well, at least we'll be walking again, instead of being cooped like chickens in this rolling pen. And who knows? George and his rebellion might—'

'*Tom!*'

He nodded, smiled, and pantomimed using a key to lock his mouth.

Jee said, 'Did ye see the princess?'

It was rare for him to ask anything, and still rarer in that wistful tone. But Jee was only a few years older than Stephanie. What images of royalty, about as far removed as possible from the lives Jee had led in the Unclaimed Lands and in Applebridge, filled his boyish mind? A princess, captured and prisoner only fifty feet away. Where I saw a pathetic child, Jee might see unimaginable glamour.

Think of others, both my father and Mother Chilton had told me.

'I did see the princess, Jee. She was sitting by her caravan with her women. And perhaps you shall see her tomorrow, when we begin walking over the mountains. She will be carried in a wonderful throne by four stout men, and if she parts the curtains around the throne to look out, she may smile at you.'

In the night gloom of the caravan I could not see his face. But I heard his soft indrawn breath as he imagined this.

'Well,' Tom said, oblivious, 'I hope they're giving her enough food and a warm cloak and a bath. No, wait. Not

262

a bath. If she smells bad enough, maybe that bastard Tarek won't go near her. I wouldn't mind a bath myself, believe it or not. And Jee, you look filthy and smell like horse turds. No princess better catch sight of you or she'll void her stomach.'

'Tom,' I snapped, 'go to sleep now.'

'Why do you sound so testy? I only said—'

'Go to sleep!'

38

And so we walked. The horses were gone, taken back to The Queendom, sold to some unseen local folk or abandoned in the mountains; I did not know. Supplies had been repacked onto a few donkeys or onto the backs of servants. The caravans were left in the upland meadow. Soldiers marched ahead and behind, and in the middle were carried the two chairs-on-poles, one for Lady Margaret and the other for Princess Stephanie with her nurse. Beside the bearers walked the captured folk of The Queendom, including Tom and Jee and me. Tom's ankles were tied with a foot of loose rope between them so that he could walk but not run. He hated this. I was left free, but my savage guard never left my side. Jee was still ignored. Perhaps the savages hoped he would just disappear, a magic illusion gone back to Witchland. I talked to none of the common soldiers, only to Tarek each night in his tent.

'Begin instruction,' the Young Chieftain said at our first session.

Never was there an atmosphere less conducive to instruction. The tent was full of people. Two guards in full battle armour stood on either side of Tarek, who lounged on a three-legged stool while I stood before him on the bare ground. The guards pointed their *guns* straight at me, the witch who had some terrible magic at his disposal – who knew what he might do to their leader? A log blazed in the fire pit, sending weird shadows over the guards' scowls and Perb's nervous face. Outside, it rained, a steady drumming on the hide roof that sounded for all the world like hooves from beyond the natural sky. Even Tarek's lounging looked uneasy, a cover for nerves stretched like lute strings.

But I had prepared. 'My lord.'

He scowled and would have spoken, but this too was part of my preparations. I would be in control here, no matter what I must do to become so.

'I know you use no such titles, my lord. But this is instruction from *my* realm, not yours. We must follow the discipline of my art. *Its* discipline.'

Perb translated. I had chosen the word very carefully, had even memorized it in Tarek's speech. The day before Perb had said that the savages' most important value was discipline.

Tarek nodded. He did not look belligerent. I pressed on, and now I spoke in Tarek's language. 'My lord, no other person must hear my lesson – only you and I. Dismiss your guards and translator. My discipline. I am *antek*.'

If he was surprised that I spoke his language, he concealed it well. For a long moment he gazed at me. Then he waved at all three men: '*Klef.*'

The guards obeyed instantly, although the stare they gave me could have wilted mountains. Perb burst into passionate speech I could not follow. Tarek repeated calmly, '*Klef*,' and the look in his blue eyes made the guards seem like house cats. Perb kleffed.

'*Jad*,' Tarek said to me. 'Begin.'

I took a stone from my pocket, clutching it to keep my fingers from trembling. So far I had succeeded. It was not very far. But *he* was obeying *me*. The savage leader of a great army and an unknown kingdom, obeying Roger Kilbourne, the Queen's fool. I sat cross-legged on the ground and gestured for Tarek to do the same. He did so without hesitation. Partly this must be due to a life of discipline – that superbly conditioned body had not happened by chance – but partly it was his own nature, so self-confident that he did not have to insist on the trappings of rank, nor try to impress others. In another life, it occurred to me, I might have liked him.

Tarek was shorter than I but longer in his muscled upper body, so that our heads were at the same height. I set the stone on the ground between us. Earlier in the day we had marched past a mountain stream, and my guard had indicated that Tom and I should strip and bathe. Jee had joined us. The cold water had stung like needles, and it had taken an hour of walking to return sensation to my frozen limbs, but from the bottom of the rocky stream I had pocketed this stone. Half the size of my fist, it was white, shot through with veins of some pink mineral and smooth from years in the water.

In my halting Tarekish (I had to give the language some name) I explained that this stone was a link between here and Witchland. To use it, one must train the mind: discipline. The first step was to learn to gaze at the rock and think of nothing else – *nothing at all* – for a full minute, while chanting a magic word.

'What is this word?' Tarek said. His tone remained cool but eagerness flickered in his eyes.

'The word is George.'

It took us five minutes before I declared myself satisfied with his pronunciation. I had chosen the word deliberately: The savages had trouble saying the 'j' sound. Five minutes of instruction time were thus used up.

'I begin,' Tarek said. 'George, george—'

'You are not saying it with the right beat,' I said, tapping my fist on the ground. 'Magic words must be said exactly.'

'Tell me again.'

Another five minutes. Tarek did not show annoyance. Discipline.

'Good. Now look at the stone. Think of only the stone.'

'George,' Tarek murmured, 'george, geor—'

'You are thinking of something else, not only the stone.'

For the first time he looked surprised. 'You know this?'

'Yes.' Of course I knew that: no one can think of only one thing for a full minute. Other thoughts inevitably wander in.

'You can see into my thoughts?'

'No. I know only that your thoughts are not solely on the stone.'

'How do you know this?'

'I am a witch.'

He nodded and returned to staring and murmuring. Time and time again I interrupted him to say his thoughts had wandered. Each time he admitted to this, and without anger. My admiration for him grew.

'Enough for tonight,' Tarek finally said. 'I will keep this stone.'

'No. It must stay with me.'

He nodded, accepting my judgment. All at once I knew what *antek* meant: one who produced something both valuable and difficult. Defence and conquering from soldiers; children from mothers; learning from *anteks*. An *antek* ruled in his own realm.

Roger the scholar.

'Goodnight, my lord,' I said.

He accepted the foreign title. 'Goodnight, *antek*.'

Back at our fire, Tom inched himself closer to me and whispered, 'Did you do it?'

Poison Tarek, he meant. I whispered, 'No. George wishes us to wait until we have a sign from him that our rescuers are nearby. For our escape, you know.'

He nodded. Everyone here – unlike in The Queendom

– seemed to accept my judgment. Everyone but me. With my nonsensical instruction, I was effectively making a fool of the leader of a great army, one who already had ample reason to kill me. How long could I sustain this travesty?

The answer turned out to be longer than I had dared hope. Perb had told me that we would reach Tarek's kingdom – the word felt unnatural on my tongue; queens should rule and men defend – in 'two more twelve-days'. For six nights I kept Tarek staring at the pink-veined white stone and murmuring, 'George ...' I interrupted him constantly to say his thoughts had wandered, thereby ensuring that his thoughts would wander. The days' marches grew shorter as the terrain became rougher. The weather turned even colder. In the mornings frost lay on the ground, on the princess's tent, on us. I dreamed every night of Maggie, pregnant with my child. Often I woke with tears frozen on my face. No rescue came from my father.

'George is taking his own sweet time getting here,' Tom grumbled.

'George, george,' Tarek murmured, and then on the seventh night, 'I think I have done this, *antek*. For a full minute.'

'Yes, you have.' The warning in his blue eyes said that I must move forward with my instruction. And perhaps he *had* been able to keep his thoughts on the stone for a full minute. Discipline. 'You are ready for the next step, my lord. Tonight, you must dream about this stone.'

All calm vanished. Tarek stood so quickly that the unused three-legged stool behind him was knocked backwards. Instantly a guard strode into the tent, *gun* pointed at my head. Tarek demanded of me, 'What do you know of dreams?'

'I . . . I . . .'

'Are they the pass to Witchland?' He used the word for the high mountain pass, through which we had marched wearily that very day.

'Sometimes,' I said. What answer would save me? Desperately I searched Tarek's face for some sign of what to say. In turn, his blue gaze raked my face, and almost I could feel it, sharp as knives.

Then he relaxed. '*Klef*,' he said irritably to the guard, who left. Tarek paced a bit – unusual for him – then abruptly returned to sitting on the ground. 'Tell me when dreams are a pass to Witchland.'

'Only for *anteks*,' I groped even as my mind filled with images of my mad sister, speaking to me in the terrible dream that, mercifully, had not recurred for many nights.

'Only for *anteks*,' Tarek repeated. 'Good.'

'My lord,' I said, trying to regain control, 'are you troubled by dreams?' I had to use the word for 'attack'; Tarekish did not seem to contain any other words for trouble.

'Not I,' he said. 'But my queen.'

Stephanie. Attacked by dreams. And Lady Margaret had also mentioned the princess's nightmares. I got out, 'What are these dreams? Who comes in them?'

'Another queen. Her slave Mar-gar-ait—' he stumbled over the name, '—says that this other queen is also a young girl, crowned in the manner of your people, and she tells my bride, "Die, die, die." And Staif-ain-ee wakes screaming.' He frowned. 'She is too old for such fear. And she is a queen. Queens do not scream.'

But I had stopped listening to him.

'Die, my baby die die, my little one, die die . . .' And Roger the child listened to the monstrous song and nestled closer, a smile on his small face and the pretty tune in his ears. 'Die, my baby, die die, my little one, die die . . . . . .'

269

Tarek said, 'Is this a witch attacking Stef-ain-ee in her dream?'

Yes. 'No.'

'Then the children of your people are badly trained.'

I said nothing. Let him think the little princess was badly brought up rather than have him suspect the truth. My mad sister had invaded Stephanie's dreams. Stephanie must have, after all, inherited the talent for the soul arts that her mother and grandmother had lacked, but that Mother Chilton said was possessed by Stephanie's great-grandmother. But Stephanie's was a talent untaught and uncontrolled. A wild card. And the talent must lie strong in her, since my sister had sensed it in that other realm.

All at once I was afraid for the little girl, more afraid than even before.

Tarek gazed at the white stone. 'Then I must dream of this stone?' he said, gazing at it. The subject of Stephanie had been dismissed; she was merely a spoiled, badly raised child with fears unbecoming to a queen.

'Yes, you must dream of this stone.'

'You will show me how to cause such dreams?'

'I will show you what you must learn to cause such dreams.' Lurching onward, I put together a jumble of instructions, scarcely knowing myself what I said. Tarek listened to all my nonsense, organized it in his practical mind and said he would practise this before he slept, in order to dream of the white stone.

'*Klef,*' he said finally, and I was taken back to my fire.

'Peter,' Tom said, in a state of high excitement. 'Great news! I have met a girl!'

39

I did not want to hear about Tom's girl, some poor kitchen maid or apprentice laundress dragged away from The Queendom to serve the princess. But when Tom wished to tell me something, there was no escaping him. While Jee, huddled in Tom's fur cloak against the cold, watched us across the fire, Tom burbled on.

'That savage bastard – the guard who watches me when you're gone – allows me much more freedom now. Well, I'm tied, ain't I? And he probably thinks The Queendom is too far now to go back to all alone, and he might be right at that if . . . Anyway, he was casting dice with two other soldiers – I wish they would let me play! Ten to six odds I could beat them all. But I watched yesterday for an hour and the rules—'

'Tom, I'm very tired.'

'Well, all right, I'll make my tale short. I took a walk in the woods by that creek and she was there and I bedded her. Oh, I feel so much better now. A man needs a woman.' He winked.

'Fine,' I said. 'Goodnight.'

'Her name is Alysse.'

'Very pretty.'

'I will meet her again tomorrow.'

'Good.'

'She has red-gold curls and breasts like—'

'*Goodnight*, Tom.'

'You need to have a woman, Peter. Truly. I say this as a friend. I know you're married but after all, hang it,

Maggie is far away. Lying with a woman would cure your melancholy.'

My 'melancholy'. I had a great ruler to whom I must teach an art I did not possess. I had a mad sister being used to divert the power of death to create those who would never die. I had a child growing in the womb of a woman I had abandoned. I had a princess haunted by phantoms from beyond the grave. I had a promised rescue that did not come. Bedding a woman was not going to cure my melancholy, which this night felt like the deepest despair.

And then it grew deeper.

She came in my dream, and *I saw her emerge from the fog. Her crown glinted gold in a light I could not see, a light bright and terrible somewhere beyond the horizon. She wore a lavender gown like my mother – our mother – and her hair was my mother's rich brown. Her eyes glittered with madness. She said, 'Roger. Brother.'*

I said, 'How can you—' but she interrupted me.

'We have your father, did you know that? At Galtryf. He is our captive. As you will someday be.' Her laugh rang through the fog, and all at once I felt myself dissolve, the flesh melting grotesquely off my bones and the bones themselves crumbling to powder as Cecilia's had, as Fia's had—

'Peter!' Jee crouched over me, a small brown shape in the dawn. The camp already stirred, and savages swivelled their heads to look at the screaming *antek*. My guard loomed by the fire, *gun* pointed at nothing, his blue eyes glazed with fear.

'You be dreaming,' Jee said. 'Wake up, Peter!'

'I'm awake.' Groggily I sat up.

The guard lowered his *gun* and the fright left his eyes. No usual enemy could ever bring fear to a savage soldier's expression, but I was a witch. Even in the confused state between sleep and waking, even in the backwash of my

272

terrible dream, I realized that such knowledge might prove useful. My guard feared witchcraft.

Jee, however, did not. He said with disgust, 'Get up, Peter. It be late.'

'Wake Tom.' Tom snored on, oblivious of all noise. Jee shook him to life.

'Oh, piss pots,' Tom mumbled. 'Morning already? By damn, but that was a short night! I was dreaming of ... someone.' He winked at me and mouthed, 'Alysse.' Jee snorted.

The horror of my dream was still upon me. My own body dissolving for all eternity ... No. It had been but a dream. I was here, alive, solid. But no rescue was coming for me; my father was captive in some place called Galtryf. I had never heard of Galtryf. But I could think of nothing else as we did the day's march. Now the land was descending; we were over the highest of the mountains; my father was captive in Galtryf. Strange plants began to appear, large red bushes with leaves sharp as swords. The air turned even colder. Where was Galtryf? No rescue was coming ...

But my sister might so easily have been lying. And she was mad.

Two more days passed. The savages became louder and more jovial as they approached home. The Young Chieftain tried to make himself dream of a white stone. His gaze began to turn on me with – what? Suspicion? Another guard was added to my original captor, and both of them hovered beside me constantly. Tom, less closely guarded each day even as I was watched all the more, met Alysse somewhere in the woods every afternoon. Cold apparently did not interfere with their amorous activity, nor did the length of rope between Tom's ankles. Jee, sensing my despair, clung to me like a shadow.

273

'Look!' Tom said one morning. 'That's her! That's Alysse!'

We had been walking for several hours, warmed by both the exercise and the sun in a welcome cloudless sky. It was nearly time to stop for the noon meal. My legs ached. I did not want to talk yet again about Alysse, but I glanced dutifully at her.

And I stopped walking, so abruptly that Jee stumbled into my legs.

This was no wanton kitchen girl. She stood twenty feet from me, holding a bucket of water, and she stared directly into my eyes. It was a gaze of complete concentration, as if she knew what I was. *Hisaf.* She *did* know. I was certain of it, although I could not have said how. Then, as I stared back, her face shifted. Only for a moment, but the plump girlish cheeks and rosy little mouth became the sparer, tauter lines of a mature woman, neither young nor old – as Mother Chilton had once been, before she changed herself into the crone Tom had talked to on the cliff above the sea. The next moment the maturity had vanished. Tom had noticed nothing; Alysse's transformation had been only for me.

She was one of that shadowy web of women who practised the soul arts. Why was she here, lying with Tom Jenkins?

My guard, not touching me, urged, *'Klef! Klef!'* His co-captor, quicker to see where I gazed, shouted at Alysse to move on. She did, with one backward gaze over her shoulder at Tom, who grinned delightedly.

'She wants me again, Peter,' he bragged.

'She's . . . she's very pretty.'

'A shame that you're married, yes?' Then, with a self-consciously sober expression, 'Although of course your Maggie is tearing fine, too.'

I had to speak with the web woman, but I could see

no manner of getting to her. I was watched every moment, and Tom would be of no use.

But perhaps Jee would.

'Only you're a long way from Maggie, after all,' Tom said. 'By damn, nobody could expect you not to have normal urges. And there's nothing like a woman to affect a man's spirits.'

'Yes,' I said. 'I know.'

'Jee,' I said when we made camp for the night, 'I have a task for you.'

'What,' he said flatly.

'It is not dangerous.' A stupid thing to say; everything here was dangerous. 'I be not afraid of danger,' he said stoutly, and my heart cracked. Ten years old, and already forced to behave like a man, with a man's pretended bravery.

'Everyone is afraid sometimes, Jee. My guards are afraid of you. You know that, do you not?'

He nodded. All around us people shouted and built fires and set up tents and cooked and fed donkeys and carried water and formed into off-duty cadres, singing. It was the best time for Jee to slip through camp. He had grown bolder about moving around now that he knew the savages would not touch him. They would not even touch me, the *antek*, and Jee the magic illusion they actively feared. Everything he did was observed, and nothing was interfered with. I suspected that he could even have walked through the outlying guard ring and so escaped, except that there was nothing to escape to.

Jee said, 'I be afraid of that girl.'

'Of Alysse?'

'She be not . . . her.' His small face creased with annoyance at not being able to articulate what he meant. Words failed him, but perceptions did not. Jee had sensed

275

something about Alysse that had completely slipped by Tom. Although that was not surprising. Tom was blinded by desire. I knew well how that felt.

Jee repeated, 'I be afraid of that girl.'

'I know. But ... but, Jee, I have no one else to help me.'

He looked at me keenly. 'Ye have the Dead.'

'No. I do not. I cannot cross over ... not any more.'

'Why not?'

I couldn't bring myself to explain to him. Mother Chilton had made me promise I would not cross over again, but against that, my father had said it could do no harm. But the truth was that I was too afraid. My sister and her *hisaf* henchmen – or controllers, or whatever they were – terrified me. In my last dream my sister had spoken directly to me, had sent that horrific image of myself dissolving for ever, lost even to eternity.

'It doesn't matter why not,' I snapped at Jee. 'Will you help me or not?'

'Maggie said I maun.' He sighed heavily, and I hated that I was bullying a small boy. But then I had an inspiration.

'It's not just to help me, Jee. It's to help Princess Stephanie.'

'The princess?' he breathed. His face changed. He had seen her once, peeping from her pole-chair. Once that I knew about, anyway. As Jee slipped around the camp at will, he might, for all I knew, have glimpsed Stephanie scores of times. His eyes widened. 'What maun I do?'

'Just find Alysse. She must know who you are. See what she says or does. Perhaps she will send me a message. Find her when no one else sees. Can you do that?'

'I can do that.'

'Thank you, Jee.'

'I want to be home with Maggie.'

'We'll get there, Jee.' I hoped it was true. I wanted to see Maggie, to talk with her, to feel enveloped in her competent and acerbic caring. To lay a hand on her belly, where my child grew. I had no right to any of these things, but I wanted them.

My guards watched me whisper with Jee, but they did not interfere, still working diligently at pretending that Jee did not exist. I rose, ostentatiously stretched and asked to be taken into the woods to piss. When I returned, Jee was gone.

Tom and I ate what was served us, setting aside a portion for Jee. Then one of my guards conducted me to the Young Chieftain's tent for our nightly instruction.

And everything began to unravel.

40

'I dreamed of the white stone,' Tarek said to me. His face was as calm as ever, but triumph shone in his eyes. 'I did all that you said, and last night the image of the stone appeared in my dream, surrounded by a ring of knives.'

'Yes,' I said and tried to smile. Of course he had. Think about anything long and hard enough and one may eventually dream of it: red boars, dancing cottages, mad sisters, pink-veined white stones. 'You are making progress, my lord.'

'But very slowly, *antek*. Your task is to teach me to bring an army from Witchland to my kingdom. That is a long way from dreaming of a white stone.'

'It is indeed. But how long did you need to become a great warrior?' *Discipline*.

'War is not witchcraft. How long did you need to learn to bring the army that killed my father?'

I ignored the glittering of his brilliant blue eyes, but my heart began a slow, hard thud. 'It took years, my lord. I told you that.'

'You do not look that old.'

'I began very young.'

'When you were a queen's fool?'

He had been discovering more about me. From whom?

Tarek continued, 'It would seem to me that an *antek* who can command such powerful witchery would not allow himself to be a woman's toy, or to sleep in the ashes of a hearth.'

'I did not sleep in the ashes of a hearth.'

'On at least one occasion you were seen there. Come, Roger Kilbourne, I will not cross knives with you. Teach me more quickly.'

It was an unmistakable command. Before I could respond, he added, 'Or at least show me that you *can* do what was said of you.'

'My lord? I don't—'

'I think you do. Enough of white stones and chants of "george". Show me, here and now, that you are indeed an *antek*. Go to Witchland and bring something back.'

'I have already done so.'

'You refer to the witch child, the servant of your servant. You brought the child back from Witchland.'

'Yes.' Let him think so, if it enhanced his estimate of my value.

'But I did not see you do so. Go to Witchland now, while I can watch you, and bring something back.'

We stared at each other. My thoughts raced. I was so far away from Soulvine Moor that surely my sister would not appear to me if I crossed over. And if I did encounter anything harmful, I could return immediately. However, my father had warned me so strongly not to bring anything back over with me. And Mother Chilton . . .

Anger suddenly flooded me. *Do this, do that*, I was told, but how could I obey such contradictory orders? I was a *hisaf*. I would decide for myself. My father's decisions, after all, had brought him only a dead wife and captivity in the mysterious Galtryf. Surely anything I chose could not be worse?

But there was still my fear. I was afraid to cross again into the Country of the Dead.

'My lord,' I said, and even to my own ears my bluster sounded weak and thin, 'the arts of an *antek* cannot be rushed. In good time I will—'

'You will do it now. Or I will believe that you cannot do it.'

'*My lord*—'

'Tarek, I would interrupt.'

It was one of the Young Chieftain's captains, an older warrior with a short feathered cape thrown over his fur tunic and urgency in his face. Our lessons were never interrupted. The Tarekish word for 'interrupt' was, in fact, the same as 'attack'.

'*Klef,*' Tarek said.

'Mar-gar-ait is dead.'

Lady Margaret. Dead.

Tarek said, 'Murdered?'

'I cannot tell.'

Tarek said, 'My queen?'

'Not harmed.'

The two looked at each other. Their impassive faces nonetheless communicated much that I knew I could not discern; I was not one of them. But I did realize that Tarek would not have been interrupted for the death of a 'slave' unless something else had occurred. He said, 'I will come.' Then he looked at me. 'And you will come too, *antek.*'

Tarek and his captain strode from his tent. His guard formed around him, falling into perfect step. I followed, immediately accompanied by my own startled guard. As the Young Chieftain paced through the camp, soldiers fell silent and sprang to attention, left fists raised in the air. The very cook fires seemed to not snap. Thus Stephanie's high hysterical screams rang clearly through the night air.

Outside her tent Tarek gave an order and his guard fell back, as did mine. The captain remained in the doorway, his knife drawn. Only Tarek and I could enter the tent of his child bride.

She sat on the carpeted ground, shrieking, trying to get

280

her thin arms around the corpse of Lady Margaret. The nurse crouched beside both, ineffectively saying, 'Your Grace, *please* now. Your Grace ... Lambie ...' There was no blood on Lady Margaret's gown, no injury that I could see to her head or limbs. But her face was contorted into a look of horror.

How long had she been dead? If I crossed over right now, before she lapsed into the mindless serenity of the Dead ...

I did not cross over.

Tarek said sharply, 'Staif-ain-ee! *Ka!*'

The little girl looked up at him, shrieked louder than ever, then buried her head in the nurse's shoulder. Her thin body shook uncontrollably. She did not cease screaming.

Tarek said to me over the noise, 'Translate. Ask the slave what occurred here.'

I stepped forward and put a hand on the nurse's shoulder. She looked up angrily, saw who I was and fell into confusion. She breathed, 'The witch fool ...'

There was no time to argue with her name-calling. I said, raising my voice to be heard, 'His lordship wants to know what— Your Grace, please stop that shrieking!'

My words had no more effect than had Tarek's. Impulsively I sank to the floor, pulled the princess from her nurse's arms – how did I dare to do such a thing! – and said quietly into her ear, 'I know what you saw. Do you hear me, Stephanie? *I know what you saw.* You are not alone with the monster.'

I did not know what she had seen. But my words made a difference. She still shook and sobbed, but her screaming ceased. Being alone is so often the worst part of pain. The princess clung to me, her tears wetting my tunic, her hair in my mouth.

Tarek said, somewhere between relief and disgust,

'Good, *antek*. Now discover what occurred here.'

Over the princess's shaking shoulders I asked the nurse, who eyed me with jealousy even as she poured out her story. 'Lady Margaret and I put Her Grace to bed, and then Lady Margaret lay down on her pallet, she was that exhausted, and I was just washing out Her Grace's things—'

A water-filled basin sat in one corner, with a small pile of sodden white linen spreading a stain on the ground.

'—when all at once Lady Margaret sits bolt upright on her pallet and cries out – her, that never complains nor makes a noise about how we have to live on this unholy journey – Lady Margaret cries out "No! No!" And my lambie wakes up at the same moment and screams, "No!" The exactly same moment! Then my lady slumps over, dead as a bucket of stones. And Her Grace goes screaming.'

I translated, and Tarek turned to his captain, still standing just inside the tent flap. 'For this you bring me here, Sufgek? For the death of a slave woman that frightened a child?'

The nurse demanded, 'What did he say?' I ignored her.

Sufgek betrayed no emotion, but he said, 'Both awoke in fear at the same moment. It may be witchcraft.' His eyes shifted to me.

Tarek's gaze also turned to me, sitting on the floor with a terrified child shaking in my arms. For a moment the brilliant blue eyes turned speculative.

'No,' he finally said. 'This is nothing more than women's *blimct*. Sufgek, you should not have attacked my instruction. *Klef*.' He strode from the tent, the captain stepping hastily aside to let him pass. Over his shoulder Tarek said to me, '*Antek*, return to your fire.' The tent flap fell.

I had only a few moments. To Stephanie I murmured, 'What did you see in your dream?'

'No! Don't go!'

She was preparing to shriek again. Hating myself, I said quickly, 'If you make noise, Tarek will come back. You don't want that, do you?'

'No.' And then, a suppressed wail: 'You said you know what I saw.'

I was threatening to take away the reassurance that she was not alone. Quickly I said, 'You saw a girl with a crown, didn't you? And she said something bad?'

Her arms tightened convulsively around me. The tent flap rose. My guard, his face averted from the women within, said loudly, '*Antek. Klef. Klef.*'

'Don't go!' Stephanie wailed.

'I must.' If I were dragged from the tent, she would scream even worse. 'But I'll come back tomorrow. And remember, you are *not* alone. I can fight the bad girl with the crown.'

I stood, and the nurse took her from me. My guard had actually advanced into a tentful of women, a measure of how far he would go to carry out orders. Yet he did not touch me. I followed him back to our fire. The Young Chieftain was probably disciplining his captain, whatever that involved, and so I was saved from proving myself until tomorrow night.

Tarek was more intelligent than his skittish captain, and he had already begun to doubt my supposed powers. He had apparently acquitted me of witchcraft in Lady Margaret's death. In this instance, he was both right and wrong. Lady Margaret's death might indeed have been due to soul arts, but not mine.

Both Tom and Jee waited at the fire. Tom, wide-eyed, said, 'The princess ... Her Grace ...'

283

'Be she hurt?' Jee demanded fiercely. His whole skinny body strained forward.

'No, Jee, she's not hurt. But Lady Margaret is dead – she died in her sleep. The princess was upset, is all.'

He relaxed; Lady Margaret meant nothing to him. Nor to Tom, who launched into a long recitation of the death-while-asleep of an elderly aunt of some girl in Almsbury. But Lady Margaret had meant something to me. Again I saw her at court, scolding Queen Caroline's ladies into order. Playing a lute by the hearth on a winter's night. Finding me unconscious in a corridor of the palace and bringing me to the safety of her rooms and the nursing of her own serving woman. I saw her at Stephanie's monstrous marriage, defying the bridegroom by walking with dignity from the throne room in pursuit of the nurse. With the little princess by a mountain fire, urging me to 'help Her Grace'. And now Lady Margaret had, by some fearsome art I did not understand, been murdered by a dream.

Be tranquil, my good lady, there in the Country of the Dead.

'Peter,' Jee said softly, under cover of Tom's cheerful babble, 'I did so. I saw Alysse. She sent you this.' His small warm hand closed briefly on mine, and then I held a packet wrapped in leaves and tied with vine.

41

The camp quieted soon after. When soldiers rise before dawn and march with heavy packs all day, they sleep early and deep. Not guards, however. The penalty for a warrior who slept on guard duty was death. Now that there was no caravan in which to lock me, my guards rotated all night long. At whatever hour I woke, one sat beside me, feeding the fire, alert to anyone coming or going from its circle of light and warmth. But I had Alysse's packet.

As soon as I unwrapped the leaves, the scent told me what lay inside. I wrapped it again and waited until Tom and Jee slept. Then I opened the bundle and pretended to nibble on the little cake within, letting tiny pieces instead slide inside my tunic. I was careful not to swallow even a crumb, but it was difficult. The cake's honey and nuts would have been hard enough to resist – long ago the army had run out of sugar stolen from the palace – but what made the mouth fill with sweet water and the tongue waggle in anticipation was the cake's aroma. The drugs Alysse used, that Fia had used, smelled like every dream of food a hungry man ever had.

Tom had gobbled Fia's honey cake and slept like a stone. I had eaten mine, spiced with a different herb, and could not remember my own name, nor the proper shapes of tree branches, nor why I could not bed that bewitching girl … But that second drug was not what Alysse had baked into this cake.

I left the rest of the cake lying exposed on its broad leaf, and I pretended to sleep.

The guard was young, but he was a soldier. He did not touch the cake. From one half-opened eye I could see his nose twitch, and once his hand moved towards the leaf, but he withdrew it. If he should choose to eat it at the end of his shift and then simply fell asleep back at his own fire ... Why had Alysse sent only one cake? Surely she could have foreseen this problem?

The guard did not eat the cake. It sat there still, resting temptingly on its leaf and giving off its strong delicious aroma, when the next soldier on duty relieved the first. The savage fed the fire, settled himself beside it, inspected us three inert prisoners. Overhead the stars shone sharp and cold. Tom snored. The savage whistled under his breath, something I had never heard any of them do, a sweet and plaintive little air. Could all of them sing tunefully then, just as all of them had blue eyes? The savage stopped whistling. A long suspended moment, and then he ate the honey cake.

Soon ... soon ... *now*.

He snored even louder than Tom. Surely someone else would hear? No one did. The only other guards were posted at the princess's tent, several hundred feet away in the darkness, and at the camp perimeter, further away still. Servants – now slaves – taken from the palace were not deemed worthy of being guarded. The chance of rescue from The Queendom was past, and there was nowhere for captives to run.

Slowly I sat up, watching the savage slumped beside his *gun*. In the dimness he looked like nothing as much as a furry boulder. In a few more moments Alysse slipped into the firelight, took my hand and led me silently to the quiet deep shadows of a clump of bushes between fires. Her fingers were cold in mine.

'Who are you?' I whispered. 'You bedded Tom to get to me, didn't you? Do you come from Mother Chilton?'

'Yes. No. It is not like that.' Her voice was hostile, which first surprised me and then did not. She continued, 'You were told to not cross over again. You promised not to do so, and you have broken that promise, just as you broke the one to Fia.'

Was there anything these web women did not know?

I said hotly, 'A *hisaf*, my father—' how strange the words sounded, spoken aloud '—said there was no danger to anyone in my crossing over, so long as I brought nothing back!'

'The *hisafs* have their beliefs about the Country of the Dead, and we have ours. Theirs are mistaken.'

'But *hisafs* can actually go there, and you cannot!' Sudden doubt shook me. 'Can you?'

'No. Our knowledge comes in other ways. We—'

'Who are "we"? What are you and Mother Chilton and Fia?'

'We are those striving to preserve life.'

'But are you women all witches or—'

'Who we are is not your concern, and I am not here to argue names with you, Roger Kilbourne. I have undergone considerable risk to talk to you, and that risk should convince you of the dire importance of what I have to say.'

'Which is what?'

Her cold hand tightened on mine, hard enough that it hurt. She was much stronger than she looked. Her voice held an intensity made greater by the dark night.

'I am here to tell you two things. The first is that no matter what the *hisafs* say, you must not cross over, not ever again.'

'Why not?'

'Will you not take my word on this?'

'No. My father said—'

'Damn your father! He now lies prisoner in Galtryf, that is all your *hisafs* have accomplished so far!'

'How did you know that? How? My sister told me—'

'Your sister is the real reason you must not cross over. You two are linked by blood. She is a great danger to you, and an even greater danger to the rest of the living.'

'You tell me nothing I have not already heard,' I said acidly. 'Surely you did not come here to say only that. Tell me exactly what she can and cannot do!'

Alysse's voice changed. She no longer scolded; now she was trying to convince me, and in her conviction burned desperation. She spoke slowly, and each word carried a terrible weight. 'The grave is not really a wall between the living and the dead, as the *hisafs* conceive it to be. That is their mistake. Not a wall, not a moat, not castle fortifications. You must form a different picture in your mind. Those living and those dead are connected, as in a vast web. How can it be otherwise, when the Dead were once alive, and the alive must someday join the Dead?'

'Mother Chilton spoke of a "web of being". But I do not see how—'

'Of course you do not see how – you are only a *hisaf*, and not a particularly able one. Just *listen*, Roger Kilbourne. Your crossing over does not, in and of itself, disturb the web of being, no. Your father told you true on that. But you did not confine your crossings to yourself, did you? When you brought back others, and their objects, each occasion upset the balance of the web. Pulled at its delicate threads, tore some loose. I do not say you caused this war, because it began before you were even born. But you have aided the enemy, oh how you have aided them!'

'It is not only I who have torn threads loose. Who sent

Fia back over, and Shadow and Shep and the other dogs?'

'Neither Fia nor the dogs are our doing. Do not attempt to accuse me, Roger. You do not know everything and I shall not tell you more – you, an ignorant boy who has already profoundly helped the enemy. Don't you understand? Soulvine Moor is destroying the web that weaves together life and death. Both have tremendous power, and that power flows along the strands of the web of being, which holds it in balance. Even your ill-begotten sister is part of that web. The rogue *hisafs* are using her, in league with Soulvine Moor. Your father's *hisafs* hope to kill her. Neither group must succeed. If the flow of web power – the strongest force in the world – should be so abruptly and greatly disturbed, what do you think might happen to the living? Or to the Dead, waiting so trustfully for—'

'For what?' I struck in. Her words dazed me. Could the barrier between living and dead really be destroyed? 'For what do the Dead wait in their circles? Tell me!'

She said simply, 'For the sword.'

I shook my head in the darkness. And then I remembered. Slowly I said, 'There was something bright and terrible, coming from the sky in the Country of the Dead—'

Alysse gasped. 'You saw the sword?'

'I don't know ... only for a moment. I'm not certain. It was the moment I brought back the Blue army, and something rent the sky, but it was so bright I couldn't look at it. Then I crossed away.'

She groaned. 'You should not have seen it at all. No one should see it except— I will not tell you more. You have no right to know. Roger, you must not cross over again for any reason.'

'But you admitted that my crossing over does not by

289

itself disturb anything.' Why was I arguing about this? I was afraid to cross over.

'It is not just what you might happen to you, Roger. It is also your sister. She was – is – at the centre of the web. The power that Soulvine Moor seeks to take from the Dead and allocate to themselves, that power flows through her, the unnatural living presence among the Dead. Do you not see why she is mad? That would drive any child to madness. And unlike other *hisafs*, faithful or faithless, you are linked to her by blood. If you remove that centre of power while you are in the Country of the Dead – if you think you must kill her to defend yourself, for instance – it could do immense harm. That must not happen. And neither must she harm you.'

'Why not?' I said bitterly. 'If I have caused so much havoc already in the Country of the Dead, if I have aided Soulvine Moor so much, if I have done such evil, why go to such lengths to protect me so? Here or there? Why not just let my sister destroy me?'

'It is not you we are trying to protect.'

'Not me? Then whom? Princess Stephanie? My sister is appearing in her dreams and—'

'Stephanie too is part of the web, and it would have been better had that poor child been shot by Tarek's soldiers. Then she could have rested quietly in the Country of the Dead. Instead she is being tormented by your sister, and she is so closely guarded that we cannot get to her to help except at prohibitive cost. But the princess cannot cause any real disruption to the Country of the Dead, and she is not the reason I am here. Not the reason I have risked so much to talk to you.'

Her voice held so much apprehension that my own chest tightened. It was difficult to breathe. But whatever I had expected, it was not what Alysse said next.

'If you somehow escape from here, Roger Kilbourne,

if you do not die at Tarek's hands, then you must not go home to Maggie. She is with her kin in the village of Tanwell, but you must *not* go there. Your sister does not know about Maggie, but if you go to Tanwell, she may find out.'

'I ... I don't understand. Not go home? Mother Chilton told me to go home to Maggie. She did!'

'I know,' Alysse said. Her voice dropped so low that I had to lean into the bushes, close to her ear, to hear her at all. Twigs tangled in my hair. 'When Mother Chilton told you to go home to Maggie, we did not know what we know now. I have come here, through dangers you cannot possibly understand, in order to tell you that under no circumstances, for no reason, can you go back to Maggie.'

'Then is Maggie the person you are trying to protect? That you have taken all these risks for? The person that Fia—'

'No. Not Maggie.'

'Then who?'

It was a long time before Alysse spoke. I had the eerie impression she was listening to something, there in the starlit night. Finally her voice came, slow and reluctant from the darkness.

'Your child will be a son.'

Then she was gone, and a rabbit hopped away from the bushes into the cold night.

42

In the morning, the savages buried Lady Margaret. At dawn Tom and I were woken by my usual guard. The soldier I had drugged with Alysse's honey cake had been hauled away, asleep on duty, and perhaps shot. I did not care. Two savages led us a short way into the woods, where a hole had been dug in a small clearing. Lady Margaret's body, wrapped in what had been the curtains of her pole-chair, already lay at the bottom of the hole.

Tom and I shivered beside the grave, uncertain what would happen next. Silently Jee slipped in beside me. The air was very cold and low grey clouds pressed down from the sky. Morning bustle in the camp was muted by the trees. I was having trouble keeping my thoughts on Lady Margaret, or on anything except what Alysse had told me last night. Two factions contended for power over the web of being: Soulvine Moor with the faithless *hisafs*, opposed by my father's *hisafs* and the web women, and the latter two could not work together nor even share information. *'Your child will be a son . . .'*

Tom said grudgingly, 'At least the savages are burying the lady. They might have . . .' He waved his hand to indicate that savages might have done anything.

I was surprised too. Despite what Tarek believed, even his senior captain thought that Lady Margaret's death had involved witchcraft. Based on their treatment of Jee, the soldiers would have been reluctant to even touch the corpse. Nonetheless, Tarek must have given the order that Lady Margaret should have whatever death rites were usual for her people, and his soldiers had obeyed. Discipline.

We stood there while the sky darkened even more and a few stray drops of rain fell. Just slightly colder, and the rain would become snow. Tom muttered, 'What are we waiting for?'

Jee said, 'Her.'

'Who?' Tom said.

'The princess.'

Of course. Jee had grasped that more quickly than I. Lady Margaret had been Princess Stephanie's senior attendant. To Tarek, neither childhood nor hysteria would be a bar to the royal duty of attending the death rites. In his own way he was behaving decently. I hated that.

Tom said, 'Don't be daft, Jee. Nobody would bring a little girl to—'

The princess emerged from the woods.

She clutched her nurse's hand, and her little face was as bloodless as the stone I had given Tarek. Panic filled her eyes. Behind her walked her guard and six or eight of the palace folk. Tom craned his neck, looking for Alysse. She was not there.

When Stephanie reached the edge of the hole and looked down, puzzlement crossed her face. It was replaced by realization, and she opened her mouth to scream.

Instantly Jee ran towards her. 'No, it be all right!' he cried, and she turned to see who had shouted. Before Jee could reach her, the princess's guards seized him and threw him against a tree. Immediately he was on his feet, shaking his head and starting again towards the princess.

'No, Jee!' I called, and ran towards her myself. So the savages *would* touch him if he approached the princess. They would kill him. But not me. These men had seen Tarek permit me into Stephanie's tent last night. They let me go to her, kneel beside her, be clung to by her trembling little arms.

'Your Grace, do not scream. I mean it. You must be brave.'

'Here, lambie,' the nurse said, trying to take Stephanie from me. She clung harder. Blood streamed down Jee's face, twenty feet away.

'You are not alone, Your Grace. Don't scream. I am here.'

She nodded. I picked her up with my one good hand and the stump of my other wrist. The nurse scowled at me jealously and the guards glanced at each other. But they permitted it. Their expression said that these death rites, whatever they were, had nothing to do with them. Let the slave folk of the conquered country complete this quickly so that the march home could resume.

Then no one did anything, and I saw that it was going to be up to me, the *antek*.

With a princess's head buried against my shoulder, I walked to the edge of the grave and said loudly, 'We commend the soul of Lady Margaret to the ... the sky, and we ... uh ... commend her body to the earth. She was a gracious lady. A good woman, who helped many and was loved by all. Lady Margaret, farewell. Nurse, take the princess away, and you others follow. *Kevel bik ben tekir, semak.*' 'You two there, cover the body with dirt.'

The two soldiers I pointed to with the stump of my wrist looked startled, then glanced at each other. But they moved towards the shovels leaning against a tree. The palace folk, equally startled to be ordered about by someone who had once been the queen's fool, nonetheless obeyed. The nurse took Stephanie from me, even as I whispered, 'Be brave. I will come to you later.' Jee followed her with his eyes. In a few moments only he, Tom, I and our two guards remained in the clearing, watching the savages shovel dirt over Lady Margaret's body.

Then Jee moved towards the grave. The guards edged away from him. The boy leaned over and threw onto the dirt a twig pulled from a holly bush. There were no flowers this late in the season, but the bright red berries and glossy green leaves glowed on the mound of fresh dirt.

There was a moment of silence. Then Tom said, 'By damn, I wish I'd thought of that. But why didn't you give the proper graveside speech, Peter?'

Because I had never heard one.

It began to rain.

All morning it drizzled, a cold grey rain that made walking a misery, especially since the rain blew from the west straight into our faces. Not that the savages seemed to mind. Each step brought them closer to home, and they marched through the mud singing, even when a booted foot slipped on the downhill trail and the soldier landed on his arse. His fellows laughed and taunted him, at least when their captains were out of hearing distance. I learned several more bawdy words in Tarekish.

Not so the folk from The Queendom. Servants, now slaves, trudged beside the one remaining pole-conveyance. Tension stretched every line of the servants' faces as they bent their heads against the rain. *What is this place we go to? What will happen to us there*? For me, the question was more immediate: What would happen to me tonight, when Tarek sent for me for the instruction he no longer seemed to believe in?

'You are quiet, Peter,' Tom said. He walked beside me, the length of rope between his ankles shortening his stride, Lady Margaret evidently already gone from his thoughts. 'There's Jee disappearing every ten minutes and Alysse not walking with the women and you with a face like a crushed potato and ... Peter!' His face, rain running down it from his yellow hair, brightened and he leaned towards me conspiratorially. 'Is tonight the night? Will you – you know?' He pantomimed drinking ale and then, with a theatricality that should have put him in a playhouse or a gaol, pretended to choke and die.

'Stop that, Tom!'

'Yes, all right. But *is* it? Is tonight the night?'

'I don't know.' True enough words. I knew nothing for sure. Although one thing I suspected: It was not Tarek who would be next to die.

'But do you think that—'

'Oh, hold your tongue, Tom!'

He scowled and adopted an injured tone. 'Just as you say. Here comes Jee – you'd probably rather tell *him*.' Tom moved away, all wounded dignity and dripping sodden hair.

Jee slipped into step beside me. The blood had congealed on his face into a fresh scab, vivid and clean in the rain. 'I saw,' he said to me now.

'You saw Princess Stephanie?'

'Yes. She pushed aside the cloth and looked out. She still be crying.' And then, very low, 'Her nana be dying next, yes?'

'I don't know,' I said. But I did know.

'Then after the nana, ye will die in yer sleep?'

'No.' But honesty took over. 'I'm more likely to die at Tarek's hands. Listen to me, Jee. If that happens, you must leave the camp. Take Tom with you if you can, but if not, go yourself. Go back over the mountains.' What was I saying? Telling a ten-year-old to cross the Western Mountains with winter coming on? But I had nothing better to offer him. 'Escape. Go back to Maggie.'

'I maun not leave her,' he said.

'Yes, that's right – you must not leave Maggie. You must—'

'Not Maggie. The princess.' He looked up at me, rain streaming down his face. 'I maun not leave the princess with these by-damn savages.'

Love. Even for a ten-year-old, it reversed loyalty and blinded sense. As it had for me over Cecilia, and Maggie over me. Still, I saw the struggle on Jee's upturned face. He loved Maggie. He loved Stephanie.

'Jee—'

But he was gone, a small shadow slipping through the rain.

Several hours later we halted for the midday meal, although there was no glimpse of the sun to say that it was actually mid-day. We ate sodden gruel and mouldy cheese. I lay down, wrapped in my cloak, and despite the drizzle fell instantly asleep.

'Are dreams a pass to Witchland?' Tarek had asked me, and I had replied, 'Only for *anteks*.' Now I tried to make myself dream of my sister, as I had told Tarek to dream of the white stone. If I could make her come to me in a dream, I might obtain more information from her without actually crossing over to the Country of the Dead. Always before I had dreaded dreams of my sister—

—*green eyes, glittering with madness, calling my name in the fog*—

—but now I sought to dream of her. Tarek had made himself dream of what he chose.

But I could not. No dreams came in that brief sleep. Then we marched again until dusk fell and the rain, mercifully, stopped. Blazing fires dried out everything, but not very much. All too soon my guard motioned me impatiently towards Tarek's tent for the nightly instruction, just as if the Young Chieftain still believed in it. This might be the last time I stood in the land of the living.

I said nothing to the others. Tom would only charge around, making everything worse, and I had already said what I must to Jee. I had told Princess Stephanie I would come to her later today, but I did not think I would be able to fulfil that promise. Like so many others.

But I did have a plan. Desperate, stupid but nonetheless a plan. 'Help her,' Lady Margaret had said of Stephanie, and Lord Robert Hopewell, in the palace dungeon, had told me it was my duty to rescue the princess. But neither Lady Margaret nor Lord Robert swayed me as much as another child: my unborn son. I could not help him, could not go to him even if I survived, lest I lead my mad sister to discover he existed. Nor could I do much for Jee. So I would do what I could for Stephanie, the third child caught in this deadly war that none of them, nor I, really understood.

We reached Tarek's tent and I entered.

43

The Young Chieftain stood in conference with one of his captains. They broke off as soon as I entered, and the captain gave his raised-fist salute and left. He did not glance at me. I might have been as invisible as Jee, from the belief that I was a witch – or as invisible as an insect, from the belief that I was both negligible and soon dead.

'*Klef*,' Tarek said.

He had not called me *antek*. The only thing I could do was strike first, hoping to catch him off guard.

'My lord, you begin to think I am not an *antek*.' The language was a barrier; I did not know the words for 'lose faith'. But I had his attention. The blue eyes narrowed and studied me. He said nothing.

'Before, you told me to go to Witchland and bring back something. I told you the arts of an *antek* cannot be hurried.'

'Yes.' His expression sharpened. Tarek, the soldier, recognized a frontal attack when he saw one.

'I will do this, but not now. Not tonight.'

'Why not?'

'Because I am an *antek*, and an *antek* does not break his discipline, not even for his leader.'

Tarek said nothing. For a long moment I thought I had lost. My gamble was that an *antek* in his own sphere did indeed owe first loyalty to his art. If I was wrong, I was dead, and Tom and Jee with me.

Finally Tarek said, 'That is true,' and I breathed again.

'When does your discipline send you to Witchland? I tell you this, *antek*: It must be soon.'

'It will be soon.'

'When?'

'It will be when you set aside the princess.'

His brow furrowed. 'Set aside?'

I had used the only word I knew of Tarekish that might fit: 'discard', as a knife that had been broken. Obviously it was not the right word. The white stone sat on Tarek's three-legged stool. Was he planning to return it to me, in dismissal and contempt? With my one good hand I picked up the stone, squeezed it hard to quell the trembling in my fingers and gathered my courage to try again.

'I will go to Witchland for you when you say the princess is not your wife and that she must go back to The Queendom.'

This time he understood. I rushed on, like a man who has entered rapids and cannot escape the river until they end.

'The queen is but a child, not a true wife for such as you. And she is without discipline. You saw that last night. Your people will not like her. She can be discarded. I say this from a big, big reason: I was wrong last night. I made a mistake. Princess Stephanie's dreams may come from another witch.'

In one stride Tarek crossed the tent, seized me by the front of my tunic and all but lifted me off my feet. I could feel both his strength and his rage, lightning running along his body into mine. The smell of him filled my nostrils: male sweat and animal fur and anger. My hand, still holding the white stone, flailed helplessly, but some primitive part of my brain stopped me from even trying to strike back.

'*Antek*, you lie.'

'I do not!' I gasped. 'My lord . . .'

He dropped me and I staggered, barely staying on my feet. Words tumbled from me so fast I scarcely knew what I said. 'Did you make ever a mistake in your art? In war? All make mistakes sometimes. I told you last night that the princess was not a . . .' What was the word for 'victim'? I could not find the words I needed. 'That no witch had killed Lady Margaret. That is true. But the queen's nightmares – I told you that only an *antek* can use dreams as a pass to Witchland. I told you! Last night I dreamed. Now I know more than last night, because of the dream. Queen Stephanie *is* attacked by a witch, and it is not me! But she is without blame, my lord. The witch seeks to attack you through her, as a warrior might conquer a weak country in order to attack a strong one . . .'

I had made a mistake.

I knew it from Tarek's face. He was not a soldier who used the weak to attack the strong; that would have been beneath him. As was torture. There was a foreign code of honour here, and I felt, like a stab in my belly, the moment I had insulted his honour past repair. I had failed.

Tarek drew his knife.

I blurted, 'Wait! I will go to Witchland now!'

It bought me a second's hesitation from him. I clamped my teeth hard on my tongue and crossed over, before Tarek could send me over permanently.

Darkness—

My father had said I could cross over provided that I brought nothing back.

Cold—

Even Alysse had admitted that a *hisaf's* crossing did not widen the breach in the wall.

Dirt choking my mouth—

The breach in the wall, the pulled threads in the web . . .

Worms in my eyes—

Then I stood in the Country of the Dead, and a figure raced towards me from fog. Not my sister, not a *hisaf*, a dumpy figure whose face contorted with fear and indignation—

Stephanie's nurse.

She barrelled into me at full tilt, nearly knocking me over, even as I struggled to understand what must have happened. She was dead. She was not yet in the quiescent and mindless trance of the Dead. Therefore she had died only moments ago.

'Roger! Where am I?'

A word filled my mouth: Witchland. I could have told her that, and she would have perhaps believed me, as Blue soldiers had once believed me. Then the nurse might stay awake here and I would have more time, endless time, to question her. But I could not do that to her. She would be alone and living among the quiescent Dead. It was too terrible a fate, and although I had imposed it before, I had not known then what stalked the Country of the Dead. So I ignored the nurse's query and thrust at her, with the immediacy and sharpness of a sword, my own question.

'What happened to you? Tell me!'

'I . . . I was asleep . . . There came a young girl. I couldn't see her clearly but she was crowned, and her eyes – they were mad, they were!'

'What did she say to you?'

'I . . . I . . .'

'What did she say?'

'She said, "Die, die, my little one." It made no . . .' And then she understood. 'I am dead. Like Lady Margaret.'

'Nurse, no. Don't—'

Her body sagged against mine and her face went slack. I laid her on the grass. Then I tried shaking her hard –

it is old women, after all, who are most willing to talk to me, but the nurse was not old enough. I could not rouse her. And what more would I have asked? She had confirmed what I already suspected.

My sister killed in dreams. She could not use dreams to directly reach anyone in the land of the living except those with talent in the soul arts, and she had found such a person in Princess Stephanie. But how had my sister killed Lady Margaret and the nurse? Desperately I tried to account for this. A web, Mother Chilton and Alysse had both said, a web of being that connected the living and the dead. Power flowed along the filaments of the web, the immense power of death that must eventually claim us all. I pictured power flowing from my sister to Stephanie as the child lay asleep – sleep, the little death. Certainly it was during sleeping dreams that my mad sister reached me.

And somehow she had sent that power through Stephanie's sleep to the sleeping Lady Margaret. Both Lady Margaret and the nurse had been intimately entwined with the princess's life, with her thoughts, with the affections of her heart. There had been no marks of injury or illness on Lady Margaret's body. Her heart had simply stopped.

Stephanie was both the conduit for these murders and the reason for them. While Lady Margaret and her beloved nana lived, Stephanie could not be taken over by my sister. But now both women were dead. Web women could not reach the princess while she was so closely guarded. But my sister had had no such barriers. She had used the little girl in the most monstrous way, and Stephanie did not even realize it. I hoped she never would.

But what did my sister want from Stephanie in the first place? I didn't know. Mother Chilton had not given me any information about the princess, or else hadn't had any. Alysse had said that Stephanie would be better off shot, but she had also dismissed the child as unimportant. My father had not so much as mentioned her. That argued that none of them had known how my sister could reach others through the princess. Only I knew. And what could I do about it?

'Help Her Grace,' Lady Margaret had said.

I kicked at a boulder, a stupid display of anger that merely bruised my foot. Why did everyone expect of me things I could not deliver? Lady Margaret, Tom, Jee, Lord Robert. All people without soul arts, whereas those that had them urged me to not use them. How was I supposed to save even my own life? I was seventeen years old and at the mercy of events I could not control.

But at least I could bring something back to Tarek. Piss on Alysse's scolding and my father's advice; it had not helped him avoid capture! I walked a little way into the fog. Best would be a soldier with some old-fashioned item that Tarek would recognize but would know I could not possibly have already concealed on my person. I searched for a tranquil warrior.

Instead I saw an entire circle of the Dead disappear before my eyes.

The fog had lessened a little. Through light wisps I spied the circle, ten strong and holding hands, and I walked towards it. In the centre was a dense dark patch of fog: Soulvine watchers. Even as I lurched backward, ready to flee, the dense patch began to whirl. Its faint humming grew louder. Faster and louder the fog rotated, until it was a spinning vortex. Then came a large clap of sound, like lightning striking the ground, and the ten Dead disappeared, along with the vortex.

Gone. Just gone.

Despite myself, I stumbled forward. The pervasive fog

over the landscape had also disappeared. I could see again for miles, along the mountains and valleys of the Country of the Dead. But there was nothing to see where ten Dead had sat awaiting eternity. The grass was not even charred. It was as if nothing, and no one, had been here at all.

What had happened? How had the watchers from Soulvine taken the solid bodies of the Dead – and to where? Did the men and women in that circle even exist any longer? Or had their power been diverted to Soulvine Moor, to be used to help Soulviners live for ever?

A chink in the wall. Power flowing along a torn web.

My vision blurred with fear.

It was fear too that finally spurred me forward. I galloped to the nearest of the Dead who still existed, an old woman holding a fireplace bellows. I didn't question why she was holding a pair of bellows when she died; I just snatched the thing from her hand. If my theft was enough to rouse her, I didn't stay long enough to see it. The bellows had a carved wooden point. I jabbed it into my thigh and crossed back over.

Tarek again stood with one of his captains. '—is dead,' the captain was saying. *The nurse.* The captain's back was to me and I could see Tarek's face over the man's left shoulder.

The Young Chieftain's eyes, for the first time since I had known him, widened in fear. I sat up, aware of the pain in my thigh, the blood in my mouth from my bitten tongue. Aware, above all, of the fireplace bellows that Tarek must have seen all at once appear in my tranced hand, materializing from nowhere, conjured by the air.

So that was how it looked to an observer.

'Tarek?' The captain turned, puzzled, to see what had so startled his leader. All he saw was the *antek* unaccountably holding a fireplace bellows where there was no fireplace.

Strange but not fearful. Anyone might have stolen any-thing from the palace in The Queendom.

'*Klef,*' Tarek managed to say. The captain, still puzzled, saluted and left.

Tarek and I stared at each other.

'*Antek,*' Tarek finally said. And then, 'What shall I do about my queen?'

'Set her aside,' I said.

'No.'

'My lord—'

'You are the *antek,*' he said. The fear had disappeared. 'You will stop her dreams. You will do it now. *Klef.*'

A call to my guard outside, and I was hustled to the tent of the twice-bereaved princess.

44

This time Stephanie was not screaming. She was beyond that. Numb with terror, she crouched beside the body of the nurse like some small animal caught in a snare. Only when I pulled her onto my lap did she begin to tremble, but still she made no sound. Her silence was more terrible than shrieking would have been.

'What happened, Your Grace?' I said as gently as I could.

She did not answer.

'Your Grace, were you asleep?'

Nothing.

'Stephanie, tell me. Were you asleep when your nana died?'

A nod against my shoulder. Then the dam burst. 'I dreamed. The bad girl came . . . She *laughed* . . .'

'What did she say?'

Now she trembled so hard I could barely hold her.

'Did she say, "Die die die"? Did she, Stephanie?'

Another nod.

I called in Tarekish, 'Guard! Guard!'

My guard put his head into the tent, eyes carefully on the ground.

'Find a woman of her people to attend the queen. Some older slave—' there was no other word '—and bring her here now. Send two men to remove this dead woman.' Another funeral. Stephanie could not stand another. I would see to it that she did not attend. Tarek would listen to me – for the moment, anyway. I owed my moment to a fireplace bellows, and I must make good use of it.

The guard withdrew. I murmured wordlessly to Stephanie, trying to calm her. This did not succeed. Her trembling grew worse, and warm pungent liquid soaked my lap. Terror had loosened her bladder. She was a child, after all, who had grown up pampered in a palace, and what did I know of pampered children? Nothing.

It seemed hours before the soldier returned, although it must have been only a few minutes. With him was a middle-aged woman with the rough red hands of a laundress. However the guard had selected her, he had chosen well. She sized up the situation immediately, and I saw her push down her own fear to take Stephanie from me, keeping the child's face turned from the nurse's body.

'There, there, Your Grace, let's just get ye out of that wet gown—'

'Roger!' Stephanie screamed.

'I'm right here, Your Grace. Go with the ... the nana, and I'll stay here.' With relief I handed over the princess.

'That ye won't, not while I change her gown,' the woman said, scandalized. 'Ye wait outside the tent until I call ye. There, Your Grace, it'll be all right. Susannah be here now ...'

Susannah did not seem afraid of me, nor even of the savage warriors who hauled away the nurse's body. I stood by my own guard outside the tent, my clothes soaked with the princess's piss, until Susannah called peremptorily, 'Ye maun come back in now. Ach, but ye smell! No, don't take her all wet like that. Your Grace, lie on your pallet and he'll sit beside ye and hold your hand. There, that's a good girl.'

Stephanie had calmed under Susannah's stern orders, but her eyes still held a frozen terror that caught at my heart. I sat beside her, murmuring nonsense, but the terror did not lessen. No one came. Finally Susannah said, 'She maun sleep, that be what she needs. I have a friend who can make a posset—'

'No! No sleep!'

It burst from me unbidden, words whose import I had not considered. How was a child going to go without sleep? But dreams were the conduit through which my sister reached her. If she—

'How be a child able to do without sleep?' Susannah demanded. 'Yer daft, ye are, witchman or no. A child maun sleep.'

'No,' Stephanie moaned. 'The bad girl . . .'

'She won't come while I am here,' I said, and immediately could have bitten my tongue. Again. I had no power to stop my sister from invading the princess's dreams. I had not even been able to entice her to invade mine.

But Stephanie believed me. For the first time some of the fear left her eyes. Not all, but some.

'Ye can't sleep here!' Susannah said, scandalized all over again. Evidently witchcraft did not scare her, but scandal did. 'A man sleeping in Her Grace's tent!'

'You're here to chaperone,' I pointed out.

'Makes no cheese ale,' she said, a country saying I had not heard in years. 'Ye go.'

'Roger stays,' Stephanie said, and for the first time I saw on her little face something of her commanding mother. The next second she was again a frightened little girl, but the tone had had its effect. Susannah shut up.

She moved around in the background, washing out the princess's soiled gown, making herself as much at home in her new duties as if born to them. I thought of Tom, capable of adapting to any place he found himself, tireless and fearless. Probably if Susannah had not been such a person, she would not have left The Queendom in the first place. Unless she had been taken by force, and then it must have been a truly epic battle.

Stephanie fought sleep. Her eyelids half closed, then flew open. Again, and yet again. But finally she slept.

I could have wakened her. But then what? Eventually she would have to sleep. The best I could do was sit beside her and stay awake myself, ready to shake her if her face or body indicated agitated dreams. But then even that possibility was taken from me, and not by the muttering Susannah.

'*Klef*,' my guard said from the tent door.

'Go away, ye barbarian!' Susannah snapped.

He did not go away. When I did not *klef*, he and another soldier invaded the tent and dragged me from it. 'Do not let her dream!' I said desperately to Susannah, who looked at me as if I had taken leave of my wits. 'It is vitally important. Wake the princess if she starts to dream. Stay awake yourself and—'

'*Klef!*' I was dragged out.

Susannah did not understand, no more than Tom did. She would sleep and would let Stephanie sleep, and my sister would breach Stephanie's dreams as Soulviners were breaching the Country of the Dead. And then what? I did not know. But it could not be good. Not for Stephanie, not for any of us.

The savages dumped me by my fire. It was very late and only embers were left. Tom slept, but Jee was absent. My guard squatted beside me. In the night darkness I could not see his face, but the jerkiness of his movements told me how uneasy he was.

No more uneasy than I.

The stars shone high and cold between patches of clouds. I stared at the familiar constellations as they appeared, the Bow and the Ox and the Weeping Woman, and I waited. For what, I did not know. But it would happen, whatever it was. An entire circle of the Dead had disappeared before my eyes. Two women had been killed by power obscenely diverted through an innocent child. In that other realm my sister walked, mad and murderous. *Hisafs* and web women performed acts I did not understand in places I could not go. Something would happen, brought about by one of them.

But instead it was Jee, a dirty and lovesick ten-year-old, who brought everything to the point where there could be no turning back.

45

'Peter,' Tom said, shaking me. 'Wake up!'

I jerked upright, expecting to see savage soldiers, *guns* pointed at me, carnage or riot. Instead there was just Tom, silhouetted against a paling eastern sky. Beside last night's fire my night guard sat cross-legged, watching us. The army had not yet been roused for the day's march.

'What is it?'

'Alysse is nowhere in camp.'

'You woke me to tell me that? What do you expect me to do?' When I had finally slept, my sleep had been deep and dreamless, the profound sleep of complete exhaustion. I wanted more of it.

'You don't understand,' Tom said. 'Alysse is nowhere at all. I sent Jee to look for her, and he did. The savages have hurt her or killed her. I know it! She couldn't have left camp all by herself!'

Yes, she could. But I couldn't tell Tom that, not about the rabbit hopping away into night shadows, or about the hawk that had dropped a stone down my chimney in Applebridge. So instead I said lamely, 'Jee looked everywhere?'

'Yes! He told me so.'

'Where is Jee now?'

Tom looked around distractedly, as if just noticing that Jee was again gone. The worry for Alysse was real, I knew, but temporary. Just so had he grieved for Fia – for a week. Then he had worked out in his fickle mind that she was not worth the grief because she had left him, and so he had gone on to Alysse. So would it be this time. Soon there would be a Sarah or a Madge or a Jane, and he would never mention Alysse again.

At least, that's how it would be if I could keep us both alive.

Tom said, 'I don't know where Jee is. That boy comes and goes, comes and goes, he don't never ... but Alysse, a defenceless girl! These piss-pot savages ...' He clenched his huge fists and stared at my guard, who ignored him.

'If she weren't so pretty,' Tom went on, 'but she is! Peter, you ain't seen this of course, but she has the most amazing—'

I followed his gaze. The guard jumped to attention. My spine turned cold.

Gliding towards us through the sleeping camp, ghostly in the pale light just before dawn, was a procession. Even at a distance I recognized the Young Chieftain from his walk, a gait of utter confidence and purpose. But Tarek never came to this part of the camp, and in the morning he led his triumphant army on their march in the opposite direction, toward home. Behind him walked two of his captains, and behind them three soldiers with full arms and shields. The six men moved in silence among the sleeping savages and the less orderly palace encampment, heading for me.

'What the ... By damn—'

'Be quiet, Tom. I mean it. Say nothing. You are my servant.'

The savages reached our fire. Tarek did not slow his pace but kept on walking. One of the captains snapped an order to my guard, who hauled me to my feet and into the procession as neatly as a hawk that grabs prey in its talons without breaking flight. Tom, already standing, scrambled alongside me.

'Tom, no.'

'I'm your *nel*, remember? This looks serious.'

Looks serious. Tom, not ordinarily given to under-statement, saying this looked serious. Laughter rose in my throat, the insane laughter of hysterical fear. I pushed it down. Whatever was happening here, in this eerie dawn silence, I would need my wits about me. Even for dying.

The nine of us walked through the camp to the prin-cess's tent. Away from the fire, the cold pierced me; sometime during the night, winter had set in. Tom kept up, despite the rope between his ankles, by employing a peculiar half-hop, half-step. The savages did not try to stop him. To the pearl of the eastern sky were added sudden streaks of pink. Somewhere to my left a soldier stirred and drew a sharp breath as we passed. In the woods beyond, an owl hooted.

Three guards lay peacefully on the ground before Ste-phanie's tent. More than peacefully – their limbs sprawled with total abandon, and all three snored loudly. Six upright guards surrounded the pole-and-animal-hide structure, *guns* at the ready. Then I saw Susannah, royal nurse of less than half a day, gagged and bound to a sapling twenty feet beyond the tent. At the sight of me she struggled against her bonds and tried to cry out, but no sound came.

Tarek did not break stride as he pushed aside the tent flap and went in, trailed by his captains. The three soldiers remained outside. I followed Tarek, Tom stumbled after me, and no one stopped either of us. So Tarek *wanted* Tom here. Why? What would we find inside that could—

We found Jee.

He stood defiantly in the middle of the tent, which was warm from the fire pit, his cloak discarded in a corner. He held Princess Stephanie's hand. Jee's eyes were wet, but at the sight of me the tears vanished, replaced by anger.

'You did naught to help her! Naught! So I maun – I maun – make them let us go!'

'Jee.' I thought I had known fear before, but it was nothing compared to this. He had ... done what? My mind scrambled to keep up. Drugged the guards, yes. So Alysse had sent more than one honey cake and Jee had kept them. All along he had hoped to ...

'You rescued Maggie but not Her Grace!' Jee accused me. Stephanie started towards me, but Jee drew her back to him. She stood tethered by his hand, reaching towards mine, staring at Tarek in complete terror. Tarek, her husband.

The Young Chieftain said to me, 'Has the witch boy defiled her?'

I turned. His eyes were blue ice. 'Defiled? My lord, he is ten years old!'

'He is from Witchland. You told me so yourself.'

And so I had, in the effort to convince Tarek that I was an *antek*. I gasped out, 'He is but a child.'

Stephanie struggled free of Jee's hand and ran to me. Tarek said to her, in our language, 'Stop.'

She stopped as if shot, halfway between me and Jee. Jee stepped towards her and again took her hand. I don't think she even realized he had done it, paralysed with fear as she was.

Then Tom – fearless, bumbling, ignorant Tom – let out a great bellow, lurched forward and swept both children into his arms. Jee and Stephanie had no more hope of stopping that great sweep of huge arms than of stopping an avalanche. What scared me was that neither Tarek nor his captains stopped Tom either. The three savages stood in the doorway, and I with them.

'You piss-pot bastards!' Tom brayed. 'Making war on children! I'd like to—'

'Be quiet, Tom! Now!' I turned to face Tarek, my back to the other three.

His brilliant blue eyes glittered with anger, but he had not yet given orders to his men. In that delay I saw our only chance. I began to talk, very fast and low, frantically groping in that guttural language so unsuited to words of leniency or compassion.

'He – the boy – he is a child, he did not touch her – I can make him go away – there will be no attack.' Why did Tarekish contain no word for 'trouble' other than 'attack'! 'It is finished – I will send the boy away – the princess – I mean the queen, she is your queen – does nothing and is not disciplined – it is finished now.'

'It is finished,' Tarek repeated meditatively, gazing at me.

Behind him one of the captains spoke. I did not understand everything, but I caught 'witch child', 'danger' and 'attack'. More, I caught the captain's expression, which transcended language. A universal expression, the same everywhere on a certain kind of person with power. *End the trouble by ending the troublemakers.*

Tarek was of a different mould. He listened as I raced on, and his eyes studied the children in Tom's arms. I could not see them behind me, and all three stayed silent, but I knew what Tarek saw. An indignant giant bound at the ankles, a trembling six-year-old girl, a defiant urchin who might be a witch child but who was also only a deluded little barbarian imagining himself in love with a queen. Three such as it would shame a great warrior to consider worthy enemies. I babbled, and I saw the blue eyes make his decision, and the captain behind Tarek said no more, somehow knowing he had already lost.

'Bring back the queen's woman,' Tarek snapped, and one of the captains immediately disappeared to fetch Susannah. And to me, 'Tell your *nel* to put down the— *Jai axteb!*'

I had never before heard an oath from Tarek. Stephanie screamed. Something snarled behind me, and then a grey shape hurtled past me towards the Young Chieftain, who went down. A shot shattered the dawn.

It had all happened so fast that I stood gaping, my mind trying to catch up. Tarek lay half in and half out of the tent, and atop him lay the body of a huge grey dog, its teeth still fastened in the Young Chieftain's arm. As soon as I saw that, time slowed, and each event, each thought, became separate and distinct in my mind, as each step becomes distinct to legs moving slowly in pain.

Soldiers rushed into the tent.

Stephanie went on screaming.

A soldier pulled the dog's carcass off Tarek. The dog that had materialized, in the savages' view, from nowhere.

My father saying to me that there was no danger in my crossing over, only in bringing something back.

The dog's teeth had torn flesh from Tarek's arm and blood gushed forth.

Alysse saying to me, 'We are those who strive to preserve life.'

Tarek struggled to rise.

The fireplace bellows I had brought back from the Country of the Dead, yes, but also my shaving knife, clothing, boots, even a chair – things that had crossed with me time after time.

Guns were raised and pointed at me and at the others behind me, the blue savage eyes above each weapon filled with fear and hate. All the repressed vengeance these men felt for me erupted now that my witchcraft had harmed another of their leaders.

Tarek rose his feet, his face rigid with the effort to deny pain, his lips parting to give an order.

My shaving knife, my boots, a chair, the bellows ...

Alysse: 'Bringing anything back from the Country of the Dead disturbs the natural order of the sacred landscape.'

The wall between the living and the dead eroding ... the threads of the web pulled and destroyed ...

Preserve life, preserve life ...

'Fire,' the Young Chieftain gasped.

But I had already turned, thrown my arms around Tom with his burden, bitten down hard on my tongue and willed.

Nobody had ever said anything to me about taking things *into* the Country of the Dead. With Tom, Jee and Stephanie in my arms, I crossed over.

46

Darkness—

Cold—

Dirt choking my mouth—

But not only mine. It was as it had been when I brought back Bat, brought back Cecilia, brought back the Blue army, and I was faintly surprised that it should feel no different travelling the other way. Beside me, Tom and Jee and the princess were prisoners of the dirt, were crawling with the worms, and though their fleshless bones could no more move than could mine, I somehow felt them and their tongueless screams. It went on for a long time, and yet even longer. Then we were through and tumbling onto the ground in the Country of the Dead.

With a great roar Tom tore away from me, dropping Jee. Stephanie still clung to Tom, her face buried in his neck. I staggered on the featureless grass, amazed at what I had done – and then uncertain of what I had done.

My own body was back in the land of the living, as always. But had I really brought these three bodily through the grave, or were their bodies dead on the other side, so that any moment now they would lapse into the mindless tranquillity of the Dead?

'Where did everybody go?' Tom bellowed. 'What did those piss pots do? By damn, there's the mountain shaped like an anvil, just like we didn't move, but where the swigging dung is the *tent*? Where is the *army*? Where are *we*?'

319

I had never seen anyone less tranquil.

The landscape looked closer to its usual state than at any time since the fogs had begun to form. When I had crossed over before, I had seen a patch of humming, dense darkness and a circle of ten Dead whirling into a spinning vortex until they were funnelled into pure power for Soulvine Moor. Afterwards, the Country of the Dead had resumed its former calm, and so it appeared now. We stood on the same western mountain slope as in the land of the living, with the same meadow and trees and rock faces and river valley below, but all else was gone. No tents. No fires. No Young Chieftain and his captains and savages. No *guns* raised at us. Merely a few random Dead, sitting serenely where once they had died.

And the three with me did not lapse into the quiescence of the Dead.

From Tom's shoulder, Stephanie spied her nurse. She let out a scream and wriggled so hard that she escaped Tom. The princess ran to her nana, and it was Jee who ran with her. Jee, who knew what I was and where we were, as the others did not.

'My lady, my lady . . .' I heard him croon, but whatever else he said to Stephanie was masked by Tom's bellow.

'Peter! Where did everything go? By damn, I thought we were dead! Those *guns*—'

The dead nurse registered on his mind. He stopped, frowned, looked helplessly at me. 'Peter . . .'

'Tom,' I said, 'sit down.' For he had begun to tremble, this reckless giant whom I had never seen tremble before.

He remained standing. 'Peter,' he said, and now his voice dropped to a whisper, 'the nurse died. Are we . . . are we all dead?'

'She is; you are not,' I said. 'Tom, sit.'

He did, cross-legged on the grass, and all at once I was reminded of the Young Chieftain during my instruction. Just so had Tarek dropped to sit when I brought back the bellows. What would Tarek now do to my body in the land of the living? Kill it, of course. *Fire.* And yet, if I were already dead there, why had *I* not lapsed into the mindless tranquillity of the Dead? Nothing made sense.

But it made even less sense to Tom, who repeated desperately what I had said to him, 'The nurse is dead but we are not?'

I sat beside him. 'No. But this is the Country of the Dead. I brought you here.'

'You ... brought me here?'

Tom's face creased into valleys and ravines more complex than the mountainscape around us. Jee still murmured to Stephanie, who at least remained quiet, clinging to her dead nurse.

'Tom, listen. I am a *hisaf.* You told me once that the old folk of Almsbury talked of the Country of the Dead, and those who could cross over to it. Those stories are true, and I am such a one. That was what Tarek wished me to teach him. I once brought back an army that attacked and killed his father and—'

'That old story is *true*?'

'Yes.'

'That was you?'

'Yes.'

'You? Truly?'

'Yes.'

'That was *you*? Peter Forest?'

'Roger Kilbourne,' I said.

'But you really—'

'*Yes.* Tom, we don't have time for this.' Which was a stupid statement because now all we had was time. An

321

eternity of time, if we were fortunate. If not . . .

Tom sat quietly, only his face wrinkling as his brain struggled to take in a situation that he could not have imagined, that until this moment he had not believed possible. But the brain of Tom Jenkins was an omnivorous creature. It could digest anything, although nothing then stayed within it for very long. Eventually his face stopped working itself into whole landscapes, and he jumped to his feet. 'Well then, we should get going!'

I looked up at him. 'Going? Where?'

'Why, to The Queendom of course! We escaped!' Suddenly he laughed, a great ringing noise that echoed off a nearby cliffside. Never before in the Country of the Dead had I heard anyone laugh, except for my mad sister, and her laugh— What would happen if she found us here? What if she found Stephanie, whose wild talent my sister had already used to kill two people?

Tom said, 'Yes, we escaped Lord Tarek! The bastard must be wondering what happened, us just disappearing like that before his very eyes! Winked out like a candle! By damn but you're clever, Pe— Roger Kilbourne. I'll call you that now – you've earned it, haven't you? A *hinaf*!'

'*Hisaf*.' I corrected, inanely.

'Whatever you like, you clever lad. All right, we should get started. Where is— Oh good. Jee has got Her Grace in hand. We can take the princess back to The Queendom now, and then you can just wink her back inside her palace, and I daresay we'll all three be heroes. Ten to one odds. The palace girls will love us!'

'Tom, wait.'

'What? I don't see no problem here, Roger. Not as long as you can keep doing that crossing-over trick. You can, can't you?'

322

Could I? I did not even know if I were alive or dead back there in Tarek's country. Although if I were dead, wouldn't I have already lapsed into mindless tranquillity? Slowly I said to Tom, 'That will not work. If I cross back over, it will be to return to where my body is, which is at the savage camp, or wherever Tarek takes me. My body is in a sort of trance back in the land of the living, and I cannot leave it more than a few days without food or water. Also—'

He frowned. 'Is my body there too? And the princess's? And Jee's?'

'No. I brought you here bodily.' *Like a shaving knife, a chair, a pair of boots*. There was no other way that someone not a *hisaf* could cross that barrier.

'Can you bring us back home?'

'Yes.' Surely bringing back someone who was not dead, surely that would not cause the same havoc as bringing back someone who belonged in the Country of the Dead? 'But then I would bring you back to wherever *my* body is when I crossed over.'

'You mean, with Tarek?'

'Yes.'

He chewed on that for a while, then burst out with, 'Well, from where I sit, you ain't thought this through very carefully.'

'I didn't think it through at all! The savages were going to shoot us all, so I just acted.'

'George would have arranged things better.'

'I'm sure,' I said wearily.

'So what do we do now?'

Jee said, 'We maun not travel to The Queendom on the other side.'

He had appeared at my side without my hearing him, and Stephanie with him. The princess's eyes were wild still, but she held tightly to Jee's hand, her shoulder pressed against his. Apparently whatever he had said had made him her protector. Silent Jee! But, at that, he would probably be a better care-taker for the little girl than I had been so far. He could hardly be worse.

Tom said irritably – he didn't like being outguessed by a boy – 'Why "maun" we not travel in The Queendom, Jee?'

'We not be *in* The Queendom. We be in the mountains. And with the living it soon be winter. We have but two cloaks and I have Maggie's two knives. We have no money. Not enow.'

Jee was right. If we travelled, it must be here. And yet, if I brought them back over the Western Mountains while in the Country of the Dead, back to where The Queendom's border began in the land of the living, what help would that be to us? The moment I crossed back over, we would all be once again wherever my body had remained. Assuming my body was still alive.

Tom argued, 'But if we travelled in the real country, we could at least find something to eat. What can we eat here? I don't see nothing.'

He was right. There was nothing edible in the Country of the Dead, where none ever ate.

Tom looked at me. 'Pe— Roger, what do we do?'

'Let me think!'

The three of them stared at me, which was not conducive to thinking. But there was only one course open to me anyway. I stood.

'We are going to walk one day's journey towards The Queendom. That is the first step. Tom, can you carry Her Grace if needed?'

'Of course. But then what will—'

'We are going to walk one day's worth towards The Queendom.' I tried to make it sound as authoritative as

I could. Finally Tom nodded. Despite wishing I were George, Tom trusted me.

I wish I trusted myself.

Jee cut the rope between Tom's ankles and we set out, Stephanie between Jee and me. She clutched both of our hands. Silently, timidly at first, three living people and a *hisaf* walked through the Country of the Dead.

Only light patches of fog veiled the landscape. The sky, low and featureless and grey, gave off its even pale light. Neither trees nor grass, the latter dotted with bushes or with clumps of pale wildflowers, stirred in the breeze. There was no breeze. To the east loomed the mountains that Tarek's army, in the land of the living, had just traversed; to the west somewhere lay the valley of his kingdom. And all around us sat or lay the Dead. There were not very many of them, this high in the mountains, where not many had lived, let alone died. But there were enough. A hunter. Two soldiers. An entire family that had perhaps lived here over time, their deaths separated by decades but occurring in the same dwelling, so that they all ended up together. Stephanie peered at a child lying tranquilly on the grass and gazing at the sky, and her hand tightened in mine.

Tom began to sing.

I almost snapped at him, but I stopped myself. I had seen the Dead, walked among them, my entire life. Tom had not. His face was ashen, with drops of sweat on his forehead and upper lip. He could do nothing about the eerie stillness of the Dead, but he could at least shatter the eerie silence. 'Oh, a lady came a-riding,' he sang, quavering on the high notes, 'all of a summer morning . . .'

And so we walked, threading our way through the

Dead, to the sounds of a lady come a-riding, a hunter come a-courting, a soldier come a-drinking, a girl come a-dancing, while the air hung quiet around us and no night fell.

47

Land stretches or shrinks in the Country of the Dead, according to need. Where many have died, a mile in the land of the living can become ten on the other side. A pond may become a vast lake, a stand of trees a huge forest. Conversely, if few have died on mountain, in desert or wild ravine, ten miles may become one. But never less than one, and even if this way back to The Queendom was shorter than the way Tarek had brought his army and his captives, it was still a great distance. After a few hours Stephanie and Jee, both with little sleep the night before, were exhausted.

'We will stop here and make camp,' I said.

Tom nodded. This was something he understood. He gathered wood, took out his flint and steel, began a fire. There was no need for a fire: there was neither cold nor darkness nor wild animals, and we had nothing to cook. Our two cloaks of savage fur were too warm to wear. But Tom needed a fire. He built a roaring blaze and settled the children to sleep beside it. I heard Jee's stomach growl, but both he and Stephanie fell asleep too quickly to protest the lack of food. Not so Tom.

'Roger—'

'You have first watch, Tom,' I said. 'Have you your knives?'

'Yes.' He flashed them at me. 'What beasts are here? Any like . . . like Shadow and Shep? Hey! If they be like our dogs, maybe we can find one to hunt for us and—'

'I don't know. I need to piss, Tom. Do not leave the children.'

'No, I will not, but Roger—'

'In a minute.' I was gone before he could question me further. Tom would not follow, not without Jee and Stephanie. I had time.

When I was out of his sight, I lay on the ground beneath the low branches of a mountain pine and drove a sharp stone into my thigh.

My promise to Alysse was already broken, and I must know what my situation was. If Tarek had kept me alive and captive, I would return to my body and then could immediately bite my tongue and cross back to the Country of the Dead. The savages might not even realize I had briefly been present. If, on the other hand, I was already dead but somehow not quiescent, I would not be able to cross over at all. I could not imagine what I would do then, but at least I would *know*. Was I alive back in those savage mountains, or was I dead?

The answer turned out to be neither.

Darkness—

Cold—

Dirt choking my mouth—

Worms in my eyes—

Earth imprisoning my fleshless arms and legs—

And then I lay beneath the same low branches of a mountain pine, but bright light blazed between the green needles. An astonished squirrel, squatting in the shade, squawked at my sudden appearance and skittered up the tree trunk. A moment later a nut was thrown down at my head.

I was back in the land of the living but not with Tarek's army.

My head whirled. This had never happened before. Not just my essence, but my body, whole, had moved through the grave. Nothing of me had remained in Tarek's camp – I had 'winked away', as Tom would have said. How could I have moved bodily to the country of the Dead, when always before my body had remained behind?

Slowly I understood, and the understanding chilled my heart. This was due to the breach that Soulvine Moor had created in what should have the impenetrable wall of the grave. As a result of that breach, *hisafs* could now truly move between the realms on either side of the grave, could even travel in one to appear suddenly and unanticipated in the other. It was terrifying proof of just how far Soulvine had come in its quest to break down the wall between the living and the dead.

So I was safe from Tarek, but dread of the future filled me. However, there was no time for dread. Almost immediately I began to shiver. The brightness beyond the pine branches was sunlight on a light fall of snow. Crawling out from beneath the tree, I pulled my fur cloak tighter around me, blinked several times and tried to think what to do next. I could cross back over immediately and so escape the winter that Jee had so pragmatically mentioned, but that would not solve the problem of feeding us.

Running warmed me. Few savages lived in these high mountains, but on the other side we had passed one large group of Dead a mile or so back. They had been dressed in different styles of rough clothing, some for winter and some for summer, which suggested that a mountain family had lived and died on that spot for a long time. Perhaps they lived there still. Perhaps I could steal food from field or orchard.

Harvest was well over. The farmhouse stood, but the small field and stunted orchard were bare. However, a herd of goats foraged on the hillside above the farmhouse, watched by two boys of nine or ten. The goats pulled at the tough-stemmed plants poking above the light snow. I hid at the edge of the woods and eyed the boys. Did they have *guns*? Could I get close enough to steal a goat?

It turned out to be surprisingly easy. I ran out of the woods and towards one of the goats. The boys shouted something. Surprise raised their downy eyebrows, widened their blue eyes. They rushed towards me, knives drawn, fierce scowls replacing the looks of surprise. They were boys, but they were Tarek's people, and I, with but one hand, must not have appeared too threatening. Still, I seized the neck fur of a startled kid, bit my tongue, and goat and I vanished from the boys' sight.

Almost, I enjoyed it.

When I emerged from the woods, Tom was pacing up and down, frowning. 'A long piss . . .' He spied the goat.

'Can you butcher a goat, Tom?'

He nodded, speechless. But Tom Jenkins was never speechless long. 'By damn, where did you find *that*? I saw no animals all day, not so much as a puny bird. She's a beauty, ain't she? I'm so hungry I could eat a—' He stopped cold.

'What is it?' I said.

Tom whispered, 'Is that goat . . . is it a Dead? Can we eat a Dead? Roger, what if doing that—'

'It's not a Dead. I crossed over and stole it from a savage farm on the other side. It's alive until you kill it, Tom.'

His face cleared. He seized the kid, which bleated piteously but without effect. I turned away to be sure that Stephanie still slept. Jee was a hunter, but it was a fair bet that the princess had never seen her dinner slaughtered or skinned. Stephanie slept on, until the smell of roasting meat woke them both.

I could do this. I could feed us by crossing back and forth. We could walk to The Queendom over these quiet mountains where weather did not exist, and I could bring them all back over, safe, to the land of the living.

I could do this. Unless we encountered the other life in this place.

Once before I had travelled with another person through the Country of the Dead. I had led Cecilia back from Soulvine Moor, through the Unclaimed Lands, to the edge of The Queendom. But that time I lived in both realms, and I had to travel in the land of the living by day, with Maggie, and in the Country of the Dead at night, with Cecilia. And Cecilia had been docile and unresponsive. Dead. Only the landscape had been alive, churning with storms and wind and quakes of the ground.

Now the countryside lay quiet, the fog still and light, the Dead quiescent. There was no sign of other *hisafs*, nor of my sister. Perversely, this very absence began to trouble me. Did they not know we were here? Could I really be that fortunate?

Yet it did not seem fortunate to be here. It seemed eerie, as it never had before, not even in the most wild of the landscape's previous disturbances. I had come here most of my life, in anger or despair or hope or refuge, but I had never come here bodily, knowing that I had left no physical self in the land of the living. And I had never come here accompanied by others to whom all this was not only eerie but unimaginable.

'So that . . . man is really dead,' Tom said as we walked towards the mountain pass to the east. It looked much closer here than it had on the other side. I hoped that was true. The Dead that Tom pointed to was a hunter, dressed in many shaggy furs, more fur bound around his feet, a primitive spear by his side. He must have died in winter. Jee and Stephanie walked ahead, where I could see them. The princess kept her hand tightly in Jee's. She had entirely stopped talking, not a single word, but she kept walking.

'Yes, ' I said to Tom, 'he's dead.'

'And he's just been sitting there since he died.'

'Yes.'

'And when we come to the place where Lady Margaret died – it's right over that hill, you know – we'll see her, just sitting there.'

I had not thought of this. It would be better for Stephanie to not see Lady Margaret. 'We will skirt around the other side of the hill, I think.'

'All right. Yes. Just as you say. Peter – Roger, I mean – I don't like this.'

I said gently, 'They are dead, Tom. They cannot harm you.'

'I ain't *afraid* of them,' he said earnestly. 'It's just that . . . well, you know, they're *dead*.'

'Yes.'

'And we're not. You are going to take us all back, ain't you? Once we reach The Queendom?'

'Of course I am.'

'You're completely sure, ain't you, that you can do that?'

'I'm sure.' *Please let it happen that way.*

'All right.' He lapsed into troubled silence. But the next time we passed one of the Dead, another hunter although from a much later time, Tom took the bow clutched in the dead man's hand and the two arrows remaining in the quiver on his back. Tom stared at me defiantly as he stole them, but I said nothing. Weapons could harm nothing in this place except the four of us; I had learned that years ago when the Blue army had been awake beyond the grave. And I could not let Tom bring the weapons back across with us. About that too I had learned

332

my lesson well. But I told him none of this now. Let him take what comfort he could from carrying the bow and arrow while we walked. He was much more uneasy than Jee, who possessed astonishing powers of acceptance. Or maybe it was merely that Jee had grown up near Soulvine Moor and was thus aware of the true strangeness of the world, whereas Tom had grown up in Almsbury, never thinking about it. And now he must. So let Tom Jenkins have what comfort he could find in his stolen weapons.

Another thought came to me. If I, a *hisaf*, could now slip bodily between the land of the living and the Country of the Dead, then surely other *hisafs* could do the same. All of us, including my father. If it was true that he had been imprisoned in that place called Galtryf, and if he chanced to discover this new ability, then Galtryf could hold him no longer. He might come to rescue me after all. But for my entire life my father had arrived too late to aid me. This was but one more such occasion. My bitterness towards him did not abate.

More walking, more Dead. Tom took a shield from a lone savage soldier, carrying it gingerly, as if it were a snake that might at any moment turn and bite him. But he kept the shield nonetheless.

48

When Stephanie could no longer walk, Tom carried her. The Country of the Dead has neither day nor night, but living bodies do. At 'evening' we made camp on the top of a small rise. Again Tom insisted on a fire. We cooked more of the goat meat. While the children slept, I studied the country to the east. The pass was indeed much closer than on the other side. We might reach it with one more day's walking, or perhaps a day and a half.

Tom wanted to talk. He sat hunched over the fire, shifting restlessly on his great haunches until he burst out, 'What's the good of being dead then?'

'What?' I was trying to figure out how long the goat would last, and if I should cross back over and try for more food. Tom ate prodigiously, fuelling his great bulk.

'I said, what's the good of being dead? If all you do is sit around for ever like some rock?'

I suddenly thought of the something bright and terrible – the sword, Alysse had called it – that had burst from the sky as I brought back the Blue army. But I did not know what it was, or what it meant for the Dead. I knew only that the memory terrified me.

'For that matter,' Tom went on, and now his voice held anger and despair, 'what's the good of being alive, if this is where you end up? You and me and George and everybody, just lumps sitting around in this awful place? Tell me that, Roger!'

'Tell you what?'

'What good is it? Death, or even life? Why bother?'

'Tom,' I said softly, 'have you never considered such thoughts before?'

'Of course not! Usual people don't think about such things. They think about hunting and farming and their dinners and bedding women and ... and usual things. But then this is where it all ends up. Here!'

I had always thought about death, had always known death. But then I had always known I was not usual. I was a *hisaf*.

Tom said, 'I wish you hadn't brought me here.'

'But then Tarek would have killed you, and you'd have ended up here anyway.'

Tom groaned, and I saw that his distress was real, and deep: the anguish of a man who truly never thought beyond the next dinner or the next girl, and now was being forced to do so. I owed Tom my life; I must do better by him.

'Tom, this is not all there is. Not here, I mean. And in the land of the living, there is much more. There is ...'

Maggie.

She burst into memory so vividly that it was as if she, not Tom Jenkins, sat beside me. Almost I could see her, touch her, smell the clean sweet scent of her fair curls. Maggie, who had stood by me and loved me and now carried my child. Maggie, whom – now, in this desolate place, talking of Tom's desolation – all at once I realized that I truly loved.

'There is *what*?' Tom demanded. But I was too shaken to answer right away. So this was love. Not the dizzying longing I had felt for Cecilia, the herb-induced desire for Fia, but this powerful sense of Maggie as the woman who should be beside me, whose life was entwined with mine, whom I wanted to not only hold but also to talk to and argue with and protect and be bullied by. Maggie.

'You have no answer,' Tom said. 'There *ain't* no more.

This is the end – sitting around like lumps, everything inside us gone. I'd rather not have been born.'

'No,' I finally managed to get out. I must give Tom some comfort, and it must be what he wanted, not what I had just discovered that I wanted. 'I don't think this is the end, Tom. Someone very wise once told me that the Dead are waiting.'

'Waiting for what?'

'I don't know. I wasn't told. But that there is more coming, eventually.'

'Who was the wise person who said so? George?'

'No. A witch.'

'Well, that's another by-damn thing,' he burst out. 'I never believed in witches before, and now here . . . and all these Dead . . . and you bringing us here . . .' He buried his head in his hands.

I tried once again. 'We will go home once we reach The Queendom, Tom. And you will have a long and rich life, with all kinds of girls. And when you do die someday, and come here, it will only be temporary. Like a . . . a . . .'

'Like an inn on a journey?'

'Just so.'

'Some inn!' He snorted and looked around in disgust, which the next moment brightened into hope. 'You mean that after this, there's another place?'

I would not lie to him. 'I don't know.'

'But you think so?'

'I don't know.'

'But it's possible?'

'Tom, anything is possible.' Too many things.

'Then, in that next place, there might be all the good things? Food and hunting and girls?'

I chose the safe answer. 'I don't know.'

'But do you think—'

'I don't know!'

'Well, don't *shout*.' He brooded for a long moment. 'I think I better ask George.'

'You do that,' I snapped, and at last he fell silent. I did not want to guide Tom Jenkins through a forest of thought that was more foreign to him than even the Country of the Dead. I wanted to sit and think of Maggie, feel the longing for Maggie that, like a slow-growing plant, had finally bloomed after years of putting forth stem, leaves, buds. Maggie, who had always been before me but whom I had never really *seen*. Maggie, my Maggie—

—whom I could not go home to, lest I lead my mad sister to my unborn son.

There must be some way around this. I had found ways around so much already. I had saved three living people by turning to the Dead. I had even transcended the usual boundaries of a *hisaf*, by crossing over bodily and not just in essence. Surely I could find some way to—

Stephanie screamed.

On that noiseless hilltop the scream shattered ears, echoed off unseen rock faces, seemed to pierce the very ground. Before I even knew I was moving, I had wrapped my arms around the little girl.

'Your Grace! What is it? What—'

Jee grabbed her hand. 'My lady, my lady, it was only a dream.'

Stephanie shook her head violently and the goat left her stomach and spewed down my tunic.

The vomiting actually seemed to calm her, and for a ridiculous moment I hoped she merely had indigestion. But then she choked out, 'The ... bad girl ...'

A dream after all, and of my sister. 'Tell me, Your Grace.'

She tried to obey, failed, tried again. In her own childish

337

way, she was not without courage. 'The bad ... girl ... she's very angry.'

'At ye?' Jee said indignantly.

Stephanie shook her head. I wished she would not do that, lest more vomit come up. But it did not. 'At ... Roger.'

'Why?' Jee said. 'What did the bad girl say? You can tell me, my lady.' He had not let go of her hand, her thin pale fingers tight in his stubby ones.

'She's angry at Roger for living. She wants him dead.'

Of course she did. She would want us all dead: Jee and Tom and me. We were the three who stood between her and control of Stephanie, we three who anchored the princess in enough reality so that Stephanie was only a passive tool, not an active ally. We kept the little girl sane, as Lady Margaret and Stephanie's nana once had done. Those two women, substitutes for the princess's dead mother, had anchored Stephanie. Now they were gone, and we three males performed the same function. But for how long?

Alysse had dismissed Stephanie as unimportant. It seemed that Alysse was wrong. My sister hunted her, in dreams if not in body. Why?

I said carefully, 'Your Grace, can you tell me exactly what the bad girl said?'

'She said, "Die, die, my little one, die." And she was talking to Roger. Only Roger was a baby.' Through the tears, the vomit, the fear, Stephanie's little face looked confused. As well she might. My sister's mad mind had mixed herself and our mother, herself and me, the infant who had been born in the land of the living and the one born wholly in the Country of the Dead. Finally I understood the source of my own terrible dream about my mother. It was not my own memory, but my sister's

338

distorted images. *'Linked by blood,'* Alysse had said of my sister and me.

Now I knew why my sister hunted Stephanie. She wanted to use Stephanie to kill me, as she had killed Lady Margaret and the nurse. Or, more likely, Soulvine Moor wanted to use my sister to use Stephanie.

'Stephanie,' I said, dispensing for the first time with her title, 'this is very important. Do you know where the bad girl is?'

She nodded. 'Far away.'

Far away. That explained why we had not been accosted in the Country of the Dead. My sister and her rogue *hisafs* must travel by walking through the landscape of the Dead, even as we must. None could subvert that, and for a brief moment I took comfort in the sheer physicality of both realms. My sister was far away.

But it was cold comfort. The princess was right beside me. And it was possible that this little girl, an unwitting conduit, could use a dream to force me to stop my own heart. Stephanie could dream me dead.

I got out, 'Do you know the name of the place where the bad girl is now?'

Again the princess nodded. 'Yes. Soulvine Moor.'

'Is she coming here?'

'I don't know.'

But I knew. Of course my sister was coming here, to claim Stephanie. And I must get my charges over the mountains as quickly as possible, so that I could return them to the land of the living before my sister or her henchmen reached us.

'Tom,' I said, 'douse the fire. We must go on walking.'

It was not easy travelling – uphill to the mountain pass, taking triple the time Tarek had needed to move his army in the opposite direction. The backs of my legs ached constantly. Exhaustion clouded my mind, which wanted only to think of Maggie and could not stay focused long enough to do so. It was worse for Tom, who carried Stephanie when she could no longer walk, which was often. Tom never complained, nor did Jee. And the princess, either infected with their courage or else drawing on her own, inherited from her formidable mother, bore quietly her own constant exhaustion.

We did not dare let her dream. So one of us must always be awake beside her, and when her sleeping eyelids began to flutter and her thin body twitch, we shook her awake before nightmares could invade her mind. 'Wake up, Your Grace,' I mumbled, often not sure that I myself was not trapped in a dream of endless weariness. 'There, there, my lady,' Jee crooned. And Tom: 'Come on now, little princess, look at Tom! Look at that pretty flower over there! Look at ... at Roger! Don't he look handsome?' Tom seemed to think that children needed constant cajoling, as if they were sheep that would not pen. I did not look handsome, and Stephanie's small pinched face squinted at Tom as if he were crazy. But she had escaped the dream.

Then more walking. More goat meat. Fewer Dead in these high remote reaches of the savage kingdom. Until we reached the mountain pass and for the first time began to descend.

'The meat be bad,' Jee announced, opening the pathetically small remaining packet of goat meat.

'Faugh! What a smell!' Tom said. 'Bury it, Jee. Roger, we need more food.'

The three of them gazed at me: Tom confident, Jee wary, Stephanie hopeful. She said, 'Can you bring some cake? Or apples?'

I tried to imagine stealing apples from a root cellar or

cake from a larder inside a farmhouse of savages. 'No, I don't think so, Your Grace.'

'Oh.' Her face fell.

'Take me with you,' Jee said. 'I will get them.'

Jee would have tried to steal anything that Stephanie wanted, from cake to jewels, but I was not going to take him. I still was not certain what would happen when I returned the three of them to the land of the living, and I was not going to do it more than once. Living people might be different from boots and shaving knives. And then what?

'Jee, you must stay here to guard the princess. Wait here now.'

'Where are you going, Roger?' Tom called as I walked away.

'Wait here,' I said over my shoulder. Why did I not want them to see me vanish as I crossed over? I told myself that I did not want to scare Stephanie, but that was not the truth. I did not know what the truth was. However, it led me a little way into a hillside grove, from where I could see a cluster of Dead in a little dell below. I lay on the ground and crossed over.

Cold—

Darkness—

Dirt—

And then a greater cold, and snow up to my knees. It was night, with a nearly full moon low on the icy horizon. Shivering, slipping, cursing, I made my way down the hillside towards a farmhouse that was little more than a hut, its shutters closed against the winter night. But there was a ramshackle chicken house beside the hut. Surely I could break into that and grab a chicken before savages erupted from the house to shoot me. Surely I could—

'Stop,' a voice said from the darkness.

I Almost screamed. A woman stood beside me, emerged

from the shadow of the chicken house, where no woman had stood before. She wore a smooth white cloak and carried a big bundle.

'Stop, Roger Kilbourne.'

'What . . . who . . . ?'

'What I am does not matter. What *you* are, does matter, and you are a traitor.'

'A—'

'A traitor, yes. What else do you call those who aid the enemy? You are no better than the faithless *hisafs* who use your sister.'

I moved closer, to peer at her face. She showed no shrinking, no fear. Under the hood of her white cloak, her face was neither young nor old, plain nor pretty, and her eyes were green. I said, 'You're one . . . another one of the women of that shadow web, those who use soul arts—'

'I am a witch. Why can you not use the word?' she said impatiently, and I recognized the tone. It was Mother Chilton's tone, Alysse's tone, even Fia's tone – all the web women who had scolded me for not doing as they instructed.

I said, deliberately avoiding the word *witch*, 'I am not a traitor. I merely need food for—'

'We know why you need food. Here.' She thrust the bundle into my arms, then leaned close to me. Her breath came frosty from between lips thinned with anger.

'You are a traitor, Roger Kilbourne, whether you know it or not. You were told to not cross over again and—'

'My father, a *hisaf*, said that I—'

'—yet you have not only done so, you have brought with you three from the land of the living. Do you suppose your father ever imagined you could do such a thing? That if he had ever imagined it, he would not have

342

warned you not to? You have even brought one with great and untaught talent, and now—'

'I tried to get Alysse to help me rescue the princess, and she said that the princess did not matter!'

'We did not know then all that Stephanie is, or how she might be used. But I am concerned with *you*, Roger Kilbourne. You were told how Soulvine Moor seeks to destroy the web that threads together the living and dead. You were *told*. Yet you have immeasurably damaged that web by your reckless actions. Three living brought into the Country of the Dead, three who are not *hisafs*, when just *one* born there has made possible such havoc! How can we make you understand what you have done?'

'The savages were going to shoot them,' I said, and despite myself it came out like a sulky boy, not a man rescuing his sovereign and his friends. Always the web women did this to me – reduced me to an erring child. They rescued me, seduced me, scolded me, reproved me. I was weary of it all.

'Yes, the savages were going to shoot them, and do you not think Stephanie would have been safer in the trance of the Dead than as your mad sister's tool to destroy both living and dead? You were told that once before. She would not be quiescent for ever, you know. Better she should be dead.'

Her callousness angered me. Or perhaps it was not callousness but, rather, an ability to look further ahead than I ever could. *She would not be quiescent for ever.* But Stephanie would have been so for a very long time, and she would have been deprived of her life here, in the realm of the living – a little girl, six years old. She might even have ended up in one of the circles of the Dead destroyed for ever by a whirling vortex from Soulvine Moor. I saw Stephanie's thin sweet face, eyes with their dark shadows of sleeplessness framed by lank brown hair, and everything in me recoiled from this web woman's pragmatic and far-seeing willingness to sacrifice the princess, and with her both Tom and Jee.

I said, carefully spacing each word, 'I ... would ... not ... let ... them ... be ... killed.'

'No, you would not. And as a result, Soulvine Moor has acquired more power from the damage you have done to the natural divide between life and death. *You must stop crossing over.* Do you even understand what your actions have enabled? It is partly because of you that *hisafs* can now cross bodily and not merely in essence. How you could take it upon yourself to—'

A shout from the shuttered hut. Sudden light spilling from an open door. The *crack* of a *gun*.

Immediately I bit my tongue and crossed over. But not before I saw a white deer, almost invisible against the snow, bound away from the chicken house and into the winter woods.

49

The web woman's bundle contained bread, cheese and dried cherries. Tom, Jee and Stephanie ate eagerly, too absorbed to even ask how I had obtained such riches, although Jee glanced at me sharply. Stephanie's lips turned red from cherries, a bit of colour in her pale face. Tom got crumbs in his beard.

But I, despite hunger, could swallow nothing. My belly churned, already full of doubts, questions, horrors real and envisioned. Was I really a traitor, aiding Soulvine Moor in its quest to rob the quiescent Dead of whatever should come next for them? Had I really made things worse in this war?

Things did not look worse in the Country of the Dead. They looked exactly the same: light patches of pale fog motionless over the ground, low even light, stillness and quiet and very few Dead in these high mountains. But more must be happening beyond my sight. How had the web woman known of those happenings – or indeed where I was in the Country of the Dead? Web women were not *hisafs*; they could not cross over. I did not understand what they could or could not do.

I did not understand anything.

'By damn, that tasted good,' Tom said with deep satisfaction. 'I'm ready now to walk ten miles, see if I'm not. And to carry you the whole way, Your Grace.'

'I will walk with Jee,' Stephanie said. The circles under her eyes were darker than ever, the tender flesh looking far too bruised for a child, but her cherry-stained lips smiled. The smile brought me no cheer.

I, Roger Kilbourne, aiding Soulvine Moor. And if – when – I brought three mortals back again to the land of the living, would I aid it still more?

Better she should have been shot.

No. Not better. No.

'Let us go,' Tom said. 'We must— What is that?'

One of the Dead walked towards us from the trees.

It was an old woman dressed in a gown so frayed and worn that patches of the skirt had weft but no warp. Her eyes were open but unseeing, and she walked in strange jerks, not with the tremors of the very old but rather as if some foreign power moved her unwilling legs. Her arms dangled loosely at her sides. Her face was serene.

Tom reached for the bow and arrow stolen from a savage soldier.

'No!' I said. 'She's not dangerous, she's—' What? Dead. She was supposed to be dead. The Dead did not behave like this. 'Stay here, all of you.'

They did not, of course. Jee remained with Stephanie but Tom followed me, even as I followed the dead woman. She lurched with that jerky gait across the hilltop and into the trees. There was no trail here. She stumbled in a straight line through undergrowth, across a shallow stream, under a stand of high pines. When she fell over, she righted herself. The falls did not tear her gown nor scratch her face.

After perhaps a half-mile she came to a group of Dead. They sat in a circle, seven strong. Before she could become the eighth, I grabbed her with my one good hand, turned her to face away from the circle, and shook her hard.

'Mistress! Mistress!'

Slowly her eyes focused, and behind me I heard Tom draw a sharp breath. He had not seen this before. But always it is old women who are most willing to talk to me.

'What want you, lad?' She spoke in Tarekish, and I switched to that guttural language.

'Where are you going?'

Puzzlement came into her watery blue eyes. She looked at me, at the countryside, at the featureless sky. 'I am dead.'

'Yes. Where are you going?'

'No place. Where would a dead person go? I am here.'

Tom demanded, 'What does she say?'

She turned towards his voice and saw the circle of the Dead. Her puzzlement deepened.

I asked, for the third time, 'Where are you going?' My belly tightened. If she could actually tell me . . .

But she could not. Old women of the savage mountains were no different from old women of The Queendom. If I had wanted her to talk of her childhood, she might have done so. But the Dead are not interested in talking about the present, not even their own present, not even enough to stay roused. The old woman's face lapsed back to tranquillity while her feet tried again to move towards the circle.

'Tom,' I said, 'tie her to that tree over there. Tightly enough that she cannot escape.'

'*Tie her?* A dead woman?'

'Yes. Tear a strip off the bottom of her gown if you've nothing else.'

'But why, Roger? She can't harm us!'

'She can harm herself.'

Tom planted himself firmly in front of me, the old woman between us. Her feet kept moving, although my one good hand easily restrained her frail body. Tom said, as he had once before, 'I do nothing more without answers, Roger. Tell me about this.'

I gazed at his troubled face. He meant it. He would obey no more orders without more information. Even though I doubted that he would accept my answers, or believe them, or be reassured by them.

'Soulvine Moor is waging a war with all the rest of us, Tom. With The Queendom and the Unclaimed Lands and Tarek's kingdom. That is the real war, not any rebellion against savage rule. The war is being fought both in the land of the living and the Country of the Dead. Soulvine Moor wants to break down the barrier between the two realms and channel the power of death into themselves, so they can live for ever.'

Tom's face flashed through several emotions and finally settled into pity.

'Roger,' he said gently, 'that don't make sense. How can death have power? Why, the woman's dead and just look at her! A limp rag that can't go nowhere.'

The old woman's feet kept moving, her bare toes brushing against my boots. I wanted to make her stop; I wanted to make Tom understand; I wanted to stop explaining what he could never understand. I was exhausted and irritated and afraid.

'That's the best I can tell you,' I snapped. 'Believe it or not, as you choose. But this war is why Stephanie is having nightmares and why Lady Margaret and the nurse were killed and why I could bring you and Jee and the princess across the grave to this place. You remember the grave, Tom? You remember crossing over? Make sense of *that*.'

He did remember. I saw it in his eyes – the darkness and worms and his fleshless arms and legs flailing helplessly – and I felt ashamed. I owed Tom as much as he owed me. But I could not give him explanations I did not have. I knew death had immense power – *something bright and terrible rending the sky* – but I did not understand how

Soulvine Moor was channelling that power. I was a *hisaf* and I crossed over, but to do something is not necessarily to understand how it is done.

Tom said, 'If this old woman sits in that circle over there, it aids . . . it aids Soulvine Moor?'

I nodded. This he could understand: us against them.

Tom took the woman from my grasp, produced a rope that must have been yet another of his thefts from the Dead, and tied her firmly to a stout oak. His broad face was very pale. Then he dragged two more Dead from the circle and tied them to trees.

'That's enough,' I said, not knowing if it was or not. 'The circles need at least ten to . . . to work. Save some rope.'

'I will,' Tom said grimly. Colour had returned to his face. He had a task to perform. Tasks always steadied him.

We walked back to Jee and Stephanie, neither of whom asked any questions. I don't know what Jee had told the princess. Then we resumed walking, Tom and Jee carrying the rest of the provisions on their backs. We saw no more circles this high in the mountains, but each time we came to a lone Dead, Tom solemnly tied him or her to a tree.

One, three, five Dead – out of all the centuries of those who had lived.

'George would be proud of you,' I said, to say something.

'Tell him when you see him,' Tom said, not looking at me. Nor did he smile. His words might have been sarcasm, or not. I could not tell. And I did not ask.

Stephanie dreamed.

We could not keep her dreamless for ever. The snatches of sleep she was allowed were not enough, not for anyone. She began to whimper and fuss. The skin

349

beneath her eyes looked so bruised that an observer, had there been one in the Country of the Dead, would have thought we beat her. Nor could Tom, Jee and I keep walking for a whole 'day' and then do without sleep as, each in turn, we watched over Stephanie to keep her from dreaming. Even Tom's great strength grew less, and we were only, as best I could judge, halfway down the eastern slope of the mountains. As we neared The Queendom, fog grew in the Country of the Dead – not yet thick, still just light wisps drifting across the landscape – but the fog too seemed to trouble Stephanie. She would stare at a drifting patch of grey mist and bury her head in Tom's shoulder or against my side.

She was stumbling along, holding my good hand, when we came upon another circle of the Dead, and Stephanie broke.

There were fifteen Dead, and they all held hands. For the last quarter-mile the fog had disappeared almost entirely, and now I saw why: it had all been concentrated in this circle. Fog obscured each of the fifteen heads. If I laid my hand on one of those heads, I knew, it would vibrate like a hive of bees. And in the centre of the circle was a dark dense patch of mist, slowly rotating.

Tom and Jee froze, staring in horror at a thing they had not yet seen. I had, and yet a shiver ran through my belly and spine. That dark rotating mist was made of watchers from Soulvine Moor, and if the mist did the same thing I had seen once before, those dead men and women would soon be—

'No!' Stephanie shrieked. 'Make it go away!'

'My lady, my lady,' crooned Jee, unfreezing and hanging over her, his small dirty face mirroring her distress.

'Look away, Your Grace, and we'll go on just like it ain't there!' Tom said, but his false cheer rang hollow to even a child. Futilely he tried to turn her face away from the circle.

'It's there!' Stephanie cried. 'It's there! I want to go home! I want my nana!'

And then a storm of tears, greater for having been so long held in. Tom's face went stony. 'Women's weapons,' he had once said of one of his bedmate's tears, Agnes or Joan or Betsy or Annie. Did he think that of the little princess, who was but six? But I was too weary to explore the corners of Tom Jenkins's brain; my only thought was to put distance between us and the circle. Tom would not be tying these Dead to any tree.

'Carry Stephanie, Tom,' I said. 'We must keep on.'

'I cannot,' he said.

Never before had I heard Tom say he could not do something.

'I must rest at least a little while,' he said. 'I ain't an ox, Roger. Though you think of me as such. Strong dumb Tom, who does your bidding.'

'I don't think of you that way,' I lied.

'It don't matter. But I must sleep, and I will. Over there.'

He started off around the side of a hill, out of sight of the circle of the Dead. I bit back a sharp retort. Weariness had made us all quarrelsome, but I could not afford a quarrel with Tom. We needed him too much. Biting back my own resentment – if he thought it hard to be a follower, let him try to lead this sorry band – I followed Tom, dragging the sobbing Stephanie.

All of us lay down. Immediately exhaustion took me. I said to Jee, 'Can you watch Her Grace, Jee?'

'Yes,' he said stoutly. And even though I saw that he too was tired, even though he was a child, I let him. I stretched out on the ground away from Tom, who even in sleep kept close the weapons he had stolen from the

351

Dead: two spears, the bow, a quiver of arrows fashioned by different hands, the shield, a *gun*. Plus one of his own two knives in his hand. Within moments I slept, the deep and empty sleep that, amazingly, had not once been troubled since we crossed over into the Country of the Dead.

And then Stephanie dreamed.

It was her shriek that woke me, but it was Jee who lay asleep – no, *not asleep*. I jumped up and ran to him. No breath stirred his lips.

'Jee!'

'She came!' Stephanie cried. 'The bad girl, she wants me to stay here.'

'Jee!'

I grabbed the slight body and shook it. Jee gave a single great gasp and then once again went limp. He was not yet dead but he would be soon, she was killing him.

I dropped Jee, raised my good hand and struck Stephanie a blow on the head.

She slumped to the ground before her small face could even show surprise. Tom yelled and the next moment I lay flat beside the princess, with Tom's knife at my throat. His eyes glittered with rage, with astonishment, with instinctive defence of his sovereign.

'Tom, *does Jee live*?'

Confusion replaced all else. 'Jee? You attacked the—'

'She was killing him! With her dream.' It was not Stephanie I meant, but even if Tom did not understand, he turned his head to look at Jee.

'Let me up!'

Tom did, but not for my sake. In a moment he was kneeling between the children. I squeezed my eyes shut tight, suddenly afraid of what my sister had done, of what I myself had done . . .

A great ragged gasp, and then a hoarse cry, as from a throat bruised and scarred. But Jee lived.

And Stephanie?

'She breathes,' Tom said grimly. 'But her senses have left her. You did it to stop her dream from killing Jee?'

'Like Lady Margaret. Like her nurse.' I could still feel Tom's knife, and I put my hand to my throat. It came away bloody. 'Tom, it was all I could do!'

'She's but a little girl!'

'It was all I could do.'

Jee still lay gasping. Only that could have kept him from the princess. I crawled to him and touched his shoulder. His dark eyes fastened on mine. Slowly colour came back into his face and his breathing grew more regular. Then he started to cry.

I gathered him into my arms. 'Hush, Jee. She could not help it. She meant you no harm; it was another working through her dreams. Hush now.'

He thrust me away, ashamed of having broken down in front of men. Anger was better than fear, so he became angry. 'What other?' he demanded. 'Ye be the witch. What other from Witchland kills by our princess?'

Tom, cradling the unconscious Stephanie, looked at me hard.

I said, 'She is the queen of . . . of the faithless ones. She lives here, in the Country of the Dead. And she is my half-sister.'

Silence.

The silence stretched on while Tom and Jee stared at me. And then another voice spoke into the stillness:

'That will do no good, Roger. Stephanie must revive sometime.'

I whipped around and there she stood, at the edge of a grove of pine trees, and with her a dark fog that raced towards us, obscuring that first sight of her slim figure and her shining crown. The dark mist obscured too the three men I had seen with her. In a moment that dark mist rising had reached us, and I could see nothing at all. But I could hear my sister's laugh, which pealed towards us from the fog, high and shrill and mad.

50

I groped in the fog, which was so thick that I lost all sense of direction. My good hand clutched air, but the stump of my wrist whacked painfully against something solid and hard: Tom. I cried, 'Do you have the princess?' But before he could answer – there was no time, when time had been all we had until a moment ago – I felt Jee's arms around my waist. Tom had been holding Stephanie's limp body; he must still be holding Stephanie—

I grabbed onto his bulk and bit my tongue, and we all crossed over. Perhaps my sister expected this, for she went on laughing, the last sound I heard before

Darkness—

Cold—

Dirt choking my mouth—

Worms in my eyes—

Earth imprisoning my fleshless arms and legs–

And we were through, standing knee high in snow, with brilliant sunlight piercing our eyes and an icy wind blowing the bare mountain trees.

Tom shouted something, his words borne away by the wind. Almost I expected to see my sister appear beside us. But she could never do that. She was marooned in the Country of the Dead and we were safe, I had done it, had brought Jee and Tom and Stephanie back over bodily.

Another figure materialized in the snow. Another. Then a third.

The three men who had been with my sister. *Hisafs*, holding knives. They stood less than ten yards from

355

where we huddled against the cutting wind. Tom dropped Stephanie onto Jee and sprang in front of me. His stolen weapons had been left in the Country of the Dead, along with our cloaks, but he had his own two knives at his belt. He hurled one at the closest man.

The *hisaf* vanished.

He had crossed over, of course. I saw Tom's expression through the white cloud of his breath as the knife buried itself in a bank of snow. The second *hisaf* stood, grinning at him, then at me. He shouted something I could not hear for the wind. Older than my father, he had a thick black beard, bald head, and eyes that—

Before Tom's second knife reached him, the *hisaf* vanished.

How long? How long to cross through the grave, take a breath, inflict minor pain on himself, then again traverse the crumbling barrier of cold and darkness and return to us to—

'Behind ye!' Jee shouted. He dropped to the ground on top of Stephanie, shielding her with his body. Tom whirled around. The third *hisaf* now circled Tom, knife in hand. I grabbed one of Tom's knives from the snow and tossed it to him. I barely had time to find the other knife before the bald, black-bearded *hisaf* reappeared, fifteen feet from us. Sunlight reflecting off snow glittered along his blade.

Tom lunged at the third *hisaf*. Younger, bigger, stronger and not unskilled in fighting, Tom managed to knock the blade from the man's hand. Immediately the *hisaf* vanished, just as the first one reappeared right next to him.

Tom dodged. The *hisaf*'s knife glanced along his left side, but Tom didn't seem to notice. He concentrated utterly on his opponent. Even the *hisaf* must have felt the fury in that huge powerful body because, instead of attacking again, he vanished.

The black-bearded *hisaf* ran towards me through the snow.

Tom was faster; he reached me first and leaped upon the man. They struggled briefly, and then the *hisaf* melted from Tom's grasp and was gone.

'What are they?' he screamed at me.

'*Hisafs!* Like me!'

Tom groaned. 'Stand back to back!' he yelled at me over the wind. I clutched his other knife, knowing that I was too clumsy to use it – *Peter One-Hand* – but with no choice. All of us were without choice. These *hisafs* could now cross over and back in body, as I had. We must kill them and send them quiescent to the Country of the Dead, or we would all four of us go there ourselves. No, three of us, for then my sister would have Stephanie, and I did not think that her handlers would want Stephanie quiescent and mindless when she could instead be put to use.

Jee and Stephanie lay between us at our feet. The third *hisaf* vanished without attacking – *why*? We waited for the men to reappear. The wind howled and froze my face. The *hisafs* did not come. Minutes dragged by. What if they just let us freeze here until—

Two of them appeared on either side of me, close enough for me to feel the warmth of their bodies, and the third a little way off. Then one had me by the neck with his knife at my throat. Tom spun around to face us.

'Attack and Roger dies!' the man shouted above the wind.

Tom hesitated.

In that moment of hesitation the second *hisaf* lurched forward. His knife flashed. A gust of wind blew snow in my eyes, blinding me, and I could not see what happened

357

until the gust passed and the *hisaf* was falling to the ground, Jee's hand on his ankle. Jee had tripped him. Tom fell to his knees and plunged his own knife into the man's chest. Blood jetted forth in a fountain, turning the white snow bright red.

But Tom had fallen to his knees, not leaping on the *hisaf* but rather —

And then I heard my sister's voice inside my head – *and I was not asleep and dreaming*. 'Don't kill Roger! Take him! Take him!'

The *hisaf* holding my neck chopped with his other hand at my wrist. My knife dropped into the snow. The remaining *hisaf*, the bald black-bearded one, moved leisurely towards us. At my feet Tom raised his eyes to the approaching man. Tom's eyes were unfocused, almost dreamy. Abruptly his gaze sharpened and he tried to rise to his feet. The black-bearded man stopped several feet away, smiled and raised a *gun*.

Then my sister screamed again. 'No!' she cried, her fury a seething red cloud in my brain. 'He is not the one! Roger is not the one!' She shrieked, and I raised my good hand to clap it over my ear, as if that could have shut her out.

Not the one.

The *hisaf* holding me hesitated. Did he hear that voice too? I had felt him preparing to cross back over, had felt the shift in his body against mine as he imprisoned me, the change in his breathing. He was going to carry me back with him. But he hesitated when my sister screamed in my head – and in his? – and at that moment the shapes fell out of the sky.

Two of them, falling with immense speed. For a moment I thought they were cloaks, but a moment later they were birds. Enormous dark birds, hurtling through the blowing snow – no, neither falling not flying but diving, as raptors dive for prey. But eagles and hawks and even owls dive with talons extended, and these huge birds dived beak first, one at each *hisaf*. They dived straight for the two heads.

I was shoved away as my *hisaf* raised his knife, the other his gun. Neither was fast enough. The birds' beaks struck the men's skulls. Then the talons were out, fastened on the men's shoulders as beaks jabbed into screaming faces, again and again and yet again. Screams, howls of pain. One beak pierced an eye and the spurting blood stained the white ground red.

I took a step forward, too sickened and fascinated to know what I did. Tom staggered to his feet. A few moments more and it was over. One *hisaf* lay dead from Tom's knife, the others from the monstrous birds, which abruptly vanished, leaving two women panting on the snow, their faces contorted with the effort to breathe. One was the white-deer woman who had brought us food, and the other was Alysse.

I had no time for Tom's gasp of recognition. Three *hisafs* had accompanied my sister in the Country of the Dead, and all three lay dead at my feet. My sister was alone. Only I could cross over to stop her from doing this again: recruiting more *hisafs*, tracking me and Stephanie and anyone else with wild talent, sending killers after us bodily through the Country of the Dead. Only I.

Filled with more rage than I had ever thought possible, not quite sane with it, I crossed over.

51

Darkness—
 Cold—
 Dirt choking my mouth—
 Worms in my eyes—
 Earth imprisoning my fleshless arms and legs–
My sister stood at the edge of the pine grove no more
than twenty feet from where I crossed through. Fog
swirled around her. Through that dark mist we stared at
each other, and all at once and for the first time her name
was in my head. My mother's name.

I called, 'Katharine!'

Her eyes widened. Mad she might be, and filled with
anger – 'She's angry at Roger for living,' Stephanie had
said – but she had wit enough to recognize fury even
greater than her own. She was without protection, and
I was finally without fear. She turned and ran into the
trees.

I raced after her. The dark fog rose around me, thickening until I could see nothing. But I could hear, and
I followed the sound of breaking branches and crushed
undergrowth. She was a solid living body even as I was,
and like me she stumbled in rhe fog.

'Katharine!'

I felt her in my mind then, a great shrieking that went
on and on. Almost I stopped pursuing her – anything to
get that monstrous noise out of my brain. The terrible
din made it harder to hear her passage, just as the darkening mist made it impossible to see her. So it was sheer

luck that the stump of my wrist brushed against her body, and I grabbed wildly with my other hand. I had her.

'No! No! *No!*'

It was the scream of a terrified little girl, and the body flailing against mine was slim and light – '*Eleven years dead*' – that of a child. But she had killed like the most ruthless soldier and she was not what she seemed. None of her acts had been childish. Desperately I named those acts in my mind, to keep my fury hot enough to do what I must.

Lady Margaret, murdered in her sleep.

Stephanie's nurse, murdered.

My father, captive somewhere.

Fia, crumbling and melting grotesquely in my arms.

'*Die die die . . .*'

'No!' Katharine sobbed. 'Roger, No!'

I flung her over my shoulder and carried her through the grove of trees, back towards the hill where Tom and I had seen her appear. Once we were free of the grove, the fog lessened a little. I could see where I was going. My sister beat her fists ineffectively on my back. The shrieking in my mind went on and on, so intense that it almost blinded me, as if sound were just more dark mist. But the actual fog disappeared as I rounded the base of the hill.

Here was the circle of the Dead that had so frightened Stephanie. All the mist here had been drawn into the rotating centre fog or else onto the heads of the Dead. All fifteen heads vibrated. I could not stop to think who they might be, these men and women about to lose eternity to the greed of Soulvine Moor, because I could not rescue them. Already the turning fog was becoming a vortex, humming loudly, whirling faster and faster.

'*Your sister is at the centre of the web,*' Alysse had told me. '*The* hisafs *seek to kill her. They must not succeed. The flow of web power – the strongest force in the world – must not be so abruptly and greatly disturbed.'*

But I was not going to remove Katharine's power from the web; I was merely going to disperse it, spread it out among many, like a raging river diverted harmlessly into the greater immensity of the sea and so unable to bury villages, knock down trees, kill the innocent.

'No, Roger! No!'

I broke through the circle of the Dead and carried my sister to the edge of the spinning vortex, even as its humming rose to an ear-shattering shriek. Her slight body writhed in my arms. Katharine beat on my back. I pulled her from me and lifted her high, higher than I thought possible with my one good hand and the stump of my wrist.

I could not do it.

She was but a girl, a child, mad through no fault of her own but rather through the horrors of her birth. She was my sister, however ill-begotten. And I was not a murderer – I was *not*. I could not do this monstrous thing, could not murder my sister no matter what she had done. My arms ached with holding her above my head and I cried out, a wordless noise like an animal in pain, in rage, in frustration. My *sister* . . . I could not do it.

Then Katharine stopped sobbing and shrilled, 'Your child is the one! Your son! And I will have him!' And she laughed.

It was the laugh that had shivered along my bones, terrorized my dreams, . . . that laugh . . . and *she wanted my unborn son*.

Before she could unbalance me, before she could give again that cry that might make me change my mind—

She wanted my unborn son.

—I lunged forward and threw her into the vortex.

A huge clap of sound, like lightning striking the ground.

362

I was blinded, deafened, knocked off my feet. When I could see and hear again, when I could rise, the fifteen Dead in their circle were gone. The fog was gone. Katharine was gone.

The grass was not even scorched.

I stood in the tranquil and empty countryside, and knew that I had won. My sister, along with the other fifteen, had been drawn into the fog of watchers from Soulvine. However she may have strengthened them, she could no longer terrorize me. Nor Maggie, nor my son. As a separate entity, Katharine had ceased to exist. I had won.

I stood on the lifeless grass and wept.

After a time, I don't know how long a time, I heard something come crashing through the trees of the little grove on the other side of the hill. Another rogue *hisaf*, come too late to rescue my sister? I did not wait to find out. I bit my tongue and crossed over. At the last possible moment I saw that it was no *hisaf* rounding the base of the hill but instead another of the grey dogs, which had no business existing in the Country of the Dead.

Nor, any longer, did I.

I crossed back into the land of the living upon the cold plain. Noon sunlight had replaced the blowing snow, bouncing off drifts to blind the eyes. Tom, Jee, Stephanie, Alysse and the white-deer woman were all gone, leaving only the three dead *hisafs* half-covered with snow.

52

As my vision adjusted to the wintry brightness, I saw that light glowed in the pine grove where, in the Country of the Dead, I had chased my sister through the fog. A fire burned there. Shivering, stumbling, I trudged towards it.

Jee and Tom huddled close to the fire. Between them lay Stephanie and the two web women, lying on a white fur cloak with another over them of white hide. *A white rabbit, a white deer, two cloaks falling from the sky* ... The women lay gasping still, chasing each breath, their faces contorted and ashen. Stephanie was still unconscious from my blow. But when Jee looked up at me, it was of neither the princess nor the web women that he spoke.

'Tom be hurt.'

'Pi-piss pots,' Tom said. 'It's ... nothing.' He toppled over onto his right side, clutching his left. It was sodden with blood. The *hisaf*'s knife had found its mark after all. Between Tom's fingers the blood, which must have slowed in the cold of the open meadow, oozed red in the firelight.

'Tom!'

He gasped for breath, sounding like the web women.

'Tom, how bad is it? Oh, how bad?'

'Bad ... enough.'

I tried to look beneath his bloody fingers and slashed tunic, but all I could see was red. Frantically I shook Alysse. 'Help him! Help Tom!' Once Mother Chilton had cured me of the poison on Solek's knife, had cut off my hand without killing me, had healed me. 'Help him!'

She opened her eyes and seemed, through her gasps, to understand. Faintly, as if it might break, she shook her head.

'But you are healers! You can heal!'

She said something too low to hear. I put my ear to her mouth and she repeated it. 'Nothing . . . left . . .'

The web women had no power left. They had used it all to become the monstrous birds that had saved our lives. But I didn't care that they had risked their lives, perhaps would still lose them, to rescue us from the traitor *hisafs*. They could not – only in my roiling mind it became *would not* – help Tom. Tom, whose strength and loyalty and courage I had relied on again and again. I could not do without Tom.

My good hand came up, descended, slapped Alysse across her cold cheek. 'Help him! Do something!'

She did nothing. Tom, oblivious to his one-time bedmate, groaned. His gaze fastened on me.

'Tom, try – oh, try!'

'Can't.' His eyes never left mine, as if he could anchor his life to another's and so not slip away. 'Going back . . .'

'No!'

'Country . . . Dead.' And then, with a huge effort, 'Tie me to a tree there. I don't . . . want . . .'

'Tom!'

'Bye, George.' He grinned then, for half a moment the old Tom, jaunty and fearless. Then his throat gave a terrible rattle, his body shuddered, and he was gone.

I let out an enormous howl. I would have crossed over to get some last few moments with him, but Jee was on me, his small face pushed up to mine. 'No! No! Don't go over, Roger! She be there.'

I ignored him. He grabbed my tunic, still half frozen, and hung on. I tried to knock Jee off me. He clung like pine pitch.

'She be there. She will kill ye!'

'No! She can't!'

'No! Ye maun not go!'

'The boy is right,' said a quiet voice behind me. I knew that voice. In grief and loss and fury, I turned my head, Jee still clinging to me and Tom dead on the snowy ground, and faced Mother Chilton.

It was only her voice that I recognized. This was not the woman of the apothecary tent in the capital of The Queendom, nor of the cliff above the pebbled beach where my Aunt Jo had died. This was the crone Tom had described, looking older than anyone I had ever seen. Her body bent forward, both spine and neck curving so much that were it not for the staff she leaned upon, she must have toppled over. Sparse grey hair straggled from under her hood. Her face, with shadows on it from the dancing fire, creased into wrinkles like the ravines of the Unclaimed Lands. But her grey eyes met mine clearly, filled with pity.

The deer woman on the ground, still panting, none-theless smiled.

Mother Chilton said, 'Roger, there is no point crossing over after Tom. It is too dangerous, and too late. I'm sorry you lost your friend, but that is the cost you must pay. As these women are paying theirs.'

'They are alive!'

'There was no assurance of that when they set out to perform their rescue.' Mother Chilton hobbled past me. Painfully she lowered herself to the ground beside Stephanie. I remembered what both Alysse and the white-deer woman had said to me about the princess: *'Better she should have been shot.'*

'Don't touch her!' I cried.

Mother Chilton kept her gaze on Stephanie, but her words were directed to me. 'Don't be ridiculous, Roger – Stephanie is in no danger from us. The situation is different now. When she was Tarek's prisoner, there was no way to reach her and control her talent, which in any case we vastly underestimated. It is different now. You have done at least that much good in bringing her to me.'

'You could have gone to her!' I scarcely knew what I was saying, except that it distracted me for a little longer from Tom's body slumped beside me on the ground. Tom, gone, among the Dead ...

'No,' Mother Chilton said, 'I could not have gone to her. I could barely come here. I am very old now, my years given to saving Tom.'

'You lie!' I cried, furious at her, at the world. Both worlds. 'You could have become a ... a ... .whatever animal you can become!'

'Not in front of the savage soldiers, I could not. They would have killed us both on the spot from terror of witchcraft. This was the best I could do, and it has cost me. Everything has a cost, Roger Kilbourne – when will you learn that? These adepts in the soul arts are paying the cost of your rescue, just as Tom Jenkins has paid it. To save you, Alysse and Elaine both took the form of raptors, which was neither of their spirit-sharers. We each do what we can, and we each pay as we must.'

'Spare me your cant! Tom—'

'Is as safe as the Dead can be. Soulvine Moor will not harm him in the Country of the Dead.'

'You cannot know that.'

'Yes. I can. Take from it what comfort you will. Ah, the apprentice stirs.'

She meant Stephanie. The princess opened her eyes, put her hand to the bruise my fist had left on her head and began to cry.

'Stop that,' Mother Chilton said, so firmly that Stephanie, starting in surprise, did so at once. 'You are now an apprentice in the soul arts, my child. We do not cry.'

Jee said fiercely, 'She be the princess of The Queendom!'

'That too,' Mother Chilton agreed. 'And you, Jee, are her most faithful servitor.'

He looked confused – perhaps he did not know the word – but his fierce stance beside the princess did not change. 'My lady, be ye warm enough? Closer to the fire.'

She groped for his hand, but her eyes were on Mother Chilton. The two stared at each other, and in that deep gaze something passed between the child and the crone, something beyond either words or my understanding. I did not care what that something was. I turned back to Tom.

He lay face up on the snow, the faint smile still on his lips, his eyes gazing at pine branches but seeing nothing. Gently I closed his eyes. How would I do without Tom? Without his courage, his cheerfulness, his endless energy? I strangled my sobs and turned my face away.

Jee's attention was given to Stephanie, as was Mother Chilton's, and it was the deer woman who struggled to put her thin cold hand into mine. It brought no comfort. I had never had a friend before, and I had none left now.

I was alone, and my friend had gone to the Country of the Dead.

We buried Tom in a little dell behind the pine grove. The ground was softer there, warmed by a thick pile of dead leaves blown in by the vagrant patterns of autumn winds. We had no winding sheet and could not spare either of the cloaks, one of fur and one of hide, but I did not want to wrap his body anyway. Tom Jenkins had lived full tilt, with no artificial barrier between him and whatever he encountered, meeting experience eagerly at every turn. Let him meet the grave in the same fashion. And, beyond the grave, he was safe. So Mother Chilton told me, and although I did not understand what she meant, I believed her because it would be unbearable not to.

We dug the grave deep, Jee and I, using stout branches as shovels, and covered it with stones as large as we could carry, against wild animals digging at it. This took hours, until sunset. I welcomed the labour. It kept me from thinking about Katharine and what I had done to her on the other side. It almost kept me from thinking. Almost.

We did not let Stephanie attend Tom's burial. Her head ached from the blow I had given her and we left her by the fire with the web women. Jee and I rolled Tom into the hole we had dug, covered him over and said a few words. I didn't remember what was said. It didn't matter. No words could have been sufficient tribute to the life-loving vitality that had been Tom Jenkins.

Before he went into the ground, Mother Chilton reached into Tom's pocket and pulling out something small. When she caught my gaze, she opened her wrinkled old hand. On her palm lay the miniature of Fia.

'It's a marker,' I said. 'That's how my sister and her *hisafs* knew where we were.'

'Also how we women of the soul arts knew,' Mother Chilton said tartly. 'Do not think always of the evil side of things, Roger.'

Stupid advice. It was all evil: my sister, the breach in

369

the wall between life and death, the rogue *hisafs*, the savages' expedition to abduct Stephanie, who since I had hit her was afraid of me.

Mother Chilton added, 'An axe may be used to cut wood for warmth or to chop off a man's legs. The evil lies not in the axe but in how it is used.'

'You do not yet know what evil I have done.'

Her old eyes sharpened. 'What? What is it you have done?'

I told her. For the first and last time I saw bewilderment in Mother Chilton's face. She quavered, 'What does it mean?'

She was asking *me*? I said angrily, the anger a mask for anguish, 'It means I have killed my sister! It means I am a murderer. It means Katharine is no longer a threat to me and mine.'

'Yes, but the web . . .'

All at once I did not care about the web. I did not care about Mother Chilton or Alysse or Stephanie or even Jee. I wanted Maggie, yearned for her with every sinew in my exhausted and murderous body, longed for her as a ship in a storm longs for nothing but the safety and peace of a sheltered harbour.

'Roger—'

'Leave me alone!' I stalked away from her twisted bony hand on my arm. I fled from Tom's grave, from everything that had happened in that pine grove, clear to the far edge of the snowy meadow. The wind had stopped but it was bitter cold. I shivered and wrapped my arms around myself.

In the valley below an army moved.

I could see horses, men and then a purple banner, from this distance a thin thread against the snow. Staggering through snowdrifts, I raced back to Mother Chilton. 'An army! Coming here!'

She didn't seem surprised. 'Ah, then they are a day ahead.'

'You knew? Who is it?'

'Lord Robert Hopewell.'

'Lord Robert?' I had last seen him in the palace dungeon, had assumed he'd been executed as Tarek's army pulled out. But no. I knew Tarek better now. To execute a vanquished rival would be to admit that the rival might not be completely vanquished. It was an admission of weakness. Or perhaps Tarek had been more subtle: I had been taken in order to teach him to bring an army back from Witchland. Tarek wanted Lord Robert alive to face that witched army under savage command, as Tarek's father had once faced a witched army fighting against him. Or perhaps the Young Chieftain had some other reason for sparing Lord Robert that I did not understand at all; I was only a *hisaf*. Or perhaps Lord Robert had fought his way free of the dungeon with the knife I had left him, stolen from the Country of the Dead. My mind seized on that idea. I wanted so desperately to have done some good to someone, somewhere.

My sister—

'His lordship's army marches to rescue the princess,' Mother Chilton said. 'They will be very pleased to have to travel no further than this and not be required to attack Tarek's forces. They will take Stephanie back with them, to resume her reign under Lord Robert's protectorship. I will go with Stephanie, at her insistence, as her nurse. And young Jee will go as well. She will make him a page.'

'Lord Robert will not permit that.' I argued, from resentment. Mother Chilton was disposing everyone as if they were dishes on her cupboard shelf: This one here, that one there. 'Pages are nobly born.'

'Nonetheless, Jee will be a page.'

'He will hate it.'

'He will not. It will let him serve Stephanie and stay beside her.'

'You can see the future then?' I said sarcastically. 'I suppose that someday she will choose him as consort?'

'No one can see the future. I tell you what will happen tomorrow, which is only the unfolding of today, and even then not a certainty until it happens. Do not be childish, Roger.'

'I am not a child.'

'No,' she said, and I heard despair in her voice, 'you are not. But you must not be here when Lord Robert's army arrives. They will not thank you for rescuing Stephanie, not when they know how you accomplished it.'

Witchcraft. That's what Mother Chilton meant. She was right, but nonetheless her words stung. 'And do you then propose to tell Lord Robert that the princess, a crone, two sick women and a ten-year-old boy just chanced to stroll out of Tarek's camp and cross the mountains in winter?'

'What I tell Lord Robert is no longer your concern. You must leave here, Roger, for your own safety and ours. You must leave now. I will take care of the others.'

I wanted to leave, and now that I could turn the care of Jee and Stephanie over to Mother Chilton, relief rose in me like a great wave, cresting from gut to belly to heart. I was free to go to Maggie.

'But before you go, I must give you three things,' Mother Chilton said, and despair was back in her face.

I did not understand that despair. Nor did I want to understand it. My own heartsickness was enough for one person.

Mother Chilton continued, 'One thing I would give

372

you is material, two are knowledge. First, this.' She handed me the white fur cloak.

I glanced at the fire. Stephanie and the two women lay asleep and uncovered on the hide, warmth from the flames dancing on their faces. Jee crouched nearby, likewise fire-warmed. And Lord Robert would arrive in a few hours.

'There is a pocket,' Mother Chilton said, 'with Tom's knives and some money. Take the water bag, and after I tell Lord Robert that you are dead, I think you may pass through The Queendom untroubled, provided that you do not venture too close to the capital.'

'Thank you. What are the two pieces of knowledge?'

'The first is this, and you must listen carefully, Roger Kilbourne. When power flows along the threads of the web of being, when it is made to flow unnaturally from death back to life, there must also be a flow in the opposite direction. Or else the whole web will become more and more disturbed, until it is destroyed. There are terrible times coming. More terrible than you can imagine. So if you never listen to me again, do so now. Until we know the consequences of what you have done to Katharine, you must not again disturb the web of being. I will not ask for your promise because you have broken so many before, but do not act again as a *hisaf*, nor communicate with other *hisafs*.'

'You distrust them because they are men.'

'Perhaps,' Mother Chilton said. 'And perhaps we have reason to distrust even good men. Perhaps you do too. I notice that you have said nothing about trying to rescue your father from Galtryf.'

'My father made no attempt to rescue me.'

'Enough.' She held up her bony hand. 'I do not want to hear it. The *hisafs* are deeply mistaken about this war, and it is well that you do not attempt to go to Galtryf.'

I scowled. Now that my father could cross over bodily, how could he be kept at Galtryf? And when I had broken my promises to not cross over, it had been for good reason. If I did not wish to rescue my father, it was because such an attempt was both unearned by him and futile. But the truth was that Mother Chilton's words did not touch me deeply. I was done with the web of being, done with the women of the soul arts, done with the *hisafs* on both sides of this war. 'Well, what is the second piece of knowledge? Be quick, Mother Chilton; there is an army on the move.'

'You intend to go to Maggie at Tanwell, do you not? I know that nothing I can say will deter you. But after you have reclaimed Maggie, keep a constant watch on her and the child. Do not let any stranger approach him, especially if they approach through you.'

'I can take care of my wife and son.'

'She is not your wife. That is a fiction Tom Jenkins created, remember? You have not married Maggie.'

'Not yet. But I shall. And this is none of your concern, Mother Chilton.'

'Nothing on either side of the grave is more my concern than your unborn child. Nothing.'

The words were said quietly, without looking at me. All at once the fight left me, replaced only with a sick coldness that reduced my voice to a whisper. 'What is he?' I whispered. 'What is my son?'

'He is our last hope.'

'He is but an infant! Not even that yet!'

'Nonetheless,' Mother Chilton said, and said no more. I wouldn't have listened anyway. I was going home to Maggie, to tell her I loved her. We would marry, and then I would take her and my son away from all this strife, from the war fought on both sides of the grave, from anything that would threaten them. Finally I knew what

374

precious good I had in Maggie, and I would not lose her again.

Mother Chilton turned her old face away from me and towards the fire. 'Ah,' she said, a soft desolate sound in the piney darkness.

53

I left before Lord Robert's army arrived, with no further warnings or scoldings or strictures from Mother Chilton, no more telling me where I should go, where I must not go, what I could or could not do, how I had failed in my duty as a *hisaf* and my obligation to the forces aligned against Soulvine Moor. Looking at her, so frail and bent that walking seemed a torture, I wondered how she could carry out her own task of tutoring Stephanie in the soul arts. But I did not doubt that she would do so. If Lord Robert Hopewell, who again would be lord protector, discovered what Mother Chilton was about, the battle between them would be epic.

Almost I could hear Tom's voice saying, 'Three to one on your grandmother, Peter.'

I said goodbye to Jee as he huddled beside the fire. 'Jee, I cannot go with you to the palace.'

His small face was solemn. 'I know. Ye maun go to Maggie.'

'Yes. And you must tell no one at court about Maggie, not ever. Not even the princess.'

'I know. They maun not find ye.'

'That's right.'

'Roger,' he said thickly.

I peered at him more closely. In the fitful light from the fire his small face contorted with anguish. Jee put one hand on my good arm and I had the sense that he did not even know he was doing so. He burst out, 'I maun go with my lady!'

'Of course you must. Princess Stephanie needs you.'

'But Maggie . . .'

Now I grasped his struggle. I said gently, 'You think that by going with Princess Stephanie, you will be deserting Maggie.'

Jee's fingers tightened on my arm.

'Hear me carefully, Jee. Maggie loves you and she will miss you. But she does not need you in the same way that Stephanie does. Maggie will have me. Stephanie will have Mother Chilton, but you can see how very old she is. Look at her. There will be much that Mother Chilton is unable to do. And you are the only one who understands what Stephanie has had to endure in the Country of the Dead. Who else could understand? Whom else could she talk to about that? The princess *needs* you, Jee. You must go with her, and I will see that Maggie understands that.'

It was the reassurance he wanted, and the excuse. His face relaxed, and in the firelight I saw his rare smile.

At least I had been able to ease the heart of one child.

And so I set out. I had a white fur cloak. I had Tom's knives, Jee's snares, a water bag and both gold and silvers from Mother Chilton, more money than I had ever possessed in my life before. But both coins and the fur cloak could be markers, and I intended to shed them as soon as I could. I wanted neither web women nor *hisafs* tracking me. This journey would be mine alone.

Floundering through the snow, screened by trees, I skirted the meadow and climbed the next hill to the north. Now I could see all the way to the vast plain of The Queendom. Far below, the advance guard of Lord Robert's army rode hard, with the main body marching one valley behind. They would reach the pine grove before nightfall. Tomorrow, or perhaps the day after to allow for rest, they would return east to the capital.

I would travel in the same direction as the army,

towards Glory, but by a slightly more northern route, and much faster. An army escorting a princess is a more cumbersome thing than a lone traveller. And perhaps I could buy a donkey along the way. Maggie would find good uses for a donkey.

In the near distance rose the smoke of an isolated farm. It was as yet only the beginning of winter, and the farmhouse would hold preserved meat, dried fruit, stored cheeses. I would wait until I saw the farmer and his sons, if he had any, leave the cabin, and then I would deal with his wife. I would buy provisions, and I would trade my white fur cloak for something simpler and unmarked. The farmwife would be at least half savage, but she would sell me what I needed. It is old women who are most willing to talk to me.

'*There are terrible times coming,*' Mother Chilton had said. '*More terrible than you can imagine.*'

But not for me. What I had done to Katharine would stay with me all my days. but now I was going home to Maggie and my son.

I started down the snowy hill towards the farmhouse.